The Sweetest Taboo

By Carole Matthews

THE SWEETEST TABOO
BARE NECESSITY
FOR BETTER, FOR WORSE

The Sweetest Taboo

Carole Matthews

AVON
TRADE

An Imprint of HarperCollins*Publishers*

HarperCollins books may be purchased for education, business, or sales promotional use. For information please write: Special Markets Department, HarperCollins Publishers Inc., 10 East 53rd Street, New York, NY 10022.

FIRST EDITION

Designed by Elizabeth M. Glover

Library of Congress Cataloging-in-Publication Data

Matthews, Carole.
   The sweetest taboo / Carole Matthews.—1st ed.
      p. cm.
   ISBN 0-06-059562-0
   1. Women—California—Fiction. 2. Motion picture producers and directors—Fiction.
   3. Triangles (Interpersonal relations)—Fiction. 4. British—California—Fiction.
   5. Los Angeles (Calif.)—Fiction. 6. Actors—Fiction. I. Title.

PR6113.A88S94 2004
823'.914—dc22   2003062977

04 05 06 07 08 JTC/RRD 10 9 8 7 6 5 4 3

To Steve Cooper,
for friendship and invaluable help with research.
Anyone who can get you onto the bridge of the
Starship Enterprise has got to be a top bloke.

One

I can tell you exactly when I fell in love. The exact place. The exact minute. The London Book Fair. Here. *Now*. Let me quickly check my watch so that I will remember it forever—3.45 P.M. I have no idea who he is—yet—nor that he's about to turn my life upside down, but already I'm bitten, smitten. He looks at me again and smiles, and my insides flood with a tingling warmth that I haven't felt for a very long time. I also have pins and needles in my feet, but that's more to do with uncomfortable shoes and the first glimmer of a bunion than Cupid's deadly aim.

"We need someone gorgeous," he tells me, and I realize that I'm staring.

He has an American accent that I can't place. East Coast, West Coast—I'm hopeless, they all sound the same to me. Drawly and sexy. And they all make me go weak at the knees.

"It'll take about five minutes. No more," the All-American man is saying to me now. "Can you spare the time?"

I want to tell him that if he asked me nicely I could probably spare the rest of my life, but only manage to stammer out, "Y—Yes."

Reaching out, he takes my elbow and guides me toward him. I gape round—having failed in the mouth-closing area—looking for approval from Nigel, the manager of the book stand where I'm supposed to be helping out. But he is busy talking numbers to a bookshop owner in a corduroy jacket and no one else is the slightest bit interested in what I'm doing.

What I am doing is some temporary work for Bindlatters Books, publishers of a highly dubious range of Technicolor horror books for the youth market that seem to involve more blood than your average abattoir sees in a week and lots of heads being ripped off.

Working for a book publisher may sound interesting—I can just hear myself dropping it into the conversation at dinner parties— but what I'm actually doing is wearing a red polyester uniform and attempting to give out leaflets to people who don't want to take them.

"Publisher?" my American asks as he eases me through a crush of people.

Would that I could claim such a lofty position. I could pretend, but what would that achieve? But maybe I don't need to admit that my knowledge of books extends to buying the battered copies that have done the rounds of charity shops to fill my long and lonely nights. I am an aficionada of dog-eared Danielle Steel. "No." How can I make this sound riveting? I have no idea. I'm not that inventive—at least not at short notice. "I'm Chief Leaflet Giver-Outer."

He tries to look impressed, as if I've just told him I'm chancellor of the exchequer.

"It's a temporary position." Oh dear. I sound dreadfully bitter. The London Book Fair is held in Olympia and it takes me forever to get here every morning—as I live in Battersea on the wrong side of the river. But it's only for a week. I have to keep reminding myself of that fact. However, what happens at the end of the week could well be worse. A big fat nothing is currently looming large on the horizon of my life.

I glance at my inadequate official badge. It doesn't bear my name—Sadie Nelson—or any of the other details that single me out from A. N. Other. Just the name of my stand. I guess the people who generally perform this thankless task don't hang around long enough to warrant having a printed name badge.

"I'm Gil," this gorgeous American says over his shoulder. "Gil McGann."

"Publisher?"

"No." He gives a dismissive shake of his head and takes a

firmer grip of my arm as we thread our way through the on-coming throng. "I'm a Hollywood film producer."

Yes, and I'm Halle Berry.

"I've just bought a great book," he continues. *The One That Got Away.* A romantic comedy—funny as hell."

"I'm here to do smiley things with the author."

Oh good. So let me just get this clear: I'm standing here in a red polyester uniform, which is designed specifically to fit some-one shorter, fatter and forty years older than me, talking to a gor-geous Hollywood film producer about his latest movie acquisition. On the plus side, I'm having a good hair day. And, despite not asking my name, he told me I was gorgeous. Any minute now, my alarm clock is going to go off and I'm not going to be able to decide whether this was a dream or a nightmare.

Currently, it could go either way.

We squeeze through the crowd and onto another exhibition stand which is a hundred times bigger and swankier than Bind-latters Books' one. It is hung with huge posters of trendy books, some of which I've even heard of, but haven't read because they haven't hit the Skid Row of the charity shops yet. There is a group of people drinking champagne in the corner and laughing loudly. A stainless-steel table with a smear-free glass top has been arranged at one side and there is a crackle of anticipation in the few people, looking decidedly like fellow minions, who are milling around.

Gil stands next to me but doesn't let go of my arm. I'm not complaining. I have goose pimples all over me and yet I'm not the slightest bit cold. In fact, you could probably grill hamburg-ers on my cheeks.

"I hope you don't think this is too much of an imposition?"

"Not at all." My hormones are nudging me to do my most winning smile. I can't—my feet are hurting too much from standing in one spot all day in high heels. My lips stretch tightly across my teeth and from somewhere in the depths of my re-serves, I send a tired smile back at him. "Though you haven't ac-tually told me what you want me to do."

"Damn," Gil says. "Sorry. We need you to pose with Elise Neils." He gives a nod of his head toward a mass of blonde curls surrounded by smooth, besuited men. "Feign adoring fan for some press photos—if you wouldn't mind."

"Oh." I suppose it could have been worse. It could have involved me perched on a stand giving out leaflets.

This, apart from my current pleasant interlude, has been the job from hell. But beggars can't be choosers, and I very nearly was a beggar before this rather dubious "opportunity" with Bind-latters knocked.

I used to work in the City—great job, great flat, great car—until due to economic downturn, world recession, plummeting share prices—blah, blah, blah—I found myself severely and swiftly surplus to requirements. First the job went, then the car, then the flat, then the fair-weather friends and, accompanying each, a slice of my self-confidence. I had slogged my guts and my liver out for that company—late nights, short lunch hours, a social life that revolved around entertaining customers with copious amounts of vodka—and it chopped my heart into little pieces to be told to clear my desk and never again darken the door of Allen-Jones Holdings by someone I had considered a good mate.

I vowed never to work in the City again. Panic set in when I realized no one in the City actually wanted me to anyway. "Recruitment freeze" was the most common term I heard. "We'd love to employ someone of your caliber, but . . ." Then I found that recruitment freezes were not confined to my chosen industry alone.

Since then I've scrabbled around with a variety of part-time, poorly paid jobs that have barely provided enough to pay my share of the rent on the slightly scrubby flat in Battersea my lovely, lovely friend Alice has very kindly let me squeeze into with her—even though she knows I'm a credit risk.

I look back at Gil. And, for once, I don't know what to say to this man. I'm not normally known for my reticence, but all my words suddenly seem to have dried up. Perhaps it's being surrounded by a surfeit of them in all these worthy tomes that's making me feel inadequate.

"Here she is," Gil lowers his head to mine and whispers close and in a faintly reverent manner right next to my ear. The goose pimples go into overdrive.

The lucky author, who has had half of Hollywood chasing her, is a bit too young and a bit too gorgeous for her own good and I could scratch her eyes out already. I wonder how far Gil McGann's "being smiley" extends?

Elise Neils is oh-so hip and oh-so tiny and bears the confident air of someone who is used to being pampered. Sliding behind her special desk as if she's done it a thousand times before, she beams a practiced smile at her waiting audience. She looks like a complete cow. *I want a job that's glamorous,* I think, shortly before I'm manhandled away from Gil by a publicity-type woman with trendy horn-rimmed glasses and plonked next to Elise Neils in order to look adoring.

"Hi," she says. Actually, she seems quite nice, but I've already determined that I won't like her. She takes up her pen and poses in a suitably authorish way, while I lean forward, looking subservient and as if my life would improve 1000 percent if she would deign to scribble in her book for me. A poster reading: THE ONE THAT GOT AWAY! overshadows us both. The cameras go *click-click-click* as we turn our heads to and fro, inducing wedding photo-style smiles, and by the time we've finished I've decided that I don't want to be a celebrity after all.

"Thanks," Ms. Hot Author says to me and benevolently pats my arm with her oh-so tiny hand. She slides out from behind her table and sashays off in the direction of the champagne, followed by a horde of devoted men.

I stand abandoned and look round for Gil. He is waiting there, thumbing through a book—the only male in the vicinity with his tongue still in his mouth. Gratefully, I wander back toward him.

"Thanks," he says. "You were wonderful."

I'm not sure if he's being sincere or teasing me, but I grin thankfully anyway.

He nods toward the scrum for champagne, where our future Booker Prize winner gives him the glad eye, but he is completely oblivious. "Shall we join the crush?"

"I'd better get back," I say with a flash of unbridled loyalty that surprises even me. What am I thinking of? Champagne with a Hollywood producer or giving out leaflets on an exhibition stand for less than a fiver an hour, and I choose the latter? I am clearly sickening for something. Or mad.

"I'll walk you back," Gil says. "Give me a moment." And he strolls to the side of the stand to gather some bits and pieces. It gives me time for a more thorough appraisal. And already I'm regretting my decision to hotfoot it back to Bindlatters Books.

Gil is tall and slender and is wearing a suit that looks like it has been squashed into a suitcase on a Transatlantic flight and worn on an exhibition stand for too many days. I don't think he's a natural suit-wearer. He isn't glowing with a typical Hollywood tan either, and I thought everyone over there was a slave to the sun. Perhaps he spends too much time inside watching movies—I don't know. It sort of suits him, though; he'd look funny if he was tanned. He's boyish in a craggy way and I'm not certain how old he is, but I would suspect that he's still this side of "life begins at . . ." He has a cute smile and enough charisma to make sure that most women are giving him a second glance. It's certainly working for me.

Gil comes back bearing a raincoat—because, as usual, this week it has been raining persistently in London—a folded copy of *The Times* and a hardback copy of *The One That Got Away*. He waves it at me. I daren't tell him that I'll read it in about five years' time, after it has done the rounds of several offices and the pages of all the sex scenes bear unsightly, unidentifiable stains. It'll probably have a few crucial pages missing too. I hate it when that happens—but then it isn't the most irritating thing about being financially embarrassed. Having a cupboard that contains nothing but Ambrosia Creamed Rice and an out-of-date tin of pilchards is much, much worse. Believe me, I know.

He hands me the copy of *The One That Got Away*. "For you."

"Thanks." I feel a flush of deep gratitude until I see a picture of the lovely, lucky and probably fabulously wealthy Elise Neils on the back.

He takes my arm again and we head back toward what I have lovingly come to know as "my stand." There are a thousand questions I should be fitting into the next two minutes and I can't think of any of them. This could be my big chance—for what, I'm not sure. But I do know that I am blowing it like you wouldn't believe.

"Well," he says.

Nigel is at the front of the stand giving me what I can only describe as "a look." Gil and I sort of hover, looking and not looking at each other at the same time. Nigel makes a point of checking his watch.

"My hotel does great afternoon tea," Gil says suddenly. "Very quaint. Very English. What time do you get off?"

"Me?" There appear to be no film stars or flighty young authors around. He nods. I have several thousand more flyers to get rid of before I'm done. Perhaps I can dump them in a wastepaper bin somewhere. "About an hour."

"Come to my hotel, Ms. Chief Leaflet Giver-Outer. Join me for afternoon tea."

"Oh." I couldn't tell you when I last had afternoon tea. In fact, I don't know if I ever have. Isn't it only tourists and blue-rinsed old ladies that do afternoon tea? "Okay."

Gil takes a business card out of a silver holder, scribbles on the back and hands it to me. And it does indeed say GIL MCGANN, PRODUCER in big, bold letters. "It's not far. I hope you can come."

"I will," I say before my brain has time to compute this and decide that one of us is barking mad.

"See you later." And he walks off into the crush of publishers and agents while I stand and contemplate the fact that I have just agreed to go to the hotel of a man who hasn't even asked my name and, although he could have his pick of flighty, flirty young authors to "get smiley" with, clearly has a fetish for women in red polyester uniforms. I watch him until he disappears, running my fingers round the sharp edges of his card.

Nigel sidles toward me. "Leaflets," he says, handing me another interminable pile.

"Leaflets," I echo. And the earth rushes up to meet me with BUMP written all over it.

Two

Gil flopped onto the bed in his tiny room. What had cost an extortionate amount of money was little more than a broom cupboard. A broom cupboard in the attic. He guessed it was supposed to be cutesy, with original beams and steeply sloping ceilings—and, more disconcerting, steeply sloping floors—but he kind of preferred rooms that you could stand up in. He'd end up with a hunchback if he stayed here more than a week—already his neck was developing a painful crick. There was no gym in the hotel and it had rained so much that jogging was out of the question. Jet lag weighed heavy in his unexercized bones. Next time he would stay at The Hempel and be damned.

Lying down was the easier option and Gil stretched out and enjoyed it briefly. Then he tensed up again. What was he thinking of? There were a million and one things that he ought to be doing while he was in town other than hitting on strange women. It had been his intention to schmooze some up-and-coming British writers. What had happened to his brain that it had been swayed so easily by a hot lady in a dreadful suit? As if his life wasn't complicated enough.

Gil couldn't do relaxing, it was too much of a waste of time. He got up and switched on his laptop. The time difference here was a pain. When he was raring to go, everyone in LA was still curled up in bed—or out at parties. He tapped in his password. The first message was from Georgina, under the heading *Urgent*.

Gil groaned to himself. Nothing Georgina ever did was urgent. Not in the real world. He clicked the message open. *Call me!* it said. *Now!*

Gil glanced at his watch. Now would not be a good time to call Georgina. He wasn't even sure she would understand that the rest of the world didn't operate on Georgina Time. She'd probably just broken a nail or something equally earth shattering.

He clicked through the rest of the messages—mainly moans and groans from the studios regarding his latest projects—and dispatched his replies with professional ease. At least e-mail never slept. Gil ran his hands over his face. A shave was definitely in order. His entire "casual" wardrobe of one sweater and one pair of jeans was spread out on the back of a chintzy armchair and he wished he had thought to pack more clothes for socializing, but then he hadn't bargained on being blown away by a beautiful blonde. How long had it been since he had felt like this? Certainly not since he'd married Georgina, that's for sure.

The digital display of his bedside alarm blinked lazily at him. Gil worried at his thumbnail. Perhaps he'd better call Georgina. Just in case it was, for once, an emergency. There was always that horrible element of doubt with Gina, that some day she might even follow through with one of her many threats. Looking at the phone, he wondered where she was right now. Maybe he should leave it as long as he could.

Gil headed toward the shower, hoping that more water would come out of it than last time. He needed to freshen up, and fast. Try to make a silk purse out of a sow's ear. For some ludicrous reason he wanted things to go right with this woman.

He also needed to do something about the situation with Georgina, but that was going to take some diplomatic handling. And he was fully aware that he had been putting it off for far too long.

Three

Mr. Hollywood Movie Tycoon could just want casual sex—I fully appreciate that. And maybe it is easier to impress one of the more lowly administrative staff by saying you're a film producer rather than a flighty young author, who might well yawn and think, not another one! I have no friends here at the Book Fair to discuss this with and I can't ring Alice as she has a real job and is busy, busy, busy 24/7. I also can't ring her because I know she would tell me that I'm being a total wimp.

I'm glad to be leaving the frantic crush of this conference behind. Only one more day to go. It's great if you're really involved in these things, but if you're on the periphery of them, doing sundry unseen tasks to keep the whole thing rolling, then it's a bit of a drag. When I was a whizzy City-type, just a few short months ago, I used to love conferences. They took me all over the world—Paris, Prague, you name it, I've been there. Aren't conferences always very little to do with work and more to do with leaving responsibility or the bosom of one's stifling familial duties behind and going mad for a while by embarking on a period of anonymous sex in an anonymous hotel room with a stranger from a rival company who you're quite sure you'll never see again? I am, of course, talking about other people—not me. I was always purely an observer of these sexual shenanigans.

This is because I don't understand the concept of casual sex. Why would you want to get your bits and pieces out for a total stranger? I am into commitment and love and loyalty in a big way, and Mr. Gil McGann, film producer, is going to be cruelly disappointed if he thinks English girls are easy. Well, this one anyway. I can't vouch for my friends. They all seem to be able to bonk anything that breathes. Or am I just being fussy? It is a criticism that has been leveled at me in the past. Some of my friends have boyfriends *and* girlfriends. What's that all about? A fashion thing? Sexual greed? I don't understand it at all. Or is it just easier to date someone whose nail varnish you can share?

Anyway, I have more immediate problems. Thankfully, Bindlatters Books have supplied me with a locker so that I won't have to turn up at Gil's hotel sporting the red ensemble. I came to work wearing black boot-cut trousers and heeled boots from the days when I could afford to splash out on posh ones. On the downside, I am also wearing a cropped T-shirt bearing an embroidered Betty Boo and the caption DIAMONDS ARE A GIRL'S BEST FRIEND! Alice brought it back for me from Universal Studios on her summer holiday to California last year—her final extravagance before she became a burdened homeowner. It seems a bit tacky wearing a Universal Studios T-shirt to have afternoon tea with a man who might well work there in a serious capacity instead of just paying up to go in the theme park and experience a multitude of different ways of getting wet and sick.

I look in my purse. It contains three pounds and fifty pence and a credit card I keep threatening to cut up. Taking Gil's business card from my polyester pocket, I turn it over in my hand. The Townham Hotel. He's right—it isn't too far from here. My stomach has a shiver of indecision. But, hey, who's in charge here? Me or my digestive system? This is the only excitement I've had in days, weeks, months! It's another thing I can drop casually into dinner-party conversations for years to come. Ha! I may not be trendy enough to have a girlfriend—or desirable enough to have a boyfriend—but this must earn me at least a few "cool" points.

Throwing on an elderly Afghan coat that has seen better days, I shoot out of the conference center and grab a Tube to South Kensington, squashing in with delegates talking in la-di-dah tones about the kind of authors you see all the time on breakfast TV. The Tube takes an age to chug anywhere from this part of the Underground, which means that every day we all have to suffer

the same smelly, dreadlocked busker singing old Simon and Gar-
funkel hits very badly. Nevertheless, in true British fashion, we
all cough up our obligatory fifty pence before we are allowed to
shuffle off at the station.

The Townham Hotel is just round the corner from here, but
before I head there, I dodge between the rows of speeding traffic
and cross the road to a little boutique that does great clothes at
knock-down—and possibly knock-off—prices. I say *boutique*, but
it's more of an upmarket charity shop. This is what I'm reduced
to, not only for my books but for all my clothing needs too. I rush
in and rummage like a woman possessed through the rows and
rows of crushed blouses. Got it! For twenty-two quid I become
the proud owner of a black lacy top with bell-bottom sleeves and
a neckline that does nothing to hide the fact that I'm a girl. Ha!
Down with red polyester!

I apologize to my credit card and give it a grateful kiss before
battering it again and rush into a cubicle at the back the size of a
broom cupboard and change out of my Betty Boo, which gets
stuffed unceremoniously in my handbag. I clip my hair up and
decide that I look a bit fab—well, better than in my red number.
I'm not sure that the twenty-two-quid top will survive the rigors
of Alice's washing machine, but it will do for now. I just wish I
had some blusher with me. I positively bloom behind a carefully
applied barrier of Raspberry Whisper.

Four

The Townham is posh. Not as posh as the Ritz, say, but I still feel ridiculously nervous, and lurk outside in the pouring rain for a moment, thinking that showing up here could be bordering on insanity.

Before I'm completely drowned, I decide that I don't care if it is or not. This could be my big chance. Gil the film producer may offer me a part in his latest movie. Why not? Some very famous actress was discovered while waiting tables in Los Angeles. I can't remember who, because I know diddly-squat about Hollywood—but it was someone really, really famous.

Here I go. Deep breath, shoulders back, head up. This isn't do or die, but it's do or go home and eat last night's leftover risotto and moan to Alice that nothing exciting ever happens to me.

I find Gil in front of a roaring log fire, sprawled out on a big squashy sofa, *The Times* discarded on his lap. The suit has gone and he's wearing jeans and some preppy, hand-knit sweater that probably cost about a million quid and came from Fred Segal or somewhere; the only thing I do know about Hollywood is that Fred Segal is a trendy shop because *Glamour* magazine says Madonna and Calista Flockhart shop there. How much more trendy do you want?

Gil's also fast asleep, but I'm quite pleased because at least he's not snoring—something that I always find very off-putting in a man. His fringe has flopped over his eyes and I want to reach out and smooth it away from his brow and I'm suddenly seized by this overwhelming feeling of love and warmth. If I was a bit older, I'd call it a hot flush, but unfortunately I can't dismiss it so easily. I look at this man I don't really know and yet I want to hold him.

I stand there and don't really know what to do. Gil looks so peaceful that I could stay and watch him for hours, but on the other hand, having summoned up the nerve to come here, I'd really like him to be awake to acknowledge the fact.

The room is dark and mellow; the only light is from the flickering fire and a scattering of table lamps. There are a couple of nut brown Chesterfields and some squishy sofas too. The night has closed in, encouraged by the pouring rain. It's no wonder he's nodded off.

My dilemma is solved by two loud German businessmen who come crashing into the lounge like an advance from the panzer division, speaking in *Achtung!* voices. They carry big brandy glasses and march across the lounge to a far-flung Chesterfield as if they are invading Poland. Gil's eyes shoot open and once they have stopped rotating in surprise they focus on me. A smile spreads across his face.

"Hi," I say.

"Hey." He swings his legs off the sofa and stands to greet me, even though he still looks a bit dazed. His fingers fold round mine and they're warm from the heat of the fire. "I must have dozed off," he says.

"Jet lag," I advise as if I know about these things.

"I guess so." Gil sits down again and pats the sofa next to him. "Join me. I've ordered afternoon tea."

Slithering out of my damp, doggy coat, I throw it at the corner of the shaggy hearthrug, which probably resembles one of its long-lost friends, and sit down at the far end of the sofa. I always find it a nightmare sitting on a sofa with a stranger. I'm never quite sure of the etiquette of correct distance. Too close and you end up sliding down the middle of the cushions. Too far to one end and you look standoffish. I try to position myself centrally in the cushion, which I'm sure gives off its own message.

"Well," Gil turns and appraises me. "You look different." By that, I hope he means better. His eyes linger on my cleavage.

"I don't think those uniforms were designed by Armani," I joke awkwardly.

"No." He laughs. "Probably not."

A tray of tea arrives. There is a bottle of champagne on the tray and no sign of a teapot. "I thought we'd do afternoon tea without the 'tea' part." Gil pours me a glass of champagne. "To tell you the truth, I'm not that fond of tea. I'm more of a coffee person."

I wonder if this is his only dark secret. I hate this part of meeting people—the part where you think they're potentially a fab human being and then you find out they've more skeletons hiding in their cupboard than a horror film and all manner of undesirable habits. I also hate the fact that I always live in hope of being wrong. Gil lifts his glass.

"What are we celebrating?" I ask. *"The One That Got Away?"*

Gil shakes his head. "I think Ms. Neils has had enough glasses raised to her." He clinks his glass against mine. "Maybe we should toast the one that *didn't* get away?"

I assume he means me, but I'm not 100 percent sure.

"I'm only here for one more night," Gil says, and he gazes at me in a very twinkly way. "I'd like to spend it with you."

I nearly spit out my champagne. Blimey, this is a bit quick. We haven't even got as far as the smoked-salmon sandwiches! Are all American men such fast movers? I manage to swallow my fizz instead of spraying it all over the place, but it goes down the wrong hole and I start to cough.

"Oh hell," Gil says. "I didn't mean it like that." He pats me with an exuberant amount of force on my back. The Germans glare over their brandy at us. Gil and I start to laugh and before he beats me to death, I get him to stop pounding my vertebrae into submission.

"I'm fine. I'm fine," I say. We fall back onto the sofa, slinking down, giggling, and I forget all about the territorial occupation of cushions; we put our heads together like a couple of naughty schoolkids.

"Shall I start again?" Gil asks finally.

I wipe the tears from below my ears, hoping that my mascara is still in the place it should be. "I think you'd better."

"This is my last night in London. I am supposed to be going to a book signing with Elise. I'd rather spend the evening having dinner with you."

He's choosing me over the cute, successful author! "Won't she be mad?"

"I have just agreed to pay her an awful lot of money, so I think she'll cut me some slack."

"We haven't eaten our sandwiches yet."

"These wouldn't feed a Cockney sparrow," he says in a Dick Van Dyke accent. "Do you have other plans?"

"Yes." I twiddle the stem of my champagne flute. "I'm supposed to be eating last night's risotto with my flatmate. I'd better phone her."

"I'll call Elise too."

"Let's do it." And with a nod, we both produce mobile phones and punch in numbers.

Alice's phone clicks straight to answering machine and I leave a garbled message while trying to keep one ear on Gil's conversation. He tells Elise that he's unavailable, but I notice that he doesn't explain why. Small point, but I wonder if it's pertinent. We both end our calls and then look at each other, vaguely embarrassed.

The Germans seem to take the hint that this is becoming a private party and leave. Gil stands up and throws another log on the fire and we listen to it crackle and hiss in protest for a while.

"I don't normally do this sort of thing," Gil admits.

"Me neither."

"Dating is a pretty weird business in California."

"I think it's pretty weird in London too."

"You're not in a permanent relationship?"

"Me?" I shake my head. "No." Would I be here if I was? I want to say that I've given up on men, but really I think they've given up on me. I have had three full-time, bona fide, paid-up boyfriends in living memory, all of whom I adored and all of whom left me for someone bubblier and with bouncier breasts. It's given me some sort of complex.

I do dating occasionally, usually when one of my friends forces me to, but I find the whole thing traumatic. At eighteen the will-he-ring?/won't-he-ring? thing is part of the deal. At thirty-two I feel that I've grown out of it. I don't want to play dating games. I don't want to spend nights in loud wine bars with people that I don't give a toss about. I don't want seven men on the go at once. I want relationships. Sensible, grown-up ones. Preferably involving two people who care for each other. I don't want posturing and playing cool and keeping my options open. I don't want to pretend that I'm something that I'm not. I try very hard not to do manipulation or deceit. I run all my relationships with a view that honesty is generally the best policy. You'd think that men would like that, but they don't. Generally, they can't cope with it at all.

"You?"

"No," Gil says. And I notice that there is no telltale white band round his finger from having hastily stashed his wedding ring away. Years of conference-going has made me suspicious. I have been approached by more married men whose wives don't understand them than I care to remember.

"I didn't really need you to pose with Elise," Gil says suddenly with a nervous smile. "I'd watched you for most of this week and didn't know how else to talk to you. Is that a terrible confession?"

"No." It's a pretty amazing one though. I'd imagined Hollywood producers being used to having a string of obliging starlets hanging on their arm, not having insecurities about chatting up someone like little old me.

"For someone who professes not to be interested in giving leaflets out," he continues with a smile, "you were doing it with a certain amount of fervor."

"Needs must," I say. "I'm at the stage where I treat every job as if it might be my last." I pull my knees toward me and let myself sink into the sofa in an attempt to convince my body I'm not as weary as I feel. "I was a City trader, but the world of financial high-flyers decided they could manage without me." I fiddle with my champagne glass to avoid eye contact. "I went from a ten-year career plan governed with the aid of a very pushy life coach to not knowing what I'm going to be doing next week."

Gil shrugs. "The movie business is like that all the time. One day you're hot, the next you're not. You have to roll with the good times and try not to take it too personally when you're as popular as a fart in a spacesuit. Successes are quickly forgotten. Failure tends to hang around."

"Like a fart in a spacesuit."

Gil laughs. "Exactly."

"Have you produced anything I'd have heard of?" I venture. I like to think I'm a bit of a film buff—as long as it's something you can watch on Sky Home Box Office. By the time I get back from work most evenings, it's all I can do to sit upright and watch television. If he does deep and meaningful movies, I won't have a clue.

"Maybe." Gil reels off a list of films that were all major block-busters over here as well as in the States: *Funny Bones, Teenage Dreamboat, Frankie and Sally, One Hot Night, Remembering Maude, Could It Be Magic?*

Oh good grief. He *is* a film producer. A hit factory. And it may well show an inherent lack of trust in men, but I was convinced he was going to turn out to be a fraud. I don't even want to examine how I came to this conclusion. I may still pop down to Blockbusters to check out the credits on the DVD covers just to make sure he's listed.

"I loved *One Hot Night*," I say and blush over the implications of the title.

"You did?" He too flushes. "It's my own personal favorite."

"I'm very impressed."

"I have to confess," Gil says, "I kinda hoped you would be."

"I have my own confession to make," I say. "I spent twenty-two pounds I don't have on this top in an effort to impress you."

"It worked," Gil says. "You look very lovely."

"Thanks."

He sighs. "Why didn't we meet up earlier?"

I don't know the answer to this. We are too comfortable too quickly, and already I'm dreading the time when he'll have to go. Then I wonder if we'd met earlier whether it would, in fact, have made things better or worse.

"How can I feel like this?" Gil says. "I don't even know your name."

And if it's a line, I am falling for it. "Sadie," I oblige. "Sadie Nelson." And, at this moment, it's about the only thing that I am certain of.

Five

Why do nights whizz by so quickly when you don't want them to? Why couldn't the hours drag by like they do when you're sitting in a dentist's waiting room? Time, as they say, does fly when you're having fun. Even if you happen to be having it while you're in the land of Nod.

We didn't make dinner—or the bedroom, for that matter. We sat chatting for hours and then, without even realizing it, we'd fallen asleep. When we did wake, it was because we were both freezing cold as the fire in the Townham's lounge had long since died. I'd like to think it was romantic that we'd cuddled up together like children and slept soundly—although several of my limbs are starting to regret it—but part of me feels that I would have liked to stay awake all night and talked. That's the unacceptable face of getting older—the mind is still very willing, but the body is a right old party pooper. Too many early nights in bed with nothing but ye olde battered paperbacks for company have made my party-animal cells go all dormant.

"Hi, sleepyhead," Gil says, and I think that he's a fine one to talk.

"Hi," I say, even though my tongue is fuzzed up to the roof of my mouth. "Ooo." Bits of me are hurting and I don't dare to think what my hair looks like.

Gil takes my hand. "I have to go," he says. "I need to call a cab, otherwise I'm going to miss my plane."

I can't think of anything to say. No, that's wrong. I can think of too many things to say.

"I wish I could take a later flight." He genuinely looks troubled. "I have work and stuff. I need to get back."

It would only be delaying the inevitable. "That's okay," I say.

"I have to go to work too." The whole world of leaflet-giving-out could crumble if I'm not at my post by nine.

"I'll be in London again," Gil says. "Soon. I usually come over to the screenings in September."

September? That's months away. Seven months away, to be exact. That's not soon.

"Great," I say.

"You do want to see me again?" Gil asks. "You do want to stay in touch?"

"Yes. Of course."

"Do you have email?"

I can borrow Alice's computer. She's a good pal. She'll realize that this is a worthy cause. "Yes."

"You still have my business card?"

I nod.

"It has my phone number and my email address on it."

I nod again. This is too rushed, too hurried, too important.

"Come to my room," Gil says.

"I . . . we . . ."

"No," Gil says. "Wait here. I'll be five minutes. Three." Then he kisses me soundly and rushes out, ordering a taxi and sprinting up the stairs without pausing.

I want to cry, but tell myself, *Don't make a scene! You're made of sterner stuff than that. This man is nothing to you. You only met him yesterday. How can you be stupid enough to cry over him? This was a pleasant evening and you must enjoy it for that—even though there's a chance that you'll never, ever repeat it in your entire life.* Standing here mesmerized, tasting his kiss on my lips, I try to work out a game plan, but haven't succeeded by the time Gil returns.

He still looks like he's just woken up, but he's wearing his suit instead of his preppies and carrying a suitcase. "The cab's here," he says, and his voice is definitely tinged with disappointment and sadness and I don't know what else.

I grab the damp Afghan from the floor and throw it on and we both head outside.

It's a gray and drizzly London dawn. The sky is the color of overwashed sheets. The sun, white and weak, is edging above the Tube station and looks as feeble as I feel. The Afghan is failing to keep me warm and I stamp my toes on the pavement in an effort to revive them.

Gil opens the cab door and throws his suitcase inside. "Heathrow, please," he says to the driver, who seems reluctant to put away his newspaper. Then Gil turns to me. "This is it."

"It's been nice to meet you," I say.

"Nice?" Gil laughs in surprise. "I hope that's traditional British reserve," he says, "because I think it's been a lot more than nice."

"Very nice." I can feel myself starting to cry. "It was very nice."

Gil wraps his arms round me. "I guess 'very nice' will have to do." He kisses me again and this time it's warm and tender and very inappropriate for a cold, hard, city street. *Don't go,* rushes up and sticks in my throat.

Gil disentangles himself and holds me away from him. "I don't want to remember you like this," he says, "looking sad and alone. And more than a little cold."

"I'm fine." I stamp my feet just to show how capable I am of creating my own warmth. "Really I am."

Gil brushes his lips against mine for a final time. "I'll call," he promises as he gets into the back of the cab.

I hope to goodness that he does. "Bye." I put my fingers against the glass as he closes the door. The cab driver, oblivious to our plight, moves off into the first murmurings of rush-hour traffic.

"Bye," Gil mouths back.

And they drive away, leaving me standing on the pavement, looking pathetically after them. Gil's cab turns the corner and he is gone.

Back in reality, I know I may never see him again. The thought sends my mood plummeting to my boots. While Gil is heading swiftly back toward the California sunshine and the mad, bad, make-believe world of movies, here in my mundane little life in miserable little downcast London, it starts to rain. If my life were a movie, the sun would be out, it would be full of love and laughter— and I'd get the guy. We'd walk off into the sunset arm in arm.

As it is, it's pouring and I have no umbrella. I am not getting the guy, I am just getting very wet. And I'm doing it without having brushed my teeth. I escape the downpour, dive into the Tube and realize that somewhere between the Townham and here I've lost my weekly pass and will have to buy another ticket. A heartfelt "fuck" is not far from my lips. *An absolutely perfect day for giving out leaflets*, I think.

Six

Alice and I are sitting in the Wing-Wah Chinese Takeaway waiting for the owner, Li, to create some wonder in our lives via the medium of sweet-and-sour pork.

"Why look so glum, lady?" Li says while putting our prawn crackers in a plastic bag.

"Man trouble," Alice informs him. "Her. Not me," she expands, with a flick of her hair in my direction.

"Thanks," I say, uncertain that I want the world and, in particular, the queue in the Wing-Wah to share my romantic troubles.

"Confucius, he say all men are total borrocks."

Li was born in Bermondsey and has lived for the majority of his thirty-five years in South London. He has never been to China and knows bog all about Confucius. He does, however, do a mean crispy duck, so we tolerate all his insane ramblings, from his interpretation of the lesser-known sayings of Confucius to the sheer brilliance of Jackie Chan—who, I'm led to believe, does all his own stunts.

"We're giving this one the benefit of the doubt," Alice says. "He's a movie producer."

While I quietly die of embarrassment, the rest of the queue nod their approval.

"And he didn't try to sleep with her on their first date."

The queue nod again.

"They just fell asleep in each other's arms."

All the faces in the queue melt into a warm smile. I smile tightly back.

"So," Li shrugs. "What probrem?"

"He's in Los Angeles," Alice continues.

There is a sympathetic "awh" from the queue.

"So what? Air travel velly cheap."

Cheap is a relative thing when you have no money. As it is, Alice is having to sub me this takeaway until my check from Bindlatters clears. What's more, having survived my stint at the London Book Fair, I am now a fully paid-up member of the ranks of the unemployed.

As Li bags up our sweet-and-sour, I look at his Chinese horoscope clock. It is just after 9 P.M. in the Year of the Pig. This thing is desperately inaccurate. I don't think Li has the foggiest idea how to set it. When the rest of the world was celebrating the Year of the Tiger, Li's clock said Rat. Whatever year it is, Chinese or otherwise, I wonder where Gil is now. His plane was leaving at some ungodly hour and the flight's about eleven hours long. And they're what—eight hours, nine hours behind us? Or is it in front? I don't know. I wish I was more *au fait* with international time travel. I haven't a bloody clue where he is. I only know that it isn't here. My lip wobbles slightly.

"Sweet-and-sour poke. Plawn clackers. Egg Flied Lice. Two steam dumpling."

Li is perfectly capable of pronouncing his r's—he only slips into this Chinese stuff for effect. Whenever we see him in the pub he talks in a broad south London accent and says "gor blimey, mate" a lot.

"We're on," Alice says and stands up to grab our goodies.

I'm not the slightest bit hungry, although normally nothing affects my appetite. I wish I were one of those people who can't eat a thing when they're stressed. Me, I stuff it all in whatever my emotional climate.

"Good luck, love," a builder-type bloke says to me from his seat by the window and gives me a thumbs up.

"Cheers," I say. I think I might need it. I'm sure that the minute Gil hits home turf and is surrounded by slender, gorgeous movie stars in the ilk of Uma Thurman, Gwyneth Paltrow and Sharon Stone, he'll come to his senses. After all, what could he possibly see in me? I will be a forgotten memory quicker than you can say, "Sadie *who*?" One day, when he's attending the pre-miére of *The One That Got Away*, he may spare a thought for the Leaflet-Giver-Outer who might have been. But, then again, he may not.

"Tell your friend to say hello to Jackie Chan," Li shouts after us.

"Yeah, right."

I plod out after Alice and she hands me the brown carrier bag while she shimmies into her shiny new Ford Fiesta, which I'm dead jealous of. I slide in next to her and look at all the bells and whistles and gadgets and I want a nice car again. Being a transport-reduced, underpaid, poverty-stricken person is pants.

Alice pulls out into the traffic. Every journey with my friend is a white-knuckle ride as she has a blatant disregard for the Highway Code. Quicker than any speed limit could possibly allow, we are at her flat.

My friend has the top floor of an Edwardian conversion which she bought in a rush due to spiraling property prices and all that guff. It looked great—on the surface—but beneath all that Farrow & Ball paint lurked a heap of unseen and extremely expensive dangers. That was the point at which I moved in. We are now at the stage of no ceilings, exposed wiring and two deckchairs in the lounge carefully arranged amidst the plaster dust.

Alice pushes the door open and kicks a dustsheet out of the way. Jerry, who we like to call "our builder," even though he never does anything we tell him, is not the world's tidiest worker.

"I'm starving," she says.

"Mmm . . ."

"Oh come on, Sadie." My friend nudges me encouragingly as she puts the takeaway in the oven with some plates to give it a blast. "He might ring. Give the bloke a chance. He's probably still over the Atlantic enjoying the delights of British Airways' plastic food."

"Yeah," I say, and feel all sorry for myself. The weekend is yawning vacantly ahead of me, and come Monday morning, I will have to steel myself to go out into the cruel world and look for menial work involving some form of ill-fitting uniform again.

I ferret around in the kitchen drawer until I find the chopsticks, while Alice dishes out, piling our plates with a mountain of monosodium glutamate. We struggle through stacked cans of oil paint to the lounge, ready to settle ourselves for a debauched night of calories and cheesy telly.

As Alice sits down, she glances over at the answerphone. "Ooo."

Its little red light is winking joyously at us.

"I wonder who it is?"

If I could tell her that, I'd be able to give up my day job and spend my time predicting Lotto numbers.

Alice prods the machine with a well-practiced blow from her big toe. It whirrs into life.

"Hi," a disembodied voice says.

I sit bolt upright—or as bolt upright as it is possible to be in a deckchair. I'd know that sexy American accent anywhere.

"It's Gil," I say.

"It's Gil," the voice on the answerphone says.

"*It's Gil,*" Alice echoes in hushed tones.

"I know, I know."

"I got back home safely."

"He's back home," my helpful friend tells me.

"I know that. Ssh!"

There is a bit of throat-clearing going on down the line. "I'm missing you," the answerphone continues.

Alice chews her lip, ecstatically. "Oh my word! *He's missing you.*"

"Shut up, Al."

"Well." A little disappointed pause. "I'll try to call you again over the weekend. Bye."

And that's it. The machine peeps and farts and rewinds and if Alice wasn't here I'd listen to the message all over again. But I can't, because she *is* here and she'd think I was too pathetic for words.

"Do you want to listen to it again?"

I put on a cool expression and shake my head. "No."

"Well, I do," Alice says. She gives the machine another kick and we listen to Gil telling British Telecom that he misses me all over again.

"He sounds very keen," she observes as she turns her attention to her sweet-and-sour pork.

So he does. It gives me a warm glow—which has nothing to do with the fact that my plateful of noodles is burning my knees.

Seven

"So? How was sunny London?"

"Wet," Gil replied. "Very wet." He was sitting in a battered trailer on the back lot of Paramount Studios grabbing a rushed lunch with his dear friend and confidant, Steve Bernard. Gil was weary with jet lag and he felt like he had scratchy stubble on the inside of his eyelids as well as on his chin.

A woman with a bald, purple head and red eyes sat in the corner of the office talking into a cell phone with a broad Brooklyn accent complaining about her last Brazilian wax.

"Martian," Steve said, flicking a thumb at her.

"I thought Martians were little green men."

"Hey, this is Hollywood." Steve shrugged. "Martians can be any color we like. Maybe the green ones clashed with the wallpaper."

Gil helped himself to half a pastrami sandwich.

"Oh man, get your own lunch!"

"No time," Gil said. "I've got a meeting with the execs in ten."

"About this new book?"

"Yeah. *The One That Got Away.*"

"Lead?"

"Hugh's the obvious choice."

"Hugh." Steve pursed his lips with approval. "Are you gonna shoot in London?"

Gil, mouth full, nodded. "Mmm-hmmm."

"Take me," Steve said. "Local knowledge. I know the places to go where it doesn't rain."

"There aren't any."

"They're well-kept secrets we don't reveal to American

tourists or movie producers." Steve looked wistful. "I haven't been home for years."

His friend was an ex-pat Brit who had moved out to LA when the British film industry went into terminal decline some time ago. Steve was an art director by trade, working on the latest— and eleventh—*Star Satellite* movie, one of the most successful and spectacular sci-fi shows of all time. Fittingly, the two men were surrounded at this moment by blueprints of fantastical buildings and star ships.

What *Star Satellite* lacked in story, plot and depth of character- ization was more than compensated for by fabulous sets, an ex- cess of pyrotechnics, state-of-the-art special effects and very skimpy costumes.

"If you go home, you might not want to come back to this madhouse." Gil brushed crumbs off a small white polystyrene model of a building.

"If you're going to take my food from my mouth, man, at least don't sprinkle it all over the Arutigan Senate."

Gil gave it an admiring glance. "It looks good."

"What do you expect from a genius?" Steve waved one of his fries at his masterpiece. "It's in Stage Ten, if you want to take a peep."

"I might just do that." Gil helped himself to a fry. Steve looked pained. "I'm helping you out," Gil said. "Otherwise you'll get fat."

"Yeah—and then what?" his friend asked. "Renée Zellweger won't want to snog me. Big deal. I'm a happily married man for heaven's sake. I don't have to starve myself. Shapely men are good. It's shapely women this town can't handle. California birds are too skinny. No meat."

"I met a nice woman in London." Gil looked up to gauge Steve's reaction. "Shapely," he added.

Steve looked round. "That was a bit stage right."

Gil shrugged. "It happens."

His friend frowned. "Not to you, it doesn't. You don't do meet- ing women. You have Georgina."

"Well, I met a woman. Big deal."

"And?"

"And, nothing."

"Is she British?"

"Yes."

"Good. Good. Good start. As you know, I'm genetically biased toward British women. Are you going to see her again?"

"She lives in London."

"This is the Golden Age of travel, mate. She could get a ticket for a few hundred bucks. She could be here tomorrow."

Gil tried not to look worried.

Steve frowned. "*Is* she going to come out here?"

"I don't know," Gil admitted. "I just got back. I've called her already. Maybe we'll email for a while."

"Oh boy!" Steve huffed. "You really know how to take risks with relationships."

"Well, I am twice-bitten. I need to take things slow."

"And there is the small matter of Georgina."

"Gina's cool."

Steve snorted. "Georgina's never cool. She is in permanent crisis mode. I don't know how you deal with it."

"Someone has to." Gil took another mouthful of sandwich. "Anyway, I'd better shoot. Don't want to engender bad feeling with the suits by being late."

"They'll keep you waiting for hours."

"That's their prerogative." Gil stood, ready to leave.

"You are the worst kind of commitment-phobe, Gil McGann," Steve said.

"And how do you work that out?"

"Because you don't even realize you *are* one."

"What a bunch of baloney," Gil scoffed. "I've been married twice—and look where that got me. I'm not a commitment-phobe. Maybe I'm just all commitmented out."

Steve grinned. "Send your English Rose a ticket. Take a chance."

Gil kissed Steve on top of the head. "You are such an old romantic," he said with a smile.

"And you're full of shit," Steve barked.

Gil ducked out of the door before he could be drawn any further on the state of his love life, and as he did so, a bit of Arutigan Senate building whistled past his ear.

"Catch you later," Gil said and strode out into the warm California sunshine.

He headed across the parking lot, past the swaying palm trees and toward the historical, sugar pink stuccoed buildings that formed the studio offices. Gil felt the sun warm his bones. The brightness of the cloudless blue sky hurt his tired eyes and he slipped his sunglasses on.

He'd only been in Los Angeles for a few hours and already chilly London seemed a million miles away. He thought about Sadie Nelson freezing her butt off back home and wondered, not for the first time, if she would come out here if he sent her a plane ticket.

Eight

Barmaid. I am a barmaid. I have a fancy title, like Liquid Refreshment Entertainment Officer or something. But I am, without shadow of a doubt, a barmaid. And I feel this is an all-time low for me. It's one of those trendy bars that has very loud music but no chairs, and I think that should be scaring me.

I am part of a TEAM, so I'm told. And we all have to work like a TEAM. Which mainly seems to involve pooling our tips and not having any tea breaks. My uniform for this job is ludicrous, and already I'm longing for the feel of red polyester again. The name of the bar is Floosies and I have a spangly Lurex skirt that barely skims my bottom and a matching cropped top suitable for someone with infinitely smaller breasts than mine. I definitely feel like a Floosie. Or a complete idiot. It serves me right. I lied on my application form and somehow convinced the manager that I was twenty-five, when in fact I am on the slippery slope on the far side of thirty. I feel twenty-five—some days—so is it such a huge lie?

When I arrived for my shift, it was apparent that everyone else had lied about their age too. Unlike me, they're all *under* twenty-five—by about ten years. Most of them are still enjoying puberty. They suit minuscule Lurex because they have no thighs and concave stomachs. I, as is natural for a person of my advancing years, have the softly rounded belly of someone who has enjoyed a lifelong attachment to all things chocolate, and burgeoning childbearing hips. They have belly rings; I am at the age where the only thing I want in my belly button is fluff. The men don't wear anything on their top at all except a spangly bow tie—at least I have not stooped so low. But it is, I admit, a very small step.

I have never been so miserable. We are in a TEAM huddle prior to the commencement of the night's festivities and there is some sort of chirpy chanting going on, which is making me too depressed for words. It comes to a conclusion with a joyful whoop and a punch of the air, by everyone except me—I jump into action about thirty seconds later. The other staff turn to look at me as if they suspect there is an "old" person in their midst, and already I am singled out by the manager as not a TEAM player. I try a weak smile and give my Lurex a tug to make it appear longer. I fail on both counts.

We are sent to our allotted stations. I am in the quiet "chill-out" bar as I am a trainee TEAM member. How can I be thirty-two and still a trainee? When I was eighteen and trekking round the major cities of Europe in my gap year before starting university, I had a vision of how my life would be. And this definitely was not it.

By now I was going to have had my fabulous and fulfilling career, have sown my wild oats along the way, leaving a trail of brokenhearted men who were, of course, grateful to have known me and richer for the experience. I was now going to be entering enthusiastically into a new phase of my life involving a rather large, detached country cottage, several blonde angelic children and a blond angelic husband who earned pots of money, but from a job that allowed him plenty of time at home to share child-rearing duties—which, naturally, he would do with aplomb and without complaint. We would still, after the children were in bed soundly asleep, be mad for it like rabbits.

I am assigned to a twenty-year-old boy, Olly, who is to show me the ropes. He has more hair gel than is good for one person and puts his hands on my Lurex at every opportunity. I am going to punch him before the night is out. No one ever drinks out of glasses anymore, so all we have to do is dole out bottles. I can read and the till adds everything up for me, so how hard can it be? The main problem is going to be staying awake until three o'clock in the morning when the rest of the world is in the land of Nod and my shift finally ends.

Before I give the impression that all is doom and gloom, there are some parts of my life that are going particularly well. One part of my life, actually. I have spoken to Gil several times since Friday and it is still only Tuesday. In between long, luscious transatlantic phone calls, we text and email each other and do all those sorts of high-tech things that lovers now do. And while it is very nice to have a "status" boyfriend that I can drop into conversations—or at least begin to compete with my flatmate—in some ways I think it is the contrast between his high-flying, glamorous, warm-temperatured lifestyle that is making me so unhappy with my low-slung, tacky, freeze-your-ass-off excuse for existence.

The thing is that I'm frightened of losing him before I even get a chance to start. I have nothing to talk to him about. He rattles on about Brad and George and Russell—I think we all know who they are. He has meetings and projects and power breakfasts at Nate 'n Al's and drinks at Chateau Marmont. I have my daily fight on the Underground and my daily fight to survive. I have nothing to impress him with. I feel I have to rehearse some funny lines to throw in, which is never a good sign. We can't even talk about the weather, because it's always bloody sunny out there!

Olly nudges me in the Lurex again and I sigh heavily. "This should be a gentle introduction," he says. And I look up and see about two hundred people stampeding toward the bar. "You'll hit your stride by the time the rush starts."

And I really have no idea whether he is joking or not.

Nine

Gil had taken a guest to dinner at Morton's. It was a huge, high-ceilinged restaurant that still managed somehow to be intimate. Everything was crisp and starched—the napkins, the tablecloths, the waiters. The lighting was subdued to a level that spoke of discretion, and tables were thoughtfully placed so that conversations from your neighbors couldn't easily be overheard. That was probably why it was one of the favored haunts of the movers and shakers of the movie industry. Gil nodded to a few acquaintances as they took their tables.

The meeting today had gone great. The execs had been more than enthusiastic about *The One That Got Away,* which was more than unusual, and it looked like this project could get a green light very quickly. The writer whom he'd approached to do the screenplay, Danny Ziemska, sat opposite Gil, nervously fiddling with his fork. Ziemska was a seasoned scribe who had written and sold six scripts, which were all stuck in development hell; consequently, none of them had yet graced the silver screen. Maybe Gil would be able to change that for him. He sure hoped so. And so did Danny Ziemska.

At the moment, Ziemska was tossing out some ideas—formed entirely on the basis that he had absolutely no knowledge of the contents of the novel. However, that didn't stop him from sounding extremely convincing.

Gil felt weary down to his bones and he could blame only so much of it on his transatlantic jet-setting. It was becoming harder and harder to find projects that excited him, and the relentless battles and struggles were starting to deplete him rather than energize him. He hoped *The One That Got Away* would get him firing on all cylinders again. If you were a producer who didn't want the cut and thrust of steam-rollering a project through to a finished movie, then it was time to cut and run, buy the remote farmhouse in the Highland Lakes of Texas, and write that novel you'd always meant to start but never did.

There was a relentlessness itching round the collar of his shirt like ants. Perhaps he was starting his midlife crisis. They were all the rage these days amongst his friends. It seemed to occur at the point where you realized you'd achieved everything you'd ever dreamed of and yet with that came the even more startling realization that there was still something missing. A vital nerve synapse connection that failed to make the jump and kick-start the happiness feeling.

But what would make him happy? Would another job put the spark to his flame? Was this the work for which he was ideally suited? His father had been in the movie business—on the other side of the camera—and Gil had followed him into it without questioning whether there was anything more appropriate for his talents. Did he want to do something else? Be someone else? But wasn't that part of the point of Hollywood? Everyone here wanted to be someone else. All the waiters, busboys and cab drivers wanted to be actors or writers. All the actors wanted to be directors. All the writers wanted to be producers. And what did the producers want to be? This particular producer wasn't really sure.

If a change of career wasn't the answer, what was? Would it be a life like his good friend Steve had? Would he be content to spend his days making models and then going home to play Happy Families with his wife and kids? Was that what was missing in Gil's life?

Gil downed his drink. He still had the wife, but they no longer operated under the pretense of Happy Families. He could never have considered bringing up kids with Gina, when his wife had turned out to be harder to manage than any eight-year-old could be. Maybe having a family would have helped her to settle down. Gil somehow doubted it. How could he have reached the age of thirty-eight, live in a place with the most agreeable climate in the world, have everything that money could buy and still not be able to say that he was truly, bone-deep happy? Perhaps he still had enough of a grip on reality—even after years of living in materialistic Tinseltown—to appreciate that happiness was indeed the one thing that money couldn't buy. If it was, why did he know so many damn miserable millionaires?

Gil looked up at the writer, who was still in full flow, unaware that he had long lost Gil's attention. "Do you have a family?" Gil asked.

Danny Ziemska stopped midstream and paused, open-mouthed, clearly wondering whether the wrong answer would affect his future employment. "Er . . ."

"It isn't a trick question," Gil said. "I'd like to know."

"I have two children," Ziemska said. "A boy of four and an eighteen-month-old girl."

"Do they make you happy?"

"Y—Yes," Ziemska stammered. "I guess so."

"Great," Gil said. "That's great."

"Do I get the job?" The writer was hesitant.

"Yeah," Gil said.

Ziemska stood up. "I'll get my lawyer to contact you to set up a contract."

"Yeah." No transaction was ever complete unless a whole bunch of lawyers were involved. The waiter hovered and Gil pushed the check and a wad of bills toward him. He needed to be out of here now.

They walked toward the door—another new and wary relationship established. Gil smiled to himself. It made him think of Sadie and where she might be now. He'd been thinking about her a lot since he'd returned from London. Maybe too much.

The writer said his goodbyes and jumped into a cab. Gil's sleek black BMW arrived courtesy of the parking valet and, handing over a generous tip, Gil took his keys and slid into the driver's seat. He swung out of the restaurant parking lot and onto Melrose Avenue, heading for Beverly Hills and the monstrous modernist glass-and-concrete structure that Gina had chosen and which he now called home.

He couldn't imagine Sadie choosing a place like that. She was too straightforward, too down to earth. That's what he liked about her the most. She had no airs and graces, no pretensions, no apparent collagen implants. She meant what she said and said what she meant—which was something that hadn't been a huge feature of his marriage to Georgina. Sadie was pinned securely to the earth, while Gina floated to and fro on the Southern California breeze, changing direction just as often. Suddenly he wanted to see Sadie again, see if the feelings he was having were real. Damn this time difference, this ocean between them. Why on earth couldn't he have fallen in love with someone from Hollywood? Gil straightened himself in the driver's seat. What was he thinking! Fallen in love?

Ten

It's just after four in the morning. I have feet the size of an elephant. They are throbbing and purple and I've no idea how they are going to resume their normal size before I'm due on my shift tomorrow night. Not even in my wildest dreams will I be able to get my poor, battered tootsies anywhere near my shoes at the moment.

I'm sitting in a deck chair in the bomb site that we call Alice's lounge with my trousers rolled up to my knees and my feet in the washing-up bowl full of cold water. I can't decide whether it is heaven or hell. It is, at least, bringing some feeling back to them—even if that feeling is pain. I am very glad that Alice is fast asleep and can't see me. My friend looks cool at all times—even in her cartoon nightdress—whereas I do not.

I sink back into the deck chair and close my eyes. There must be an easier way to earn a living than this. I've got to get my life back on track, and if I wasn't so exhausted by the process of trying to earn enough to put food in my mouth then I could possibly contemplate a major career change. How did I ever manage to hold down a respectable, well-paying job when I can't even cope with standing up behind a bar for eight hours? I'm just going to sit here for another five minutes and then head for my bed—and hopefully dream of Gil.

There is an alarm going off in my head and I've no idea where I am. Oh shit, my feet are in a bowl of cold water. Arrgh! I've remembered the pain. What's that bloody ringing? It's the phone. Good grief, what time is it? It's still pitch black outside. I fall off my deck chair and lurch for the phone before it wakes Alice. The bowl tips over and the water winds its way round the dustsheets and seeps in between the floorboards. I stub my toe on Jerry the builder's Black and Decker sander.

"Damn it!" This had better not be someone selling double glazing or conservatories. I snatch up the phone.

"Hi." It's Gil's voice and I sink to the floor.

"Hi," I say and all my anger floods out of me, just like the water in the washing-up bowl.

"How are you?"

"Awful," I say. "Very awful. I have a crap job, a crap life and I'm living in the power tools section of Kmart."

Gil laughs and I can't help but smile too.

"How are you?" I ask.

"Missing you."

That's me gone to pieces again and suddenly all the pain in my feet dissipates in a warm rush of something nice. I make a bad job of stifling a yawn. "What time is it?"

"Time you came to visit me," Gil says, and this time he doesn't laugh.

"Yeah, right," I say. "I'll get Harold to fire up the Lear jet."

"I'm serious. Will you come?"

"Gil, how can I? I am what is commonly known as financially embarrassed."

"I'll arrange it," he says. I wish I could see his face, because he sounds as if there is no smile in his voice at all. "You can pick up the ticket at the airport."

"I can't do that!" I lean back against Alice's still unpacked tea chests.

"Why not? You said you were having a terrible time. You could be on a plane tomorrow night."

"You are definitely from Planet La-la." My feet are getting cold and I wrap them in one of Jerry's dustsheets—which aren't dusty because Jerry hasn't yet done anything workmanlike enough to produce dust. "Real people don't just jump on planes willy-nilly. We think about it for months. Shop around. Complain that we're being ripped off. And then, and only then, after weeks of deliberation, do we finally get round to booking a ticket. Even when I had the money to, I wouldn't have dreamed of flying off at a moment's notice. Real people don't do spontaneity."

"Maybe you should try it."

"I have a job."

"You're working in a bar," Gil points out.

"I can't let them down. Tonight was my first night. I'm part of a TEAM." Although there wasn't much TEAMwork going on when dear Olly slipped off to the Gents for a sneaky smoke and left me to face a bar full of thirsty and increasingly aggressive ravers all by myself.

"You have a very misplaced sense of loyalty."

I sigh. He may well be right.

"Don't you want to come?"

"Of course I do. It isn't that."

"Then what is it?"

"I don't know." And I'm not really sure why I'm not jumping at the chance. Is it because I'm as pasty as a milk bottle and I couldn't face putting my unfit body into a bikini until I've had at least half a dozen sunbed sessions and twenty hours of remedial therapy with a personal trainer? I can't remember when I last saw the sun or the inside of a gym. What if I get out there and Gil discovers I'm not the wonderful woman he seems to have decided I am? I'd only have to stand next to one of those toned, tanned, salad-eating, stick-thin women and the game would be up. What if he realizes within five minutes that I'm really just a fat milk bottle with a rapidly decaying brain, and wants me to go straight home again?

"Am I rushing you?" Gil says into the space my whirring cogs are creating.

"Yes. Well, no. Why the sudden urge?"

There is a big transatlantic pause. "I haven't felt like this for a long time," he says. "I want to see if what I feel is real."

Ah! See? So he *does* want to check out whether I'm a fat milk bottle.

"I'll email you the details later, but a ticket will be waiting for you at Heathrow tonight. I promise," Gil says decisively. "I hope you'll be there too."

And without even saying goodbye, Gil hangs up. Ooo. Now what?

Alice and I are sitting on the deckchairs having a wholesome and nutritious breakfast—a nourishing bowl of Cocoa Puffs and that other well-known delicacy, strawberry Pop-Tarts. Alice is booted and suited and ready for work. If I came across her all power-dressed like that, I certainly wouldn't mess with her. I, on the other hand, have reverted to dressing-gown slob mode. We're watching *Good Morning London*, but not giving it our full attention.

"Tonight?" Alice asks.

"That's what he said." I have a spoonful of chocolate milk and pretend that all this glugging in my stomach is due to my dubious diet.

"Impulsive." Alice nods in a way that indicates she's impressed, and it takes quite a lot to impress Alice. "I like that in a man."

I give her my best worried look. "He's paying."

"Even better," my flatmate says. "Does he have a brother?"

"I don't know what to do."

"Why?" Alice starts on the Pop-Tarts.

"I don't want to appear desperate."

"You *are* desperate."

"I know, but I don't want him to think I am."

"So what if he does?" My friend gives a careless shrug because, let's face it, it's not her life we're discussing. "What have you got to lose?"

"I don't know that either." I stare out of the dirt-streaked window into the pewter-colored day, looking in vain for inspiration. "Except that it could all go horribly wrong."

"I love your positive attitude," my friend notes. "Anyway, if it did, at least you'd know. He could turn out to be a complete cokehead. It would stop you pining your life away for him."

"Mmm." I hadn't even considered that Gil might be a cokehead. That's a very positive thought, Alice! "How would you feel about me going?"

"Great," she says. "I could get a lodger who actually pays me rent."

"Thanks." I try not to be hurt. "My bed isn't even cold before you've got someone else in it."

Alice folds her arms and stares at me in a very fierce way. "Sadie, you are such a sad sack."

"And this I don't know?"

She trundles on without acknowledging my inferiority complex. "Life has been poohing on you from a great height for months now and finally you meet this absolutely great bloke— this Hollywood producer-type hunky-chunky man who wants to whisk you away to a better life. This could be a turning point, and you're behaving as if he's asked you to saw your left foot off for him. I don't understand you. I'd have my bikini and my fake tan packed and be humming old Beach Boys' hits in the departure lounge at Heathrow before this guy could change his mind."

I bite the end of my spoon, nervously. "Do you think he *will* change his mind?"

"You are so pathetic." Alice crunches into her Pop-Tart with a certain amount of venom. "Why are you even hesitating?"

"Because this sort of thing only happens in the movies."

"He *is* in the movies. He's a Californian. It's an accepted fact that they all have a very weird view of the world. Too much sun," she says by way of explanation. "It changes your concept of reality. This could just be an everyday thing for him and here you are making a great big deal out of it."

"So you think I should go?"

"Grr . . ." Alice bounces over to my deckchair and I duck because I think she is going to hit me. Instead, she leans over and kisses me. "I love you. You are my best friend. And when I get home from work, I don't want to see you here," she says. "Do this, Sadie. Do this and be damned. If you don't, you'll be damned anyway."

Damn. I don't want to be damned. I *am* making a big deal out of it. It is a big decision. I help myself to the last Pop-Tart in the hope that it will help me to make it.

Eleven

Gil sat outside the dingy, impersonal building set back on a corner of Sunset Boulevard waiting for Georgina and nibbling away the skin at the side of his thumbnail.

This was terrifying. He looked up at the sky for no other reason than he wasn't sure what else to do. There weren't even any jet vapor trails he could lock onto. If Sadie had picked up the ticket, she should be on her way by now, but he hadn't heard anything from her. He hoped there hadn't been any problem or last-minute change of heart. For whatever reason, it had been very important to him that she come out here.

The plain black door opened and a straggle of people wandered out, blinking as the sunshine hit them in the fraction of a second before the sunglasses reflex kicked in. A less-than-discreet row of limousines waited along the side street and the household names who owned them scuttled into the backs of them, shading their faces, hoping not to be seen. Gina, dressed from head to toe in white and carrying a silver vanity case, came out last. She waved at him and tottered across the parking lot on yet another pair of impossibly sexy five-inch stilettos from Diavolina.

"Hi," she said as she slid into the BMW, air-kissed him on both cheeks and threw the case into the back seat.

"Hi," Gil said. "How did the meeting go?"

Gina lit a cigarette and blew the smoke out of the window. A dozen gold bangles jangled on her wrists and her cigarette bore the imprint of her full lips. It looked like blood. "I don't go to AA because I'm an alcoholic," she snapped. "I don't have a drink problem."

"You're strictly a wheatgrass-only girl—these days."

"I go because it's a great place to network. Do you know who goes to this class?"

"Yes, I do," Gil said. "I just saw some of them scuttle out. It's nothing to be proud of, Georgina. And it isn't a 'class.' People are trying to straighten out their lives."

Gina stared out of the window. "You called because you wanted to talk to me," she said. "If I'd known it was going to be a lecture, I'd have declined."

"Do you want to go for a coffee?"

"No," Gina said, rearranging her diamonds on her fingers. "I'm busy. I have an artwork booked for this afternoon."

"You have a dog to do."

Gina glared at him. "You always reduce things to their most base level, Gil." She fluffed up her hair. "But, yes, I have 'a dog to do.' You may drive me there if you like."

"Thanks." Gil pulled out of the lot.

Georgina was on her seventh career reincarnation in as many years, still seeking the Nirvana of a job she enjoyed for more than seven weeks—or even seven days, in some cases. She had lasted as a holistic manicurist for less than seven hours—which was a personal best—after she had tried to persuade her clients that it was all due to the toxic effects of nail varnish that the ozone layer was being slowly but surely destroyed. Now she was working as a creative canine stylist, transforming the pooches of the rich and famous into more than just fur-babies. Who, after all, wants to be seen out and about with a little cute 'ums who isn't completely color coordinated? In a town where money was no object, the cost was astronomical. At least it kept Gina in wheatgrass. The rest of her expenditure still came from Gil's checking account.

"Where are you heading?"

"Bel Air," Gina said and relaxed back into her seat.

That was great. Exactly in the opposite direction to where he wanted to be heading. With a sigh, Gil swung out onto West Sunset Boulevard.

"So. What do you want to talk to me about?"

Gil could feel himself grip the steering wheel tighter. There was only one way of saying this. He took a deep breath. "I want a divorce."

Gina spun round. "You want a divorce? Just like that?"

"It's been overdue for a long time."

"I don't want a divorce."

"Life isn't always about what you want, Gina."

"Everyone in Hollywood is divorced." She fluffed her hair again. "I don't want to run with the crowd."

"You left me for the pool man." Gil turned to look at her. "Two years ago."

"He wasn't the pool man," Gina said. "He was an actor. A very good one."

Not good enough to be able to give up working as a pool man, Gil thought sourly.

"You could have given him a job."

"Why would I want to give a job to a man who was sleeping with my wife?"

"You always think of yourself first," Gina complained.

The scruffy drag of Sunset Strip disappeared as they hit the boundary of Beverly Hills, and the dust and garbage on the sidewalks gave way to palm trees and manicured lawns.

Gina's lip still stuck out obdurately. "Why so sudden, all this talk of divorce?"

"You're living with someone else," Gil pointed out. He also wanted to point out that after two years of separation, talking of divorce wasn't sudden. The affair with the pool man/actor hadn't lasted. Gina had soon realized that despite her protestations, Kurt was better at dealing with chemical levels and leaf blockages and whatever pool stuff pool men did, than he was at acting. The only great act he had managed to do was convincing Gina otherwise—however briefly.

"What does Noah think?" Gil went on. "Doesn't he *want* you to get divorced?"

His wife was now living with an aging British rock star, Noah Bender. Gil didn't know if Bender was his real name—or even Noah, for that matter—or whether it was a summation of his proclivity for dressing up on stage in leather garter belts and going on benders. Noah was five feet, three inches without his heeled boots and his concealed lifts. He had dyed blond hair with a mullet cut and skin so tanned that it would have made great shoe leather. He and Gina had met at a Narcotics Anonymous meeting, so maybe Gina was right about the networking thing. When Noah was sober he adored Gina. When he wasn't, he couldn't remember exactly which particular tall, leggy blonde he was supposed to go home with. But then after all the drugs that had gone up one rather large nose into one rather small brain, Noah Bender couldn't even be relied upon to remember the lyrics of his greatest hit song—the royalties of which had bought him his Beverly Hills home. He was a neighbor of Jack Nicholson. He also had Kurt the actor as his pool man—although Gil didn't think that Noah knew that.

"I'm happy as I am." Her pouty mouth didn't exactly scream inner serenity or contentment. "Noah appreciates my need for security."

"Get secure with *him*," Gil suggested in as reasonable a tone as he could manage. "Divorce me. Marry him."

"Noah's a free spirit," Gina said. "I respect that. He doesn't want to be tied down by the convention of marriage."

"There's nothing conventional about our marriage," Gil said.

"Then why do you want to end it?" Gina flicked her cigarette butt out of the window, ignoring the fact that it was likely to earn her a ticket in this town for constituting a fire risk. She turned toward him, squeezing her breasts together with her arms to enhance them further than they had already been enhanced. Gil knew Gina's breasts weren't her own, because he had paid for that too. He'd liked them a lot better when they were natural. Some sort of gold Chinese symbol nestled in her ample cleavage.

For some reason and in spite of the air-conditioning pumping away for all it was worth, Gil's palms were clammy. "I think it's time to move on."

Gina let her cleavage sag. "You've met someone else."

"That has nothing to do with this."

"Who is she?"

"No one. I met her when I was in London."

"And she's no one?" Gina pursed her scarlet lips. "I bet she'd like to know that."

"She is someone," Gil capitulated. "Someone very special."

"And how are you going to have a relationship with her in London? You can't even make it home to Beverly Hills most nights."

"She's coming here." He glanced over at Gina, who took in this information with a flinch. "Tonight," Gil added, hoping he was right.

"We're nearly here," Gina said unnecessarily. "Make a right here. We're heading for Bellagio Road."

Obediently, Gil swung the BMW into the narrow winding row dotted with barely visible multimillion-dollar homes, secreted behind tall hedges and security gates and monitored by twenty-four-hour CCTV. Billionaires Row.

"It's here," Gina said. Gil stopped at the electric security gates and waited while Gina gave her name to the little black speaker box on the wall.

The gate swung open soundlessly and Gil drove up the sweeping driveway to a chateau-style house that looked as if a tornado had blown it here, perfectly intact, all the way from France. Gil stopped at the door just as a liveried butler came and opened it. Three boisterous little Bichon Frises bounded out. They were currently lemon with pink ears instead of the customary white, but no doubt Gina would soon change all that.

His wife reached into the back of the car for her vanity case full of doggie dyes.

"Don't you want me to be happy?" Gil said.

"I want nothing more." Picking up her case, she got out of the car. She shut the door and looked in through the window. "But how can you be happy if I'm unhappy?"

Then Gina moved away toward the house, her "enthusiastic" smile fixed firmly in place.

Gil opened the door and started to follow her. The Bichon

Frises nipped at his ankles. For fluffy white poodles they were fe-
rocious little bastards. "Why does my seeing another woman
make you unhappy?"

"You are my husband, Gil." Gina smiled at him—her "gen-
uine" look fell into place. "I still love you."

And with that she disappeared into the cavernous house. The
dogs yapped and snapped some more.

"Oh hell," Gil said as he kicked them away. The butler gave
him a sympathetic look. He whistled to them and with a mod-
icum of persuasion from the soles of his Patrick Cox loafers they
left Gil alone and scampered after Gina into the house as fast as
their little yellow legs could go.

Gil got back in the car and headed off toward the studio,
where he had an important meeting for which he was going to
be inexcusably late. He was all wound up and there was a sour
swirling in his stomach. Reaching into the glove box he popped
another Alka-Mint antacid tablet, which he seemed to be eating
like candy these days. But at least it was the only drug habit he
was cultivating.

This situation couldn't go on. He really had to do something
about Gina. How had he managed to get himself in this situation? He was perfectly capable of manhandling multimillion-
dollar movies into life. He had enough box-office hits under his
belt to prove that. He could deal with petulant stars, petulant directors and petulant studio heads. And yet his petulant wife
stamped all over him in her stilettos. His love life was like a low-
budget B movie, going straight to DVD oblivion, and it was something that worried Gil immensely.

Twelve

Los Angeles from the air looks as if someone has upended several hundred of those slot machines with forty different colors of flashing lights and laid them out end to end. You can tell that it is a place that positively teems with life before the pilot has even thought about lowering his undercarriage.

On the ground it's equally manic. LAX is like Heathrow Airport on steroids—all careering courtesy buses, Terminator-type taxi drivers and honking horns. After an eleven-hour flight, I am in no fit state to cope with this assault on my nerves. It's getting on for midnight local time, which means it is some ungodly hour in the morning for me and my body clock.

Gil said "come" and, lo and behold, I'm here. And at this moment, I am wondering exactly where *he* is. I tried to call him to let him know that I was brave enough to take him up on his offer of a plane ticket, but he wasn't there. I've left a message on his answerphone, but you would have thought that he'd be around to collect me. He was the one who booked the ticket—he should know when my plane was due to touch down. And I kind of expected him to be waiting here with open arms and transport—not necessarily a dashing white charger, but maybe a top-of-the-range sports utility vehicle.

I'm feeling vaguely numb. This is the start of a new life for me, and I feel I should have done it with considerably more planning aforethought than this—but then I probably would have talked myself out of it too.

I phone Gil's number, but my stupid mobile doesn't work over here. Alice did try to warn me about this, but I was in too much of a rush to leave our green and pleasant land to listen to a technical download on the merits of tri-band phones. And this is probably a bad time to admit it, but I have absolutely no idea where Gil lives, other than in the Hollywood Hills. Where the hell is that?

I have no American coins and I don't see any sign of a payphone. I could sit here for a while and just hope that Gil turns up, but the police here look terribly mean and moody and I don't think they'd take kindly to me loitering here for too long. It would be better, even with my meager resources, for me to book into a hotel for the night and then find out where the hell Gil the Elusive is tomorrow morning, when I've had a good night's sleep and don't look and smell like someone who has wandered off the set of *Dawn of the Living Dead*.

This is not how I imagined my first night in LA. Not at all. In my fantasy it involved chilled champagne, a warm bubble bath with some frangipani-scented muscle rub or some such, cool sheets and a hot man. Still, I might be on for the bubble bath if I can find a hotel room that won't bankrupt me.

Thirteen

Gil was in a panic. He jumped into the BMW, smoothing down his wet hair with his free hand. His plan had been to arrive home early, fix the house up a little—to make up for his housekeeper Maria's inadequacies in that direction—relax by the pool with a cool drink and generally be in a great frame of mind, ready to go and collect Sadie from the airport. Instead, due to a rash of unscheduled meetings, he'd barely managed to get back to his house in time for a quick shower and shave.

Now he was all kind of hyper and he didn't know if it was anxiety or excitement. Sadie's plane would be landing shortly and he'd need to get a move on if he was going to get to LAX in time.

Gil eased the BMW into gear and began to back out of his driveway, foot flat to the floor in the time-honored style of movie car chases—just as a large black Jeep Cherokee screeched into the driveway; its driver also had their foot flat to the floor in the time-honored style of movie car chases. The resulting crash was spectacular. Gil catapulted forward over the wheel, sounding his own car horn and inflating the air bag in his face.

"Oh man," he said, checking his neck for whiplash injuries as he got out of the car, untangling himself from the sagging balloon on his lap. There was only one person who could cause this much damage on his own driveway.

The front of the Jeep Cherokee was smoking gently. He opened the door and Gina, doing a great impression of a rag doll, flopped out. Her face was smeared with lipstick, her sunglasses were skew-whiff and she clutched a bottle of vodka in her hand, which could never be considered a great omen. At the very least, it showed that she'd remembered little from her AA meeting—save the contact numbers of a few minor stars.

"I thought you were sober now." Gil caught the vodka bottle as she let it drop. "What are you doing here? You shouldn't be driving when you're drunk."

An incoherent stream of invective came from somewhere in the scarlet mess that was her mouth. Her eyes rolled alarmingly.

"Oh jeez." Gil shook his head. He put his arms round Gina and heaved her up off the pavement, and she promptly knocked them both into a heap in the driveway, her weight falling squarely on top of him.

Gina started to cry. "I love you, Gil," she muttered an inch from his face.

"You have a very strange way of showing it," he said, and set about trying to push Gina off him.

She wailed louder. "Noah doesn't love me."

"Yes, he does," Gil said. "You've just had another fight." He managed to hoist Gina to her knees.

"This is different."

"No, it isn't." Except that this one came complete with extraordinarily bad timing. "I need to get you inside before the security patrol swings by and decides I'm trying to murder you." It was a tempting thought.

"I don't think you love me anymore."

"I don't, honey," Gil said, abandoning all attempts at decorum and heaving Gina over his shoulder. "I care for you. Very much. In a past tense sort of way."

"No one loves me."

"They do," Gil insisted. It was just that he'd be hard-pressed to give her a list at the moment. And that was the problem. Gina had no one else to turn to when things went ass-upward, which they frequently did. She had very few friends, and they all seemed to mysteriously fade into the background whenever there was a crisis. Perhaps it was because the crises were so very regular. So, Gil was always the one that she ran to. Much as it pained him to admit it, the running to bit sometimes involved going straight to his bedroom. Gina called it her comfort sex. She said she needed other men for excitement and adventure, but she always came back to him for warmth and tenderness. Gil never knew whether he should view this as a compliment or not.

It was a long driveway and when they reached the steps to the house, Gil was grateful to lower her from his shoulder. "Put one foot in front of the other," he instructed, while Gina tried to co-ordinate her Jell-O legs. Gil checked his watch. He should be long gone now if he was going to make the airport in time. "Come on," he said, and he dragged his limp wife up the steps.

"What's the hurry?" she slurred.

"I have to go to the airport."

Gina stopped dead and looked up. "Airport?" She sounded surprisingly coherent.

"Sadie's arriving." He looked at his watch, more for show than the fact he needed to check the time again. "Now."

"I'm going to throw up," Gina said, flopping again.

"Goddam!" Gil dragged her to the nearest bathroom and with-out ceremony pushed her inside. "You do what you have to do while I prepare the guest bedroom."

Gina's head snapped up again. Her voice sharpened. "Guest bedroom?"

"Sadie's arriving. Now," he reiterated. "I guess she'll expect to be the one in my bed."

"Does she know about us?"

"Gina, there isn't an us. We haven't been in a relationship for two years."

"We're married."

"What the hell does that matter?" Gil wanted to bang his head against the white Italian tiles that Gina had insisted on importing from Tuscany. "You live with another guy."

"You're jealous of Noah?"

"No, of course I'm not. But just because we aren't divorced, it doesn't mean that we're still married." He was sure that was log-ical somewhere, but his head was starting to spin just as surely as if he'd drunk as much as Gina. "This has to end. You can't keep coming back to me."

Gina slumped by the toilet. "Thanks for kicking me when I'm down."

"Noah will be here tomorrow." *When he's sobered up too,* Gil added silently.

"And you'll be back together before you know it."

Gina sniffed and looked pathetic. "He's sleeping with someone else. A twenty-year-old UCLA student named Tyler."

"And you have Kurt, the pool man," Gil reminded her. "And very occasionally me. I'd say you were about quits."

Gina made a sound that indicated imminent barfing. It was time for him to see to the guest room. The minute anyone vomited in the vicinity, he had a dreadful, uncontrollable urge to join in. "I'll be back in a minute," Gil said and shot out of the bathroom toward the brief sanctuary offered by the call of household duties.

Gil lay down on the bed, enjoying a moment's respite. How was he going to make Gina see that this situation couldn't continue? With Sadie here in person for a few weeks, maybe she'd finally take the hint that he was moving on with his life. After studying the ceiling fan for a few minutes, Gil got up and closed the drapes. Gina should be finished by now. It should be safe to go back into the bathroom. But it wasn't. When he pushed the door open, Gina lay sprawled on the floor. Next to her was a bottle of pills, its white and possibly lethal contents spread out in front of her.

"Oh no, Gina," he said. "Not pills again." He picked up the bottle and scanned the label. Usual stuff. Prescription sleeping pills. Gil massaged his temples. It had been a long time since Gina had gone down this route. He knelt down next to her and shook her.

"What?" Gina mumbled.

"Did you take any of these?"

Gina lolled against him.

"Tell me, Gina. Did you?" He counted the pills. There were supposed to be twenty and it pretty much looked like there were twenty on the floor. "Tell me or I'll have to call 911."

"I didn't take any," she mumbled. Her eyes fixed on his and they were clear, unclouded by drugs. "But I thought about it."

"One day," Gil said, "you won't have to kill yourself. I'll be quite happy to do it for you."

Gina sobbed. "You don't mean that."

Gil caved. "No," he said. "You're right. I don't."

From the depths of her despair, somehow Gina still managed a seductive smile.

"This is ridiculous." Gil heaved Gina to her feet.

Gina touched her head gingerly and leaned against him. "I feel kinda funny," she said.

"Let's get you settled and then I can go to the airport."

"You're still going to the airport?" Gina said. "You're *leaving* me?"

"I have to. Sadie's arriving. You know that." And Sadie would be wondering where the hell he'd got to. It wasn't a great start to their relationship, but he'd make it up to her.

Gil led Gina to the guest bedroom. Without protest, she slipped out of her clothes and slid, naked, between the sheets. When she wasn't being a complete pain in the ass she was still a very beautiful woman. Her face looked pale against the white pillow.

"Okay?" He stroked a strand of blonde hair from her face. "Go to sleep," Gil said as if he were speaking to a five-year-old.

"Don't leave me," she begged. Her eyes filled with tears. "I don't want to be alone."

"I won't be long. You'll hardly notice that I'm gone," Gil said, and eased himself away from her. "Close your eyes."

Gina snuggled down under the covers and obediently closed her eyes. Leaving when she was like this was hard. She was so weak and vulnerable. It tore Gil's heart apart.

Tiptoeing out of the room, he glanced at his watch again. Nightmare. He should have left an hour ago. He could call the airport while he was on his way and let Sadie know what had happened. Surely she'd understand.

He closed the front door quietly behind him and with a brief glance at the damage Gina had done to his car, he maneuvered round the wreck of her Jeep and headed off toward the airport. There should be very little traffic on the road at this time of night, and with a bit of judicious speeding he could be there in half an hour. He could only hope that Sadie was still there too. Where else would she go?

Fourteen

I'm still wandering round LAX, nursing my abandonment like Linus's grubby security blanket. Heaving my case along the ground, I wish that I'd taken time to oil its wheels. But I didn't have time to do anything. It was sheer good luck rather than good management that I even remembered to bring my underpants. I just rushed headlong out of my old, crappy life into this new one—which is starting off in a rather crappy manner, it has to be said. I console myself with the fact that it would have been worse if I'd arrived in this brave new world knickerless.

The first cab driver that I give the glad eye to gives me the finger for reasons that elude me. Tentatively, I wave at the next one and he stops dead in front of me, even though I'm nowhere near the taxi rank. Is this a good sign? The driver gets out, yanks my case from me and stuffs it in a boot that appears to be already full of tools and ropes and dirty oil cans. I'm not sure that I want my case in among that lot. Too late. And equally too late, it is not until I'm ensconced in the back seat that I realize he's Armenian and is still romantically attached to his native tongue.

I know that he's Armenian, because when I say, "Could you please take me to a nice, comfortable but affordably inexpensive hotel as near as possible to Hollywood Hills," my driver grunts in return and says, "Armenian."

Call me peculiar, but I haven't been to America before, and I sort of expected everyone to speak American, not Armenian. So, in true British style when in strange and foreign land I then shout, "Hotel."

The Armenian grunts louder.

"Hotel."

"Grunt?"

"Hotel! Hotel!"

"Grunt? Grunt?"

This continues until we are waved out of the road by an irate traffic cop and a voice crackles over the radio—a voice that, mercifully, speaks American. The Armenian hands me the radio microphone.

"Hi," I say. "Can you tell me where there's a decent, cheap hotel in Hollywood?"

"In Hollywood?" There is a disbelieving laugh at the end of the static.

"Well, as near as possible." The woman rips off an address, then shouts at the Armenian in what I presume is Armenian. He hands me the map and sets off at breakneck speed, while I try to peel myself out of the fur fabric seats and work out which way up the map is.

After a frenzy of bouncing along a motorway/highway/freeway— I don't know what defines one from the other—that has seven weaving lanes of traffic, the hotel that I am deposited at feels like an oasis of calm. It is two streets down from Rodeo Drive, shoppers' heaven, so as swanky as you can get on a budget and somewhere in the vicinity of The Missing Boyfriend, I think. I curse Gil silently for leaving me to my own devices on my first night, when it is becoming clear to me that my devices are not really up to much.

I explain to the mad and grumbling Armenian in a variety of sign language, shouting that I'd like him to heave my case out of the boot while I go and check whether they actually have a room available. And, believe me, I could weep with relief when Mary Ann, the lovely, neatly coiffured and manicured receptionist, tells me that I can bag the last one and at a price that is only marginally outside my reach. I hand over my credit card and go back out onto the deserted street—just in time to see the Armenian and my case driving away into the wide blue yonder.

Now I could really weep and not with blessed relief. But I

don't, I stiffen my British upper lip and soldier on. I plod back inside. Because anything more than plodding is now beyond me.

"Do you have luggage?" Mary Ann asks on my return.

"I did," I say, but haven't the strength to explain further and, instead, with my most world-weary smile, take the key and head toward my room. How wrong I was to think that my man and this city would be ready and waiting to embrace me. If nothing else, the hot bath is still on the agenda.

The stairs are my last barricade to sanctuary. I climb them, unlock the door to my room and once inside, lean against it—glad that my trials and tribulations are over at last. My head hurts, so I decide against the light—not that I can find the switch anyway—and opt instead to fumble my way straight to the bathroom. If I lie on the bed first I'll never get up.

I do manage to find the bathroom light and my heart sinks to my very tired knees when I see that I have the wild-eyed stare of a woman completely out of her own time zone. There isn't a humongous bath after all, but a rather clinical and cold-looking shower cubicle. Which is not the fantasy my aching limbs and my cheese-smelling feet had entertained. My heart sinks a bit further when I look in the mirror and a large, naked and very sleepy man appears behind me.

"What the—?" he says, scratching his testicles.

"What the—?" I echo, wishing he wouldn't.

"Get the hell out of my room before I call the cops."

"*Your* room?" I look at my key. Right room, right key. By this time a very bemused woman with a skew-whiff wig and a pink negligée has joined him. "Sorry. Sorry," I say, backing out, inching past them. Luckily, they are so sleepy that they're having trouble focusing.

When I get out of the room, I hear them double lock and bolt the door. Quite right too. I clonk downstairs to reception.

"There are two people asleep—two people who *were* asleep—in my room."

"Oh my," says Mary Ann, hand to mouth. "Maybe we haven't got a room left." She taps furiously at her computer and then

gives me a horrified look. "You're right," she says. "Mr. and Mrs.
Lubisky are booked into 109. I'm sorry, but we haven't got another room," Mary Ann says.

This is truly the final straw.

She smiles sympathetically at me. "But then your credit card
company has refused authorization."

No. *This* is the final straw. Even my favorite piece of plastic has
deserted me. At this point, all my brave stoicism departs. I lie
down on the floor in reception and cry. Big, loud crying.

"Hush, hush," says Mary Ann and I don't think it's because
I'm causing a scene in her nice, calm reception. She rushes from
behind her desk and helps me up, ushering me to a convenient
plush velvet sofa. When I wail louder, she rushes off and brings
back a cup of lukewarm water with milk in it and a tea bag.

"Oh my, oh my," she says again. "This will make you feel better." She plonks down the tea and rushes off again to bring me a
plate of chocolate-chip cookies. Now that *is* making me feel better. I can feel an involuntary smile tease my lips.

Mary Ann sits down beside me, patting my hand while I tell
her my sorry tale and regain my equilibrium with the aid of bis-
cuits which Mary Ann bakes herself and brings in for the hotel
guests because she's clearly that kind of person. I give Gil an
extra bit of stick in the course of my regaling because—let's face
it—this really is his fault. And despite it being two o'clock in the
morning, Mary Ann hands over the reception phone and I fish
his number from my handbag, which has thankfully escaped Armenian hospitality, and call him. The phone goes straight to
voicemail and I leave a tearful message telling him where I am.

"You lie down here, dear," Mary Ann says, and she somehow
produces a chenille throw from somewhere and covers me as if
I'm her favorite child. For the first time in a long time, I want to
suck my thumb. "I'll wake you as soon as the other guests start
to appear."

Gratefully, I lie down. At least Mary Ann hasn't abandoned
me in my hour of need. Where can Gil be? Surely he can't just
have forgotten I was arriving today? This does not bode well for

future convivial relationships. I toss and turn a bit, trying to make myself comfy. Mary Ann gives me a sweet, sympathetic look. Though how on earth she thinks I'm going to sleep cramped up on the sofa, with my mind buzzing like this, heaven only knows. I can quite honestly say that's the last thing I remember.

Fifteen

LA was enjoying an unseasonably hot spell for this time of year. Even at this time of night, you could feel the pressure of warm air on your skin. Gil liked to think that the ambient temperature was responsible for the tiny beads of perspiration that had dampened his forehead, but it wasn't.

Screeching the car to a halt at LAX, he left it by the curb next to a hundred signs telling him not to. He would risk whatever wrath parking control could throw at him—it would probably be less damaging than Sadie's wrath. Racing inside the airport terminal, he hurried to the arrivals area—but there were no disarmingly attractive, disgruntled British blondes waiting there.

This was disastrous. What would she think of him? He had dragged her halfway round the world only to leave her waiting at the airport. It was like being jilted. But then maybe she had decided not to come at all and hadn't actually got on the plane. Gil punched her number into his cell phone, but it rang unanswered until the answerphone clicked in. Did that mean she was over here or still at home but in bed? Gil rubbed his hands over his eyes. Why was life so goddam complicated?

Gil went over to the information desk. There had been no messages left for him. Nothing. And, of course, they couldn't do anything useful like let him know whether Sadie was actually on the flight.

He did a final lap of the terminal, but she definitely wasn't there. Sadie, like Elvis, had apparently left the building.

It took Gil two hours and fifty-six dollars to retrieve the BMW, which was in the process of being towed away when he'd emerged from the airport terminal empty-handed. Both he and the car had suffered enough indignities for the night, so he had followed it to the pound on a courtesy bus and had quietly paid up. It seemed a bargain under the circumstances as a tow-away downtown would have cost three times the price. Nevertheless, the journey back to Beverly Hills was a somber one. Somewhere in this sprawling city, Sadie could be searching for him. If only he knew where she might have gone.

There was a light on inside the house when he pulled into the driveway. Gil sighed. He didn't think he could face any more histrionics from Gina, and hoped that she had calmed down and sobered up by now. His wife was sitting in the kitchen as he let himself in through the front door.

"Hi," she said. She was sipping a cup of hot water and looking very sheepish.

"Hi," Gil said. "Feeling okay now?"

"Better," she said. "Thanks."

"Noah will be back tomorrow."

"Maybe," Gina said. "Or maybe not. Who wants to hang out with a thirty-four-year-old woman, when every day there are busloads of skinnier, prettier, more obliging females arriving to make their fortune? What man will continue to look at me when faced with that? Noah's only human."

Gil didn't want to point out that Noah was not only human, but an aging rock star—which seemed to be a particularly fragile form of human.

"I need to be twenty-four, max," Gina complained. "I hate getting old in this town."

"Let me fix you some coffee." Gil put his hand on her shoulder and she touched it tentatively, giving his fingers a squeeze.

"I don't need coffee," she said. "I need more bruising liposuction. Another little squirt of Botox here and there. A plump of collagen."

Gil poured them both a coffee and sat down opposite her. He didn't want the coffee—it tasted stewed and bitter. "You look fine as you are."

She had looked even better before she'd had everything enhanced. There was something intrinsically more attractive about women whose faces and breasts moved.

"You're a one-off in this place, Gil McGann." Gina examined the coffee and pushed it away. She sighed wistfully. "A lovely, reliable man with monogamous tendencies."

Gil didn't remind her that she'd spent most of their married life pouring scorn on his loveliness, reliability and monogamy.

"Sadie's very lucky," she said. Then a light clicked on in her brain. "Where *is* Sadie?"

"I don't know," Gil admitted. "But wherever she is, she wasn't at the airport."

Gina hung her head. "This is all my fault."

For once, Gil didn't feel like rushing in to correct her. It *was* her damn fault. He glanced hopefully at the answerphone. "Any messages?"

"No." Gina gave him a sympathetic look.

"I'm going to bed," Gil said. "I'm just about done in."

"Thanks again, Gil," his wife said. "I didn't know where else to go."

He was too tired to point out that she always came here, no matter what the crisis.

Gina toyed with her hair. She looked at him from beneath spiky, mascara lashes and it crossed Gil's mind that she had reapplied all her makeup, as the lipstick smears and gray tracks of her tears had all disappeared. He would never understand women. Gina's life might be crumbling around her, but she was always concerned that her nails were well manicured while it did.

"I'll see you in the morning," she said.

"It is the morning," Gil said and gratefully made his way toward his bed. This was definitely not how he had imagined Sadie's first night in LA.

Sixteen

I wake with loo-brush hair and dead badger's breath and I get up, ignoring my aching bones, which have spent too many hours on a plane and on a couch. Creaking over to the reception desk, I give my throw back to Mary Ann, who crinkles her eyes sympathetically.

"Thanks," I croak.

"Room 111 has checked out," she says in her sweet singsong voice. "You've got a half hour before the cleaners arrive. Wanna use it to freshen up?"

"I'd love to," I say. "No messages?"

Mary Ann shakes her head. "Why don't you call him again?"

And even though I'm not in the mood to speak to Gil, I really have no choice. There could be a perfectly feasible explanation for why he forgot to come and collect me when I have given up everything I have ever known to be with him. I won't dwell on the fact that one of those things was dressing up in a Lurex costume to serve bottled beer to drunken yobbos. I am, after all, feeling very aggrieved.

Mary Ann roots behind her counter and produces a toothbrush. She gives me a little wave with it. I don't like to ask whether it is a new one or one from the lost property—at the moment I don't care. I just hope it didn't belong to someone who had mouth ulcers or herpes or a deadly disease. What can you catch from toothbrushes? I'll have to make sure that I run it under the hot tap.

I take it gratefully, despite my doubts about its pedigree, and go up to Room 111. Peeping round the door, I'm relieved to see that there aren't any residual occupants, and go inside and crash out on the bed. What I wouldn't give for another couple of hours in here! But Mary Ann has been so kind already that I move my bum and head into the bathroom to indulge in a short but much-needed scrub. After that I hope I'll have found the strength to phone Gil.

Gil shot awake at the first hint of a ring. It had to be Sadie. He grabbed at the receiver. "Hi," he said.

"Were you sitting on it?" Sadie's flat British vowels were a joy to his ears.

"Yeah." Gil swung his legs over the edge of the bed. "I've been out of my mind. Where are you?"

Sadie reeled off the name of the hotel. "Why weren't you at the airport?"

"I was." Gil leaned back against his headboard, relieved that Sadie had turned up unharmed and in relatively good spirits. "But I was hideously late, and I guess by then you'd given up on me. I had an emergency."

Gil rubbed his tired eyes like a bad actor doing a waking-up scene. When he removed his curled-up fists, he felt his eyes catapult out on stalks and ping back into the sockets. "Arrgh!"

"What's the matter?" Sadie said.

"Nothing. Nothing." Gina was lying in bed next to him, also trying to pull herself from sleep.

"Hi," she said, inching toward him.

Gil clasped his hand over the mouthpiece. "What are you *doing*?"

Gina smiled. "Keeping you company."

Gil jumped out of the bed, then realized he was stark naked and covered himself with the body of the phone. "I don't need company!"

"You don't need what?" Sadie said.

"Nothing. Nothing." Gil kept edging away from the bed. "Stay exactly where you are," he said. "I'll be right with you." Then he hung up the phone.

Gina rolled over seductively. "Shall I stay exactly where *I* am too?"

"I want you out of here now, Gina. By the time I am showered and dressed, you need to be gone."

"I can take a hint." Gina pouted.

"You seem to have made a remarkable recovery," Gil observed.

His wife looked completely unabashed.

"I won't let you spoil this for me."

"I don't know what you mean." She rolled over in the bed, exposing some more flesh. "I want to meet Sexy Sadie."

"All in good time," he assured her. As soon as he'd managed to broach with Sadie the fact that he still had a wife.

Seventeen

Washed, scrubbed, but still wearing yesterday's underwear—albeit inside out—I venture back down into the reception area of the hotel.

"He's on his way," I say to Mary Ann and she looks so pleased you'd think I told her that Gil had proposed rather than just remembered that I exist.

"Do you think it will work out with him?" Mary Ann squeezes my hand.

"I don't know," I admit. "I certainly hope so."

Mary Ann tears a piece of paper from her jotter and scribbles on it. "Take this." She pushes the paper toward me. "It's my daughter's address. She lives in Larchmont Village." I have no idea if this is good or bad. It could be a complete dump. "Daniella's looking for a housemate. I think you two would get along fine."

I take the piece of paper.

"Men are not reliable," Mary Ann advises me in a conspiratorial tone. I have managed to work this out for myself, but her concern for me brings a lump to my throat.

"He seems very nice," I say, for some reason rising to Gil's defense.

"If you get problems, call her. I'll tell her your name."

"Thanks."

"Do you have work?"

I think I'm going to adopt this woman as my new mum—*mom*. "No. Not yet."

"I could maybe fix you up there too," Mary Ann says with the contented nod of one of life's fixers. She scribbles on another piece of paper. "A friend of mine runs this agency. She's looking for some help. Call her when you've settled in. Tell her Mary Ann recommended you."

This woman should be on commission.

At that moment, Gil crashes through the doors at full speed.

I give him a little wave. "Hi."

He comes and crushes me with a bear hug, lifting my feet off the floor. "I'm sorry," he says. "Really sorry."

He doesn't know the half of it yet.

"Where's your bag?" Gil says, looking round for it.

"Gone," I say. "I got a taxi when I realized you weren't coming to the airport. The driver stole my case."

"He stole your case?"

"Mary Ann let me sleep on the couch."

"You slept on the couch?"

My new best friend and surrogate mother nods. "He stole her credit card."

"He stole your credit card?"

I nod in agreement. No point in admitting that the damn thing's gone *boing!* of its own accord.

"This is terrible," Gil says. "You should have called me as soon as you got here."

"I did," I say. "I called from the hotel. My mobile doesn't work here. I left a message on your machine."

"You did?" When I nod again, a dark and menacing frown crosses his brow. He leads me to the door.

"Wait."

I go and hug Mary Ann. "You've been an angel."

"It's been so nice to meet you," she says. "Call me."

Gil and I head toward the door.

"You look after her," Mary Ann warns.

There is a black BMW parked at the curb and it shocks me because it suddenly brings home to me how little I know about this man. I didn't even know what car he drove, and yet I've entrusted my life to him. Before I can voice my disquiet, Gil ushers me into it.

"How was your flight?" this stranger says.

"Fine. Thanks." This is hard. Gil still looks absolutely gorgeous. He hasn't gone bald, acquired a toupée or a bulbous nose since I last saw him. Things in my stomach are still going *wee-hee!* But it feels like we're different people on this side of the world. If you discount the crushing bear hug, we haven't touched either. Is that odd? Is it me or is it him?

"So what was the emergency?" I ask, settling into the plush leather.

"Emergency?"

"The one that left me stranded at the airport."

"Oh, *that* emergency!" Gil focuses on the road. "It was a friend," he says. "I had to help out."

What about my emergency? I want to ask but don't.

"I'll make it up to you," Gil says. "I promise."

I try not to look too doubtful, but am sure I fail. I'm also trying not to be tense, but that's not going so well either. And it's a shame, because if I could force my shoulders down from my ears, then I'm sure I'd be delighting in my surroundings. On first impression, I think Los Angeles gets very bad press. I'd expected ghettos and shootouts and rundown housing estates—and I guess there's plenty of that too—but at the moment I seem to have landed in a little slice of paradise. The temperature is not too hot and not too cold, but just right. The buildings here are painted enticing pastel shades and there are trees bearing lemons and oranges on the grass verges right by the roads—I'm resisting the urge to check that they're not plastic. The sky is so blue, it's heartbreaking. My only prior knowledge of Beverly Hills is that it's where the Beverly Hillbillies lived. I can see now why they loaded up the truck and moved to Beverly Hills. I can't believe that I'm going to live here too. I'm going to love it!

Gil pats my leg—really, he does—and I wonder where all the passion from the phone calls and emails and our one night in London has gone. We're awkward with each other and I'm not sure why. For the moment I put it down to getting off to a bad start.

"We'll go back to my house," Gil says and does a U-turn complete with screeching wheels, which is just *so* American. "You can freshen up."

I don't really like to tell him that—apart from a change of clothes—this is about as fresh as I get.

We head off into Beverly Hills, where the palm trees line the streets and the grass is so lush it just invites you to roll in it, and there is no litter anywhere! I try to remember when I was last on a street without litter. Every home is begging to have a movie star living in it. They have quaint porches and leaded windows and elaborate sprinkler systems that twist and turn as they water the lawns, as if they're dancing in time to some silent music. Never before have I found the process of lawn maintenance so marvelous. Lavish mansions are ten a penny. It's like a real-estate theme park for the incredibly rich.

We pull up outside a huge, modern glass-and-concrete place. There is a Jeep with a wrecked bumper bar in the block-paved drive. Gil frowns.

"Is this your house?"

"Er . . ." Gil says. There is something like fear in his eyes. Maybe this isn't his house, he's just going to pretend that it is. "Yes, it is my house. I think," he says enigmatically. He turns to me and appears to look at me for the first time. "I think we'll take you shopping."

"Now?"

"You have nothing to change into," he says. "I'll take you to Rodeo Drive."

"They won't be open yet, will they?"

Gil checks his watch. What I want is a sit-down and a nice cup of tea—but that is so British I can't even bring myself to say it. The last meal I had was a plastic tray full of squashed rubber spirals that were supposed to be pasta. I could do with some brekkie—hot waffles, cinnamon toast, pancakes dripping with maple syrup. These are the things I'm fantasizing about.

"I don't have any money to go to Rodeo Drive with," I say. Has Gil forgotten the fact that I don't have any money at all? How embarrassing would it be to get your card bounced in Armani?

"My treat," he says. "It's the least I can do."

I hope he's not going to be the type of guy who tries to buy himself out of "situations." I hate that. Although at this particular moment, I'm prepared to be bought.

"Can't we go into the house for a short while?"

Gil chews his lip. "The pest control man is still there."

"You have pests?"

Gil pulls away from the house. "Only one," he says. "But it's a very large one."

Eighteen

Rodeo Drive is sparkly in the morning sun. No wonder this is called the Golden Triangle. The shops are all glitzy, gaudy, glittering walls of glass, all dressed up in gold. And they are all closed. Only the street cleaners grace the pavements.

Every shop is a fat fashion magazine name: Prada, Escada, Versace, Gucci, Armani, Tiffany. Excess on a scale that I never knew existed. I can't cope with this opulence on an empty stomach. We find a small deli and coffee house that is cool and dark and we go inside.

The waitress shows us to a quiet booth, and Gil sits down opposite me. She hands us the menus and disappears. We both take a tense, deep breath and then smile.

"This isn't how I thought it would be," Gil says.

"Me neither."

He takes my hand across the table. "Let's get back on track," he says, and his eyes crinkle when he smiles.

"I'd like that."

The waitress comes back and I order my pancakes. Gil does the same. For the first time since arriving, I'm starting to relax.

"How long are you planning to stay?" Gil asks.

A big bubble of disquiet inflates in my brain.

"I could take a few days' vacation. Show you around," he offers.

"That would be nice." Is it at this point that I remind him that he sent me an open-ended ticket? I thought that was more or less the same as being one-way. I had rushed out here to be with him, not thinking that it was a temporary assignment, a holiday. I had been planning to stay indefinitely. Gil, on the other hand, looks worried that I might stay a fortnight.

The pancakes arrive. They are luscious, golden fluffy clouds piled high, smelling like heaven. "Oh yum."

I can't eat a mouthful. How can I have got this so wrong? I thought he was gagging for me to be out here. What happened? Stuff happened, that's what.

Gil tucks into his without hesitation. "I'd like to see as much of you as possible while you're here."

"That would be nice." I need someone to whack me on the back of the head to jog my needle along the record. "I could stay for a while," I say with more confidence than I feel. "If you wanted me to." His fork has ground to an abrupt halt halfway to his mouth. "I have the offer of a job."

"Oh." Gil looks like he might cough up his pancakes. "What sort of job?"

"At an agency," I say, wishing that I had looked at the scrap of paper that Mary Ann kindly gave me so that I could tell him what type of agency.

"That would be nice," he says. Good grief, now he's doing it!

We both stare at our food. I push my pancakes to one side. The sweet smell is making me feel sick. Gil pushes his plate next to mine.

"Let's go shopping," I say, and I'm out of the booth before he can argue.

Nineteen

We arrive back at Gil's house and the wrecked Jeep of the pest control man is still there. Gil blanches slightly when he sees it. There is definitely more to this pest-control-man business than meets the eye.

After a moment's hesitation, Gil swings into the drive and stops the car. "I have something to tell you."

I have been steeling myself for this. "Do you want me to go home?"

"No. No!" Gil looks horrified. "Why ever would you think that?"

I shrug. My emotions are far too complex to put into words.

"It's more complicated than that," Gil says, rubbing at his chin. I want to rub at his chin for him. Preferably with my lips. He looks very desirable when he's anxious. "You know that I helped out a friend last night?"

I nod.

"Well, that friend is still here."

"Is that a problem?" I'm not sure that I'd be so cagey if I was taking Gil back to meet Alice.

"She can be very difficult."

She? "So can I."

Gil laughs nervously.

"She's the pest control man?" You can't pull the wool over this girl's eyes.

"Yes," he says, although it clearly pains him to.

I put on my jaunty face. "Let's go and meet her then."

Gil's "pest control man" is tall, slender and blonde. She's wearing white Lycra and full war paint. Not the usual outfit for exterminating cockroaches, I wouldn't have thought—but then this is LA. I wonder at what point Gil would have expected me to twig that he was telling sweet little lies.

Gil is shuffling from foot to foot. We are standing in a magnificent glass atrium and he's behaving as if it isn't his house at all. The pest control man is sitting watching morning television with her feet curled up against her on the sofa. I'm laden down with bags from some of the trendiest—and most expensive—shops in the world. I feel like I'm in *Pretty Woman*. Gil is Richard Gere and I'm the scruffy hooker with a heart. I am now the proud owner of two thousand dollars' worth of clothes—none of which I really wanted. I have underpants worth what I could live off of for a week. I drop the bags on the floor. The pest control man looks round.

"Hi," she squeals and stands up. She has an awful lot of leg. When the pest control man bends over to turn off the television, her bottom is a small, underripe apricot, and she's wearing Capri pants that are so tight I don't know how she managed to sit down in them. They are definite SROs—standing room only. They also show that she's wearing no underwear even though she probably hasn't had it stolen. To continue the fruit theme, her chest sticks out like two very firm cantaloupe melons. It is gravity defying. The only other chest I have ever seen like this is Barbie's. I hate this woman already. The concept of sisterhood is currently eluding me big time.

She saunters over to us, licking yoghurt from her fingers. "You must be Sadie!"

"Yes," I say.

She holds out her yoghurty, sticky hand. "Gina," she says, grasping mine. Her eyes scan me like one of those metal detectors they use at airports to find hidden manicure scissors and tweezers that might come in useful for terrified passengers during terrorist attacks. She is clearly taking in my visible panty line, lack of melonious chest and bottom like a bagful of walnuts. I knew I would hate this bloody place the minute I arrived.

I have a quick scan of myself. I probably do look a bit like a Bosnian refugee. "I had my clothes stolen," I say in my defense.

"Oh." She takes in the shopping bags and scowls at Gil. "Well, it sure looks like you've been having fun replacing them." The labels get another examination. "I don't know that Gil has room in his closet. But I can always move some of my clothes."

The pest control man flutters her eyelashes. None of us speaks. "You *are* staying here?" she asks.

"No," I say, to which they both look suitably stunned. I have to say that I'm a bit stunned myself. "I have a place organized."

"Oh," Gina says, faintly bemused. And I notch up one tiny little victory, even though it feels very hollow.

"You must stay here," Gil says, ignoring me completely and looking directly at the other contender. "I invited you." I was beginning to think he'd forgotten. "Gina will be leaving very soon."

"Well, you know what they say," I quip. "Two's company, three's a crowd."

"In LA they say two's company, three is a lot of fun." She gives me a sultry and very superior look.

"I like my own space," I say. Oh yes. This from the woman who's been living in her friend's deckchair for the last three months.

"Come on," Gina says, whipping up some of my shopping bags. "I'll show you the guest room. Gil, honey, fix us all a nice cool drink."

Without protest, Gil disappears into the kitchen.

Gina totters along in front of me while I trail behind, wishing my bottom wiggled more. We enter a bedroom that is the size of Alice's entire flat. It has one wall made completely of glass and it overlooks a swimming pool that looks like something out of a David Hockney painting. Beyond that are yet more palm trees and the Hollywood Hills. I would like to stay here very much.

I lay my new clothes down on the bed. I'd really like to follow them and have some more z's—jet lag is making my eyeballs as heavy as marbles. Perhaps I'll feel better when I've changed. But there's no way I'm going to get undressed in front of this stick insect.

Then I realize, if I am going to hang around, it would be

worthwhile getting on more amenable terms with Gina. She may not be my idea of friendship material, but she is quite obviously going to make sure she stays part of Gil's life.

I'll try the friendly tack. Something innocuous. "So how do you know Gil?" I ask.

Gina opens one of my designer bags—a tiny little carrier from Saks Fifth Avenue that contains an even tinier lacy thong. She looks at it with disdain and then up at me without altering her expression.

"Didn't he tell you?" The disdain changes to a faintly demonic grin. "I'm his wife."

Twenty

"You told her *what?*" Gil said. Things hadn't got off to a great start with Sadie; now they were going from bad to worse.

"Only what you hadn't," Gina snapped back.

"You are *not* my wife," Gil insisted.

"Show her the divorce papers."

"She'll wonder what in hell's name she's come to. Let's return to sanity," Gil pleaded. "Go back to Noah."

"I can't. He doesn't want me back." Gina stifled a sob. "And now you don't want me."

"Gina." Gil spoke quietly and reasonably. "Sadie is important to me. This relationship is important to me. Don't spoil it for me."

Gina pouted. "She had to find out sometime."

"Yes, she did. But not this way."

Gina sidled up to him and slid her arms round his waist. "Why can't we all stay here together? I won't be in the way."

"We want some privacy to get to know each other," Gil said. "I'll buy you your own house. Anything."

Gina looked thoughtful. "Where?"

"Anywhere. Have this house."

"Isn't it a little small?"

"It has six bedrooms. There are six bathrooms. You should know, you chose it. How many of the damn things do you want?"

"There's no need to get cranky." Gina checked her watch. "I have a doggie to do." She grabbed her bag and car keys. "Catch you later." She blew a kiss to Gil as she skipped out.

"Move out!" Gil shouted after her.

"A few days, Gil," she shouted back. "You can't deny me that."

Gil sighed. The main problem was that he seemed unable to deny Gina anything.

Twenty-one

Welcome to Tinseltown, where everything is fake. Especially the people. I fit in very well. I'm wearing DKNY embroidered jeans and an Armani T-shirt that cost over two hundred dollars and I don't have a penny to my name. I do look very cool though, and more than a match for Gil's wife. I wish. Being a complete coward, I haven't dared to venture out of the bedroom to find out exactly what the situation here is because I don't think that I want to know. I just know that I have to get out fast. Oh, won't I have a lot of fun recounting all this at the pub? Alice will laugh her socks off.

This is madness. I pull out the two crumpled notes that Mary Ann gave me and try to decipher her writing. Job first, then accommodation when I'm sure I've got something to pay for it with? I dial the number from the bedside phone, not caring that I'm abusing my host's hospitality now that I know he's a lying bastard.

"Cunning Stunts," a voice says. "For all your stuntwork requirements."

"Oh." I did wonder. "Can I speak to Bay Cavendish please? Her friend Mary Ann told me to call," I say. "My name's Sadie Nelson. I've just arrived from London and I'm looking for some work."

Message relayed. "Come on down. Bay will see you right away. Where are you coming from?"

I have absolutely no idea. "Beverly Hills?"

"We're on Wilshire Boulevard." The woman rips off the address, rattling on about boulevards and cross streets, midtown, uptown, downtown, while I frantically try to remember the directions and search in vain for a pen.

"Thanks," I say. "I'll be there in a little while."

With a little flutter of panic I hang up. Gil stands at the doorway. "Where?"

"Job interview," I say, standing up and smoothing out my new jeans.

"You look great," he says.

"Thanks. I'll pay you back." What with I'm not quite sure, but I'm becoming a master of the grand gesture.

Gil shakes his head. "It doesn't matter. Money I have plenty of."

"You seem to have quite a few women on the go too," I observe in a surprisingly calm way when I really want to hit him round the head with my shoe.

"That is just *so* not true," Gil says. "What can I say? Gina is not my wife." He sits down on the bed. "Not in the real sense of the word."

"Why didn't you tell me?"

"She left me two years ago for the pool man." Gil attempts a laugh. "Now she lives with an aging rock star. They fight. She drinks, takes pills and turns up on my doorstep." He looks as weary as I feel. "I know I should, but I can't turn her away. I'm the only one who looks out for her. She'd be a mess without me, and I can't have that on my conscience."

I sit down next to him. "Bollocks," I say with a heavy sigh. I don't know about the Golden Triangle, I seem to have walked straight into an *eternal* triangle.

"This is simply very bad timing," Gil says with a sanguine air that I don't share. "Bear with me," he begs.

"I think you need to sort this out with her," I say.

"Stay here while I do."

I get the feeling that he won't be able to pluck up the courage unless I'm around, but I'm not prepared to be used as a battering ram. "I can't sleep in the next room to your wife," I say. "It might be very LA, but I can't get my head round it at all."

I realize this is tantamount to saying, "It's me or her!" But that's how I feel, and at the moment, it doesn't look like it's me who's winning. "I need to get to my job interview," I say.

"I'll take you."

"I can walk." My legs have forgotten what it's like to move.

"No one walks in LA," Gil says. "You'll get arrested. If you want to walk we can go to a gym."

"Okay," I say. I can't fight. I'm a defeated little mess. My Prince Charming has toadlike tendencies as all of them have. When will I learn that all is not what it seems? And if there's any place I should be more aware of that than usual, it's here.

Twenty-two

Bay Cavendish, owner of Cunning Stunts and Double Take talent agencies, is in fact plain old Barbara Cavendish from England. She may have dropped her boring name for a more glamorous pseudonym, but her accent is pure North London.

"Hello, duck," she says, shaking my hand. Bay is of indeterminate age—fifty going on thirty, buxom and bottle blonde. If there was ever anything that made me wish I was a brunette it's coming to LA. Brown hair appears to be in very short supply. Bay could be Jackie Collins's other more portly sister. It doesn't seem to matter to her that the 1980s have long since gone—she's wearing leopard-skin Lycra leggings and a black chiffon shirt that shows her bra.

"Can you start now?"

"That's my interview?"

"We don't stand on ceremony here," Bay says. "Mary Ann reckons you're okay and I can pay you cash under the table."

What more can one want in an employee? From outside, the office building is a chic black glass affair, tiered like a child's building blocks. Bay's agency has the top floor with views over a major traffic intersection on Wilshire Boulevard. The inside is less prepossessing: a jumble of gray desks, piles of portfolios and a spider plant in a state of near death.

"Exactly what does the job entail?"

"Min looks after Cunning Stunts." Bay nods at a pretty Chinese girl, who smiles at me. "We provide stunt actors for action movies—people who are prepared to throw themselves off tall buildings in order to get paid." Bay looks bemused by the idea. "Anything that involves danger and daring. You'd run Double

Take. Anyone who needs a bottom or boobs comes to us—Julia, Gwyneth, Cameron. Although I think J-Lo does her own bottom."

It's an interesting thought.

"We also do famous look-alikes. Brad, Bill—Clinton," she adds so that I'm in no doubt. "Fergie's always popular. Irish girl, Bernadette, who lives on La Brea. Very good value. Posh voice and everything. She can do fat Fergie or thin Fergie."

I don't want to know how. I don't even want to know how the real Fergie does it.

"Bernadette did a book launch last week. Couldn't tell the difference. Quite at home with the champagne and canapés. I'd rather do that than have someone set fire to me for a living," Bay observes. "Well, are you going to join us?"

I laugh. "I'd love to."

"Great," Bay says, slapping me on the back. "Min, get the kettle on and then show Sadie the ropes."

A wave of delirium sweeps over me. I can't believe this. One day in LA, and already I've lost a boyfriend and gained several designer outfits and a new job. All I need now is somewhere to live and some money.

"We'll have a lot of fun," Bay promises.

And I'm sure that we will. I'm just glad that I'm not the one who has to answer the phone and say, "Cunning Stunts" with a straight face.

Twenty-three

"Please don't do this," Gil says as he drives me to Daniella's house. Daniella Silverstone is Mary Ann's daughter and my new landlady for the foreseeable future. Guilt is written large on his face.

"I have to." I'm clutching my collection of designer carriers, like an upscale bag lady. "I can't share a house with your wife."

"She isn't my wife."

She certainly acts like it.

"Gina isn't my type of person," I say, which is the most tactful I can manage for "Gina is a manipulative bitch."

"She isn't my type of person either," Gil insists.

We pull up outside Daniella's house. She lives in a small one-story home on a quiet back street in Larchmont Village. It has a tidy patch of lawn, a front porch with lots of planted terra-cotta pots and a smart SUV in the drive. This is more my size of house. More bijou, less hotel. You could fit the whole thing into Gil's atrium. I've only spoken briefly to Daniella on the phone, but I'm hoping that she's as nice as her mother.

"Let me come in with you," Gil says. He is looking agonized.

"No." I shake my head. "I'll be fine."

"This will only be for a few days," he promises. "Gina will go back to Noah and she'll be off our backs."

And onto her own back. Thinking catty thoughts always makes me feel better. I will, of course, believe this when I see it.

"I bought you a new cell phone." He hands it over to me. "It has my numbers programmed in."

He presses a few buttons to demonstrate, and a string of different numbers pop up. Six different office, home, mobile, health club, etc., etc. I'll never keep track of him.

"You must stop buying me things, Gil."

"It's the least I can do."

It's the most irritating thing you can do, I think. But wisely say nothing. Mind you, I do have a slight cash-flow situation. "I need to ask you a favor." It pains me to do this, but I'm getting very good at pride swallowing.

"Anything," Gil says—which I think is a very rash statement given our current predicament.

"I need a loan," I say. "Until I can get myself sorted out." I may have struggled through my first afternoon with Double Take, but I won't get paid until the end of the week and I don't suppose Daniella will take kindly to an IOU. "Can you lend me a few hundred dollars? I think Daniella will want a deposit from me."

"It's yours," Gil says as he pulls out his wallet and peels off a thousand dollars.

"I don't need all this."

"Have it." Gil presses the money into my palm. "Keep it as a contingency fund."

I take the money. Even though it feels awful, I have no choice and I remind myself that it's a temporary measure. "I'll pay you back."

"You don't have to," he says. "It's only money."

Spoken in the typical blasé way of someone who has some. It's true that money isn't everything, but it's an awful lot more when you haven't got any. And besides, it isn't Gil's money I want, it's his time, his attention and half of his double bed. It's not his money, nor his wife in the spare room. I want a one-woman man. Is that too difficult to ask for?

"I'll have another talk with Gina tonight," he says.

Apparently.

"I'll sort this out."

Methinks that if he hasn't managed to sort it out in two years, I'm best not to hold my breath. And I thought it was supposed to be women who were complicated.

"I'd better go and get settled in," I say, and wonder whether I should have marked this all down as a bad job and got on the next plane home.

"Can I see you later?" Gil asks as if I haven't come all this way just to see him.

"I'm tired," I say. Too tired to face Gina again is what I really mean.

"There's a restaurant just around the corner," he says. "A small Greek place. Very good food. You'll like it. Let's have dinner if nothing else."

It seems as if nothing else is very much on the menu.

"That's fine," I say and we look at each other for a bit. We haven't had a kiss or anything yet and the longer we leave it, the harder it seems to get to bridge the gap between our lips.

Gil appears as if he might be considering giving it a go and then changes his mind. Is this reticent creature the same man as the one who was mad for me and declaring undying love on our one night in London? It certainly looks like it.

Twenty-four

Gil and Steve were sitting in the Arutigan Senate—a massive plywood construction in Sound Stage Ten—perched on two packing cases and drinking machine coffee. The set was nearing completion, and a painter "marbled" the pillars to the constant sound of hammering from the carpenter laying a cardboard "slate" floor.

"It sounds like you're making a complete bollocks of this, mate," Steve commented after due consideration. "If you don't mind my saying."

"That's why I came to you for advice," Gil said. "I knew you'd be constructive."

"Well, what do you expect?" Steve said. "She's dropped every-thing . . ."

"She has dropped nothing," Gil interrupted.

"She has flown all the way over here," Steve corrected, "just to be with you, and she turns up to find you still shacked up with your mad, not quite ex-wife."

"Don't you start." Gil was exasperated. Why could no one understand his situation? Why couldn't *he* understand his situation? "I am not shacked up with her. I'm helping her out in a crisis."

"Gina has a crisis every other day and twice on Sundays," Steve pointed out. "And you're always there to bail her out."

"I can't help it," Gil said. "I feel responsible for her."

"Just as well," his friend observed. "She doesn't seem to feel very responsible for herself."

"She may be a *little* unstable," Gil agreed.

"That's like saying Julia Roberts is a *little* gorgeous."

"I'm frightened that she'll do something stupid if I point-blank tell her to leave."

"So in the meantime you are doing something stupid instead and jeopardizing a potentially rewarding, not to mention lustful, relationship with the best thing that's happened to you in a long time." Steve gave Gil a knowing glance. "There are some quotes in there, you know."

"You think I'm being stupid?"

"Just a tad," Steve said.

Gil stared at the pillars. On the screen this would look like a million dollars' worth of intergalactic real estate. People in cinema seats all over the world would gasp when they saw it. In reality it was nothing but some lumps of wood and cardboard with a fancy paint job. Nothing was what it seemed in this town. "I don't know what's wrong with me." Gil shook his head.

"I know what's wrong with you." Steve wagged his finger. "She isn't mad enough for you. Sadie's probably just too normal," his friend said, ignoring him. "English women are like that. Down to earth. It's all the rain. It keeps them soggy and consequently very grounded." Steve was warming to his theme. "California women are airheads. They dry out and float off."

"I'm beginning to wish I hadn't asked now."

"Plus, you're too good-looking for your own good," Steve continued, unthwarted. "It's meant that you can spend your life having gratuitous sex with a bevy of young, willing, Botoxed women—while the rest of us have to do it once a month while the kids are on a sleepover. Don't you ever get fed up with meaningless sex?" Steve slapped his forehead in disbelief. "What am I saying?"

Both men laughed. But the truth was that Gil was heartily sick of meaningless one-night stands. He did it more because it was what was expected of him, rather than for any real enjoyment. How tragic was it to admit that?

They watched the painter put the final touches to a flimsy make-believe pillar that looked as if it was supporting an equally make-believe marble ceiling. She stepped back to admire her work and they gave her a round of applause.

"Tell me," Steve continued in a more serious tone, "when did you last have a real relationship?"

"With Gina?"

"No. *Real* real," Steve stressed. "Your wife—and I use the term loosely—she had a dozen different men while you were married, and never failed to tell you all about it. I think this has left you with a deep-seated fear of becoming involved again."

It was something his shrink told him regularly. So regularly that Gil had stopped going to him. Nor did it help that his first wife had left him for an actor ten years younger than her. It had given him a pathological fear of all tall, blond males with high cheekbones and chiseled jaws. And a fear of being hurt again.

"It could be the male menopause," Gil said. "It's a very real phenomenon."

"You're too young."

"I'm beginning to question everything in my life."

"How old are you?"

"Thirty-eight."

Steve took a sharp intake of breath. "You're right. That *is* a bad age to be in this town. The movie business is filled with people who never get past thirty-five. Some of them start counting backward. At least mentally."

Gina's fears were justified in some ways—as a guy, the older you got, the younger the arm candy had to be. Gil felt his bones weighed down with weariness. "Don't you ever get tired of this industry?"

"Mate," Steve said, "yesterday I took a piss with a one-eyed, ten-foot pink beetle with eight arms. How can you get tired of that?"

"There are days when I don't know what I want," Gil admitted. "But you . . ." He shrugged. "You don't buy into the whole thing."

"That's how I keep sane. Otherwise you start to think that it matters. And it doesn't. It's an illusion, just like that pretty pillar."

His friend had it nailed, but it was so difficult to remember, when you'd been steeped in the industry as long as Gil had. None of it mattered—they weren't curing cancer, they weren't saving lives, they were entertaining people and sometimes not very well.

"You've spent too long here." Steve spoke into his thoughts. "This is the most fickle of fickle places. Everyone is waiting for the bigger, better deal. Sometimes you have to bite the bullet and decide that nothing else is ever going to be any better."

Gil chewed his lip. "Like Sadie?"

"Only you can tell that." He patted Gil's knee and then stood up and stretched. "Don't leave it too long though," he advised. "Or someone else might realize that she's a hot property too."

Twenty-five

"If there's one thing more irritating than sitting on the end of an automated phone service," I say with feeling, "it's finding out that your dream boyfriend already has a wife."

"Tell me about it," Daniella says, taking a contemplative gulp of wine. "It sucks."

She has opened a bottle of California grape juice of impressive vintage and a bag of Doritos to celebrate my arrival and my status as new housemate. Already we have been friends for twenty years.

Daniella dips a Dorito into her wine before eating it. "Gina sounds nuts."

"Not so nuts. She's managed to get her husband exactly where she wants him."

Daniella goes all dreamy. "Really Gil's like Mr. Rochester in *Jane Eyre*. He has a sad, mad wife tucked away in the attic."

"Guest bedroom."

"How romantic."

"Not for poor old Jane Eyre," I remind her.

My bags have been unloaded into Daniella's spare room, which is very nice, very Shaker, with a patchwork quilt on the bed. It even has its own *in-suite* bathroom. And no *in-suite* wife.

My new friend examined, minutely, the contents of all my carriers and judged me to be suitable lodger material. The deal was done. I feel that my American "adventure" is starting to take a turn for the better. Daniella reluctantly hands me the bowl of Doritos.

"I'm on a Doritos-only diet." Daniella examines her rounded belly. "I don't think it works."

My new friend is small, slightly pudgy and has strong, dark eyebrows that frame dazzling, deep-blue eyes. Her nose is extraordinarily cute and child-size, and the thought occurs to me that it might not be her own. She takes the Doritos back before I have the chance to eat any.

"My own Mr. Rochester still lives with his wife too," she says with a sigh. "He's a mad movie mogul. I was young and silly. He spends his days surrounded by beautiful, long-legged creatures who will do anything to get a part in a movie. And I mean anything," she adds with an air of disgust. "He told me I could be a movie star and that I meant the world to him. I couldn't believe that he loved me even though I had Donald Duck syndrome."

I throw her a questioning look.

"Short fat legs, waddly ass," she explains. "Turns out I was right. He didn't love me at all." She chain-eats Doritos. "Long-legged creatures don't get attached," she says. "They just move on to the next sucker. I proved a little harder to detach."

She holds up a framed photograph of a little girl who looks about ten years old. "Alexis," she says. "My daughter. And Mr. Rochester's."

I take the photograph. Alexis is a mini-Daniella—small, rounded with puppy fat and inherited genes. Her dark hair falls in long lazy curls to her waist and she has her mother's button nose—and I feel mean for thinking that Daniella had parted with good money to have hers surgically adjusted. I guess not everyone in Hollywood worships at the altar of cosmetic surgery.

"She's adorable," I say, and suddenly it hurts that I am older than Daniella and have no picture of a daughter to show in return.

"He never sees her," she says, returning the photograph to fit in the shiny gap made by an absence of dust on a table. "When I like him, he's affectionately known as the Mad Movie Mogul."

Maybe she sees my eyebrows raise.

"No names," she adds. "He's a big cheese in this town. One of the movers and shakers. Alexis is our little secret." There is a hint of bitterness laced with regret in her voice. "To make sure I keep it that way, he pays for all this." She gestures to encompass the house. "All of it. And I take it. It helps to remind him that we exist."

"Do you still see him?"

She shakes her head. "Rarely."

"But you still love him?"

Daniella laughs without humor. "Love is an illusion in this town. Everyone wants something and they only love you for as long as you'll give it. Remember that." She stands up and pours us some more wine, which is going down far too well. "I am not under any circumstances to restart the heart of this dead relationship. If I show any sign of weakness, stop me," she instructs me. "This is one that must die."

If it hasn't died after ten years of neglect, it must be a tenacious little bugger. Like the spider plant at Double Take. "I think Gil is a mad movie mogul in training," I confess.

"You are doing the right thing," she says. "Believe me. Play hard to get."

"I can't play games, Daniella. I'm not that sort of person. What you see is what you get."

"Then you'll be eaten alive here."

It's not a great thought to relish—the fact that *I* could be the relish.

"You're seeing Gil for dinner, right?"

I nod.

"Be late."

"I'm never late."

"Try it," Daniella cajoles. "See what happens."

The doorbell rings. It's Mary Ann with Alexis, and I'm saved from admitting that I can't wait to see Gil this evening. I was actually planning to be early. How naïve can I be?

Mary Ann hugs me, while Alexis shyly eyes me with interest.

"Thanks, Mary Ann," I say gratefully. "I really don't know what I'd have done without you."

She shrugs. "My daughter calls me meddlesome."

"That is *so* not true." Daniella kisses her warmly. "I love you interfering in *other* people's lives."

"Alexis," Mary Ann says, "say hi to Sadie. She's come all the way from England."

"Hi," Alexis says. "Do you know the queen?"

"Not very well," I admit.

"Oh," she says, indicating that I'm clearly a disappointment to her. "Would you like to see my collection of Barbies?"

"I try to discourage her," Daniella says, "but she takes after her mother. Anything pink and glittery and she's gone."

"I'd love to," I say and with a wave to Mary Ann, I'm led away wishing that I could remember the days when all my problems were pink and glittery.

Twenty-six

Before I leave the house, I have a ten-minute discussion with Daniella, who tries to dissuade me from walking to the restaurant in the interests of my personal security, even though it's in the very next street, and that makes me late.

Now I'm sitting in Zorba's, breathless with anticipation and from doing a speedwalk in three-inch heels. And guess what? Gil isn't here. Even though I am late, he is later.

The restaurant is small and chic with enough Greek taverna touches to make it accessible. It's busy, but not bustling. Most of the tables are taken up by couples holding hands and talking in hushed tones. There are olives on the table and I amuse myself by spearing a few to show that I'm unconcerned about being here alone.

The waiter comes over. He is tall, with floppy brown hair and the sort of chiseled, square-jawed look that is very common among MTAs—models turned actors. I'm delighted that I've learned something useful in my first afternoon as a talent agent.

"Hi," he says in chirpy American style. "I'm Tavis, and I'm your server for this evening."

And I know that I'm in America and there are an awful lot of people here who have American accents, but it just works for me and my knees go all sort of silly. I can never understand why Americans seem to like Brits so much—we're rude and surly and very gray. Here everyone is as sunny and bright as the weather.

"I have a message for you," Tavis says, still sounding as if I've just told him he's won the Lotto. "Mr. McGann says that he's running late and he'll be here in five. He tried to call your cell, but it's turned off."

"Oh," I say, rummaging to find my mobile phone. "I'd better have a drink then."

"What will it be?"

"Wine. White. Please."

The lovely Tavis disappears and it gives me time to rearrange my hair and my thoughts. This isn't quite how my fairy tale was supposed to work out, but back here in reality I'm glad that I've moved in with Daniella. She's a great person and I think we'll have a lot of fun and I don't feel compromised by being there. I don't owe anything to anyone except Gil—and that's only money, as he says.

Tavis reappears with my wine and a wide smile. I wish waiters were as handsome and friendly in the UK.

"Thank you," I say.

He lingers. "You're from England, right?"

"Yes," I say. "How did you guess?"

"I'm an actor," he continues. "I like to specialize in English accents."

I don't dare ask why.

"Hello," he says, sounding rather like Prince Charles. "How are you this evening? Isn't the weather fine for this time of year?"

I crack up, but in fairness he's quite good.

"Very funny," I say.

He looks crushed. "It isn't supposed to be funny."

"Oh." I bite my lip. "I suppose it sounds funny to hear someone imitating us."

He looks mollified.

"I promise not to do my New York accent for you," I say. "It's a killer."

"What are you doing in LA? Vacation or business?"

Tricky. What *am* I doing here? "Well," I say, still trying to formulate an answer, "I came out here to be with someone I met in London. But it doesn't seem to be working out."

"Mr. McGann?"

"Mmm." I nod.

Tavis's eyebrows shoot up and his eyes do a Jim Carrey pop. "*The* Gil McGann?"

"I don't know." Damn, I need to know more about the movie industry.

"He's one of the best producers in the business."

"Is he?" Tavis looks at me as if I'm from a different planet. Which I think in some ways I am. "I know that he's produced some well-known stuff," I say, trying to rescue myself.

There is a small, but perceptible shake of the head.

"Have you done anything with him?" I have no idea what the correct terminology is.

"Would I still be waiting tables, if I had?" he says with a laugh. "If I could get Gil McGann to notice me, it would be my dream come true."

It would also be my *dream come true,* I think ruefully, but say instead, "So you're an actor?"

"Yeah. I was a model, but for the last six months I've been in *Happiness Hospital,*" he says with pride. "Dr. Robert Carrington."

I try not to look too blank.

"That's where I use my English accent. My character's an aristocratic heart surgeon," he says. "Except I got killed in a car wreck last week. Nurse Cathy had dumped me."

"Oh. Too bad."

"It happens." Tavis shrugs. His shoulders sag a little more. "Frequently."

"She doesn't know what she's missing," I offer, and he laughs.

"Sometimes they resurrect characters who have died and hope the viewers don't notice. Just because I'm dead, it doesn't mean I'm buried yet. I was very popular."

"Well, I hope you don't stay dead for long."

"I'd better get back to work," he says. "The guys here hire me again every time I get screen-dumped or die. I don't like to take advantage. It's been nice meeting you."

"Yes," I say. "Likewise."

Tavis walks away. He has a very tight, neat bottom. Not that I'm looking. But I can just imagine him in hip-hugging Calvin Kleins strutting his stuff in *Vogue* and I have to say that it brings an involuntary smile to my lips.

*   *   *

"Hey," Gil says when he eventually arrives and kisses me on the cheek. Cheek! "I'm sorry I'm late."

"Problems with Mrs. McGann?" I know that I sound bitter and twisted, but I don't care. I'm fueled by a rapidly dwindling bottle of wine and half an hour of sitting on my own. I wonder what Gina would say if Gil left *her* sitting on her tod for that long? I know that he left me a message, but I don't really want to see the good side of him at the moment.

"No." Gil takes my hand. "Work."

He orders a bottle of wine and out of the corner of my eye I see that Tavis is busy, but he's gawking in our direction and I can't tell if he's looking at me or Gil.

"I've been meeting with a director about *The One That Got Away*. I'm keen for him to do it, but he doesn't seem to share my enthusiasm. Anyway," he says, taking a sip of the wine that's been poured for him and nodding in approval, "let's not talk about that now. I want to know how you're settling in and I want to assure you that I will sort this out. It will be my utmost priority." He reaches out and takes both of my hands in his. "Gina is not going to be a problem. I want this to work between us, and I hope you feel the same too."

His fingers are strong, warm and comforting and his blue eyes are dazzling in the candlelight. There is a fairly revolting wine bottle on the table overflowing with a dozen different colors of wax and it's melting, slowly but surely—just as I am. I'm gradually being transported away from Battersea and the greasy Labor government and the rain. I feel the tension ease from my shoulders. At this very moment I could quite believe anything Gil tells me.

Twenty-seven

There was a huge white stretch limo with blacked-out windows in Gil's driveway when he arrived home and Noah Bender was weaving his way very unsteadily toward it with a large joint hanging from his lips and a bottle of Jack Daniel's in his hand. Gil parked the car and hurried over to catch him before he disappeared.

"Hey, Noah!" Gil shouted.

"Gil, my man," Noah mumbled back.

Gil smiled to himself. Noah Bender was a raddled old drunk, but there was a certain roguish charm about him that meant you couldn't help but like him.

"You've been to see Gina?" Gil sounded too hopeful even to his own ears.

"That is one hell of a stubborn bitch." Noah waved his bottle in the direction of the house. He grabbed hold of Gil's jacket and leaned against him. Gil reeled as the smell of stale booze and soft drugs wafted toward him. Noah narrowed his eyes and tried to focus on Gil. "Get her to come back to me," he begged. "I can't talk to her."

"I can talk to her," Gil said, "but I don't think she listens anymore."

"I love her," Noah said, sounding as if he was about to sob. "Your wife is my world."

Gil didn't have the strength to point out—again—that Gina's being his wife was a mere technicality.

"If she doesn't come back to me I don't know what I'll do." Noah swayed unhappily in front of him. It occurred to Gil that it didn't matter how rich or famous you were, it didn't mean that you had a better handle on life. If anything, it was often infinitely worse.

"Why not come back tomorrow when you're more . . . less . . . when you're feeling better?" he settled on.

Noah peered at him through his halo of smoke, only one eye left open as a slit. "I'm going to go and get seriously blind drunk."

Gil didn't think he exactly had twenty-twenty vision as it was.

"Take it easy," he suggested. "Go home. Get some sleep. Alone." Then he helped Noah to find his thirty-foot car, which appeared to have a disco going on in the back seat. "Everything will seem better in the morning."

"I love you, man," Noah said. "I wish you were a bird, and then I'd marry you."

A light bulb went on in Gil's brain. "Have you asked Gina to marry you?"

"No, man." Noah appeared to have sobered up several degrees. "Too heavy."

"It would work," Gil said, realizing that he sounded too desperate.

"I'll sleep on it," Noah said, easing himself into his car.

"You can't keep running round with teenage blondes."

Noah looked horrified. "I can't?"

"It messes up Gina's head." Gil leaned on the car roof. "She needs security."

"She has you for that," Noah said and with a wink, he closed the door.

Gil watched as the car rolled down the drive and made its way toward the Hollywood Hills, then went inside.

Gina was stretched out on one of the white leather sofas. There was a bottle of vodka on the table and six full shot glasses lined up. She was drinking one after the other. Gil watched her for a moment, unobserved, and wondered how long she could keep this up. In some ways she and Noah were well suited and in other ways they seemed to bring out the

worst in each other. Neither could embrace the concepts of so-
briety or monogamy.

"Hi," Gil said, taking off his jacket and throwing it over the
nearest sofa.

"Good dinner?" Gina asked, glancing up from the TV.

"Yeah." He sat down next to her and gave a pointed look at the
shot glasses.

Even more pointedly she picked one up and drank it down in
one. "Join me?" she said.

Gil shook his head. "No. I'm too tired." Gina snapped off the
TV. "I saw Noah. In the driveway."

"Did you have a cozy chat?" Gina huffed.

"He said he wants you back, but you aren't interested."

Gina stared at the wall.

"Gina," Gil said. "You can't stay here forever."

"This is about her, isn't it—Sadie?" His wife curled herself up
into a ball. "You want me out because she's here."

"It isn't about Sadie," Gil said. "Not entirely. It's about me. I
need space. Privacy. I need closure on our marriage." Gil rubbed
his hands across his eyes. *I need peace,* he thought. He'd had a
long day working on the film and an equally long evening trying to woo a lovely lady, and at the moment, both projects
seemed like a lot of hard work. Except that wasn't really fair to
Sadie. She'd come a long way and given up a lot to be here with
him. And she wasn't here with him—Gina was, which was unfair to both of them. "If you were free, perhaps Noah would
propose."

"Have you talked to him about this?" Gina turned to glare at him.

"Not in as many words," Gil admitted. But I am very hopeful,
he added to himself. "I know how much he wants you back."

"Noah wants me back only on his terms," Gina stated.

"Which are?"

"I don't want to be having this discussion with you, Gil," she
said firmly.

"I don't want you to be living in my house," Gil said, "but you
are, and I need to find a way for this to work for all of us."

"This is not your house," Gina pointed out. "It is *our* home." Clearly, ownership wasn't dictated by the person who paid all the bills. "I chose it. I remodeled it."

"You can have it," Gil said. "I don't want to live here anymore. *I'll* move out."

A look of panic crossed Gina's beautiful features. "You can't do that."

"Why? If you like it so much, you stay. I'll go."

Gina snuggled against him. "The reason I want to be here is because you are."

"If that's how you feel, why did you leave me in the first place?"

"You're too normal, Gil." She sighed.

He didn't think it was one of the more usual grounds for divorce. "Too normal?"

"You're upright. You never let your hair down."

If he continued to let his wife rule his life, he soon wouldn't have any hair left to let down.

Gina wrapped her arms round him and Gil eased himself away.

"I may be too normal for you, Gina, but I may be perfectly fine for someone else."

"This is back to that Sadie, isn't it?"

They could spend all night going round in circles and Gina would never see his point of view. It hadn't really mattered before because it had never really impinged on his life—other than on his wallet. Gil laid his head back on the sofa, which he didn't like either, and closed his eyes.

Gina leaned closer to him. He could smell the scent of her perfume, a heavy and oppressive cloud that enveloped her. She twined her fingers through his hair. "Spend the night with me," she whispered. "I know how to relax you."

That was certainly true. The only thing that had kept them together for so long was the fact that they had great making-up sex. "I don't think that's a good idea," Gil said.

He felt Gina stiffen. She wasn't the only thing that was stiffening and right now he didn't want her to know that. He hadn't got laid for months and he wanted Sadie. He wanted to lie with her and make love with her. Instead he had come to a harpy of a wife and a sterile box that he laughingly thought of as home. What was he doing with his life?

Gil stood up. "Talk to Noah in the morning," he said. "We need to sort this out."

Gina picked up the vodka bottle, poured herself six more shots and fixed Gil with a glare that was as steady as her hand. "I'll think about it," she said.

Twenty-eight

I had a fantastic evening with Gil—marred only by the fact that I can't take him back to my new home and I won't go to his. We had a passionate good-night kiss in the BMW and then chastely went our separate ways. Daniella's advice to play hard to get might be sound, but it is rather difficult to put into practice. Alexis had left me a Barbie—Ballet Star Barbie—on my pillow to keep me company. Which was so sweet, but somehow it wasn't the same.

I did, however, get a great night's sleep and now feel up to spitting in the eye of jet lag. I root in my designer shopping bags and find something suitable to wear for my first proper day at Double Take—though I realize that whatever I wear, I will look underdressed next to Bay's leopard-skin Lycra.

Daniella is sitting at the kitchen table, tapping away at a fairly battered-looking laptop. It's a gloriously sunny room that overlooks a small patch of garden filled with the sort of stuff we consider houseplants. She takes off her glasses and studies me. "You were back early."

"I was tired."

She leans on her hand and examines me closely. "He didn't invite you back to his place for coffee?"

"No. A bit of rampant snogging in the BMW love bus and thank you and good night."

"Hmm," Daniella says.

"It was like being fifteen again," I note. "In a very depressing way." I wouldn't mind being fifteen again if it meant I could regain slim hips, the ability to eat anything and the chance to live my life over with the knowledge I have now. If it means just snogging in cars, then you can keep it. I wouldn't be that age again for the world.

Daniella resumes tapping.

"What are you doing?"

"Trying to buy my freedom from the Mad Movie Mogul." She stops again. "I'm a scriptwriter."

"Really? Anything I'd know?"

"No. I've never sold a script," she admits. "Although I have come very close a few times. I've only been doing it for ten years." She gives me a bright, theatrical smile. "Sometimes it can take fifteen years to become an overnight success."

"Can't Three Ms help you?"

"I wouldn't ask," Daniella says with a flick of her hair. "He gives me enough that I don't have to lap dance, do phone sex or wait tables to make ends meet while I'm waiting for my big break—a lot of people aren't so lucky." She gives me a rueful smile. "If I showed this to him, he'd buy it. Right off. Because it was me. I'd get a huge check and then he'd add it to the pile of scripts at the bottom of his office closet, never to come out again. But that's not what I want. I would actually like someone to think that I've got enough talent to do this."

"Good for you," I say.

"Yeah." She gives a resigned shrug of her shoulders. "Like everyone in this town, I'm hoping to make it big one day so that I can tell someone else to stick it."

"Is the script nearly finished?"

"Not far off," she answers. "It depends how much I get side-tracked by the gym. We must sign you up too."

"I need to get some money behind me first."

"Then you'll be too old to do your crunches."

"I'd better go," I say. "I'm not sure how long it will take me to walk."

"You can't do this," Daniella says. "You'll wear out your legs. You need wheels."

"I like walking."

"It's not good for your image."

"I don't have an image."

"Everyone will think you're an eccentric Brit."

"You were just telling me I need more exercise."

"Walking doesn't count," she insists. "I'll swing by your office at the end of the day and take you to a car lot. The only thing you can buy round here are Mercedes. On your budget we need to go outta the Beverly Hills area."

"On my budget we need to go to 'Outta' Mongolia. They'll have to be giving them away."

Daniella winks at me. "We can see what miracles our feminine charm will work."

Outside, it is another day of blue skies, white fluffy clouds and seventy degrees, and I realize that you could never wake up here and blame your bad temper on the weather. My sunny mood lasts all morning, despite the fact the phone rings again the minute I put it down. So far, I've been asked to find a Barbra Streisand for a cocktail party, a Cindy Crawford for a swimwear launch, and a Marlon Brando as the Godfather for a private birthday bash.

Gil has called three times and left messages on the whizzy new mobile he gave me. I know it's him because he's the only person who has my number. I'm not being cool by failing to return his calls—I simply haven't had the time. There is a little envelope symbol flashing at me too, but I haven't got an instruction book, nor have I the time to sit and fathom out how it works. Still, Bay and Min have made me feel right at home and I have my own desk—my own little space in LA—and an insane grin because of it.

The buzzer on the office front door rings and we all glance up. This is the first caller we've had all morning. Bay answers and invites our guest in. A few minutes later a face pops round the door. Despite my only being in LA for five minutes, it's a face that I recognize. Who said this was an anonymous place?

"Hello," I say in surprise. "What brings you here?"

"Hi." Tavis looks equally surprised. "I didn't know you worked here."

"New girl," I admit. "First day."

Min claps her hands to her mouth. "It's Doctor Robert," she squeals. "You're my favorite character," she gushes. "Are you really dead?"

" 'Fraid so." Tavis looks fairly pissed off about it. "That's why I'm here. I've come to register with Double Take."

"My department," I say with a ridiculous rush of pride. Although I can't say that at the moment Tavis bears a striking resemblance to anyone. "Do you have a portfolio?" I say, trying to sound as professional as possible.

"I do." Tavis clears his throat and looks anxiously round the office. He pulls the bag he has over his shoulder closer to him.

"May I see it?"

"Oh." He opens the bag and pulls out a neatly typed resumé, which I take and examine. I've never heard of any of these commercials or programs, but he has quite a long list, so I try to nod knowledgeably. Tavis is fidgeting uncomfortably. "These are my pictures."

They are in a brown folder and without thinking I open it on the desk. My face goes the color of tomato ketchup. The folder is full of pictures of Tavis in various states of undress—mainly completely undressed. I slam the folder shut. "Fine," I say tightly. "Fine."

"I thought I could do some work as a butt double, or do some underwear modeling."

"Y—Yes," I stammer. "That's what I thought too. I'll keep you on file."

"Great," Tavis says. "I heard this is a good agency."

"Oh yes," I say, trying to get my mouth to form coherent sentences. "If anyone wants a bottom, I'm your man . . . woman." Good grief, I'm a blithering idiot. "You have a very nice bottom," I add, just to compound my humiliation.

Tavis has the grace to smile. Min has hidden under her desk, which barely muffles her sniggering. For a small and very pretty person she has a very witchy laugh. Bay is licking her lips lasciviously behind Tavis.

"That's a professional assessment," I tell him hastily.

"Thank you," he says. "That means a lot to me."

"Well . . ." I cough, hoping that he takes the hint that I'm really, really busy. I can't wait to get to the file to have another peek at his bum. I pick up and put down other folders to show that I'm frantic.

Tavis turns to go and I feel my breath release. He changes his mind and I inhale sharply. "Would you like to have lunch with me?"

"Me? I can't," I say. "I'm very busy. This is my first day."

"Go on, honey," Bay says. "You need a break. I'm not a complete slave driver."

"It looks like you have a lunch date," Tavis says, and I hate how quickly he has regained his cool when I most definitely have not regained mine.

"Thanks." I shoot a glance at Bay which she ignores, and grab my sweater.

Technically, this could be considered work, I suppose. From my vast knowledge of the London Book Fair, I'm sure agents are supposed to schmooze their clients. I stuff my mobile into the depths of my handbag. Gil will think I've disappeared off the face of the earth. If I get a minute I must try to call him.

Twenty-nine

Gil tapped in the number of Sadie's cell phone for what felt like the seventeenth time. This was meant to make it easier for him to reach her, but it would sort of help, he guessed, if she answered it. For once, he had good news to impart and he couldn't wait to talk to her.

"Answer it, goddam." Gil shook the phone. But the phone steadfastly remained unanswered. He stuffed it into his pocket. Maybe he'd stop by her office later and give her the glad tidings of great joy.

He was due at a meeting with an exec from the studio and he didn't want to be late. Gathering his script and papers together, Gil decided to take one last look to make sure that he wasn't hallucinating. He walked down to the guest bedroom and sure enough, the closets were still flung open and they were still devoid of every single scrap of Gina's not inconsiderable wardrobe. She'd gone. There was no note, no message, no goodbye. All that was left was a trace of makeup on the white linen sheets. It could only mean one thing. She'd finally seen sense and gone back to Noah. Gil felt as if his heart had wings—not dinky little Cupid wings, but great big Boeing 747 ones. This was fantastic. More than fantastic. It meant that Sadie could move out of her rented room and into his arms. Things were finally going his way. He felt so optimistic today, he was sure that he could swing a deal with the studio for *The One That Got Away*.

He closed the closet doors with a small thrill of glee. Today was the beginning of the rest of his life. He was going to contact his lawyer, get the divorce moving, pay Gina off and then get on with the equally important business of making things right with Sadie.

As he headed toward the door, he noticed how the sun shining through the atrium picked out the sparkly bits in the black granite floor. It looked like the pavement on the Hollywood Walk of Fame, and for the first time Gil didn't feel as if he were living in a fishbowl.

He flicked down the automatic top on the BMW, enjoying the warmth on his face. Life was good. Life was very good. He was going to cook dinner for Sadie. He'd go to Bristol Farms deli and buy all the stuff himself. This would be the whole nine yards—sumptuous food, soft lights, champagne, something sexy on the CD player. They could start over again on the right foot. And he wanted to do that more than anything.

Thirty

Tavis drives one of those big bus-type cars—the sort that you see in road movies or films like *American Graffiti*. It's an ancient, rusting, turquoise-colored thing the size of a small boat, and I think I'd like a car just like his. We lurch and wallow into a parking space on the main street in Larchmont Village and he feeds a meter.

The big, bold white HOLLYWOOD sign gazes benevolently down over the entire street from its lofty hill and makes me feel as if I've really arrived.

Tavis has brought me to Zorba's for lunch. He insisted it was going to be his treat, and when I agreed, insisted also that it had to be Zorba's because he doesn't have to pay here.

The restaurant looks as if it has a much livelier atmosphere at lunchtime, and the tables on the pavement are mostly full. As we approach I'm really quite pleased that my luggage was stolen and that my wardrobe is now packing a wide selection of designer labels—I'm not sure that I would have been at home here in last season's charity-shop finds. Everyone has mobile phones clamped to their ears and they all look very spruced up. Tavis, although he's sporting the relatively informal ensemble of a baseball cap and embroidered cargo pants, is still managing to turn heads. I don't know—maybe his look is supposed to be dressed-down movie star. He has the long rangy stride of a catwalk model and hips that are barely big enough to keep his pants up—hips that I would die for. It's very nice to be seen with someone so utterly gorgeous.

Tavis is hugged and kissed like a long-lost son, and we're seated at one of the few remaining tables, under a striped awning that protects us from the searing heat of the sun. My skin hasn't seen the sun for so long that I'll probably do a Count Dracula and shrivel up on the spot if any rays inadvertently hit me.

"Let me choose some of the house specials," Tavis says and I nod—I have no idea what half of the dishes on the menu are anyway. I'm sitting here quietly toasting and am quite happy for him to take charge. In fact, it all feels rather nice. But then I wonder what I am actually doing here with Tavis. This is the sort of thing I should be doing with Gil—but where has he been when I've needed him? Absolutely nowhere in sight, that's where.

"I didn't realize you'd only just arrived in LA," Tavis says. He leans back on his chair looking much more relaxed than I am.

"Two days ago," I admit. Although it already feels like half a lifetime in some ways.

"And you came here to be with Gil McGann?"

"That was the plan," I say, and I wonder whether that's why Tavis is taking such an interest in me. Is it only because of who I know? More than likely. The thought makes me relax somehow, even though I should probably be pissed off. "Only it's not quite working out like that."

"Can I ask why?"

"I'd rather you didn't at the moment," I say. "It's complicated."

Tavis grins. "I love your accent."

"Yours is very cute too."

My newfound friend laughs. Our food arrives and Tavis spoons several delicious-looking dishes onto my plate. "So how come you're working at Double Take?" he asks as he ladles.

"Sheer fluke," I say. "I think I'm going to enjoy it, though."

"Maybe you can put some work my way?"

"I'll certainly try." If anyone rings up asking for a peachy male bum, I'll know exactly where to look.

"I owe my roommate so much rent." Tavis shakes his head. "We fund each other's 'resting' periods," he tells me. "Luckily, we've had very few times where we're both out of work."

"That must be hell."

Tavis gives me a slow smile. "We manage to scratch by."

"Is it a very precarious profession?"

"I think there are more of us waiting tables than acting," he says with a hint of irony.

"Have you been an actor for long?"

He sighs. "Long enough to have been more successful by now, but not so long that I've been written off yet." He pushes his food round his plate. "I moved here five years ago," he says, "from New York. Along with thirty thousand other hopefuls."

"That's a lot of hope."

"Yeah," he says. "And there's thirty thousand more who leave here every year, their dreams in tatters."

"Tough." It makes my little problems look like chicken feed.

"Now you can see why I wouldn't mind being someone else's butt. Maybe someone will be so impressed by how my butt performs, they might like to check out the rest of me."

"I hope you get your big break," I say, and I mean it. Tavis is so laid-back and unaffected and so *not* up his own butt that he deserves to succeed.

"Thanks," he said. "I don't want to be Doctor Robert for the rest of my life."

"Or death," I note.

He chuckles.

"I'll try to introduce you to Gil," I offer. "Would that help?"

"Sure," he says. "That'll be great."

"It's the least I can do after such a lovely lunch."

Tavis fixes me with his eyes and it is truly mesmerizing. I think he's been watching too many Clark Gable films. "Sadie," he says, "you're a very nice person. You're a dying breed."

"Yeah. Me and dishy hospital doctors."

Dishy? Did I really just say dishy out loud? Not that Tavis seems to notice. He's probably more than used to women falling at his feet. He must be a crap actor, otherwise he'd have been snapped up ages ago.

The sun is warm on my neck and my eyes are starting to roll. I could quite happily stretch out here and have several winks.

"I'll get you back to the office," Tavis says as he stands up, and we walk back to his car.

"I hope things work out for you and Gil."

"Me too," I say, but for now it seems less important than it did. I'm just one person waiting for my big break, I don't have to compete with 29,999 others. I have only one rival.

Thirty-one

Daniella collects me from the office and drives me to Ralph's Wrecks—a beat-up car lot in an area that's an awful lot scruffier than Rodeo Drive. It's one of those scary places that has wall-to-wall cars with strings of tinsel bunting draped over them. If there was a breeze, I guess they'd be fluttering. I think this is much cheaper and nastier than even Daniella had in mind.

"That one looks okay." I point to my favorite rusty heap.

"You cannot be serious," Daniella says as she looks at the range of cars in horror.

"Tavis told me it was a great place to buy a cheap car."

"What is this guy? A starving actor?"

"Yes," I say. "Come on. I may not be a starving actor, but I have the budget of one."

"You cannot do this."

"Fine." I shrug. "We can go home. I don't even want a car."

"Don't be ridiculous," she says as she climbs out of her shiny SUV.

"This will be an experience for you. You can write about it one day."

"I don't do horror movies," she says, tiptoeing across the lot. "I'm hyperventilating just looking at this."

We pass something old and pink, a convertible. It has *grease* written all over it—in grease, probably. This is exactly the sort of car that one of the Pink Ladies would drive, and I can see this is where Tavis bought his wheels too.

A fat and slimy salesman comes out of the rundown prefabricated hut that functions as an office.

"You cannot buy a car from this man," Daniella hisses under her breath.

"You like this one, ladies?" he smarms, pointing at the sexy little two-seater that probably once was smart. "Try it for size."

"I'm going to puke," Daniella warns.

He opens the doors for us. I slide in, followed by Daniella, who only takes her place in the passenger seat after she has examined it for deadly diseases. If she had some antiseptic wipes with her, she'd probably have given it a good going-over.

The man, whom I assume to be Ralph of Ralph's Wrecks, hands me the keys. I start the engine and there is a lot of clattering and smoking. This does not sound like the sweetest automobile melody I've ever heard—as if I know what I'm looking for. I wish I'd had the sense to ask Tavis to come with me instead of Daniella. He would have known if it was a dud or not.

"I should have brought Tavis," I say, thinking out loud.

"You're talking an awful lot about this man," my friend remarks. "You must have mentioned him a hundred times on the way over here. Tavis this . . . Tavis that . . . Tavis a-bit-of-the-other . . ."

"Huh!" I snort.

"Huh, indeed," Daniella says. "I know where he works, what he looks like and too much detail about his butt."

I remain silent, in case anything else I say is taken down and used in evidence against me.

Daniella nudges me in the ribs. "Is he very cute?"

I give a reluctant smile. "Kind of."

"Is that why you didn't think to bring Gil?"

"I don't think Gil would know about wrecked cars. He's not the sort."

And this certainly is a wrecked car. One of Ralph's finest moments, I feel.

"This is utterly grotesque," Daniella whispers.

"I'll take it," I say, and count five hundred of my borrowed dollars into Ralph's sweating hand.

"I think walking may have been a better alternative to this," Daniella says, curling her lip.

"It'll be fine," I say. "I feel like Olivia Newton-John."

"You look more like a piece of trailer trash who sleeps with her cousin." She runs her finger over the plastic door panel and examines it for dirt. There is plenty.

"Alexis will love it." I wiggle the steering wheel about. It groans in protest.

My friend wrinkles her dainty little nose. "I think we ought to check the glove compartment thoroughly for suspicious white packages."

Ralph pats the wing. "Look after her," he says with a smile. I swear I hear a bit drop off somewhere.

"I bet he treats his wife like this too," Daniella says. She gets out of my new car and slams the door. Something else creaks. "Jesus," she mutters as she walks back to her SUV. "Follow me. But not too closely."

"I don't have any insurance."

"Do you really think that matters?" Daniella asks as she gets into her car.

I putter out of the car lot behind her, chugging and smoking, and I think the radio has more poke to it than the engine.

And suddenly I want to drive round to Tavis's house and show him my new wheels. He'll like it, I know he will. He'll think it's ridiculous and fun. And he'll think I've got a great bargain and an original car—not that I've been completely and utterly ripped off.

Thirty-two

Tavis took off his baseball cap and threw it on the nearest chair, and followed it immediately with the rest of him.

"Hi, gorgeous." His roommate, Joe Mavers, abandoned his typing and came over and kissed him affectionately on the cheek. "Busy day at the office?"

"Hell," Tavis said. "I signed my ass away as a double."

"You'll get something soon." Joe patted his shoulder sympathetically. "You always do."

"I wish I had your optimism," Tavis admitted.

"If you lose that, my man, you might as well move back to Boise, Idaho, and get a job pumping gas."

Tavis shook his head. "There are times when I think about it."

"Yeah," Joe said. "And you'd die within a week."

"That's why I never do it," Tavis said.

Tavis and Joe went back a long way. They had both arrived in LA at the same time and had bowled up at the same Hollywood acting class. When, after a few months scraping a living, Joe had landed a plum role in a soap, they had wound up sharing the same top-floor apartment in a tidy and consequently expensive block on La Brea. Joe had helped Tavis a lot over the years. Many's the time he would have packed it in and gone home—if not to Boise, Idaho, then back to his native New York—if it hadn't been for Joe's unceasing strength and support. It was like having a great older brother and a little bit more.

"Beer?" Joe asked, already on his way to the fridge. He threw Tavis a bottle of ice-cold Bud. Tavis juggled it in his hands and then snapped off the top on the window ledge.

Joe was a "character" actor—not classically handsome enough to play a leading man. He was tall and blond, but despite hours in the gym, the sauna and as many hot tubs as he could find, he was still more than a little chubby.

Joe had left his own home in smalltown America when his effeminate ways and theatrical tendencies had made his folks uncomfortable and attracted the attention of too many prejudiced fists. In a land full of dirt-poor cattle farmers, Joe was never going to fit the mold. He had drifted through a variety of states working at menial jobs and dating menial men until he landed in LA. The hick accent had gone, groomed out through hours of practice, and he only lapsed back into it for effect when he was particularly drunk or stoned.

Tavis still had the support of his family—moral, spiritual and occasionally financial. His folks had always tried to understand his leanings, no matter how alien they were to them. Joe had no one. His two older brothers had ostracized him the minute he came out. His folks never called. Tavis was the nearest to family that Joe had.

Tavis took a refreshing slug of his beer. "I met a great contact today," he said.

"We all could do with a few more of those, darling."

"She's Gil McGann's girlfriend. A very fine lady," Tavis said thoughtfully. "Very fine."

"I thought you'd given all that up."

"I have. It's far too distracting. Nothing is going to matter in my life but my career." Strong words and very easy to say, but then it had been a long time since anyone of the opposite sex stirred his interest.

"So what shall it be tonight, my friend?" Joe asked, resting his beer on what one day would undoubtedly be a paunch. "The Viper Room? The Polo Lounge? The Sky Bar?"

"Or why don't we go to our acting class and be humiliated like we always do?"

"Good idea," Joe said. "Do you think your new friend can get you an introduction to the big cheese himself?"

"I hope so." Tavis nodded in what he thought was a hopeful manner. But then, it wasn't so much who you knew in Hollywood, but who knew *you*—he was more than aware of that. Just as he was more than aware that Sadie's hair had smelled of vanilla.

Sometimes when you'd been kicked down so many times, it was very hard to make yourself stand up again. He tried to laugh about Doctor Robert getting bumped off and he tried even harder not to take it personally. *Happiness Hospital* was a crap program with a crap script and a bunch of crap actors—but he had been good, given the material he had to work with. He was sure he'd been good. But he wasn't sure that simply being good enough or determined enough was ever going to get him where he wanted to be—and that was right at the top of the tree.

Thirty-three

Gil wanted to sing. And dance. And maybe do a bit of shouting from the rooftops. He felt as if he had lost a tremendous weight—from around his neck and from around his heart. When he arrived home laden down with groceries, he had had a certain amount of trepidation: Perhaps he'd only imagined that Gina had gone, and she was, in fact, still firmly ensconced in his guest bedroom and his life. But no, there was still a gap where his ex-wife used to be.

Now he was attacking a bunch of scallions and looking forward to seeing Sadie again. If only she would call!

The meeting at the studio had gone great. The reluctant director he wanted for *The One That Got Away* had said yes. The scriptwriter was tapping away nicely and Gil was hoping against hope that the script would be delivered on time. They had a big-name actor lined up for the lead. Steve was keen to do the production design. Being a movie producer was a truly fabulous thing. Gil picked up his glass of fine California wine and took an appreciative sip. Gina had gone. Sadie was coming back. He had hired a divorce lawyer. Everything in his world was lovely.

Dinner was going to be fabulous. He didn't cook very often, mainly due to lack of time, but he could rustle up a few signature dishes when required. And he was pulling out all the stops tonight with spaghetti vongole, his favorite dish of pasta with steamed clams. Not great for the breath, but weren't clams supposed to be an aphrodisiac—or was that oysters? Virtually the same thing, Gil decided. Both small and fishy. He rubbed his hands in satisfaction.

Just one last check on his *pièce de résistance*. Gil whipped off his apron—no need to scare the neighbors. Particularly when his neighbors were the sort of people who didn't even know where their own kitchens were.

He skipped out of the side door and through a passageway that led to the drive. And there it sat. All gleaming in the sinking evening sun. Gil felt a thrill of anticipation. Sadie would love this. The garage had delivered the small, sporty Mercedes this afternoon after a few frantic phone calls. It had a soft top, cream leather upholstery, sleek black lines and a big red bow tied around it. If her heart had been hardening toward him, this would surely melt it.

Thirty-four

"Oh bollocks!" I press a few more keys on my snazzy new mobile and half of the messages disappear. "I can't get this thing to work!"

"Give me that," Daniella instructs, and does the one-finger punch of an expert.

We are back at the ranch in Larchmont, lying on the sofa, feet up, drinking iced tea—a complete anathema to me, but when in Rome, etc. Alexis is home from school and is on the floor trying to persuade Super Gymnast Barbie to put her legs round her neck.

Daniella holds the phone to her ear. Her eyes widen. "He says that Gina's gone."

"Gone?" This certainly makes me sit up straight. "Does he really say that?"

She nods.

"Gosh." I have to admit I'm taken aback. "He must have talked to her."

"Either that or he's put an axe through her head and she's under the deck."

"You write too many movies," I say.

"Ssh," Daniella instructs. "He says to get a cab up to his house as soon as you can. He's going to make dinner. And he has a surprise for you."

"Ha!" I say. "And have I got a surprise for *him!*"

Delores—my new and faithful mode of transport—behaved herself impeccably and peeped and farted all the way back here without breaking down once.

"He's more likely to have a heart attack if you turn up in that thing," she warns. "The LAPD will probably arrest you as a star stalker."

"She's lovely," I say defensively.

"Is it a car, Aunt Sadie?" Alexis asks.

"Yes," I say. "It's a very nice one. She's called Delores. She's a classic."

"Museum piece," Daniella mutters. "Anyway," she says, "why are we talking about that piece of S.H.I.T., when the fact that the other piece of S.H.I.T., having moved her ass out, is much more interesting?"

"Mommy, that spells *shit*," Alexis informs us brightly.

"Great," Daniella says. "There's nothing wrong with your spelling. I only wish your math was as good."

I stand and stretch. "I'd better get myself up there then." What I really want is a long hot bath and an early night.

"Try to sound a little more enthusiastic," Daniella says.

"I'm tired." But if I'm truthful, I sort of wish that we are going to meet up at Zorba's again. I want to see Tavis and tell him about my car. He wouldn't think it is a heap. He'd like it—I know he would. I just hope Gil likes it too.

"It's a good thing that Cinderella wasn't this reluctant to go to the ball," Daniella remarks.

"No," I say. "Although she might have felt differently about kicking her shoes off if she'd known all along that Prince Charming was married."

Thirty-five

There is a slinky black car outside Gil's house, and for a moment my heart stops and I think about turning round and going straight back home. And then I realize that *home* now means Daniella's house and not London, and the knot of my tension unravels slightly. If Gina is here, I'll just have to face her.

I pull into the driveway with a few expressive farts from Delores and park as far away from the chic automobile as possible in case Delores decides to scratch its eyes out while I'm gone.

I smooth out my swishy chiffon skirt—these designer shopping bags are bottomless, I swear. The more outfits you pull out, the more keep appearing. Surely we didn't really buy all this stuff? Shuffling from foot to foot, like some fidgety four-year-old, I ring the bell. Maria, Gil's housekeeper, comes to the door immediately and shows me into the vast atrium, muttering incomprehensively in Spanish as Gil comes to the door of the kitchen.

"Hey," he says softly and pulls me to him.

Maria blends into the background.

"You look great," Gil says with a most welcome sigh of admiration.

"Thanks." Gil also looks good. He's wearing a baggy T-shirt and shorts. He's the first man I've seen in about twenty years who looks great in anything that stops mid-thigh. All the men at home have spaghetti legs with knobbly knees and pale blue dead-fish skin from lack of sun. Or is it just my ex-boyfriends who have been so afflicted? In contrast, Gil's legs are strong and tanned. It's suddenly got very warm in here.

"I'm glad you're here," he says, and tugs me into the kitchen. Beautiful garlicy smells waft up from steaming pans. I'm glad I'm here too, now that I think of it. I might not have been jumping for joy earlier, but little bits of me are starting to bounce happily.

He hugs me close. "You like your car?"

I smile. He must have seen me arrive in my old jalopy. "Yeah," I say. "It will do for now."

A look of disappointment crosses his face and I feel a pang of disloyalty toward Delores.

"It's fine," I say, squeezing him. "It will get me from A to B. Just about."

He still looks a bit put out.

"I'll pay you back, I promise. You can have a down payment as soon as I get paid."

"It's a gift," he says rather tightly.

"Don't be silly." I give him a jocular punch on the arm and he looks at where I hit him. "You wouldn't choose anything so tasteless!"

Gil disentangles himself from me. Despite his initial enthusiasm, I'm sure he loathes Delores. I knew he would. Probably not LA enough for him.

"Shall we eat?" Gil says rather crisply.

I'm starving and could probably eat a horse. "Mmm," I say. "It smells wonderful."

"Spaghetti vongole," he says proudly.

I don't know what a vongole is. Perhaps it is a horse. It sounds more like small rodent—a mole or vole. California is doing its best to make me feel ignorant in the ways of food. There are always so many weird things on the menu. "What does that involve?"

"Clams," he says.

Are they like mussels? I'm allergic to mussels.

"It's my specialty," he says.

It looks like I'm about to find out.

"So." I perch on a kitchen stool. "Where's Gina?"

Gil looks up from his preparations. "Gone," he says. "Didn't you get my message?"

"Well, yes. Sort of."

"She went this morning," Gil continues. "Noah came down

last night, begged her to go home, and this morning she'd gone. Along with all her clothes—which is definitely a first."

My word. Maybe Daniella was right—she has got an axe in her head somewhere.

"I have started divorce proceedings."

Ooo. This *is* news.

"And not before time," he admits. And then Gil gives me a large glass of wine, which I want to gulp straight down. "I think we should celebrate," he says.

"I'll be driving later."

"I kinda hoped that you'd stay," he says with an uncertain laugh. "Didn't you bring your stuff?"

"What? All of it?"

"That was the idea."

It may be your idea, pal. But it isn't mine!

"I want you to move in with me."

"But I like being at Daniella's," I say.

Gil frowns. "You don't know her."

"I don't know you."

"But you came halfway around the world to be with me!"

I thought he'd conveniently forgotten that. "I did," I say calmly, and decide that I *do* need the wine—Delores probably has some sort of automatic homing device. She's that type of car. The wine goes down in one. "And when I got here," I remind him, "I found a little more than I bargained for."

"Gina," he says.

I shrug, Gil walks over to the nearest kitchen cupboard and bangs his head slowly against it.

"I'm not saying I won't ever move in," I point out before he suffers brain damage. "Just that I don't think we should rush it."

Gil looks deflated. He's a man who's used to getting his own way. At work, at least. "Whatever you say. I guess I have to earn back your trust."

Just when I think he's being a shithead, he turns round and comes out with something like that. And now I feel mean and ungrateful.

"Dinner looks lovely." I get off my stool and tenderly kiss his cheek. He smells of cinnamon and spring onions.

The smile eases back to his lips, but I can tell that this is not going the way he planned it. "It's just about ready," he says.

I'm going to have to eat this vongole stuff come hell or bloody high water, I think, *and suffer the consequences.* Otherwise this entire night could turn out to be a complete disaster.

Thirty-six

The spaghetti vongole was actually superb and I'm feeling very replete and not at all nauseous—for which I'm eternally grateful. Gil and I have moved into his cavernous lounge and are snuggled up on one of his white leather sofas, which would easily seat an entire coachload of people.

I think it must be the several glasses of wine and the bursting stomach that are helping, as I'm feeling surprisingly mellow. My eyes and limbs are heavy, but not in a dead-tired way, and I lean against Gil and sigh.

"This is what our first night should have been like," he says ruefully.

"I know," I say, snuggling into him. "Let's try and get back to that."

I feel him nod and his lips toy with my hair. After a little persuasion, my shoulders give up their knots. Gil's lips follow the line of my neck, his breath hot in the air-conditioned room. His kisses travel softly and slowly along the line of my jaw and over my cheek, my eyelids, the tip of my nose. And I'm burning up even though my goose pimples have goose pimples. His lips find mine and he takes my wineglass and without breaking the kiss puts it down somewhere—less worried than I am about his white leather. Our arms fold round each other and I can feel his heart pounding through his T-shirt. Oh, how I have waited for this! His hands, hot and searching, cover my body and I'm definitely beginning to wish that I'd brought my toothbrush.

My fingers wander underneath his T-shirt, tentative, easing it from his body. It is so long since I've done this that my mouth has gone dry with anticipation. This boy has a fine set of abs and a toned chest as smooth as silk. In between being a hot-shot movie producer and his wife's keeper, he clearly finds time to work out.

Over the gasps of our breath there is a screeching of brakes and the headlights of a car illuminate the atrium, making the plants look like something out of *Jurassic Park*. Gil and I part and watch the lights, breathing heavily. There is a moment of quiet, followed immediately by the most almighty smash. Gil jumps up, pulling his T-shirt down, and rushes to the door.

"Goddam it, woman!" he shouts into the night, and shakes his fist for good measure.

I tug my clothing back to a more modest arrangement and follow him.

"She hit your goddam car!" Gil is beside himself with rage and I'm not far behind either.

"Delores!" I cry. "Not Delores!" And I rush out into the drive, pursued by Gil.

Gina is sitting in her new SUV, slumped over the steering wheel. Steam is puffing from her engine. The lovely, sleek, black and shiny Mercedes now has a deep, crumpled *V* in its boot.

"Jesus!" Gil says and rushes to snatch open Gina's door.

How has she managed to hit this car as well as Delores? I rush to see my baby, and she is still parked unobtrusively in the corner of the drive, tucked under a large bougainvillea bush, rusting quietly but otherwise unscathed.

"Look what you've done to Sadie's car!" Gil yells. He is shaking Gina, but she is blissfully unaware of the fact.

"That's not my car," I say quietly.

Gil spins round. "What?"

"Delores is fine."

"Who?"

"Delores. My car." I'm aware that I'm swallowing most of my voice. "She's fine."

Gil follows my eyes and I see him recoil as his eyes rest on Delores's well-rounded, terra-cotta-spotted curves.

"Jesus," he breathes.

"That's my car," I reiterate, because he's suddenly gone very pale.

"*This* is your car," he says, and points at the sleek, black wrecked one. At the moment it looks in a rather worse state than Delores.

"It's not," I insist. "I don't know whose it is. I thought it was Gina's."

"It's yours." His voice is rising alarmingly. "I bought it for you." His hands look like they are shaking. "That's why it's got a big red bow on the front!"

Oh. I hadn't seen that. Even if I had, I wouldn't automatically have assumed it was for me. "Don't shout at me," I shout. "I don't want a car with a big red bow on the front!"

"I bought it for you!"

"I don't want it!" I shout louder. "You can't buy me."

"I'm not trying to buy you! I want you to be happy."

"I *am* happy." I'm still shouting and sound anything but. "With Delores!"

"You can't drive around in that heap."

"It's all I can afford." Technically, I can't even afford Delores, and it is Gil's money that paid for her, but at the moment I'm prepared to gloss over that fact.

"What do I have to do to say I'm sorry to you?" Gil is breathing heavily, and not in the same passionate way he was a few minutes ago.

"Just that!" I can feel my nostrils flaring and it isn't attractive. "Say you're sorry. Don't buy me things."

Suddenly Gil is very quiet. "It was done with the best intentions," he says. "I thought you'd like it."

I want to cry. Why are we making such a mess of this? "I do," I say. "Very much. The front is very nice."

Our eyes take in the beautiful and extremely dented car. We both start to smile.

At that moment, Gina slides from the driver's seat and is loudly sick on the driveway.

"Oh hell," Gil mutters and we both hotfoot to where her inert form has landed.

Gil hoists her up.

"Sorry," Gina mutters.

"Sorry?" Gil has gone white with anger. "You have wrecked three cars in two days, you stupid woman. I've had it with you, really I have. This is it."

Gina slumps onto his shoulder. I go and bear the weight of her other arm, and between us we drag her toward the house. For someone who looks as if nothing more solid than a lettuce leaf ever passes her lips, she weighs a ton. She is not a pretty sight either. The last time I saw her, the layer of foundation she was wearing was immaculately applied—now it's rubbed round her face like a mugged clown. Her eyes are bloodshot slits and she has absolutely no control over her limbs.

We bounce her up the steps, a bit more vigorously than is strictly necessary in my view, and when we get into the atrium, she throws up again.

"Maria! Maria!" Gil shouts. Gina groans. The sound is splitting my head, so heaven only knows what it's doing to hers.

The diminutive Mexican housekeeper appears. She is wearing a housecoat and rollers, which she is trying to hide under a chiffon scarf. She is also doing a very good impression of a headless chicken, running round, crossing herself and wailing incomprehensible Spanish laments at the top of her voice. It's not really helping the proceedings.

Gina groans and barfs again.

"Get a bucket for Mrs. McGann," Gil instructs and we exchange a glance after the word *Mrs*.

Once we get Gina to the guest bedroom, Gil throws her onto the bed on her back. She lies there, comatose.

"Maybe we ought to turn her onto her front," I suggest. "She may choke on her own vomit."

"Good," Gil snaps.

Maria appears with a bucket. It has a mop in it. "What I wouldn't like to do with that," he says, eyeing it and his wife malevolently.

"Is there anything else I can do?" I ask. Now I feel like a spare wotsit at a wedding. And I don't mean bridesmaid.

"No," Gil says wearily. "Maria will help me to clean her up." He looks at me sadly. "It won't be the first time." He comes over and hugs me. "Thanks."

"I think I'd better go."

"Stay."

"She needs you," I say, shaking my head. I can't sleep with Gil in the room down the hall from his drunk and disorderly wife. It's unnatural. How can he not see that? He steps toward me and I step away. "I'll call you in the morning."

"Sadie . . ." his voice is hoarse. "I don't want Gina to come between us."

But that is exactly what she is doing. And I wonder how much of it is calculated. I take another step toward the door.

"Sadie . . ." He looks from me to the comatose Gina, then to Maria, who is trying to make herself invisible. "There are things I want to say." He clears his throat. "But now isn't the right time."

"No," I say. "I'll call you tomorrow." And I blow him a sad kiss before leaving.

In the driveway the wreck of the Mercedes glints in the moonlight. It is a beautiful warm night and I know that I've had too much to drink to be driving, but I've not had nearly as much as Gina, so I reckon I'll be okay.

I go over to Delores and pat her fender. "We need to go home," I say as I jump in and start the engine. "I hope you know the way."

Like the old trouper she is, the car creaks and groans out of the drive, the corsets of her suspension pinging with the effort.

"Well done for staying out of the heat, old girl," I say. I plant a kiss on the steering wheel. "If only your owner were half as clever."

Thirty-seven

This may not be the most rational thing I've ever done, but I don't care. Right now I want someone to love Delores—and if I analyze it a bit closer I'd like someone to love me too.

I know someone who would love this car as I do and I want him to see it. There's only one person I can turn to in my hour of need. I'll drive past Tavis's apartment—just the once—and if the light's still on, I'll risk it.

Scooting down Santa Monica Boulevard, I'm amazed that the traffic is so light. Rush hour in London seems to last 24/7, and you can't go anywhere out of second gear. Delores's speed limitations are more to do with a self-governing engine: If you accelerate above thirty miles per hour, it sort of peters out. I enjoy the warm air on my face and the wind ruffling my hair, and spare a thought for my friend Alice back at home, who will be somewhere shivering her bum off.

I turn into La Brea, cruising to find the right apartment block, and when I find it, the light is indeed still on in Tavis's window. He is strolling backward and forward in front of it at a measured pace, holding what looks like a script. He's not wearing a shirt.

I park Delores and totter up to the door. Is it the done thing to turn up unannounced in LA? The label by the doorbell says MAVERS-JONES, and I give it a decisive press.

"Hi." It's Tavis's disembodied voice coming from a little box on the wall.

"Er . . . hi," I say, leaning close to it in a furtive manner. "It's Sadie."

"Wow," Tavis crackles back at me. "You're the last person I expected."

"I'm sorry," I say, Dutch courage seeping out of me. "I know it's late. I have something I wanted to show you."

"You wanna come up?" I hear the door buzzer sound.

"No." I check to see that Delores is looking her best and wish that she hadn't mussed up my hair so much. "I'd like you to come down."

"Okay," he says. "Give me five."

It takes him two and he steps out into the street, still not wearing a shirt—or shoes. He looks genuinely pleased to see me, and you don't know how relieved I am. I do a "lovely assistant" pose and present Delores. "Da—da!"

"Oh man!" Tavis coos, and without bothering to open the door, he jumps over into the driver's seat. "This is so cool," he says, fiddling with Delores's bells and whistles. "Mmm-mmm!" He gives Delores a hearty thump on her rump.

"I thought you'd like her," I say proudly.

"What are you waiting for?" Tavis jerks his head. "Get in. Where haven't you been yet?"

I shrug. "I haven't been anywhere."

"Then we must go and look at the moon over Venice Beach."

"Okay." I open the door and get in next to Tavis in the more traditional way. He's still not wearing a shirt. "Won't you be cold?"

"You sound like my mom," Tavis says.

"Sorry. In Britain you can't go to the beach without wearing an anorak. Even in summer."

"Well, now you're in Cal-i-forn-i-a!" he shouts.

And I'm really quite glad that I am.

He grinds Delores into gear and grins at me as we pull away. Delores—the shameless flirt—purrs up to fifty without pause. Tavis clicks on the radio and the Beach Boys blare out. We fly down La Brea, then chew up the miles and spit them out on Venice Boulevard, singing "California Girls" at the top of our voices.

Twenty minutes later, we park up at the beach. Tavis comes round and helps me from the car. The night is as black as new tarmac and a big, shiny moon looks as if it has been hole-punched into the sky. I can hear the sea lapping at the sand, but can't see it.

"Come on," Tavis says.

I take off my shoes and we stroll out over the sand toward the Pacific Ocean. I try to remember when I last went to the seaside and fail. Long enough to have forgotten what it is like to taste salty sea air on my lips and feel the gritty sand work through my toes.

"Sit." Tavis does just that and as he pats the sand next to him, I join him.

"I think this is the first time since I arrived in LA that I don't feel I'm running around like a loony," I say with a hearty huff.

"You need to kick back and come down to our pace," Tavis advises, and I'm sure he's quite right.

He lies on the sand and I follow suit, trying to block out the thought that sand is nothing more than pretty-colored dirt and crushed-up shells. Is this a sign that I'm too stressed? I wiggle my toes into the damp layer beneath the top powdery stuff and eventually I start to enjoy the rough texture of the sand and the coolness on my back. It feels so good, I could weep with weary joy. I'm probably still hideously jet-lagged.

Tavis turns toward me, drawing circles in the sand with his finger. "Are you enjoying LA?" Moonlight does wonderful things to his bone structure. He's wearing cut-off combat trousers and a leather friendship thong is plaited round his ankle. Delores has given his hair a battering too.

"I don't know," I say truthfully. "It's not working out quite as I planned." I give him a rueful smile.

"Don't talk about it if you don't want to," Tavis says.

"I'd like to," I admit. "I have so many things going round in a loop in my head, I feel as if I'm going potty."

"Potty is bad, right?"

"Potty's very bad." I look up at the moon. The moon is responsible for all kinds of things—the pull of the tides, were-wolves, irrational moods. But it just hangs there looking rather attractive and as if it isn't doing very much. Its lure has driven men crazy for centuries. "It's Gil," I say, digging my toes a bit deeper. "I really like him." I give Tavis a look that says it's probably more. Why would I have dragged my arse all the way out here to LA otherwise? "I want to be with him."

"But?"

"He has a wife."

Tavis raises an eyebrow.

"She's supposed to be long gone and shacked up with someone else, but I can't see much evidence of that." I sigh. "She seems very much still attached to Gil."

"And what does Gil say?"

"That he's sorting it out. But it looks to me as if she has him exactly where she wants him."

"And in the meantime?"

"I'm hanging round like a lemon."

"These Hollywood wives can be very tenacious," Tavis warns. "She may not want him, but she may want to make damn sure that no one else gets him."

"He didn't like Delores either," I confess. "He called her a heap."

"The man clearly has no style."

I don't tell him that Gil had just bought me a Mercedes and probably had every right to feel a bit piqued that I preferred my rusty old bone shaker.

"I'm making him sound awful," I say, feeling guilty. "He's not. He's really nice."

"I guess he must be if you're prepared to put up with all this."

"I'd like you to meet him."

Tavis brushes off his shorts. "I'd like that too."

"I suppose we'd better get back," I say. "I hope you don't mind me calling on you unexpectedly?"

"I'm glad you came by." Tavis is smiling, but he looks sad. I can't remember what color his eyes are, but they're glinting black in the night.

"I knew you'd understand," I say. "I don't know how, I just

did." I want to hug him or something, but have no idea how to cross the six inches of sand between us. "Thanks."

Tavis walks his fingers across toward mine and I meet them. We touch them together like a chaste kiss. Tavis takes my hands and pulls me to my feet and we stand so close that I can feel his body heat. He is one hot guy. And he's tall. Very tall. And all sort of skinny and muscle-y at the same time. It must be the last vestiges of alcohol kicking in, because suddenly I feel all warm and swimmy and my legs don't want to stand up anymore.

Tavis puts his hands on my shoulders and they scorch my skin like the heat of the midday sun. He's so close that I can see a pulse beating steadily in his throat and when I look up toward him, his face is serious. He turns me away from the pull of the sea and the lure of the moon and back toward the car park.

"Come on," Tavis says in a husky movie-star type voice that makes me shiver all over. "Delores will be missing you."

And I wonder if Gil is too.

Thirty-eight

Tavis stops outside his apartment building and turns toward me. He hands me back the keys to Delores.

'Thanks," I say. "It's been great."

Tavis bites his lip. "Come in for coffee."

"I should get home. Daniella will be worried." Like hell she will—she'll be fast asleep in the land of Nod, thinking that I'm having a rampant night of unbridled lust with Gil. Little does she know! Still, it's a great excuse. I don't know if I want to get into all the complications that coffee might imply. I have definitely taken more pleasure than I should have done in watching Tavis drive my car back bare-chested, and I don't want him to feel that I'm leading him on. He might be utterly bite-the-back-of-your-hand gorgeous, but I want an uncomplicated friendship with him. Is that ever possible with a man?

"Big decision?" he teases. He can see I'm tempted. Tavis is such easy, laid-back company. Whenever I'm with Gil, I feel like I'm walking a tightrope.

"One quick drink won't hurt," he says and jumps out of Delores using the unconventional route.

"A quick one," I agree.

"Wait there like a good girl," he says to the car.

And, also like a good girl, I follow him up the stairs and into his building.

A tall, blond man is waiting at the door of the apartment to greet us, and it takes me by surprise. "Hey," he says, clapping Tavis on the back as he approaches. "Great car."

"Delores," Tavis informs him. "This is her owner, Sadie." As he eases me into the apartment, I notice that he exchanges a look with the man. "Girlfriend of the great Gil McGann."

The man bows in mock reverence. "Respect," he says.

I laugh. "Sometime girlfriend," I correct.

"Ah," the man says. "The course of true love never runs smoothly. At least not in Hollywood."

"This is Joe Mavers," Tavis says. "My partner in crime."

"Yes," Joe says, hugging Tavis to him. "This guy and I have been together for years. We've stuck it out through thick and thin, haven't we, darling?"

Tavis looks slightly bashful.

"Oh. That's nice." This is a revelation. I had absolutely no idea that Tavis was gay. But it's quite clear from Joe's territorial manner that their partnership extends to more than mere crime.

Something inside me sags a little. What a waste! I don't want to appear fickle, particularly considering my situation with Gil, but I did feel there was a bit of "chemistry" going on back there at the beach. At the very least I thought Tavis was a "red-blooded" male.

My judgment seems all to cock these days—no pun intended. But in some ways it feels nice to know that he was merely being understanding and protective and a good mate and not in any way trying to qualify for an inspection of the contents of my underwear.

"Coffee?" Tavis says and I realize I'm staring.

"Yes, please. That would be lovely."

"I adore your accent," Joe says and he shows me to the sofa and I sit down. I feel a bit of an idiot now. I've got loads of gay friends at home. Well, two—Crispin and Paul. And I guess Crispin's a bit of a gay name. But they both *look* really gay—if you know what I mean. There'd be no mistaking Crispin for someone who'd want to jump your bones. Or even potential boyfriend material. Is anyone in this town what they seem to be? Sometimes I feel very naïve in the ways of the world.

"Joe is in one of our major soaps," Tavis shouts from the kitchen area.

Joe tries to look modest and fails.

"Fantastic." I'm really weary now, and I shouldn't have come back here as I haven't the wherewithal to make small talk.

Tavis comes back into the room and gives me a steaming mug. He sits on the chair opposite me and I study him. He still doesn't look gay, even though I now know that he is. I'd hazard a guess that Joe is a few years older than him. Tavis's boyfriend is an attractive guy and I would have said he was quite rugged, but when I look more closely there's a softness to his features, matched by a softness round his middle. As soon as he opens his mouth, there's no doubting Joe's persuasion. He has a gentle, effeminate way of talking and he camps it up outrageously. I think he's someone who would be fun to have around. But try as I might, I cannot find it in me to see these two as an item.

Joe stretches theatrically and makes a loud yawning noise. "I'm going to leave you two sweet things," he says. He comes over and kisses my cheek. "I'll say goodbye for now, but you and Gil must come to dinner. I won't take no for an answer."

"That would be very nice. Thank you."

"Your accent kills me." Joe hugs himself. He goes to Tavis and kisses his cheek too. I can feel myself blush and I look away to study the curtains, which I have to say are a bit flowery for my taste. "Not too late, Tav." Joe wags his finger. "We have sides to do."

"I have it." Tavis nods.

Joe blows me another kiss. "See you again," he says.

"I hope so."

And when he leaves, the room seems suddenly quiet.

Tavis smiles at me over his coffee. "He's the best," he says with open admiration. "I don't know where I'd be without him. Off my head. Up my own ass. I don't know."

"He seems nice." I'm not sure what else to say. Tavis is observing me intently. "What are sides?"

"Oh." He shrugs. "Lines." He picks up the script from the end table next to him. "I have an audition tomorrow morning. I need to go through them before then."

"And I'm keeping you from them?" I put down my coffee. "I feel terrible."

"Sadie . . ." Tavis smiles at me and it is warm enough to melt an ice-lolly. "I wouldn't have had it any other way. I've really enjoyed tonight. It's been a blast. I love Delores and . . ." he frowns as he glances at me, "and . . . I think an awful lot of you too."

"Thanks. You're a mate."

"A mate?" he says it in queen's English and laughs. "I'm a mate."

I throw a cushion at him. "Stop taking the piss out of my accent!"

"Help me out," Tavis says. "This character is English. You could listen to my lines."

I curl my feet up on the sofa and snuggle down into the corner. "I'd love to."

Tavis opens his script. His fingers are long and tapered. "Are you sure you're not too tired?"

"No," I say with a shake of my head. He is such a beautiful person, I could lie here and look at him forever. "What's it about?"

"It's about a man who is desperately in love with someone who doesn't even know he exists."

"Ha!" I say. "That I can relate to."

"Me too," Tavis says quietly. He wiggles about on the chair and jiggles his shoulders until he's comfortable. That boy still isn't wearing nearly enough clothes.

Tavis looks nervous and he clears his throat. His eyes sparkle, animatedly. "Here goes."

His voice, strong and clear and very English, flows over me and all thoughts of sleep are forgotten.

Thirty-nine

"What the hell are you doing?"

Gil glanced up without breaking from his task.

Gina stood in the doorway, hands on her hips. She looked better than she did last night, but that wasn't saying a great deal.

He had his suitcases open on the bed and was stuffing clothes into them as fast as he could. "I'm packing."

"I can see that," Gina said. "What I want to know is why?"

"Why?" Gil wanted to beat his head against the wall. "Do you remember what you did last night?"

A dark shadow crossed Gina's face and the pout on her lips transmogrified to a tight pucker. "So, I got a little drunk."

"You are ruining my relationship with Sadie," he said. "I want my life back, Gina. One that doesn't have you *crashing* into it. Literally."

"Well, that's very nice."

"It's how it has to be." Gil slammed the lid shut on one case. This was easier than he'd thought. The only thing that was nipping at him was why he hadn't thought of it earlier. He glanced at the bed. Only one side was messed up and he hadn't slept a wink all night for thinking about Sadie and what they might have been doing if Gina hadn't been dead to the world and snoring in the guest bedroom.

"You can stay in the house," he said, "until we get the financial side of our divorce finalized."

"Our *divorce?*"

"You can have the house if that's what you want. I don't even like the goddam thing."

"Don't you want to know why I was upset last night?" his wife demanded.

"No," Gil said. "Because if I know, it will involve me and I don't want to be involved."

Gina slithered down the door until she was sitting on the floor, long, shapely legs splayed in front of her. "Noah asked me to marry him."

Gil stopped mid-pack. "He did?" He felt a rush of levity to his heart. "That's great." Gina didn't look like she thought it was great. "Isn't it?"

"He asked me to sign a pre-nup." Gina's face screwed up as she prepared to cry. "Can you believe it?"

"And that's why you're upset?"

"Wouldn't you be?" she snapped.

"This is LA, Gina," Gil said. "Everyone signs pre-nups."

"I don't," Gina said.

"You'll get a fortune from me," he pointed out. "You'll be a wealthy woman."

"How wealthy?" Gina wanted to know.

"Very," Gil said. "Enough to keep you happy." But he wondered if any amount of money would ever keep Gina happy. "Sign it. It's only sensible," Gil tried to push the point home. "Noah is worth millions. Millions and millions. He's had how many wives? Three? Four?" Maybe a few he's forgotten. "He'd be working as a busboy at Wolfgang Puck's if he hadn't got pre-nups."

"Trust you to see it from his side."

"Get a good lawyer. Negotiate yourself a great deal. Then kit yourself out with diamonds. Have them put in all of your nails or your teeth. Or both. You'll never spend your way to the bottom of Noah's money."

Gina seemed to brighten slightly. "You really think that's what I should do?"

"Of course."

"You're not just saying that?"

Gil dropped a shirt in his case. It was one that he never wore and he had no idea why he might be packing it. "I'm outta here."

"Where are you going?"

"To a hotel."

"You can't live in a hotel," she said.

"I can't stay here with you," he said. "It's too cramped." Which was a fine thing to say about a home with more rooms than you could shake a stick at.

"What about me?"

"You can do what you like. You're on your own, Gina."

"Don't be like that, Gil," she begged. "I need you. I need you to be my best friend."

"And I need you to be *my* best friend," Gil said. "I need you to stand on your own two feet. No drink. No drugs. No stupid threats."

"You're right," Gina said. "You're absolutely right. You always are."

Gil was stunned.

Gina held up her hands in surrender. "I should go home to Noah and tell him yes. Right now."

Yes! Gil felt like punching the air.

"You should stay here. This is your home. I won't hear any more talk of hotels. I must go right now," Gina said, starting to fuss.

"I'm going to San Francisco," Gil said. "You have the weekend."

"No. No," Gina insisted. "I'm out of your life right now."

Gil moved toward her, but she held up her hands.

"Apologize to Sadie for me," she said. "Noah will pay for the damage to her car."

So some things never change. She kissed Gil on the cheek distractedly. "I love you," Gina said. "You're the best husband I ever had." She lowered her eyes and took in the bed. "I don't suppose we could have a last . . . for old time's sake?"

"I don't think so," Gil said.

Gina shrugged. "I must go and shower. Noah will wonder where I am." And with that she strode out of the room.

Gil frowned. He was getting too old to deal with Gina. He spent his working days dealing with tetchy technical crews, diva directors, lachrymose leading ladies and libidinous leading men; he needed to come home to a wife who was sane, normal and not into severe substance abuse. Someone exactly like Sadie.

Gil glanced at his watch. She hadn't called and she said she would, but then again they hadn't parted on the greatest of terms. He wanted to send her a huge bunch of red roses to apologize, but would that be construed as buying her something? He punched in the number of her mobile. It was switched off. Typical. He called Daniella's number and Sadie's new friend answered it after a couple of rings.

"Daniella?" he said. "Hi, it's Gil. Can I speak to Sadie, please?"

"Hi, Gil," Daniella said. "Sadie's not here. I thought she was with you."

"With me?" Gil shook his head even though he was on the phone. "She left here around ten last night."

"Oh." There was an uncomfortable pause.

Gil scratched his chin. "And she didn't come home?"

He could hear the hesitation in Daniella's voice. "Not as far as I'm aware."

"If she turns up, could you ask her to call me?" Gil said.

"Sure," Daniella said brightly, but he could tell she was worried.

Gil hung up. He should never have let Sadie drive away in that goddam heap. He just hoped that she wasn't wrapped around a palm tree somewhere on Beverly Glen. And if she wasn't, then where the hell was she?

Forty

"Wake up, sleepyhead." Tavis is sitting next to me. He's damp from the shower, his bare chest covered in perfect movie-style droplets of shimmering water. The only thing protecting his modesty—and mine—appears to be a very insubstantial white towel.

I try to open my eyes a little bit farther, but they just won't cooperate.

"Oh jeez!" Tavis breathes. He drops down next to me and smoothes my fringe from my eyes, looking vaguely alarmed. "What happened to you?"

"What?" I say. "Where am I? What happened?"

"You're on my sofa," Tavis says. "You fell asleep. My rendition of thwarted lover apparently bored you to death."

"Did it?" I have absolutely no recollection of this.

"You were gone within five minutes." And he looks a little disappointed about this.

"Why didn't you wake me?"

"You looked like you needed the sleep," he says.

I can't argue with that, I suppose.

"I don't know what the hell else happened," Tavis says, shaking his head. "But I hope it's not my fault. I'll get you a mirror."

"What? What?" It feels like someone has glued my eyelashes together. Tavis patters out and comes back with a shaving mirror. I hold it up to my face. My eyes are red and swollen and almost closed. My face is covered in scarlet blotches. I put down the mirror. "Clams," I say.

"Clams?"

"Spaghetti vongole. Gil's favorite."

"This is an allergic reaction?"

"Looks like it." I'm lucky I didn't go into ana . . . anaphye . . . anaphylact . . . whatever that thing is you get with peanuts. Instead I just have beef tomatoes where my eyes used to be and measles for blusher.

"Does it hurt?"

"Only when I laugh," I say. We both giggle. "So Doctor Robert, can you come back from the dead and tell me what I should do about it?" Now that I know it's there, my skin's starting to itch.

"I'll get dressed and take you to the drugstore. Let's see what they come up with. Are you going to work?"

"I can't let them down on my second day," I say. "I have to." Besides, I can't afford not to work. The amount of money I owe Gil is racking up daily. And it's Friday, so I've only got to last until tonight.

"You look terrible," Tavis says.

"Is that a professional opinion?"

"No," he says, "but this is." Tavis sucks his breath in. "Maybe I shouldn't be saying this, but I don't think you're destined to be with Gil."

"What?" I feel stunned with shock. This is more than I can take with my eyes glued together.

"Some relationships are meant to be," Tavis continues in a rush. "The universe smiles on them. Everything goes right. You always have a great time. There are no obstacles in your way. The sun always shines."

"Are you trying to tell me the universe is pissing on me?"

"Maybe it's trying to tell you something." He clears his throat and hesitates before he speaks. "He might not be the right man for you, Sadie. There may be another reason why you're here."

That sounds like California mess-your-head-up stuff to me and I've never been one for self-help books. Oh, don't get me wrong. Like everyone else, I buy loads of them, but I never read them and then they just help to make me feel guilty by sitting looking at me from the bookshelf, gathering dust. There are a lot of self-help books on Tavis and Joe's bookshelf and they don't have a speck of dust on them. Either one of them is a demon with a duster or they get an awful lot of usage.

I don't have a great knowledge of actors, never having met one before, but I understand that the general opinion of them is that they're not on this planet. California ones may be worse.

"I don't know what to say."

"I shouldn't have raised it," Tavis admits. "I had it on my mind. I guess I'm just trying to help."

"At the moment the most helpful thing you could do is find something to stop my eyeballs burning, Doctor Bob."

"We have cucumber in the refrigerator," Tavis says, standing up. "I'll cut you some slices and you can give that a try while I get dressed."

I give him a weak and feeble smile, which I hope will hurry him up.

"I could be wrong, Sadie," he says.

"Yeah," I agree. "Very wrong."

"He could be perfect for you."

"Yeah." I lie back and close my eyes.

Tavis takes the hint and pads out to the kitchen while I consider the things that are pissing on my relationship with Gil— such as his inability to get rid of his clinging wife and my allergy to small and otherwise inoffensive mollusks.

"Perfect," I say to myself. "But then again, I could be wrong too."

Forty-one

My day at Double Take is, thankfully, uneventful as I sit in the office with sunglasses on in the manner of people all over the world who are hoping not to be recognized. Bay and Min think it's very funny that Tavis drove Delores to work and had to lead me in like a blind person and, I must admit that apart from pouring a large amount of cold water—along the lines of the Pacific Ocean—on my relationship with Gil he has been most helpful and charming. You could almost believe that he was once a real doctor.

"Tavis was voted America's Sexiest Medic," Min says approvingly as he leaves the office to rush off for his audition.

"Really?" I don't tell them that I know firsthand that he does have a rather good bedside manner. I do, however, remind myself not to keep falling asleep on sofas with strange men.

I book Tom Cruise, Tom Jones and Tom Selleck look-alikes for what must be a "Tom"-themed cocktail party on a yacht in Marina del Rey. I call Gil three times and he calls me back, but we never manage to talk once. Daniella calls and we arrange to meet in Larchmont for a coffee after I leave work. I wish Tavis would call and tell me how his audition went, but he doesn't and I don't like to call him even though I have his folder out on my desk with his mobile phone number on it circled in highlighter pen.

I book a Pamela Anderson look-alike lap dancer for a bachelor party, and fake Fergie is delighted to get another airing. I take off my sunglasses at regular intervals and fill my eyes full of some anti-allergy drops that Tavis bought me at the chemist or whatever they call it here. I still haven't managed to get Tavis's bottom any work, even though I think it's the least I can do for him.

When four o'clock comes round, Bay presses an envelope into my hand, and as soon as she disappears, I check how much it is and am quite pleasantly surprised even though I've only been here two days and my eyes were only fully functional for one of them. It's hardly going to clear Third World debt, but it means I can give Daniella some of my rent.

At four thirty a small, independent film company phones. Their leading man has gone all shy and won't get his togs off for the love scene. Apparently he has unexpectedly become afflicted with a pimply arse. It happens even to the best, I guess. Can I help? *Can I help!* I tell them I have America's Sexiest Medic on my books—not a pimple in sight—and rush Tavis's resumé round to them by courier.

By five o'clock Tavis's bottom has got a job lined up for tomorrow, and I'm a happy but still bloaty-eyed woman. Now I have a legitimate excuse to phone him, and as I bash in the number I wonder why I think I need one. He's not picking up, so I leave a message and take the paperwork, ready to drop it into Zorba's for Tavis later. I leave dead on five.

I feel very LA, as I pull up in Larchmont Village at a parking meter. I could have walked here in ten minutes, but no, I have brought Delores with me, although she is being a bit more temperamental than when Tavis drove her. I feel like telling her that Tavis is gay and she's wasting her effort.

Daniella is sitting outside a trendy little coffee shop, sipping from a monster-size cardboard cup.

"Hey," she says.

"Hey," I say back, entering into the spirit. My friend and I do the air-kiss thing.

"Get a coffee and pull up a chair," she instructs.

"What's that?" I point at her bucket of beverage.

"A tall, skim, decaf caramel macchiato."

"Right." How will I ever begin to understand the men when I can't even get a grip on the drinks?

"What's it like?"

"Good," Daniella says. "It's good."

I make a mental note to get the smallest size they do, otherwise I'll spend the rest of the evening weeing. I go inside to get myself a whatever-it-was coffee. The giant bucket thing *is* the smallest one they do, and once I've managed to plow my way through a truly bewildering choice of beverages without recognizing anything, I've forgotten what Daniella said it was and decide on a boring old cappuccino—the first thing on the list—and rejoin Daniella in the beautiful blistering sunshine.

As soon as I'm settled, I take off my sunglasses and give her a flash.

"Oh my goodness," Daniella says, taking in my red, screwed-up eyes. "What happened?"

I do my "clam allergy" routine and after much commiseration from my buddy, she looks at me over the top of her DKNY sunglasses and says, "So where did you get to last night, girl?"

I sigh.

"Gil called first thing this morning," she continues in a rather censorious tone. "He sounded very anxious."

I've consumed half of the bucket of coffee before it's even touched the sides. "Gina turned up again. Drunk." I take a moment to relive the events. "I had to get out of there."

Daniella looks duly sympathetic. "And?"

"And then I went to show my car to Tavis." This comes out in rather more of a rush than I anticipated.

"Was he impressed by you turning up—presumably unannounced—in the dead of night?"

"It wasn't that late."

Daniella doesn't back down from her questioning look.

"We drove out to the beach."

"Which beach?"

"Venice Beach."

"You drove out to the beach with someone you didn't know?" Daniella takes off her sunglasses and peers at me. "This isn't sleepy little London," she says. "This is LA. That's crazy."

"I came to live out here with someone I didn't know . . ."

"And look where that's got you!"

"London doesn't have a beach," I point out in an effort to use diversionary tactics. "It isn't a situation that's previously arisen."

"Did he hit on you?"

"Who?"

"*Tavis.*" Daniella mimics my accent. Very badly.

"No."

Daniella snorts in disbelief.

"He's not that sort of man."

"They're all that sort of man."

"Not Tavis," I say, and wonder why I sound so disappointed. "I went back to his place for coffee."

Daniella shakes her head in a very drama-queen way and flings herself back in her seat. "This just gets worse!"

"I met his partner," I say calmly. "Joe."

"Partner? Joe?"

"Joe."

"Joanne? Jolene? Josephine?"

"No. Joseph. Male Joe." That's wiped the frown off my friend's face. "Tavis is gay," I confirm.

"Oh."

"He's a really nice guy." I gulp some more of my bucket of coffee. "I fell asleep on his sofa. He took me to the chemist to get me allergen-relief eye drops."

"A guy who knows about eye drops must be gay," Daniella feels moved to inform me.

"He is." I can feel that little saggy feeling again and try to ignore it. I nod sadly. "It's a hell of a waste, though." And I don't know if it's against client confidentiality or what, but I whip Tavis's file out of my chi-chi designer bag and plonk it on the table, flicking it open at a rather attractive photograph of a buck-naked Tavis.

"Ooo!" Daniella hurriedly puts her sunglasses back on for a better look. She points at Tavis's bottom. "That's gay?"

"Yeah."

"Goddam it!" She holds the folder up to get better light and then shakes her head. "It's Doctor Robert," she says. Her mouth has dropped open. "Doctor Robert's gay?"

"And from last week he's dead too."

"Shit," Daniella says, and I'm not sure which revelation she's more pissed off about. "He's an actor," she puffs, slapping the folder back down. "They're all gay."

"Isn't that a hideous stereotype?"

"Which in this case happens to be true?"

She has a point.

"I should have warned you," Daniella says.

"I didn't need warning. He's just a friend." I close the file before Daniella slavers on it. "He works in the restaurant down the street." I nod in the direction of Zorba's, which is about three doors away. "I got his backside a job this afternoon. Come with me while I tell him."

Daniella slugs down her coffee. "Drink up. Drink up," she says.

"Why the rush?" I could spend another week getting to the bottom of this cup.

"We have work to do," she says.

"What?"

"Some gay men are less gay than others."

Tavis is leaning on the bar, flicking through a magazine, but comes over to us as soon as we enter Zorba's door. He lifts up my sunglasses. "Ooo," he says.

"They feel better," I assure him. "The eye drops are doing a great job. Thanks for that . . . and for everything."

"My pleasure," Tavis says.

"It was fun."

"Yeah," he agrees. "We should do it again."

Daniella is staring at him in a very goo-goo, ga-ga way. I nudge her and she tries to look slightly less mad. "This is Daniella, my new best friend and my landlady."

"Hi," Tavis says and he shakes her hand.

I swear Daniella hangs onto it for longer than necessary and flutters her eyelashes and goes all girly. This must be her way of checking out how gay he is. I nudge her again.

"Hi," Daniella says, as if she's out of breath.

"I have good news," I announce and pull the necessary piece of paper out of my bag. "I got your bum a job."

"Great," Tavis says and snatches the paper with glee.

"The leading man has got pimples on his. I told them you don't."

Daniella has gone all dreamy again. I nudge her harder.

"This is great," he says and kisses me affectionately on the cheek. "Really great."

Ooo. Ooo. That's made *me* go a bit dreamy. "Well," I say, "it's hardly the leading role in *Four Weddings and a Funeral,* the sequel, but it will keep the wolf from the door." It's ridiculous, but while I'm yammering, I want to reach up and touch where Tavis kissed. I can still feel its warmth—and other bits of me appear to have gone quite hot too.

"One day as my agent and you got me a job," Tavis is clearly pleased. "I have to phone Joe," he says, and Daniella and I exchange a glance. "He'll be delirious. I can pay him rent." He rakes his hair and looks so excited that I get a rush too. It is a pretty decent paycheck for what should be a few hours' work.

"Let me buy you ladies a drink," he says. "We need to celebrate."

"White wine," Daniella says without pause for thought.

I shrug. "Same."

Tavis ushers us outside into the sun again and seats us at a prime table under a striped umbrella. After a moment he brings us two very large glasses of chilled white wine, dripping with condensation.

"Thanks, Sadie," he gushes as he places them in front of us. "I appreciate this."

"You're welcome," I say. I lift my glass to him. "I appreciate *this.*"

"To Tavis," Daniella says, and she's got that silly look again.

"To Tavis." You can't say fairer than that.

"To me," Tavis says, and joins in the toast even though he hasn't got a glass.

Daniella and I throw back our wine in unison.

"Now I must phone Joe," Tavis says. "Excuse me, ladies." And he disappears into the depths of the restaurant.

Daniella leans toward me. "He was flirting with you."

"No," I say. "I think that's just the way he is."

"Gay," she says as if to remind herself. She takes another sip of her wine and tuts. "He doesn't know what he's missing," she says in disgust.

I haven't really got an answer for that one. "Maybe he tried it and decided he didn't like it," I suggest.

"He didn't try it with *me*," Daniella says. "I would have convinced him."

"Joe's really nice," I say. "They seem happy."

Daniella groans miserably.

"Anyway," I say brightly. "What did you get up to last night?"

Daniella shrinks slightly. "Nothing."

It is the sort of "nothing" that means "something."

"Nothing?"

Daniella, rather theatrically, checks for eavesdroppers. "You mustn't tell a soul," she says. "Especially not my mother." Then my friend lowers her voice to confessional level. "I went and sat outside the house of the Mad Movie Mogul."

My eyebrows rise in surprise.

"For an hour," she adds.

"Bad," I say.

"More than bad," Daniella hisses. "It's ridiculous. What would I do if he saw me? What would I say?" She looks up at me. "Mary Ann would *kill* me if she knew."

"I think *I* might kill you," I say.

"I can't help it." Daniella's eyes fill with tears. "It's like an obsession." She dabs underneath her sunglasses with the back of her finger.

"Think of his wife. What has she done to deserve this?"

"She doesn't understand him."

"Can you please say that again and try not to sound like a bad cliché?"

"He can't be happy with her," Daniella says, but I'm not sure that she's aware that I'm listening. "She's been his *only* wife. They've been married for over twenty-five years. How weird is that? She is fifty-four years old!"

"A lot of women are," I point out.

"They're not married to movie moguls!" Daniella sniffs. This is clearly a subject that she's thought a lot about over the years. "He's fifty-five," she continues. "*I'm* nearly too old for him!"

"Perhaps he loves her?" I venture.

Daniella glares at me in disgust.

"Or maybe he's trying to be loyal?"

"Loyal?" Daniella looks at me as if it is an alien concept. "Who cares about loyalty when you could be sleeping with a twenty-two-year-old babe with silicone breasts?"

"Would you really want to be with someone like that?"

"Yes," she snaps. "It's the way things are done here! Don't you read Jackie Collins?"

I reach out and take Daniella's hand and give it a squeeze. "I don't know what to say."

A tear escapes from beneath her sunglasses and cuts a lonely track through her foundation. She wipes it away as it reaches her full red lips. "I'll get over it," she says. But if she hasn't managed to shake these feelings in ten years, then I somehow doubt it.

Tavis comes back.

"Is Joe pleased?" I ask.

And he grins with such pure joy that it makes the strings round my heart tighten. "Can I get you ladies anything else?"

"I think we might need some more wine."

"Stay for dinner," he says. "On the house."

"Thanks. That's sweet."

"I'll bring you menus." If he puts as much into his acting as he does waiting tables, the boy is sure to be a star.

"Tavis," I say as he turns away. "I hope it goes well tomorrow."

"It will," he says and he holds my eyes with his. "This is the universe working for us, Sadie."

I flush as he walks away.

"What did that mean?" Daniella misses nothing.

"I'm not really sure," I lie.

She watches Tavis as he chats to other women while he seats them. And I admit to having a sneaky glance myself.

My friend is looking pained. "That guy will make it big one day," she says. She drains her glass. "Are you absolutely sure he's gay?"

I nod.

"God, I hate this town," she says.

Forty-two

Gil and Steve were sitting on a low brick wall in Paramount's parking lot. All the cars had been moved out and a huge crew of technicians were in the process of flooding the area with water. Another crew painted the towering wall at one end with a pastel blue cloudless sky.

In this episode of *Star Satellite* the rescued Arutigan emperor would crash down spectacularly into the sea, shortly before he emerged to save the earth. Et cetera. In reality the parking lot would become the Pacific Ocean and a flimsy fiberglass pod, containing the hot and sweating character actor Billy Moreno squashed into a livid scarlet alien suit, would be hurled from a crane into a few feet of water. And once again the public would be blissfully unaware of the tricks of cinematic photography.

Steve kept one eye on the proceedings as he talked. "So boomerang wife has bounced back for the final time?"

"I sincerely hope so," Gil said.

"And now you can turn your full attention to the lovely Sadie?"

"I sincerely hope that too," he agreed. There was much hustling and bustling as cars were moved out of the vicinity. "You remember that show we worked on together—*Henry's Luck?*"

"The one where all the crew went down with salmonella and the leading man got a black eye from fooling around with a basketball?"

Gil nodded.

"The one where the leading lady got knocked up and spent every day honking with morning sickness?"

"The same one."

"The one we filmed in the Mojave Desert, where it rained

every day for three weeks?" Steve pondered. "And the director was a raging drunk?"

"Mmm."

"And the studio spent every day trying to pull the plug on us for going over budget?"

"Uh-huh." Gil sipped his drink.

"No," Steve said. "I don't remember that."

"Well, I do," Gil said. "And currently, I feel my relationship with Sadie is in a worse state than that picture was."

"It was a huge box-office smash," Steve recalled. "The guy got the girl. Everyone forgot that the production was a bag of shite."

"Nearly everyone," Gil said.

"Sadie will too," Steve assured him. "You need to start over again."

"Did you and Sarah start out like this?"

"No," Steve said wistfully. "We were love's young dream."

"That was not the answer I was looking for."

"Come out to the house this weekend," Steve suggested. "I'll incinerate some steak. We'll have too much beer and a few laughs. Let your old buddy charm her for you."

"Tempting though it is," Gil said, "I can't. I have to go up to San Francisco. The writer's threatening to lie down in Lombard Street and let cars run over him."

"That bad?"

"I guess."

"This is not a good start," Steve said. "Your first weekend to-gether. Your first Gina-less weekend and you're swanning off to San Francisco?"

"I'm not *swanning* anywhere. This is work—urgent work."

"Take Sadie with you."

"You know I can't do that."

"Take a day off from being a movie producer for once in a while."

"You know I can't do that either."

"Priorities, mate," Steve said. "And may I suggest that yours are slightly skewed?"

"I don't know what you mean."

"You're not trying to hide behind something else, now that Gina has conveniently disappeared?"

"No," Gil said. "I am *desperate* to see Sadie tonight. I've put off leaving until the morning especially. But she isn't around. I've been calling her all day, but she never has her damn cell phone on."

"Turn up at her place unexpectedly," Steve said. "Women like that sort of thing."

"It's not my style," Gil said. "I've spent too long with Gina. If you turn up unexpectedly, the surprise is usually on you." Usually in the form of some other guy's ass bouncing up and down.

He didn't want to share the fact that Sadie, for whatever reason, hadn't been at home last night. Where had she gone to? As far as he was aware, she knew no one in this town. It was a horrible feeling when you were sure that you could fall head over heels in love with someone, if only you were sure that they wouldn't hurt you. He'd seen too many women who were happy to feign love for money, status and an easy life. But those weren't accusations he could currently lay at Sadie's door. She had been nothing but straight with him—so far.

His cell phone rang and he snapped it open, putting it to his ear in one practiced move. "Hi." His face broke into a grin. Steve grinned back at him. *It's Sadie,* Gil mouthed silently.

Steve went all gooey. *Sadie.* He wrapped his arms round himself and turned his back to Gil, giving himself a mock passionate embrace and making slurpy kissing noises.

For someone who wanted to help, Steve was going the wrong way about it. *"Man!"* Gil hissed, his hand over the phone. But it was no good, Steve was too engrossed in snogging himself to care about his sensibilities.

"Where are you?" he said to Sadie. "I'll be right there."

He hung up. Steve stopped his one-man kissing demonstration. "Good news?"

"I think so."

"She's still in LA?"

"She's in Larchmont Village. At Zorba's."

"Then run to her," Steve said.

The Arutigan emperor was remonstrating with the crew, who were trying, unsuccessfully, to coerce him into his escape pod. The director looked as if he was moving in to strangle him. "He'll never save the world at this rate," Steve sighed. "Time for me to make a sharp exit."

"I can't blame him," Gil said. "Would you want to be dropped on your head in a flooded parking lot?"

"No, mate," Steve said. "But then I've no idea why anyone in their right mind would want to be an actor."

"Kissing Julia Roberts," they said together.

Gil stood up and stretched his legs. "I'm not going to mess this up," he said decisively.

"I'm pleased to hear it." Steve patted him on the back.

Gil just hoped that he was right.

Forty-three

"I think I'm drunk," I say to Daniella.

"Me too," Daniella agrees. "But it feels kinda nice." She pushes away her empty plate, which bears no trace of the moussaka it previously bore. "Bang goes my Doritos diet," she says, gently massaging her stomach. "I need to thank Tavis and then I need to go. Alexis will be home from ballet class and as hungry as a horse."

I think she has inherited her mother's constitution. The restaurant is becoming busy now with the evening crowd and all the outside tables are taken.

"Wait," I say. "Gil's on his way. He'll be five minutes. I'd like you to meet him."

"I'd like to meet him, too," Daniella says. "As well as giving him the once-over, I might well be beating a path to his door with a script."

"He's here," I say as his car pulls up outside and Gil gets out. He's wearing a black T-shirt and black jeans and is looking pretty cool. I still get a thrill when I see him.

Daniella adjusts her sunglasses. "Mmm-mmm," she says approvingly. "You are one lucky lady. He's young, good-looking and loaded."

"Money isn't everything," I say defensively.

"No?" Daniella tears her gaze from Gil and fixes me with it. "There are certain things in life that are better when they're very rich," she says. "Coffee. Chocolate. And men."

I laugh.

"I'm not joking," she says. "Poverty sucks. I've tried it."

I still have a foot very much in that camp.

"Hey," Gil says as he sees us. He kisses me on the cheek. "I've missed you."

Daniella is doing "crumbling" behind him. "This is Daniella," I say. "My new best friend."

"Hey, Daniella." Gil shakes her hand and slides into the seat next to me. "Thanks for looking after Sadie for me."

I'm not sure that I like that, but manage to keep the frown from my forehead. The only reason I'm at Daniella's house is because he's looking after Gina rather more than he is me. My friend might like her men rich, but I definitely prefer them attentive.

"I'm going to leave you lovebirds," Daniella says. "Are you coming home tonight?"

"No," Gil says before "yes" is out of my mouth. This time the frown wins. "If that's okay with you," he adds.

"I was going to get an early night."

Clearly this idea is not very impressive. "Late one last night?" he asks tightly.

"I'll catch you later," Daniella says, wisely extricating herself from her seat. "I won't wait up." And she clip-clops out into the street in search of her car to drive the hundred yards to her home.

The silence hangs between Gil and me. "So," he says eventually, "where did you get to after you left?"

Tavis comes to the table and I glance up at him.

"I was at Tavis's apartment," I say. Gil follows my eyes. "Tavis Jones. I'm his agent." It seems sensible to fill him in quickly. "At Double Take. He's an actor."

"Oh." Gil's look says, *Isn't everyone in this town?*

"I took Delores to see him."

"Isn't she great?" Tavis is looking uncomfortable.

"The car or Sadie?" Gil says.

"Can I get you a drink, Mr. McGann?" Tavis says.

"I think we're just leaving."

I gather my belongings. "Hope it goes well for tomorrow," I say. "Call me and let me know."

"Sure," Tavis says. "And thanks."

"You're welcome. Thanks for dinner."

I can see that Gil is getting impatient.

"Hope your eyes clear up," Tavis calls after us as we start to leave.

I wave at Tavis as Gil steers me by the elbow toward the door. "Your eyes?"

Out on the street, I dip my sunglasses. From Gil's reaction I can tell that they still look pretty bad. "I'm allergic to something."

"I hope it isn't me," Gil says.

I daren't tell him that it's probably his spaghetti special. "That's why I wanted an early night."

"Come back to my place," Gil begs. "Gina has finally gone. We can have a quiet time together, just the two of us. You can rest your eyes. We can get to know each other again."

Why am I hesitating?

"I'll cater to your every whim," Gil promises.

"Now you're talking." He puts his arm round me and we walk toward the car.

"What about Delores?" I ask. "I can't leave her here all night."

"If you're worried about someone stealing her," Gil says with a cheeky smile, "I really don't think you need to."

I take a lingering look at my mechanical soul mate. "Won't she get towed away?"

Gil glances at her too. "We can live in hope."

We head out of Larchmont and Gil takes me past the fancy wrought-iron gates of Paramount Studios on Melrose Avenue so that I can see where he is spending most of his working days. The pretty pink building is bounded by uniform lines of palm trees, and despite being the only studio left in Hollywood, it still has an air of glamor, as movie studios should.

The air is heavy with the sweet scent of bougainvillea and the bite of car exhaust fumes, and I still have a feeling that I'm just on holiday here and that it isn't quite part of my life.

Gil turns to me and strokes my cheek. "I want to put everything that's happened behind us," he says softly. "Start with a clean sheet."

"Sounds good to me." His lips are looking particularly kissable. And I think I just might stay the night after all. "We can spend the weekend chilling out," I suggest.

I'd like to see Venice Beach in the daylight and think it's probably not a good idea to mention that I've already seen it by moonlight. Hanging out on the sand at night with a guy doesn't conjure up a great picture—even if that guy happens to be gay. I think this is more information than Gil needs at the moment.

"Er . . ." Gil says. "That might be a little difficult. I have to fly to San Francisco in the morning."

I can feel my face fall.

"I'll be back as soon as I can. Maybe Sunday morning. Or evening," he admits. "It's hard to tell. I have problems there."

"You seem to have problems everywhere." I think he can tell that I'm not best pleased.

"Be patient," he says. "Now that Gina's gone, everything else is a walk in the park."

We pull up outside his house. All the lights are on. "Wow." There is a white stretch limo the size of a small street of terraced houses taking up most of the drive. "Whose is that car?"

"Oh no!" Gil exclaims. "Oh no. Oh no." And he's out of the car and racing to the front door before I get an answer.

"Gil." I chase after him, wobbling slightly in my heels due to excessive California chardonnay consumption.

Gil bursts through the door, followed shortly by me. He stops in his tracks at the entrance to the lounge. I don't, and cannon into him.

"What the fuck are you doing?" Gil shouts.

I peer over Gil's shoulder and it seems quite obvious to me what the *fuck* they are doing.

A small, wrinkly man with long hair is lying on the floor in Gil's lounge. He is wearing Gil's cooking apron and Maria's yellow rubber gloves. He's also wearing stockings and suspenders and treacherously high heels which may well be his own. Even though my eyes are suffering a severe allergic reaction, they manage to open to astonishing widths. It looks like . . . my good-ness, it is . . . it's Noah Bender. England's answer to Rod Stewart. I have another look just to check. It's definitely him. Strange. I thought he was a lot taller than that.

"What am I doing?" Gina roars. "What are *you* doing here?"

Gil's wife, on the other hand, appears to be wearing nothing but whipped cream on her chest with what seem to be strategi-cally placed cocktail cherries. She is sitting astride Noah Bender and is brandishing a wooden spoon.

I don't really know where to look and almost wish that my eyes were still swollen shut.

"You said you were going to San Francisco!"

"I changed my mind," Gil yells. "I'm going in the morning. You said you were leaving!"

"I am," she says. "Noah came to collect me and we . . ." She looks down at the man underneath her.

"Hey, man," Noah says and flicks a peace sign at us both.

"Get out," Gil says. "Get out now!"

"Goddam it, Gil," Gina says. "You'd think you'd never seen a man in women's underwear before."

"I haven't," Gil said. "Not Noah, anyway. And not in my own lounge."

I can safely say that I haven't seen a man in women's under-wear before. Not at such close proximity. It's not a pretty sight. The color doesn't suit him at all.

"You're ruining my rug," Gil complains.

"Your rug?" Gina is indignant. "You are always so uptight." In Gina's position I think I would be a lot more embarrassed and a lot less put out. And to be fair to Gil, there does seem to be whipped cream all over it.

"Get me a towel," she barks.

"I'll get you one." I'm volunteering primarily because I'd like to be out of here.

"Thank you, Sadie," Gina says.

I rush off to the nearest bathroom and grab a couple of tow-els. I'd heard about these Hollywood goings-on, but never thought that I would crash one of them. Noah Bender! The tabloids would pay a fortune for this.

When I get back to the lounge, Gil is standing as far away from Gina and Noah as possible, staring out of the window. Noah is sitting cross-legged on the sofa looking very drunk. I hand Gina the towel and she takes off her cherries and gives them to Noah, who duly eats them. Then she rubs herself down vigorously. She has a fantastic body, but I'm not sure that I want to be seeing so much of it.

"Hi," Noah says to me, plus peace sign.

"Hello," I say. "Nice to meet you. I'm a big fan. I love your music."

"Cheers, darlin'," Noah says, looking very pleased with himself.

Gina is throwing on her clothes.

"Shall I put the kettle on?" I venture.

"Great idea, darlin'," Noah says.

"No." Gil snaps his head round. "You will not put the kettle on. Noah and Gina are leaving."

"Come on, Noah," Gina says. "Put this on." And she throws him a voluminous coat that will certainly help to hide his dubious taste in lingerie.

Gina yanks her boyfriend toward the door while he's still dressing.

"You will be hearing from my lawyer," Gil shouts after them.

Noah gives Gil the peace sign again and Gina gives him the finger.

The door bangs and the room is suddenly very quiet.

"Well." I walk over to Gil. "Another ordinary day in Hollywood."

"I don't need any wisecracks right now," he says.

Actually, I think that's exactly what we need.

Gil turns to me. "I like your music?" he says. "What was that about?"

"What did you want me to say to him? That I thought his knickers were a size too small?" I sink down onto one of the white sofas and then realize that I should have checked it for surplus cream first. "Given the circumstances I think I coped admirably."

Gil says nothing.

"How come *I'm* suddenly the baddie?"

Gil rubs his forehead as if he has a headache coming on. And who'd be surprised in the circumstances. "I don't know," he says, and comes over and flops down next to me. "I'm sorry."

"We seem to be saying it a lot."

He takes my hand, but doesn't really look at me. "I know."

"It was pretty funny, though," I say. "Once you get over the shock."

"I don't think so," Gil says quietly. "How do you think I feel, knowing Gina prefers that to being with me?"

"There's no accounting for taste," I quip lightly, but I can see his point. "I wouldn't take it personally."

"Is there any other way I can take it?"

"I gather you and Gina didn't . . ." I glance rather furtively at the rug.

"No," Gil says, and I'm rather grateful for that.

Gil stands up. "I'd better take you home."

"Oh." I shrug. "I don't mind staying." I rather had my heart set on it.

"I think I'd prefer to be alone," he says.

"Oh. We don't have to . . ." My eyes wander to the rug again. "We could just have a cuddle. You look like you need one."

"I have an early start," Gil says crisply. "But thanks for the offer."

"You're welcome." I'm not really sure what else to say other than Gina is proving to be one of the most efficient contraceptives I've ever come across.

Forty-four

I should ring Gil, but I'm sulking. And anyway, he's quite capable of ringing me and he hasn't. It's 9 A.M. and the sun is already competing with the air-conditioning in my bedroom. Alexis sneaked in beside me when I was still half asleep and then fidgeted and kicked me for ten minutes until she was sure I was fully awake. We are now playing with a select few of her two dozen Barbie dolls—Barbie Birthday Wishes and Fairy of the Garden Barbie. I wonder if there is an Unlucky in Love Barbie.

"Hey." Daniella comes in wearing a lurid silk kimono and a hangover face. She gives Alexis an exasperated look. "What are you doing in here?"

"Aunt Sadie was lonely," Alexis explains. How true.

"She's also very patient," Daniella says. "You wriggle like a worm." Daniella grabs her daughter and tickles her until she's a shrieking heap.

"You should kick her out," my friend says to me.

"She's fine," I say. "I really don't mind." And a sudden pang makes me feel that I'd like my own daughter to rough and tumble with. What am I thinking of? I haven't yet snared a man and my womb seems to have gone into nesting mode.

Daniella hugs Alexis to her. "How would you like to spend the weekend with Grandma?"

"Yeah!" Alexis is out of my bed and on her way to pack her overnight bag, fickle child that she is.

Daniella sits on the edge of my bed. "I'm off to a scriptwriters' convention."

"Oh," I say. "You never mentioned it."

"It was fully booked," she tells me. "A place came up at the last minute."

"That's great."

"It will be useful for my career," she agrees. "I can make some contacts. I guess you'll be seeing Gil."

"You guess wrong," I say with a sigh. "He's out of town. San Francisco."

Daniella's face falls. "Your first proper weekend in LA and you'll be all alone?"

"It doesn't matter," I say. But inside me somewhere there's a little bit that thinks it does.

"I feel terrible," my friend says.

"Don't. This is important to you." I squeeze her hand. "I'm not your responsibility, and I can quite easily entertain myself."

Daniella looks doubtful.

"Delores and I will hit the road," I say. "I'll even remember to drive on the right side of the road."

"That Gil," Daniella says, "he might be cute, but he sure is messing you around."

"You don't know the half of it." I sink back on my pillow.

"How did it go last night?" Daniella asks. "I heard you come home."

"Not good," I admit. "Not good at all." Noah Bender in his stockings and suspenders appears in flashback behind my eyes. "I'm not sure whether this relationship is ever going to get off the ground."

"Well, I'll leave you to get ready."

For what, I wonder.

Nevertheless, I get up and plod into the shower pondering what to do with a weekend that now stretches emptily ahead of me. Probably exactly the same thing I did with all my empty weekends back in London, but with more sun.

I wonder whether I should give Tavis a call to wish him good luck. I know he hasn't got anything exciting as lines or the like, but I feel very nervous for him, like a parent sending her child off to the dentist unaccompanied. I think I will say hello, just to let him know that I'm rooting for him.

I pick up the phone as I rub myself down with a towel. Tavis answers after the first ring. "Hi," he says. It's a shame he's not got any lines, because he has a very sexy voice.

"Hello." I'm sort of embarrassed to be ringing him now. "It's Sadie."

"Oh, hi!"

"I just thought I'd wish you well for today."

"Gee thanks," he says. "I can't wait."

"Well, that's all I wanted really," I mumble. "Good luck."

"Wait," he says. "I guess you're busy?"

"No." Chance would be a fine thing. "Not very."

"Have you been on a film set before?"

"Er . . . no."

"I don't suppose you'd like to come with me?"

"Well, yes. I would."

"I'll pick you up," Tavis says. "In a half hour. Be ready."

"I will," I promise. Tavis hangs up.

I fling my towel to the corner of the room and contemplate which designer shopping bag I'm going to raid first. What should I wear—casual or chic, casual/chic, chic/casual? Think back to documentaries about filmmaking. Don't they all wear baseball caps? I don't need to rummage in my bags to tell me I don't have one. This is ridiculous! I feel like I'm going on a date, when all I'm doing is accompanying one of my clients to a job. I must try and stay cool.

"Daniella! Daniella!" I shriek, doing my best impression of a cat with a scalded bum. "I need help! Quick!"

Forty-five

Tavis's bottom is a vast improvement on the leading man's—even though I could be accused of being ever so slightly biased. The leading man is sitting glowering moodily in the corner and he looks as if he might think so too.

We are on the massive Universal Studios set, cocooned in the square box of a vast sound stage just opposite the incongruously pink Back Lot Café—and deep in the heart of the cinematic make-believe.

Tavis, my client and my reason for being here, is writhing about on a fur rug with an extremely nubile young actress and he looks as if he's thoroughly enjoying it. That boy must be a very good actor.

He isn't the slightest bit embarrassed about the fact that we're in a studio the size of a small football stadium and there are about seventy people watching him romp around in the nip simulating a jolly good shag. I can't even contemplate making love to Gil with his ex-wife and his housekeeper in the same building, so what does that say about me?

This is supposed to be a steamy sex thriller—*Killers Always Come Twice*—and it certainly is very steamy at the moment and thrilling. I can hardly bear to watch, but perhaps that's because I'm enjoying it rather too much than is good for me. I'm finding it very hard to keep an objective professional opinion. That is one hell of a cute butt.

"And cut!" the director shouts. I know he's the director because Tavis told me he was hot stuff. To me he looks about fourteen years old and totally incapable of directing a school play, let alone a movie. He's wearing a baseball cap back to front. Tavis and his friend stop in their tracks. "Good job," the director says.

The crew clap and I join in a bit too enthusiastically. Good grief, I need a drink and a lie down in a dark room.

Someone rushes up and hands Tavis a towel which he wraps deftly round his waist. The teenage director goes over and shakes his hand and then Tavis walks over to me. He's looking very pleased with himself.

"That was great," I say and to my horror I sound all breathy and girly.

"Thanks," Tavis says. His cheeks are flushed and his pupils dilated. His hair is even more messy than normal. "The director was real pleased." He winks at me. "But then it's not hard to fake it with someone who looks like that."

The tiny Asian leading lady—similarly attired in a towel—waves at Tavis and he waves back.

"I wish all my women were as easy to please." He laughs.

I laugh back, but I'm not sure why.

"I'll be back in five," Tavis says and he wanders off, presumably to restore himself to his rightful clothing.

I stand there and look like a lemon while the crew move round and set up for another scene.

Eventually Tavis appears again amid much back-slapping and high-fiving and we are loaded into a stretch golf cart of all things and are driven away from the sound stage. I'm so excited I could bite my own legs off and it's very hard to stay looking cool. We head off down James Stewart Avenue between rows of low beige bungalows.

"Those used to be dressing rooms for the stars," he tells me. "Now they're offices for writers and producers."

Daniella would be in writer's heaven if she ever landed an office here. The stars, it appears, do their ablutions or whatever they do in glorified caravans nowadays.

We sail past a tour bus full of punters ogling a street set where an episode of *The O.C.* is being filmed and I feel a frisson of glee that I have even one tiny toe in this world and I haven't had to stump up twenty dollars to get in here.

I think Tavis sees my joy, because he turns to me and says, "Do you need to get back?"

"No." If only he knew. "Not especially."

"Hey, buddy," Tavis says to the driver. "Spare five minutes and take us on a tour."

"Sure," the man says and we whizz off through the narrow streets filled with bits of scenery and trucks and empty trailers.

We bump and jiggle along and Tavis rests his arm across the back of the cart to steady himself. It does nothing to steady me. I know this sounds ridiculous, but he has such presence that he's making me all hot and cold and weird inside. And I know that he's not interested in me and I'm not interested in him either, but the fact that he is completely unaware of the effect that he might be having on me—*if* I were interested and *if* he were interested— is completely unnerving. I'm not even sure if that makes sense. Out of all the boyfriends I've had, I've never felt as comfortable as I do with someone who's gay. And is it simply because we can become mates with no agenda? Oh bollocks. I don't know. I'm just going to enjoy the ride.

"We shot *Happiness Hospital* here," Tavis informs me. "Over there." And he gestures at a building that has a banner with *Happiness Hospital* strung up above the massive doors. A shadow crosses his face. "I kinda miss it."

I touch his arm. "It won't be long before you get something else."

He grins at me gratefully, and I hope that I'm right. I can see the attraction of losing yourself in a world that is both glamorous and not quite real. The sort of world that ordinary people don't really get to experience.

We take in the Bates Motel from *Psycho*—I can imagine Gina being quite at home here. Then the set for *The Best Little Whorehouse in Texas*—I'm not even going to comment on that one— before scooting through a Mexican pueblo complete with a fake flash flood.

And just for a moment, I feel very sad. Even this isn't how it should be. A boy and girl bouncing round in a buggy laughing as if they haven't a care in the world. But it's the wrong boy. Gil should be showing me this world.

"Okay?"

Perhaps he has seen my smile die. I nod.

"Nothing is ever quite what it seems here," Tavis says, meeting my eyes. "Remember that."

And before I can say anything else, we jiggle away again to take in a steamy, bone-strewn bit of *Jurassic Park* before the driver zips past the monstrosity of a car park that's disguised with painted trees and deposits us at the main gate. Tavis tips the man generously and we leave fantasy land behind and step out into the real world once more. Traffic whizzes past us.

We cross the road to the parking lot located outside of the inner sanctum and stand next to Tavis's heap of a car—complete with real rust and real worn tires. I don't know what model it is, but it is in a marginally worse state than Delores. No wonder he has such an affinity for her. He opens the door and I get in.

"What does the rest of the weekend hold?" he asks as he pushes the gear stick into reverse with an alarming *graunch*.

"Not much," I admit. "Gil's away in San Francisco. Some problems with the movie he's working on. Daniella's gone to a scriptwriting convention."

"Oh," he says. "Too bad."

"I thought I might do sightseeing and stuff," I say, trying to sound as if I'm not pissed off.

"Alone?"

I nod. We pull away and head out on the Hollywood Freeway and down Vine Street toward Larchmont. The Eagles blast out from the radio and I lean back in the seat, letting the breeze cool me down. Tavis is deep in thought.

When we stop outside Daniella's house, Tavis turns to me. "I have the weekend off—the first one in months. I'm heading out to visit with my parents," he says. "Why don't you come with me? They live out in San Juan Capistrano. It's cute. We can drive out on the coast road and I'll show you some of the sights. We'll be back tomorrow."

"Overnight?"

"You can pick up a few things."

"Won't they mind?" You have to book in to see my parents about three months in advance, so that my mother has time to lay in stocks of apple pie and starch the sheets in the spare room so that they slice you in half when you lie in them.

"Why would they mind?"

"I don't know." I shrug. "What about Joe?"

"Joe's working," Tavis says. "Hey, two actors, both employed. Our luck could be changing!" He fixes me with imploring eyes. "Come on," he says. "I can't leave you all alone on your first weekend in LA."

The thought piques me that it didn't seem to bother Gil this much. And I hate to say this, but I'm sort of glad to have a break from him and his whining wife. I could sit around on said rump waiting for Gil to ring—or I could not.

"I'd love to come," I say. "Give me a few minutes to grab some stuff." I jump out of the car. "What shall I bring?"

"Whatever you normally wear to barbecue and laze round the pool."

Oh right. Clearly, Tavis has no idea what my life in London is like.

Forty-six

On Saturday in California people hang out at the beach—surfing, skating, cycling and any other activities that involve the wearing of skimpy, color-coordinated clothing. At home I would probably be wrapped up in my warmest coat, shoving a shopping trolley round the supermarket, looking for marked-down produce and snarling at any small children or doddery old people who got in my way. Stressed, *moi?* This is an infinitely more pleasurable way to spend the day.

"We'll take the scenic route," my friend says and drives us out of LA, winding his way through a bunch of identical-looking streets flanked with Dunkin" Donuts, KFCs and McDonald's until we eventually pick up Route 1, the Pacific Coast Highway to San Juan Capistrano, and catch a glimpse of a glittering blue sea.

Tavis hangs his arm out of the side of the car and steers with one hand, which is just so American. Sunny surf music blares from the radio, accompanying us all along the route and, as Tavis sings along at the top of his voice, I sink back into the torn, worn vinyl of his car seats, realizing that this is the happiest I've felt in a long time.

Tavis turns to me and gives me one of his movie star melt-your-underpants smiles. "Okay?"

"Yes." And this time I don't get the feeling that I'm doing this with the wrong man.

Before long we're turning away from the coast and climbing into the hills. San Juan Capistrano is a sleepy little town that looks like a modern version of the Mexican pueblo we saw at Universal Studios and is about as different as it could be from the sprawling big city.

"Let's stop in town before we get to my parents' house," Tavis suggests. "Once we get there, they'll never let us sneak away."

And I like the idea of sneaking away with Tavis. We park outside a coffee shop and stroll down the street where there's a bar with a wedding celebration in full swing.

"Ever come close to tying the knot?" Tavis asks.

"No." Not even remotely close, I want to add miserably, but restrain myself.

"You?" And then I realize it was a pretty stupid thing to say.

He laughs at the very idea. "No."

We stop at a crosswalk and he takes my hand to stop me jaywalking. His hand is warm and strong. When the little white man appears on the sign, he tugs me across. We window-shop in a very coupley way and buy a huge, colorful bunch of flowers for Tavis's mother before retiring to the coffee shop to sample their wares. And I try not to notice that Tavis is still holding my hand despite the fact we crossed the road eons ago.

In the coffee shop, after trawling through another five hundred variations on America's favorite beverage, I plump for whatever it is Tavis orders—something involving chocolate chips and a mountain of whipped cream. One day I will be grown up enough to make my own beverage choice, I'm sure, but now is not the time. I'm quite nervous about meeting his parents—probably because I hardly know Tavis and this seems like a very intimate thing to be doing. I only used to risk taking boyfriends home when I considered them "serious"—mainly because my parents are extremely embarrassing.

We sit on tall bar stools at a table in the window and watch the wedding guests dance down the street.

"What are your parents like?"

"Fine," Tavis says. "Middle-class, middle-aged worriers. You'll get grilled by my mother. She'll think we're getting married."

"She will?" I'm so surprised that I misjudge my mouth and end up with whipped cream on my nose. Tavis takes a napkin and wipes it off for me. "Doesn't she know about—"

"Gil?" he says. "No."

"I didn't mean Gil," I say. "What about your . . . your . . . lifestyle?"

"They tolerate it." He laughs. "But I guess every mother is secretly yearning to be a grandma." He stirs his coffee thoughtfully. "Except mine doesn't do it secretly. She keeps hoping that I'll have a sudden revelation and change my ways."

I bet there are a few women out there who have felt like that. Particularly if he goes around doing that affectionate, hand-holding business.

"She'll probably be examining you to see if you've got good childbearing hips."

I give my ample rump a hearty smack. "She won't be disappointed then."

"But she will, won't she?" Tavis says sadly. "A wife and children are definitely not on my shopping list."

"No." I dig farther into my cream. "But you shouldn't write it off entirely. One day you might . . ." How do I put this delicately? ". . . change your proclivities?"

Tavis laughs. "I might," he says, chuckling out loud. "Come on. We'd better go before Mom sends out a search party."

We jump down from our stools and head out into the sunshine once again. Back at Tavis's car, he opens the door for me while I get in. He comes round and hops in next to me, eschewing the door as an optional extra. He puts the key in the ignition, but doesn't start the car; instead he turns to me and wearing his serious face, says, "Sadie, I wanted to let you know that if I ever did change my . . . proclivities"—he smiles at the word—"it would definitely be for someone like you."

"Oh." I'm not sure what the right response to that is. It makes me feel like scratching my head, for one thing. "Thanks."

"You're welcome." Tavis grins at me and guns the clattery engine and we set off to do the parent thing—but not quite.

And I don't know whether I feel happy or sad that I'm exactly what Tavis would be looking for in a woman, if only he weren't gay.

Forty-seven

I'm still rooted to the chaise I've been lying on for the best part of the day watching Tavis's bronzed, toned and near-naked body as he swims effortlessly up and down his parents' pool.

"That happened in the last earthquake," his mother, Alma, says.

"Pardon?"

"The tiles," she says, pointing at several large fissures in the terra-cotta tiles that surround the pool. "We're lucky it didn't crack the pool."

"Oh."

"When that ground shakes, we know all about it!"

The earth moving is something I haven't experienced for a long time, but I don't feel this is the right time to share it. I push my sunglasses farther up my nose. It brings a smile to my lips to think that Tavis's mother assumes I'm looking at the state of her flagstones rather than the powerful, graceful movements of her beautiful son. Perhaps she is aware that I'd be wasting my time. I console myself with the fact that there's no harm in looking.

I sink back into the chaise and follow the few wisps of hazy cloud that drift across the sky in the hope that they might ease some sensible thoughts into my brain. I'd forgotten how debilitating the sun can be to a body that's been starved of rays for too long. Even thinking is proving an effort. But this is the first time in longer than I care to remember that I've had the chance to simply lie and think. I've spent the last few months careering from one part of my life to the next.

"Careering" is a good place to start. Like the majority of

women in the new millennium, I felt I was defined by the success of my career. I was reasonably happy on the treadmill of little black suits, bonuses and backbiting—until that treadmill was forcibly removed from me. Having thrown myself into a whirlwind of making ends meet, I no longer know whether I really and truly want to go back to long hours, missed lunches and stress-related insomnia in pursuit of a high salary. Instead I've been working long hours, missing lunches and having stress-related insomnia in a wide variety of menial roles that pay peanuts. What comes first—the chicken or the egg? What's the worst scenario—having bags of money but no time to enjoy it, or not having enough money to pay your bills and bags of time to dwell on it?

I'd built up a lovely barrier of capable career woman and was making a very good job of hiding behind it. Now that's been blasted into the water, I'm not sure I have the strength to rebuild it.

It's also been a long time since I've had strong family relationships, and being here with Tavis today makes me realize that I've been missing that too. My nice high wall seems to have had a lot of wobbly bricks in it for a lot longer than I thought. His parents nag him ceaselessly in the proud way that parents do, and I've decided that I want children of my own that I can nag and be proud of.

It troubles me to think that I've reached the ripe old age of thirty-two and, while I've been kissed more than a few times, I've never yet had a proposal of marriage. Not a real one. What's wrong with me? That's what I want to know. Why am I not marriage material? I haven't got bad breath or a hideous disfiguring disease. But nor do I have the talent for beguiling men.

In my twenties I was very keen to settle down—before I had done anything remotely wild—get married and have children. I used to tell everyone this, including men whom I had only seen, and ever did see, for one night. My friends—and my mother in particular—blamed my desperation for my marriage-free state. That was when I abandoned the idea altogether and convinced myself that what I secretly wanted was to be a self-sufficient career woman all along. As soon as I was self-sufficient and suitably and successfully "careered" and still no men came along, my friends—and my mother in particular—blamed my self-sufficient vibes for my continuing marriage-free state.

I'm useless at the political maneuvering between the sexes. I have read all the books—*The Rules, Men are from Mars, Emotional Intimacy, The Surrendered Single*—basically anything that would give me a clue about how to turn your average shag-monster into a sensible, caring husband. And what did I get out of them? Not a sausage, that's what.

All these self-help books give such conflicting advice. If you follow *The Rules*, you don't let any sad sap, no matter how hard he begs, get the better of you. And never ever should you think about bringing up the "M" word, other than for the purposes of pouring scorn on the poor idiots who indulge in it. For *The Single Surrendered*, playing hard to get is an anathema. She smiles at all men, however dubious-looking they may be, and wears short skirts. She offers to clean his flat. After half a dozen dates, you should be flashing your ring finger.

Whenever I've played hard to get, the object of my coolness has just lost interest and gone chasing after some tart who's gagging for it. When I've appeared compliant and in need of a man, they've run in the opposite direction—usually after someone who doesn't give a damn about them. When I've just sat there and been me—veering between hard to get and needy—that's given them the collywobbles too. I am becoming *The Resigned Single*. The nunnery beckons.

Take Gil. What does he see in Gina that I don't have—apart from the fact that all her body parts appear to be hardened up with silicone? Isn't a bit of healthy wobble more attractive than someone who is permanently drunk or high? Gil's wife/ex-wife seems to play it all by her own rules and it works perfectly. Certainly for Gil—no matter how many times she changes them or how badly she behaves. Instead of treating her like a leper, maybe I should be asking her for lessons.

At this point in my thoughts, Tavis pulls himself out of the pool. He comes over and sits down on the chaise next to me and grabs a towel. He's even more attractive when he's damp than when he's dry. And it occurs to me that I've seen a lot more of Tavis naked than I have of the absent man purporting to be my boyfriend.

His mother stands up. "I'll fix something to eat."

If we eat any more we'll all explode.

"Watch your skin, honey," she says to me. "Your cheeks are a little pink."

I can't be entirely sure that this is down to sunburn. Alma goes into the house, leaving us alone.

Tavis gazes at me. His eyes are very unnerving. They don't flicker at all. I get a very strange rush in places where I shouldn't be having strange rushes. "You're looking very pensive," he says.

"Yes. I'm thinking about my life and the mess I'm making of it," I admit.

"Gil isn't making you happy." And I'm not sure whether it's a statement or a question.

I try to smile. "It's a bit hard when he's in San Francisco."

"I think that's a suitable way of dodging the issue," Tavis says with a smile.

I stretch out and avoid Tavis's eyes as well as the issue. "Is there a code of dating conduct for gay men?"

"I have absolutely no idea." Tavis looks slightly surprised that I've voiced this. "Why do you ask?"

"I'm trying to think of a way to snare my man, and I'm failing," I say. "I wondered if it was easier for gay men."

Tavis frowns. "Is that what would make you happy? Snaring Gil?"

"I don't know," I admit. "If I can still have dark and brooding thoughts while lying beneath a careless blue California sky, perhaps there's no hope for me."

I'm going to have to do something about my selection process. I have a habit of falling in love with the wrong types, but this time I've outdone myself. I am head-over-heels in love with a man who is still fixated on his wife/ex-wife. And if I'm not very, *very* careful, I could be performing similar acrobatics for a man who is gay. I could analyze this a million times, but it all comes down to the same thing: I'm not really giving myself a fighting chance.

Forty-eight

"Ooo. Ooo. Ahh. Ahh." I feel I must mention that this isn't being said with any form of passion. *"Aaahhhh . . . !"*

"Keep still," Tavis instructs. My torturer tips more calamine lotion onto his cotton wool and resumes dabbing with zeal.

"Ahh. Ahh. Ooo. Ooo." Every bit of me that was exposed to the strong California sunshine is doing a passable impression of a parboiled lobster. My nose looks like it has been slammed in a door. "Ahh. Ahh!"

"I'm sorry," he says. "I should have given you some sunscreen."

"I was wearing sunscreen." Some pathetic little weedy factor only strong enough to keep out feeble British sun. This California bugger has fried all my skin off. I'm going all hot and cold.

"Are you going hot and cold?"

"No."

"I don't want you to get sunstroke."

Oh. That's what it is. And there was me thinking it was down to Tavis's stroke. I never guessed it would be so erotic, being rubbed all over with damp cotton wool. Or it would be, if it didn't hurt so much.

"I might be a bit hot and cold," I admit. I feel like crying at my own stupidity. I can't even do suntanning right—and how hard can that be? I sniff miserably. I bet Gina's never roasted her own nose off. "I'm going to be peeling for years."

"No, you're not," Tavis says. Doctor Robert stands back and admires his handiwork.

I look in the mirror and all I can see is one of those scary Aborigines all dolled up in full war paint. I've got pale pink chalky stripes all over me. "Fuck!"

"It's not that bad," Tavis assures me, but his face says that it is. He gives up the trying-not-to-laugh option and chortles loudly.

"I'm such an idiot," I say.

"It can happen to anyone."

"Has it happened to you?"

"No." Tavis gets a glare for his honesty. "I've been lucky," he adds quickly.

We're in the guest room of his parents' house and it isn't quite on the same lavish scale as Gil's myriad of guest rooms. The bathroom is down the hall and there are two small beds, one either side of a rather dilapidated-looking chest of drawers. This fact is helping to keep my mind from some of my pain. Is this where we are sleeping? Together?

Tavis follows my gaze. "I'll sleep on the sofa if you're not happy with sharing."

"No. No," I say, before my brain has time to think about the implications. "I can be grown up about this."

Tavis chortles again. "Are you sure you can resist the temptation?"

To what? "I think so." God, what if I fart or snore? Or both?

"I'll leave you for a while." Tavis puts the lid back on his calamine lotion and heads for the door. "To get yourself ready."

For what?

"For bed," Tavis says, even though I haven't spoken.

"Yes. Right." I wonder if the after-shampoo conditioner I'm using that guarantees thickness is working on the right part of my body.

My roommate departs with another giggle to himself, and gingerly, I peel off my clothes. Oh good grief. I look like a zebra that's been painted by some colorblind, artistically challenged five-year-old. With a promise to have a proper wash in the morning, I slide into the cool sheets, every inch agony on my burning body.

I switch off the light and lie in the dark, trying not to move, fidget or itch. It's hot and I want to throw the sheets off, but I'm lying in the nip because I can't bear a T-shirt near me either. Oh goddam it! Why was I born so stupid? The air-conditioning unit is clattering away, humming at a soporific level. I'm just about to drop off, when the door creaks open and Tavis tiptoes in. I lie still but crack one eye open. He's stripped down to his boxers and it's a very unnerving sight. I screw up my eyes again. I'm not sure I can be grown up about this after all. I wish Tavis was out of harm's way on the sofa, but it seems a little too late to voice this.

"Sadie?" Tavis whispers. "Sadie, are you awake?"

I keep my mouth shut. Which is not something I do often enough. I can hear him pad toward my bed and I stay stock still.

"Sleep tight," he says and plants a cool and tender kiss on my fevered forehead.

And I think that's possibly the one thing that will guarantee that I don't sleep a wink all night.

Forty-nine

Gil threw down his bags on the bed and took time to survey his new home. No one could say that living at the Beverly Hills Hotel was slumming it, but it was certainly cramped compared to what he was used to. *Cramped,* however, was only a rich person's word for cozy. Two rooms instead of ten. And it was definitely all the better for being a Gina-free zone.

It was Sunday evening. Not as early as he'd planned, but not too late. The director, actor and writer hadn't, in the end, indulged in fisticuffs. The movie was shooting again. Crisis averted. At least this particular crisis.

Gil glanced at his watch. He'd planned a wonderful evening with Sadie. And there was only one thing missing. Sadie.

He hadn't found the time to call her until this afternoon—which was remiss of him and he wasn't sure why he'd hung out so long. But now he was sorry that he had. Her cell phone had steadfastly remained unanswered. He'd fixed to have a romantic dinner on the private terrace of the bungalow—flowers, candlelight, champagne on ice—the whole nine yards. But now he wondered whether he should cancel it. Gil tapped in her number again.

This time when it rang, a young girl answered. "Hi."

"Hi," Gil said. "Who's this?"

"Alexis. I'm ten," she said.

"I'm Gil," he responded.

"How old are you?"

"I'm thirty-eight."

"That's old."

"Yes." He felt much older, but he wasn't about to explain why. "Alexis, is Sadie there?"

"No."

"Are you sure?"

"Yes." Alexis sounded very sure.

"Do you know where she is?"

"With Tavis," Alexis said.

Gil could feel the hairs on the back of his neck stand up. "With Tavis?"

"Mmm-hmm."

He was sure he should know who Tavis was.

"Would you like to speak to Magic Jewel Barbie instead?"

"I don't think so, honey." Wait! Wasn't Tavis the far-too-handsome server at the restaurant? What was she doing with him? "Do you know where she's gone?"

"They're away for the weekend. She left a note."

This was not sounding good. "What does it say?"

"It says . . ." Gil heard Alexis take a deep breath. "Hi Daniella and Alexis. Hope you had a great time at your convention and at Grandma's house."

Gil could feel his patience ebbing away. There was another deep breath. "Is Mommy there?"

"No," Alexis said. "Grandma is. Do you want to talk to Grandma?"

"No. No. Could you just cut to the important part?"

Alexis's fuse sounded shorter than his. "This *is* the important part." Another deep breath. "I've gone to Tavis's parents' house. Back Sunday. Love you both. Sadie."

"Thank you," Gil said.

"And she's put three kisses on the bottom."

Gil wished that Sadie would put three kisses on his bottom.

"Can you take a message?"

"I'm not supposed to talk to strangers."

"Isn't it a little late for that?"

"Barbie could take a message," Alexis suggested.

"Fine." Gil sighed. "Does Barbie have a pencil?"

"Mmm-hmm," Alexis said.

"Could Barbie tell Sadie that I'm at the Beverly Hills Hotel, and I want her to join me for dinner at eight o'clock?"

"Barbie says you're talking too quick."

"Could you tell Barbie that I don't have all day?"

"Barbie's ten too," Alexis informed him sharply. "She's going as fast as she can."

"Maybe you could get Sadie to call me?"

"Okay," Alexis said. "Bye." And she hung up.

Gil sat on the corner of the bed, feeling dazed by his conversation. Why didn't he have the knack with women—of any age? He guessed that he should be pleased that Sadie hadn't just hung round in LA waiting for him to call, but he wasn't. The minute his back was turned his women always managed to find someone else to entertain them. He hoped that this time it was going to be different. Maybe he was wrong.

Gil surveyed his impersonal hotel room. So what to do now? He could unpack the parts of his life that he'd brought into his new "home." He could take a shower. He could read the guest information brochure. And then what? He could wait and see whether his date turned up.

Fifty

"Hey." Tavis gently shakes my shoulder.

I jump myself awake and quickly check my shoulder for drib-ble. No matter how hard I try, I forget that I have no need to im-press Tavis at all.

"We're here," my driver says with a grin.

And we are here. Back outside Daniella's house. We didn't get into genealogy, but Tavis's mother is definitely Italian or one of those Mediterranean races where they like to overfeed you. We both had a huge plate of spaghetti before we left and I've obviously slept like a baby all the way home. Who needs a Star Trek transporter-style machine when you have an Italian mother? It could also have been the two very large glasses of Chianti that helped.

The last thing I remember is the traffic lights in San Juan Capistrano. Which is just as well, as I didn't get a wink of sleep last night. Tavis's breathing was just too close and too disturbing to allow me to relax. Coupled with the fact that my skin was try-ing to melt itself off and failed. It's now retaliating by being ex-traordinarily painful. I'm sure I've got more pain receptors than most people, because no matter how much calamine lotion I've dotted all over myself, it still hurts like hell. It serves me right if in years to come I end up looking like George Hamilton's Nana.

"I must have dozed off," I say with typical British understate-ment. Bet I snored like a pig.

"You snored like a pig."

Sometimes the truth hurts.

Before I have a chance to hit him, Alexis comes skipping out of the house. She's dressed from head to toe as a fluorescent pink fairy. It's an alarming sight, but Tavis looks completely unfazed.

"Hi," Alexis says. "Who are you?"

"Tavis." He high-fives her. "And you must be the Perfect Princess Barbie."

Alexis beams, clearly impressed by this assessment. I do not want to know why Tavis is a Barbie expert.

"Cool," Tavis says, and the life-size Perfect Princess treats him to a brief run-through of her favorite ballet positions and then gives a cursory swish of her wand over Tavis's car. If she is her mother's daughter, she's probably hoping that it will change into a Porsche.

"Are you Sadie's new boyfriend?"

"Alexis!" I cry, not knowing where to start in explaining to a ten-year-old that it's perfectly acceptable to have men as friends. And just because you share a bedroom, it doesn't mean that you're in any way—whatsoever—romantically attached.

"No," Tavis laughs. "I'm not."

She's not to be dissuaded from this line of interrogation. "Do you *want* to be Sadie's boyfriend?"

"Alexis!" I splutter. The few bits of me that aren't burned to a crisp are going red. "Tavis already has a boyfriend of his own."

Oh my word, what am I saying? Tavis starts to guffaw. I wonder if he learns his wide range of laughing techniques from his acting class. He certainly has the right one for every occasion. This is a perfect sound to accompany me making an arse of myself.

Alexis looks at Tavis. "Yeah, right."

Tavis is shaking with mirth.

"Look, let's go inside," I say, fumbling for the door handle.

Perfect Princess Barbie leans against the car. "If Tavis isn't your boyfriend, can I talk about Gil then?"

"Gil?" I say. "Gil? Of course, you can talk about him? Why?"

"He left a message," Alexis says. She's wearing her best concentration face. "He said you had to go to his hotel for dinner. Tonight."

"Which hotel?"

"The Beverly Hills."

Tavis looks impressed. "When did he say this?"

"He called on your cell phone. It was on your bed."

Damn. I never remember to take that thing anywhere and when I do, I don't switch it on.

"I'd better call him." I can hear the panic in my voice. I check my watch and can't believe the time.

"He said to be there at eight o'clock." That means I've got exactly five minutes to get there. Alexis looks at her watch. It is a big pink daisy, but seems to work just as well. "You don't have time," she says.

"I'll take you straight up there," Tavis says.

Damn. Decisions. I can arrive on time and looking like a bag lady. Or be late and look like a zebra in a cocktail dress. Maybe it isn't such a difficult decision.

"Alexis?" I have to ask this. "Are you sure you got the message right?"

"Mmm-hmm," she says, not upset by the fact that I'm questioning her powers of memory.

"That's really very good."

"I lie on the telephone for Mommy all the time," she says brightly and does a fairy-type twirl.

Tavis and I exchange a smile.

"Where did you say Sadie was?" Tavis asks his favorite fairy friend.

"I said she was away for the weekend with another man."

Tavis's understanding of the little folk is obviously more advanced than mine. I have a protracted heart-sink moment. "Oh good. Good girl."

Tavis puts the car into gear, high-fives Alexis again and pulls away. He glances over at me. "I think you'd better tell Gil that I've got a boyfriend too," he advises. "Quickly."

And I think it's probably a very good idea.

Fifty-one

I think we are both a bit embarrassed as Tavis chugs up to the front of the Beverly Hills Hotel. It's an opulent oasis of palm trees. A pretty pastel palace. Alexis would love it here.

Tavis glances over at me. "One day I'll come back in a Mercedes," he says with a determined air. And I don't know if it's for my benefit or if he really means it.

The man in charge of valet parking tries his best not to look horrified as we cruise along to the expanse of red carpet that sweeps up to the entrance. I feel Tavis's car doesn't serve him well. It shudders to an ungainly halt. It may be reliable, but it looks like a wreck. Delores, on the other hand, is a wreck with attitude.

Tavis sighs enviously. "That's some boyfriend you have, Sadie."

"Is it?"

"Anyone who is anyone in the movie business hangs out here."

"Do they?"

He looks at me as if I'm mad not to know this. "You'll be knee-deep in movie stars."

"Will I?"

My friend gives me an exasperated look. Ooo. I get a little shiver of excitement.

I've been in LA for days and days now, and I've not had one single sighting of a real live movie star. I've seen a few who look like them at Double Take, but that's not nearly enough. Now I'm going to be knee-deep in them!

I have a sudden attack of the wobbles and grab Tavis's hand. "Come in with me."

"I can't." He looks at the state of himself.

I look down too. Possibly worse. "Don't leave me alone," I say. "Supposing Gil's got fed up and cleared off. I'd be stranded then."

He's caving.

"Five minutes," he says, and instead of jumping over the side of his car, he gets out of the door: That's how intimidated Tavis feels. "I'll get your bag," he says and scurries round to the back of the car.

He swings my bag over his shoulder and the valet parker makes a lunge for his car keys, clearly relieved that he's going to be able to spirit it away and hide it behind a bush so that it doesn't spoil the view.

Our courage departs as we head into the reception area, which does manage to make us look unutterably scruffy. As we approach the main desk, Gil rushes toward us.

"Sadie," he shouts across the quiet expanse. His face brightens and then dulls again as he catches sight of Tavis.

"Hi." He embraces me and kisses me on the cheek, but it's a bit halfhearted and his eyes don't leave Tavis. My friend shuffles uncomfortably.

"I'm sorry I'm late," I say. I'm not actually late and I'm not sorry at all as I had no idea when Gil might deign to come back from San Francisco, but I thought it might help to get off on a conciliatory note.

"That's okay," Gil says, looking at me for the first time. "You're here. Now."

The "now" is slightly loaded, but I let it pass.

"What happened to you?" Gil looks askance at my char-grilled proboscis and medium-rare face.

"Sunburn," I provide limply. What did he think had happened? Did he think I'd been trying a bit of self-barbecuing for sadists?

"I'll delay dinner so that you can clean up."

He clearly thinks I need to. I wonder how I'm going to eat when I'm already stuffed full of pasta. Maybe if he delayed it until tomorrow I might be able to find a little space.

Tavis drops my bag to the floor. "I'll be going," he says.

I think it would be nice to invite him to stay, but I'd probably be the only one.

I plant a kiss on Tavis's cheek. "Thanks," I say. "I really appreciate it. You've been great."

"Anytime," he says and kisses me back. "It was fun."

Out of the corner of my eye I see Gil tap his foot.

"I'll catch up with you in the week," I add as I pick up my bag. "Thanks again."

"No worries," Tavis says and he waves to me and then Gil and walks away.

Gil and I stare at each other for a minute. It's like one of those moments when you get in a lift with someone who looks a bit dodgy and you don't know quite what to do.

"Could you do me a favor?" Gil says. "Speak to the desk clerk. Delay dinner. I just want to catch Tavis."

"Why?"

"I want to thank him personally," Gil says. "I didn't say the right things. I was a bit taken aback."

Oh. Phew. And I thought things were going to be tricky.

"Is half an hour okay?"

"Fine," Gil says. "Are you hungry?"

I do my best seductive smile. "Famished."

Gil grins. "Give me a minute."

I make myself a promise that I will give him my undivided attention for the rest of the evening.

Gil caught up with Tavis as he waited for his car to be returned. If there was anything Gil hated more in the world than men who wore embroidered combat pants it was good-looking guys in embroidered combat pants who had been entertaining his girlfriend for the weekend.

"Hey," Gil shouted after Tavis. "Hey, you!"

Tavis spun round.

"I want you to stay as far away from Sadie as you possibly can," Gil snarled. "If I hear that you've been breathing in the same air space I will make it my personal business to ensure that you never breathe again!"

To Gil's utter annoyance, Tavis merely burst out laughing. "Hey man," Tavis said. "She's acting as my agent. I'm going to be seeing her."

"Not if I can help it."

Tavis snorted with disbelief. "If you're so paranoid about what your lady's up to, spend a little more time with her."

"What I do is none of your business!"

"Hey." Tavis's smile had disappeared. "You made it my business. It was Sadie's first weekend in LA. You were planning to leave her all alone. You should be pleased that I stepped in. I was trying to help out."

"Well don't," Gil said. "Don't help out. Butt out."

"You don't know how lucky you are, man," Tavis said. His car arrived and he tipped the valet and jumped over the side into the driver's seat. "She's come a long way to be with you. The least you can do is make sure you pay her some attention. Otherwise someone else just might."

"Don't you threaten me."

"It's not a threat, it's advice," Tavis said. "I'm not interested in taking your lady. Next time you might not be so fortunate." He revved the engine and it coughed, spluttered and backfired into life.

Gil pulled out his wallet and peeled off a fifty-dollar bill. "Here." He threw it into Tavis's car. "For your trouble."

"It was no trouble," Tavis said tightly. "It was fun." He picked up the money and tossed it onto the sidewalk. "And I don't need your money."

Then Tavis drove away, leaving a stream of noxious smoke in his wake and the resonant sound of pistons begging for oil.

Gil was determined that he wouldn't bend down and pick up the money, so he turned on his heel and headed back into the hotel, leaving the fifty-dollar bill fluttering in the breeze, and a broadly smiling parking valet.

Fifty-two

Gil marches back into the reception area looking a little more purple than when he left.

'Everything okay?" I ask.

"Fine," Gil says, smoothing down his hair, which is standing up like the back of a cat's neck when its hackles are raised.

"Sure?"

He nods tightly. "I just wanted to straighten up a few things."

"Tavis is a good bloke," I say. "He's got a really nice boyfriend too."

I wait for the reaction, which seems to be different in every recipient. Except for females over the age of consent who generally seem to view it as a tragic waste—me included. A small but noticeable gulp travels along Gil's throat. "Boyfriend?"

"Mm. Lovely couple," I add to load it.

Another gulp follows.

"I went with him to a job yesterday at Universal. Body double. And he could tell I was really miserable. You were away. Daniella and Alexis were away. I was going to be all by myself."

A flush of embarrassment rushes to Gil's cheeks.

"His boyfriend was busy too, so he whipped me to his parents' house up the coast for some R and R."

"His parents' house?"

"Yeah." Gil is clearly in some discomfort about this. "They're really nice too. I feel so much more refreshed." And stuffed like a little pig. "How did your business go?"

Gil has sagged a little. "It was fine," he says. "I'll take you with me next time." Gil gives me his I'm-a-complete-heel look. "I promise."

We're starting to attract attention in the reception area and I remember my earlier promise to him. "Come on," I murmur. "You can take me to your room and show me your etchings while you tell me exactly what you're doing here."

"Hey! Hey! Gil!" The shrill sound of a woman's voice carries across the area. Both of our heads snap up simultaneously and in time to see the young and lovely author Elise Neils, curls and bosoms bouncing as she dashes headlong toward us. I hear Gil groan and hope that she hasn't heard it, too.

"Hi!" She rushes up and kisses Gil full on the lips. I think he can tell that I'm less than pleased.

"I didn't know you were in town," Gil says.

"I've been trying to call you." Her eyes widen. "You never reply to your voice mail."

"Sorry," Gil mumbles. "I've been away. Fighting fires. It's good to see you."

"I just arrived," she gushes. "I'm staying here. My publishers dragged me out here for another book fair." She is definitely the sort of person who couldn't be dragged anywhere that she didn't want to be. "I'm sure I told you I'd be flying out here. Are you staying here?" Elise takes in the opulence of her surroundings and is obvious in her appreciation.

"Yes," Gil says, but he looks as if he was thinking he might deny it. "Temporarily."

I wonder how long that means in Gil's dictionary.

"This is Sadie." He sort of yanks me forward.

Elise frowns and it is the cutest thing you ever did see. "Don't I know you?"

"We met at the London Book Fair." I sound as sheepish as I feel.

"I remember. You had your photograph taken with me. Are you here for the Fair too?"

"Er . . ." I look to Gil for an adequate description of what I'm here for.

"Er . . ." He seems at a loss to describe it too.

"Oh," she says. "I didn't know you two were . . ."

I'm not sure that we're . . . either.

"Let's catch up while you're here," Gil says and starts to steer me away from her.

"Yes, let's."

"I'll get my office to call you."

Elise screws up her tiny little nose. "Do you have anything planned for tonight?"

"Well . . ." Gil says, giving a delicate cough that might as well be a shout across the room that he's planning to shag his girl-friend.

"I'm only here for a few days." Elise has gone all girly. "My diary is pretty full. Tonight would be great."

"Well . . ." Gil gives a sideways glance at me. He might as well wave my knickers in front of her nose.

"I'm sure, er . . ."

"Sadie," I provide.

"Sadie wouldn't mind."

I do mind, desperately. "No. Not at all." I even do a broad grin to enforce it.

Gil looks at me as if I have just rolled all of my marbles across the floor.

"That's settled then," my involuntarily celibate boyfriend says tightly. "Dinner it is."

"I changed it to nine o'clock." Which is just as well, because we've frittered half an hour away standing here.

"Ooo. That's lovely," Elise says. "Just time to change." She takes in my outfit and tiger-stripe sunburn and makes no audible comment.

"Nine," Gil says and takes me by the elbow and walks me toward his room. "Why did we just agree to that?" he mutters under his breath.

I have absolutely no idea. But if this were a game of tennis, I'm pretty sure it would be game, set and match to Miss Smiley Author.

Fifty-three

We are on a lovely private terrace behind Gil's bungalow, seated at a candlelit table which is now set for three. The candles are hardly even flickering in the balmy evening and there is barely an undercurrent of breeze. There are, however, plenty of other undercurrents. The smiley author doesn't realize that she's supposed to be the gooseberry here and instead is making the unsmiling girlfriend feel like one.

My head and my sunburn are throbbing in equal measure. Every one of Elise's giggles is high pitched enough to shatter the crystal glasses and my brain. I'm not sure which is going to give first. She hasn't mentioned that the end of my nose looks as if it's had an unfortunate coming together with a barbecue, but she keeps looking at it.

Gil is treating me coolly and I'm trying to work out why this whole thing is my fault. I've always had this feeling that everything is my fault and I sort of assumed that I'd grow out of it, but I've not. All of my boyfriends have left me for other women and I've never hesitated to find some reason in myself for this betrayal rather than the fact they were feckless, faithless bastards. I wonder if I will ever have a man all to my little self.

Gil says that he moved into this hotel to get away from Gina, but we seem to have acquired a replacement in the blink of an eye. Elise, like Gina, is clearly used to having men fall at her feet. I'm not. The only thing that falls at my feet is my face. My relationships are always fraught and complex and I always love him more than he loves me. I've never been pursued wildly by someone who I didn't give a jot about, but I never give up hope.

Elise has all the right poses and postures at her fingertips—

which, naturally, are beautifully manicured. She has the hands of a writer and she flutters them over the conversation like pretty little butterflies. She's very nice and I detest her. I try to entertain myself with visions of her in years to come with a great fat bottom because of all the hours she's spent sitting at a computer.

Gil's watching me toying with my food and it's not because I'm sulking—which I admit I am—but is more to do with the fact that Tavis's mother decided that I was about four stone underweight and set about correcting that deficiency with a vengeance. I have a raft of pasta in my stomach that will probably take about two weeks to digest.

Our tiresome threesome is on to dessert and heading rapidly toward coffee, for which I'm eternally grateful. I just hope Elise doesn't invite herself to spend the night. My boyfriend and my new enemy are having an in-depth discussion about film, having moved on from an in-depth discussion about books.

I'm an ignorant bystander in a world that I'll never be a part of. I don't need to say this out loud. Both of them have stopped talking to me and, instead, are engaged in mutual ooo-ing and aah-ing, while I sit here trying not to go to sleep. I'm bored to tears and am thinking about getting rat-arsed drunk just to annoy Gil. The God of Love is sitting up in the heavens peeing on my party. I can't see Gina putting up with any of this and I wonder if this is why she left Gil in the first place.

I miss Tavis. Even when we're not talking we have a laugh. He doesn't have any intellectual muscles to flex. He's just quietly knowledgeable about nothing in particular—pizza toppings, the best place to park for which beach, the sharpest beer, all the lyrics to Madonna songs. Normal stuff.

When Elise giggles again I wonder how much more of this I can tolerate. Not much, is the answer. I catch Gil's eye and even in the candlelight it looks flat. There's a dead spot where the pupil should be and I can tell that he's not enjoying this as much as he's making out. I smile at him and we both light up again. He squeezes my knee under the table. Elise is expounding the virtues of some arty-farty French film I've never heard of and I look away so she can't see me grinning.

And as I do, who do I see crossing in front of the luscious pool area but my luscious friend Daniella. I nearly call out, but something about her demeanor tells me not to. She's being furtive and I know enough about furtive to last me a lifetime. Her handbag is clutched to her chest and her eyes dart left and right, but in the shadows and the soft candlelight she can't see me. However, I see *her* and I wonder what the hell she's doing here. Whatever it is, it doesn't involve writers or a convention.

Fifty-four

"I thought she'd never go," I say to Gil.

He sighs and flops down on the bed, massaging his face with his hands. "Me neither," he agrees. Then he looks at me and twitches his eyebrows with evil intent. "Alone at last."

I think of Daniella again and can't wait until I see her to find out why she told me she was on a writing course when she's clearly been on a sneaky, secret assignation. I smell the scent of a Mad Movie Mogul in the air.

"Come here," Gil says and I go and sit down next to him. He wraps his arms round me. "Sorry about all this." His look tries to encompass the past week, the hotel suite, the ex-wife, the trip to San Francisco and the smiley author. And it very nearly works—until he squeezes me tightly.

"Arrgh! Ouch!"

"What? What?"

"Sunburn." It feels like being rubbed with a cheese grater or being caressed with a steam iron. I think I've got whatever degree of burns is the worst—is it first or third? I can never remember. "I fried myself in Tavis's parents' yard."

"Is it that bad?"

"Excruciating." I lift my top up, baring my midriff.

"Medium rare," Gil says.

I nod.

Reluctantly, he eases my T-shirt back into place. "Let's go onto the terrace and have a drink," suggests the man who could be the love of my life if only we didn't keep making such a mess of it.

I nod again. Champagne is as good a painkiller as any.

We take up our places on the terrace and pull our chairs together and face the sky. Gil pours us two glasses of fizz and we sip them in a silence that may be contemplative or not. I don't know if there's an atmosphere—despite all that has happened, I still don't know Gil well enough to tell.

"I thought there was something going on between you and Tavis," he says candidly.

"He's gay."

"I know." Gil stares at where the stars would be if there wasn't too much competition from the twinkling, artificial lights of LA. "He just doesn't look gay." I'm not sure that it's politically correct, but he does have a point. "He looks like a movie star," Gil says, and there's a certain amount of envy in his tone.

I snuggle closer to him. "Let's not talk about Tavis," I say. There are already too many people in this relationship; I don't want Tavis to crowd it too. Not now.

Gil strokes my hair. He looks as if he might be going to say he loves me, but doesn't. His lips find mine. First lightly, tentatively, then deeper, searching.

"Arrgh!"

"What?"

"My nose. My bloody nose! Ow. Ow. *Ow!*" Gil's stubble has scratched all the fried skin off it. I'm clutching it and I think it might be bleeding. There's only one thing I can do. I stick my nose in my ice-cold glass of Dom Perignon and whimper with relief.

Gil sighs and slumps back in his chair. I have a feeling the moment is broken. He hands me a napkin without taking his gaze from the heavens, for which I am grateful.

Sunburn, I think, is going to be as good a contraceptive as Gina.

Fifty-five

"I like these Hollywood power breakfasts, don't you?" Steve asked in the middle of his ruminations. He was digging into a mammoth plate of potato pancakes and scrambled eggs with something approaching ecstasy.

"Yes," Gil said. "They're lovely." He looked at his strawberries and granola without enthusiasm.

"It's the only time I don't end up wearing mine," Steve said, admiring his stain-free polo shirt proudly. "My kids could grow up to be champion cereal throwers."

Gil didn't want to have breakfast with Steve. He wanted to have breakfast with Sadie. Preferably after waking up in bed with her after a wild night of mutually satisfying sex. He sighed into his freshly squeezed orange juice.

"It's not going well is it, mate?"

"No." Gil indulged in more sighing at the British propensity to understate everything. "I wanted everything to go smoothly this time. Instead it's all going wrong."

"Take Sadie to the Oscars."

"The Oscars? It's four hours of boredom and being trapped in a seat so that you can't even go to the bathroom. How is this going to improve my relationship?"

"You only feel like that because you've been a million times. Sadie will love it. It's not every day you get an invitation to the Oscars. It will blow her away. Trust me, I'm a married man with loads of experience with women."

"I didn't think the two went hand-in-hand."

"You need to get her a great dress."

"A great dress?" Gill shook his head. "Sadie isn't that shallow. She hates me buying her things."

"She's a woman."

"Yeah, but she's different. A dress won't make the slightest bit of difference."

"It will," his friend insisted. "They go all gooey. Women love that sort of surprise."

"Surprise? How the hell do you buy a dress as a surprise? That way spells danger. What if I get the wrong size? If it's too big it'll be because *I* think she's too fat. If it's too small, *she'll* think she's too fat. No, no, no. I can't do this."

"It's simple, mate. You steal some clothes from her wardrobe. Make sure you get ones that fit."

"She doesn't live with me." Gil was already beginning to spot flaws in the plan. "How do I get access to her wardrobe?"

Steve brushed his objections aside with a wave of his hand. "You're a Hollywood producer—a good one. It's your job to fix things. You'll think of something."

"I'm glad you have such confidence in me."

"Then all you have to do is take the stolen frock to a boutique. A nice one. Choose a dress. A class one. Find an assistant who fits Sadie's stolen frock. Get said assistant to model same-size classy dress. Buy it. Giftwrap it."

Gil frowned. "It can't be as simple as that."

"She'll love you forever," Steve said. "And forever can be a very good thing."

"This is Hollywood," Gil reminded him. "Forever lasts around five minutes."

Fifty-six

This is just *so* LA! I'm doing a lunchtime Pilates class with Daniella because she's worried that I'm turning into a couch potato after a whole week of no workouts. The fact that I've walked farther than she does in an entire year doesn't seem to figure in the equation. Walking only counts if it's done on a treadmill, not on honest-to-goodness pavements.

The equipment looks as if it came straight from a medieval torture chamber. Daniella is lying on the Reformer—yes, it really *is* called that—a long low bench to which she appears to be shackled. My friend is being "reformed" by Kerry-Emma, who is wearing a leopard-skin all-in-one jumpsuit in the style of the late Elvis Presley and still managing to look fantastic. She also disappears when she turns sideways. If this is what Pilates can do for you, then let it do its worst! Kerry-Emma puts Daniella's legs behind her head and pulls on a variety of straps and pulleys. Daniella groans. That looks pretty bad.

I'm right next to her on the Cadillac. If the name suggests a degree of comfort, then it is misleading. I'm being hung, drawn and quartered by Monica—a small Chinese woman with a wide cruel streak. There are pinging noises coming from inside my body from things that I don't think should go ping. My sunburned skin is trying to tear itself apart and even a vision of Tavis soothing me with calamine lotion isn't enough to stop me from wanting to scream. Whatever we are paying for this, it's too much.

After ten minutes, I'm ready to confess to anything. I'm hoping Daniella feels the same.

"How was the convention?" I ask, absorbing my pain silently as Monica hoists my legs up and out of their sockets.

"Fine." I can tell that Daniella's teeth are gritted in agony.

"Worthwhile?" I gasp.

"I think so."

"Where was it held?" I'm going to pass out in a minute.

"A seedy hotel out of town," Daniella says, puffing effusively.

"Not at the Beverly Hills Hotel then?"

A sharp intake of breath. Daniella turns to look at me and something in her neck goes ping. I think she is ready to crack. "What were *you* doing there?"

"Probably not as much as you," I manage.

Daniella lets out an unhappy groan.

"Three Ms?"

"Who else?" she says miserably.

"Would you still class it as worthwhile?"

"I don't know," Daniella says. "I can't think straight anymore."

It's not a good time to tell Daniella that Gil has finally left Gina. It may be rubbing salt into wounds that are very raw. I could tell her that I spent the weekend with Tavis, but somehow that won't come out either. Alexis will probably spill the beans for me on that one. I have spent most of the morning staring out of the window at Double Take and trying not to think about Gil or Tavis.

"Why do women want unavailable men?" Daniella huffs.

"Perhaps because the available ones are available for a reason. Arrgh!"

"True," my friend agrees.

"What a pair we are," I say. The pain now is excruciating.

"We have to do something about it," Daniella says decisively.

"We do," I agree. "What?"

"I don't know."

We both moan simultaneously and not with pleasure.

Daniella's mobile phone rings. I don't know how she manages it, but she ferrets it from somewhere in her shorts and answers. Her face goes pale. "Yes," she says tightly. And that's all she says before she hangs up.

We do some more enforced acrobatics before she speaks. "It was Three Ms' wife," she says. "She wants to meet me."

My eyes widen, but this is partly because my knees are touching my ears and I had no idea I could do that. "And you said yes?" I ask, when I can eventually breathe again.

"I need to confront this situation." She sounds very convinced.

I hate confronting situations. I don't like the idea of Daniella confronting her situation either, because it makes me think that I should confront my situation. And I'm not sure which part of my situation needs the most confronting.

Just then, Monica does something hideous with one of the pulleys. All my vertebrae snap into line. Four gallons of blood sprint to my brain. I get up feeling all giddy and lightheaded and as if I'm floating about a foot off the floor. This is such a fabulous rush. If I could do Pilates like this on a daily basis I'd never need to trouble myself with men ever again.

Fifty-seven

One of Sadie's dresses had been secured via the services of a well-versed miniature exponent of espionage. But not without coercion. Alexis—Gil's small but effective partner in crime—had driven a hard bargain. The price had been one Kennel Care Barbie. As Gil paid the shop assistant for it, he studied the grinning doll carefully. It came with its own fluffy poodle, a workstation and a tray full of stuff to manicure dogs with. It bore an uncanny resemblance to Gina—with the notable exception that Kennel Care Barbie didn't have a bottle of vodka stashed in her grooming kit. He stowed the doll in a shopping bag along with Sadie's stolen dress and headed down toward Rodeo Drive for some serious shopping.

Gil had known nothing about women's shopping—which was a terrible admission after two wives. Maybe that's where he'd gone wrong. Steve seemed to think that the way to a woman's heart was through a series of well-timed dresses. In affairs of the heart, Gil himself had always found things a lot more complicated. When Sadie had arrived in LA sans suitcase, he'd phoned one of Gina's more rational friends and had solicited some advice. She'd recommended, among other things, a one-off boutique run by a hip California designer hidden away among the less-radical Chanel and Prada. The sort of place where you'd pay twice as much for half the amount of material. Definitely the place to buy a dress to impress.

Gil found the boutique and sidled inside. There was a dazzling array of merchandise within, which almost took his breath away—and his courage.

"Can I help you, sir?" a pretty blonde assistant asked.

"I sincerely hope so," Gil replied, presenting his totebag. Never in his life had he felt more like he needed help.

One hour and several outfits later, Chloë, the blonde assistant, emerged from the dressing room in a long white dress that literally did take Gil's breath away.

"Wow!" he gasped.

Chloë twirled. "You like it?"

Gil thought there was a note of relief in her voice.

"I *love* it."

The dress was covered in tiny crystals that caught the light and sparkled with rainbow colors. This was a head-turning dress. An Oscars-Night dress. A dress that would make Sadie feel like a million dollars. He had a feeling it was going to cost him a good proportion of that, but she was worth it.

He'd like to say he'd chosen it, but he'd left all the hard work to Chloë. And she seemed to have come up trumps.

"Would you like it if someone bought you this dress?" Gil asked tentatively.

"Are you kidding me?"

He could never quite tell how Sadie would react—but wasn't that part of the attraction?

"It's fabulous," Chloë assured him as he sat and nervously chewed at his fingers. "Whoever this is for is a very lucky woman."

"And it will fit like that?"

Chloë twirled again. "I don't see any reason why not."

"I'll take it," Gil said.

And before he changed his mind, he rushed to the cash desk to pay for it.

Five minutes later, Chloë was back in her own clothes and bearing a large white shopping bag containing a giftwrapped box holding the sparkly dress. Gil and his credit card were on the verge of a nervous breakdown.

"Enjoy," Chloë said and handed over the bag.

"Thanks." Gil clutched his purchase to his chest. If dollars could be directly related to happiness, this dress should make Sadie absolutely delirious. If only he could be sure he was doing the right thing. "Thanks for your assistance." He pressed a large tip into Chloë's hand and rushed toward the door. He needed strong coffee. Strong, black, reviving caffeine. Lots of it.

He waved his thanks again and pulled open the door. As he did, he ran headlong into Gina. He wasn't sure which of them was the most startled.

His wife recovered first. "Hey," she said.

"Hey," Gil responded, realizing that he sounded cagey.

"No kiss?" Gina said with a pout.

Gil dutifully kissed her cheeks. Her eyes traveled to the bag. "I hope that's not for you," she said.

"No." Gil felt very self-conscious. "It's for Sadie."

He thought he saw a dark cloud flit across Gina's brow, but her wide smile stayed in place.

"Oscars night?" Gina tilted her head.

"Mmm-hmm."

"She'll love it," Gina said. "Noah and I may be there too."

"How are things with you and Noah?"

Gina tossed her blonde hair. "Oh, you know." She flicked her eyes heavenward. "Life is never easy with a rock star."

Gil had decided it wasn't easy whoever you were with—there were just different types of struggle. Some people were too poor, some were too rich, some were too unfaithful, some were too dependent. The perfect partner seemed to be someone whom you could rub along with most of the time—if you were lucky.

"Come for a coffee," Gil said impulsively. "I was just going across the street."

"Okay." Gina beamed as she took his arm. "You can buy me a late lunch. I had to skip mine. As you would say, I had a dog to do." She giggled and led him out into the street.

Gil thought guiltily of Kennel Care Barbie in his other shopping bag and hoped that Gina didn't notice that too. When she was like this—sober, sweet and not playing the seductress—there were times when he wondered if they could have made it work between them. He glanced at Gina as they waited at the crosswalk. There was too much water under the bridge. Too much sadness and far too much instability. Gina could stay like this for a week, a day, an hour, a minute—brief respites of calm before the inevitable storms. In the end, it was all too wearing.

He hadn't called Sadie today—which was stupid and crass. As soon as he'd finished with Gina, he'd call over. Maybe if he dropped by Daniella's house, he could deliver Alexis's fee and return Sadie's clothes to her closet before she missed them.

They went to the nearest restaurant and the hostess showed them to a booth. As they passed other diners, the men turned their heads to watch Gina, admiring her catwalk sashay. She sat down opposite Gil and tucked her hair behind her ears, grinning coyly. Several men in the vicinity had stopped eating. But there was no stirring in his heart or in his loins. At that moment, Gil realized that for him it was over. He was moving on.

Fifty-eight

Tavis's abs are as bankable as his bum. I've booked them out on a martial-arts shoot for a *Matrix*-style film without the budget to benefit from Keanu Reeves. The middle-aged male star is, by all accounts, a bit flabby round the midriff. Tavis is very definitely not.

My friend is on his way over to collect the details, and Bay and Min can hardly contain their joy. I hate to admit this, but I'm having a bit of a struggle with mine. I love working here and feel like I've been here a lifetime already. I'm as much a part of the furniture as the knackered spider plant.

Gil hasn't phoned me all day, but that's hardly surprising as we're not exactly love's young dream at the moment. I'm still miffed about the smiley author muscling in on our smoochy dinner, and he's obviously still miffed about the sunburn thing. They both seem so petty in the cold light of day, but at three o'clock this morning I was pretty pissed off. I couldn't help the sunburn thing, but he should have been able to find a way to scare off Elise Neils.

While I'm mulling over the ebbs and flows of my love life, Tavis turns up and reduces my colleagues to giggly, girly messes.

"Hi," he says and kisses my cheek. Bay and Min swoon. I give them both a superior grin.

I hand him the job sheet, which he quickly scans. "This is great," he says.

It isn't great, but it's a job. I wish I could do something to make him a star, but I'm having enough trouble making my own dreams come true, let alone someone else's.

"Hey," Tavis observes as he points at my nose. "You can hardly notice the burn."

"Thank you for that."

"What did Gil say?"

"Nothing very complimentary." I have spent the afternoon discussing my celibate state with my colleagues, who agree with me that it's a crying shame. Next time, I will use lotion with a higher sun-protection factor.

"Did you have a good dinner?"

"You could have stayed and joined us," I say. "We had company."

"Oh." Tavis seems at a loss for words. "Are you seeing Gil tonight?"

"No," I say. "Not that I know."

"Come to my acting class," he suggests. "Joe will be there and he's been beating up on me to see you again."

"What time?"

"Now," he says and looks hopefully at Bay. She nods graciously. Well, it would be gracious if she didn't have her tongue lolling out of her head. "It's in Burbank. We need to get a move on to jump the traffic."

"I'll get my coat." Which is a joke because I haven't worn a coat since I got here.

This part of Burbank doesn't look too salubrious and I'm glad I'm not on my own here at night. I've driven us out here in Delores because Tavis says the classes go on for hours and hours and I'll probably be bored to death; this way I can just go home when I've had enough and he'll catch a ride with Joe. He seems quite nervous to have me with him. Although I'm supposed to be concentrating on the road, I can see that he keeps giving me surreptitious little glances.

Eventually we pull up outside an inconspicuous and anonymous door opposite a run-down pool hall and get out. I feel like clinging on to his arm, but don't.

I think everyone takes acting class in LA. Min does them. Bay does them. Daniella doesn't do them now, but she has done in the past. No one ever seems to be just pumping gas, waiting tables, valet parking, driving cabs—everyone is an actor waiting to be discovered.

Inside, there is one large room that looks like a theater. There's a makeshift stage and rows of beaten-up crimson velour seats in which rows of brow-beaten, would-be actors lounge. Joe is there already. He has his feet hooked over the seat in front and is reading his lines. We go over to him and Joe kisses me on both cheeks. He holds me away from him, beaming widely. "Good to see you again, Sadie."

"Good to see you."

"Okay, people!" An older handsome man comes out to the front of the stage. "Our leading man is in the building!"

There is a chorus of decisive hoots and hollers and Tavis takes a mock bow.

"Thank you for joining us, Mr. Jones. Shall we begin now?"

"Hey," Tavis says. "Take it easy. I have a guest."

More hoots and hollers, and I feel my cheeks flush and hurriedly sit down next to Joe. "Take no notice of them," Joe advises. "They're uncultured animals."

"I hope I'm exempt from that," the man says.

"This is Jake Le Fevre, my acting coach," Tavis says.

"Pleased to meet you." Jake shakes my hand. "You'll have to choose another leading lady," he tells Tavis as he nods toward the entirely male motley crew assembled in the makeshift theater. "Jackie called in with a head cold."

"Great," Tavis says as he eyes his choices.

"Want to run through it with Joe?"

"Not particularly. He thinks I'm in love with him already."

More jeering.

"You should be so lucky," Joe chips in.

"Take Mohammed." There's a seventeen-stone, bearded man squeezed into a seat at one end. "It'll be a great test of your acting skills."

"It'll be a test of my sanity," Tavis says. "Sadie'll do it."

I suddenly become alert at the mention of my name.

Tavis turns to me. "Won't you?"

"Do what?"

"Read these sides with me."

In front of all these people. These proper actors! You must be having a laugh!

"Well, I'm not . . ."

"Great." Tavis pulls me onto the stage and Jake thrusts a bunch of papers at me, which I try to get the right way up.

Oh my good grief. I'm Juliet, and Tavis is Romeo. Bollocks. *Bollocks.* Thank heavens I read this at high school so I'm not completely at sea. I always knew that some day, in some very special way, my Shakespearean set text would come in useful. Unfortunately, I haven't read it again in the intervening fifteen or more years.

"Don't worry about this," Jakes tells me.

It's easy for him to say that, when he's the boss and tells other actors what to do. "Just read it straight to feed your lover the lines."

"Right," I say, and I'm not sure my voice is even audible or what reading it straight entails. There's a cloudy mist swirling in front of my eyes and I'm pretty convinced I'm experiencing my first anxiety attack.

"Let's take it from . . ." Jake flicks through the sides. My knees are trying to do the steps to the cha-cha all by themselves. ". . . 'But soft! What light through yonder window breaks?' "

I look at the sheets, which are blurring merrily in front of me and am relieved to see that Tavis is on first and his part is much bigger than mine—if you'll pardon the expression. A hush falls over the audience. I don't think they're going to be able to hear Tavis over the sound of my labored breathing. Good Lord, *Romeo and Juliet*! Why couldn't we be doing a bit from *King Lear* or *Hamlet* or anything that's not as lovey-dovey as this? I'm going to feel like a right idiot.

My friend winks at me and helps me to stand up on a box that forms my balcony. "You'll be fine," he whispers in my ear. He can't possibly know that. I rustle my pages into order. " 'But soft!' " he says, sounding exactly like Romeo should, " 'What light through yonder window breaks? It is the east, and Juliet is the sun!' "

My tongue has turned into a crispbread. I listen to Tavis, the musical lilt of his voice, and for the first time the words of William Shakespeare are making absolute sense. Passion is pouring out of his pores. I'm sure it was never like this in Mrs. Gregory's English lessons. He's so intense, it's making all the little hairs stand up on the back of my neck. If Juliet was faced with even half of this, no wonder she was swept off her feet.

When it comes to my bit, I take a deep breath and launch forth. " 'O Romeo, Romeo! Wherefore art thou Romeo? Deny thy father, and refuse thy name . . .' "

Personally, I always thought that "Romeo, Romeo" bit was rather naff, but I'm amazed at the strength with which I project it, and I can sense the audience sit up in their seats as I suddenly turn into Helena Bonham-Carter—before she started dressing up as a monkey. We carry on with the rest of the scene, moved by the emotion of the words and the hopelessness of the lovers' plight.

Tavis climbs up onto my box with me, which I'm sure isn't in the script, and he sweeps me into his arms and kisses me long and hard, his body pressed the length of mine. And I'm like a Hershey's bar beneath a radiator—soft, squidgy and melting at an alarming rate.

" 'Sleep dwell upon thine eyes, peace in thy breast!' " he continues. " 'Would I were sleep and peace, so sweet to rest!' "

His breath is hot and hard against my cheek. I'm sure that Mrs. Gregory didn't explain that Romeo was a hot-to-trot sex machine. This must be the X-rated version. I feel like I've been kissed from the inside out. All my fluttery bits are all aflutter. For someone who is gay, Tavis does a very good impression of enthusiastically snogging a woman. I can't ever recall being snogged so thoroughly. He must be a damn good actor. It takes me a moment to remember that there are about thirty people watching us. Tavis is clearly less daunted than I am. He is still gazing at me intently. I'm trying to get my eyeballs to stop rotating. Any minute now they're going to rack up three lemons and ping loudly when I've hit the jackpot.

"Thank you, Mr. Jones," Jake says wryly. "Wonderful improvisation. How could Juliet fail to fall in love with you?"

I'm wondering that myself. Tavis stands me upright again and I adjust my clothing until I look less like I've just been ravished by a rampant Montague.

"Move to Romeo's death scene," Jake instructs. "Let's see what you can do with that."

Tavis and I shuffle our pages.

"Juliet, you're assumed dead and in your tomb," Jake tells me.

"Lie down." Tavis lowers me gently and I lie prostrate on the floor, glad that I'm not having to stand upright for too much longer. My heart is beating very loudly for a dead woman.

"Take it from 'Dear Juliet . . .' "

" 'Ah, dear Juliet . . .' " Tavis kneels beside me and takes my hand. He starts his speech while I try to make myself behave dead. Do the deceased normally blush?

" 'Eyes, look your last!' " Tavis intones. " 'Arms, take your last embrace!' " When I've just about got myself together again, Tavis takes his last embrace and I collapse to a splotch of goo. " 'And, lips, Oh you . . .' "

Oh no!

" 'The doors of breath, seal with a righteous kiss . . .' "

And he does seal my lips with a righteous kiss. Well, not so much righteous as searing and lingering. Romeo's heart is going at a fair old pace too.

" 'A dateless bargain to engrossing death? Come, bitter conduct, come unsavoury guide! Thou desperate pilot, now at once run on the dashing rocks thy seasick weary bark!' "

I'm feeling decidedly seasick.

" 'Here's to my love. O true apothecary! Thy drugs are quick. Thus with a kiss . . .' "

Oh no! Not another one! Tavis smothers me with another heart-melting kiss. Our hearts pulsate together. This could well have killed Juliet if she'd been a bit of a shrinking violet. I don't remember there being so much snogging in *Romeo and Juliet* either.

" '. . . I die.' "

Tavis utters Romeo's last words, and as he releases me from his kiss and his embrace, I try not to gasp out loud, which I still have the sense to realize isn't entirely befitting for a corpse. I fall back and Tavis slumps over me. Oh my goodness!

Tears fill Tavis's eyes, whereas my tears are stuck firmly in my throat. The theater is absolutely hushed and then the motley crew breaks into rapturous applause and whistling. A few, including seventeen-stone Mohammed, wipe tears away with their sleeves and then they all spontaneously rise to their feet and give Tavis a standing ovation. Joe is blubbering openly into his handkerchief.

Tavis helps me to my feet and takes a bow. Then he clasps my hand and makes me bow with him. My heart is pounding and I want to cry and laugh simultaneously. For the first time I can see the attraction of doing this for a living. Jake is clapping hard too.

It seems to take forever for the noise to die down.

"Gentlemen, that's the way to do it," Jake says with an appreciative tilt of his head toward Tavis. "If anyone can make it in this town, it should be you."

Tavis's colleagues hoot their agreement. Jake's eyes twinkle. "Try sleeping with the right people?"

Tavis shakes his head. "I'm not sleeping with anyone."

I'm sure Jake's eyes flick over me, but I can't be certain. "Maybe you should." Then the coach claps his hands. "We've work to do, people! It's a tough act to follow. Who wants to be next up?"

Two guys from the end of the row shuffle forward. Tavis is still holding my hand and he leads me outside. The air is cool on my brow and I suddenly feel drained, as if all my emotion has poured out of me.

My Romeo takes both of my hands and squeezes them. "That was great," he says.

"I don't think so." I shake my head. "It's you they were cheering."

The door closes behind him and I'm left alone. I dampen my parched lips and whisper into the night: " 'Parting is such sweet sorrow that I shall say good-night till it be morrow.' "

I get into Delores and sit and hold the steering wheel for a bit. My hands are trembling and I can't make myself do the driving thing. No wonder leading ladies and men always fall in love with each other. Tavis is a marvelous actor, there's no doubt. For a minute there, he had me absolutely convinced that he was in love with me. And I was in love with him.

Fifty-nine

Tavis and Joe were sitting in Mel's Diner on Highland Avenue—
a traditional twenty-four-hour, seven-day-a-week establishment
that sold burgers and fries with everything. It was the early hours
of the morning and the only people in there apart from the two
of them looked highly undesirable.

Joe had expended all his energy on being Daddy Capulet for
the night and was slumped back in his seat being less theatrical
than normal. He slurped noisily on a chocolate shake. This had
become their post–acting-class routine—a way to wind down
from the emotion and recover from the constructive abuse that
Jake normally doled out to them, although he had been kind to
them tonight. They would give a data download on each other's
performance, rebuild their shattered confidence, smooth over
any insecurities that had surfaced and generally indulge in some
brotherly back-patting.

Tavis's burger lay untouched on his plate. Tonight, it wasn't
good-old American fast food that would sate his hunger.

Joe picked at his burger with his fingers and studied Tavis intently.
"You looked like you were getting well into your role back there."

"Thanks. I felt it went well." He could still feel his hands
shaking.

"Hm. Great acting."

Tavis nodded.

Joe pursed his lips. "If that's what it was."

"Oh man." Tavis closed his weary eyes, momentarily blocking
out the glare of the hard white light.

"I thought you'd given up all that girl stuff."

Tavis blew a steady stream of air through his nose, which was a completely inadequate way to encompass fifteen years of love gone wrong. "So did I."

"Maybe it was just the emotion. You were pretty good," Joe said. *"Romeo and Juliet."* He shrugged. "It doesn't come much stronger than that."

"I think it was maybe more than that."

"How long is it since you kissed a woman?"

Tavis dredged his mind back. "So long ago, I'd forgotten how fabulous it can taste."

"Better than chocolate milkshake?"

"Beyond compare."

"Mmm," Joe said, puckering his lips in disgust. "I wouldn't know."

"You've never tried it?"

Joe shook his head vehemently. "For me this is genetic, not a statement."

Tavis couldn't believe how weary he felt. He should be pleased with his performance, except that in his heart he knew it wasn't the skill of his acting that had moved him to such dizzy heights. All those things about Juliet being the moon and the stars, they'd flowed out of him with such passion that he felt as if he was the first person who'd ever spoken them.

"Maybe you should have taken Mohammed as your leading lady after all," Joe suggested.

"I certainly wouldn't be feeling like this now," Tavis agreed.

"So what are you going to do about it?"

"Nothing."

"Because she's already with someone else, or because of your pact with the devil?"

"I don't know," Tavis said. "I've given up women. They're too much hard work."

"That didn't look like too much hard work back there."

"That was acting."

"Of course," Joe said. "I forgot."

Tavis studied his burger. The colder and more congealed it became, the less appealing it looked. What good was love, if even the merest hint of it could put you off your food?

"I have something to tell you." Joe leaned back in his seat, his loud Hawaiian shirt perfectly at home in this place. "I've met someone too."

Tavis sat up.

"He could be important to me," Joe said.

"Wow," Tavis said. "This is news."

"We've been seeing each other for a few weeks," Joe went on. "He thinks I'm cute."

"He has good taste," Tavis said with a smile. "I think you're cute too."

"Ah," Joe said. "But the difference is, you could never love me as I want to be loved."

"No," Tavis admitted sadly.

Joe shrugged. "I'd long since resigned myself to that."

"So," Tavis asked, "where does that leave us?"

"I love you," Joe assured him. "Like a brother. I always will. Nothing changes that."

"Do you want me to move out?"

"No." Joe shook his head. "I never want you to stop being a part of my life. A big part of it."

"We're family." Tavis punched his arm affectionately. "Almost."

"We would be if you could get it together with my daughter," his friend said, resuming his role as father of Juliet.

"That's only make-believe," Tavis pointed out. "Real life is a lot more complicated."

"She's a fantastic woman," Joe said.

"Aren't they all when you first start out?"

"This one could be different."

"I don't want any distractions. Two years ago, I very nearly gave all this up for a woman—you know that. You were the one who had to scrape what was left of me off the ground. She loved me but hated my job. It was the hardest choice I ever had to make, but to give up my dreams would have been the biggest mistake of my life. I'm nothing if I can't act. I vowed then I'd never let anything—*anyone*—take me away from what I love most." Tavis held up his hands. "My heart is on ice."

"Oh really?" Joe said. "Seems like there's been a slight thaw to me."

Tavis hung his head. "I know. And that's what worries me."

His friend looked at him earnestly. "It doesn't matter about past mistakes. It doesn't matter what you've promised yourself. If this is really what you want, don't let her slip away."

"What I really want is to become the best actor I can be."

Joe took his hand and patted it. "Make sure that you don't become the loneliest one along the way too."

Sixty

I'm on the verge of tears. My hormones are definitely on overdrive at the moment and there's nothing I can do to convince them to calm down.

"It's fabulous." The dress is covered in tiny crystals and it glitters majestically, grabbing at every ounce of sunlight coming through the window and turning into a million miniature rainbows. "Just fabulous." I've never seen anything quite so beautiful. This is a movie star's dress, not a dress for a displaced, dysfunctional dipstick with a South London accent. I want to be cheerful, but my body is telling me to weep and I don't know why.

"Is it?" Gil looks terrified, and if I'm not mistaken there are tiny beads of perspiration on his forehead. "You don't look happy," he says nervously.

"I am," I sob. "I am."

"Do you think it will fit?"

"I don't know." I sniff. It does look like a skinny person's dress. "But I do hope so."

We're in my bedroom at Daniella's house. Gil called me a dozen times today to declare undying love and I finally feel like we're getting back on track. And it has helped me to rationalize my performance as Juliet—a passionate but misguided woman in love with an unattainable and highly unsuitable man. Tavis and I will never be anything but good friends, despite the fact that he could beat all his opposition hands down in a Kisser of the Century competition, if there were such a thing.

"When can I wear it?" I hold this creation against me. "Isn't it a little dressy for the office?"

Gil clears his throat. "I thought we'd go to the Oscars ceremony tomorrow night," he says cautiously. "If you'd like to."

I nearly drop the dress on the floor. "If I'd *like* to?"

"It can be really boring," Gil says.

"Boring?" This man has no idea of boring. Queuing up for a takeaway from the Wing-Wah Chinese in Battersea is boring. Sitting in every Saturday night watching something utterly vacuous on TV is boring. Having to Nair your legs every week is boring. Giving leaflets out at the book fair is boring. A night at the Oscars is a long, long way from my idea of boring. "I could live with boring," I say.

"Great."

Cinderella is going to the ball! I can't wait to ring someone and tell them about this. Anyone. "Shall I try it on?"

"Maybe you'd better," Gil says, sounding somewhat reluctant.

"Wait there!" I rush off into the adjoining bathroom, I whip off my Cinders rags—in this case Armani jeans and T-shirt—and slide into the dress. I pile my hair up and clip it with the nearest hair grip I can find and then look in the full-length mirror by the shower.

Even without my full war paint or coordinating Jimmy Choo accessories, I look like a million dollars. I can't believe this is me. I'd only ever expected to look as fabulous as this on my wedding day. The dress hugs every curve and even manages to give me some that I didn't know I had. The lobster red of my skin is fading fast and with a judicious application of St. Tropez cream, I should be able to pass muster as a naturally bronzed beauty. Thank God for the person who invented fake tan! In this mood, I have every reason to believe that by this time tomorrow, my fried nose will have faded enough to resemble rather fetching freckles.

I take a deep breath and prepare to present myself.

"Da-da!" I say as I emerge into the bedroom.

Gil's eyes widen with surprise and stay fixed and dilated as his brain clearly tries to assimilate this vision he sees before him with the disheveled old duck who normally frequents his life. His mouth opens but words fail to come out.

"Do you like it?" I ask, and I don't sound nearly as confident as I feel.

Before he has a chance to answer, Alexis sidles into the room. "Wow," she says, jaw dropping in awe. At ten years old she's not had time to develop the same inhibitions as a thirty-eight-year-old man. "Auntie Sadie," she breathes in open admiration, "you look like Princess Sparkle Barbie."

"Do I?" That's a good thing, isn't it?

"Alexis helped me out with your dress size," Gil admits as soon as his brain can form words again. "She gives great rates for espionage."

"Good girl," I say.

"Are you going to dress up like Prince Sparkle Ken?" Alexis inquires of my boyfriend.

"I hope so," Gil says with a grin.

I sincerely hope not! Have you seen Prince Ken? He looks like a cross between a leftover glam rocker and Liberace without the piano. But then anyone who thought Ken was the ideal name for Barbie's prince really didn't have their finger on the button, did they?

"I'm going to go and find him," Alexis says and marches out of the room, leaving us looking at each other in a slightly dazed way.

"You look stunning," Gil says with something approaching wonderment. I certainly don't think I've scrubbed up too badly.

"There are a few more bits and pieces," he says and pulls out another carrier bag from behind the bed. "I had to take a guess on the shoe size, but we can exchange them easy enough."

He unwraps a pair of Jimmy Choo's from the neatest little box you ever did see. They match the dress exactly and I hope to God that they fit. Gil kneels down and offers up the shoe. My foot slides in, nestling perfectly in the soft satin. The slipper fits. I am indeed Cinderella.

Gil stands and hands me a small clutch bag. He has thought of everything, and I want to wipe out all the previous bad things I thought about him. It doesn't matter what the dress has cost—although it's clearly a substantial sum. For all I care, it could have been from a charity shop, it's the fact that he's taken so much trouble over getting it right that is moving me so deeply. I don't think anyone has ever gone to so much effort on my behalf. If I'm not careful, I'll start myself off blubbering again. Perhaps Gil is my Prince Charming after all. And I thought this kind of thing only happened in the movies.

"One more thing," Gil says and he produces from his jacket pocket an elaborately padded jewel case. My mouth goes dry. "This was my mother's," he says cautiously. "I hope that isn't too corny."

"It's not corny," I say. "But it's too much, Gil."

He opens the box and a beautiful diamond necklace glints back at me. I bet Princess Sparkle Barbie doesn't come complete with these, otherwise she'd need her own bank vault.

"I can't wear that."

"Don't you like it?"

"Gil, it's fabulous. But the cost . . ." You could probably buy a house with the proceeds. Two, probably. "I don't think I can do them justice."

"You'd make me very proud."

He takes the necklace out of the box and tenderly clips it round my neck. "You look lovely."

I study my reflection again. I don't look lovely—lovely is the sort of word my mum uses to describe a pleasant outing to the garden center or a cup of tea from a seaside café. I look stupendous, sensational and sizzle-your-socks-off sexy. The sort of bird worthy of taking to an Oscars ceremony.

"I don't know what to say."

Gil comes toward me. "Don't say anything." He takes my hair clip and throws it to the floor, letting my hair fall round my shoulders. "You are a very beautiful and desirable woman." He breathes against my neck. "I haven't had the opportunity to show you how much I need you."

I'm feeling a bit needy too. "Help me unzip the dress," I murmur as Gil covers me with insistent kisses.

Without a word, he unzips the back and eases the teensy,

weensy, oh-so insubstantial straps from my shoulders. I'm having the chocolate-and-radiator sensation again.

The door flies open. "I found him," Alexis announces and marches in clutching Prince Sparkle Ken in a viselike grip with one hand and Princess Sparkle Barbie in full regalia in the other. "You can play with him now."

"Maybe not right now, Alexis," I say, sounding a bit more breathy than I would like.

"Gil would like to," she says without doubt as she plonks herself down on the bed and affects a pose that indicates she's there for the duration. "Wouldn't you, Gil?"

And despite the stricken look on his face, Gil still has the good grace to laugh.

Sixty-one

Joe was working in Book Fever—his work on the soap was drying up and he'd taken some extra shifts in the local bookstore to ease the pain of rejection and increase his chances of bumping into Spielberg over a copy of *Adventures in the Screen Trade*.

He'd left a message for Tavis to call him, but it was just as easy for Tavis to swing by, as he'd nothing else on the agenda. Maybe Joe would have some time for lunch at Clafoutis or one of the other coffee shops on Sunset Plaza.

It was Tavis's day off—from everything. A rare occurrence. No shift at Zorba's, no sides to learn that couldn't wait a day or two, no auditions, no buttwork, no housework. Nada. A blissfully unencumbered day stretched ahead of him and he thought, like a true Californian, he might take a ride out to the beach.

The shop doorbell announced Tavis's arrival. "Hi, bro," Joe said, high-fiving him.

"So where's the fire?" Tavis asked.

"No fire, but how would you like to go to the Oscars party?"

"You're kidding me!"

"Would I joke about something like that?"

"How did you swing it? Was this your new friend?"

Joe looked shady. "Not exactly."

"Wait," Tavis said, holding up his hand. "There's a catch to this, right?"

"Isn't there always?"

"With you? Yes."

"What is the worst possible job at the Oscars?"

"You got us a job? Oh man, why do you do this to me?"

"You need the money."

"Don't I need my dignity more?"

"No," Joe said. "So what's the worst job?"

"Valet parker."

"We don't have to go that low," Joe assured him.

"Waiter. Waiting tables."

Joe clicked his teeth. "Got it in two!"

"That would kill me."

"Prepare to die."

"No way, man!"

"Come on, it will be fun. It'll give us something to aspire to. What else were you going to do tonight?"

"I don't know. Watch TV. Wash my hair. Wash someone else's hair."

"You are very ungrateful, my friend."

"Aw, come on, Joe," Tavis begged. "Don't lay that on me."

"What other way are you going to get to go to the Oscars party?"

"I'm going to become a movie star, remember?"

"Yes, and back in real life, at least this way we can go to our graves saying that we were there."

"I don't think being hired help is the same as being there."

"Now you're getting picky. Just think of the stories you'll be able to tell your grandchildren."

"Are we ever likely to have grandchildren? Look at us," Tavis said. "You're a raging old queen and I'm a . . . I don't know what I am."

"A freak of nature," Joe obliged.

"Thank you."

"Just think of the *Movie Premier* magazine headlines. 'Waiter to Winner!' Wouldn't that make an interesting piece? I can see it now."

Strangely enough, Tavis could see it too. He held up his hands. "I'll do it," he said. "But only because you're my best friend and because it beats watching it on TV."

"You'll enjoy it," Joe assured him. "It'll be a blast!"

No, Tavis thought. A blast would be *winning* an Oscar—and one day he was going to make sure that he did.

Sixty-two

This is my big night. I've taken the day off from Double Take especially to prepare myself. There isn't going to be one single bit of my body that hasn't been puffed, plucked, polished, painted, preened and pampered in the line of duty. By the time I've finished, it will be impossible to tell where I finish and Gwyneth Paltrow begins. Bay and Min could hardly contain their excitement, and I'll never dare show my face in the office again unless I take several thousand compromising photographs of the stars.

I am back at Daniella's watching some hideous daytime quiz show and having a quick tuna sandwich before the serious work of my makeover commences, when the doorbell rings. I peep through the curtain and my heart does a funny little lurch when I see Tavis standing there. Off I trot to let him in.

"What are you doing here?"

"That's a nice welcome."

I stand aside and let him in. "We're friends," I say. "We don't need pleasantries. How did you know I'd be here?"

"I used all of my potent psychic powers to detect where your aura was in the universe."

"Only Brits do irony," I inform him.

"I swung by the office and they told me you had the afternoon off."

"Guess where I'm going?"

"To the beach with me."

"No."

"Ah, come on. I have the afternoon off too. Joe can't play, he's working at Book Fever."

"Take another friend."

"I don't have any other friends." Tavis turns puppy eyes on me. "You're my only friend in the world."

"That's because you work too hard."

"So where are you going?"

"To the Oscars ceremony!" I can hear myself squeaking with delight.

"Oh." Tavis doesn't look quite as thrilled as I do. "With Gil?"

"Who else?"

"And to the Governor's Ball afterwards?"

"Of course."

Tavis picks up the Prince Sparkle Ken that Alexis has abandoned on the sofa and flops down. He purses his lips and quietly says, "I'll be there too."

"Fantastic!"

"Not so fantastic." He looks up at me, wrenching Ken's arm backward with a certain degree of brute force. "While you're having fun, moving and grooving with the stars, I'll be waiting tables."

I sink down on the sofa next to him. Now I feel like smashing Ken's face in too. "Oh, Tavis."

"It may be the only way I ever get to go there."

I put my arms round him and give him a big hug. "Don't talk like that. You're brilliant. A fantastic actor."

He smiles reluctantly. "You're just saying that."

"No, I mean it. Last night was . . ." What was it? Unnerving, that's what. "It was superb. You're very talented."

I fall silent.

Tavis grins at me. "Keep going."

I tut. "You know I'd do anything to help."

"Come to the beach with me," Tavis begs. "That would make me feel a lot better."

"I can't." I try an Alexis-style whine. She seems to win every argument with it. "I have to get ready for tonight."

"How long will that take?" Tavis says. "You already look fabulous."

"I don't," I protest. "I'm a mess. I have to do hundreds of girl things before five o'clock." This is the designated hour of white stretch limo arrival. "It's nearly twelve now. That is six short hours away."

"What are you going to do in six hours?" Tavis is aghast. "You could repaint a street of houses in that time, not a few toenails."

"I'm a high-maintenance babe."

"You are not." Tavis snorts. "The natural look is very fashionable. Come with me," he pleads pathetically. "I have to go to work early too. Before then I can show you some good old-fashioned California entertainment."

"Like what?"

"Rollerblading." He looks pleased with the idea.

Somewhere inside me a little bit of resolve weakens. "I've never been Rollerblading."

Tavis is already on his feet. "You'll love it," he says. "How can you come to California and not Rollerblade?"

"Gil will go bonkers if I'm not back on time." Worse still, he'd probably go without me.

"We'll be back in plenty of time. Joe will go *bonkers* if I'm late for work."

"It's not difficult, is it?"

Tavis takes my hand. He fixes me with those damned Romeo eyes, and my last inch of willpower crumbles to dust. "It's a piece of cake," he assures me. "Would I lie to you?"

I feel my insides sigh. Last night, as Romeo, this man was willing to lay down his life for me. You don't forget that sort of thing too easily. I feel that I owe him.

"Rollerblading it is," I say. I hate myself for it, but I've always been a pushover when it comes to doe-eyed men.

Sixty-three

Venice Beach is packed with hippies who came in the 1960s, tuned in, turned on, dropped out, chilled out and never went away again. There is an extraordinarily large population of sixty-year-old men wearing long ponytails and tie-dyed vests.

A woman who is possibly ten years older than my nan whizzes past on silver Rollerblades in minuscule Nike shorts beneath a cropped top and nearly takes me out at my knees. She is the only eighty-year-old I've seen with thighs of steel. But then she's also the only eighty-year-old I've ever seen on skates. It can't be that difficult then, can it?

I've got my skates on—ten slithering wheels that are determined to have a life of their own. And I'm clinging onto Tavis for grim death.

"Take it easy to start with," Tavis urges.

I don't think I could take it any other way. Does he think I'm going to go whizzing down Venice boardwalk at ninety miles an hour on my first outing?

We set off. Gingerly.

Help! The minute I move, it feels as if all the wheels charge off in different directions. I wave my arms around in an attempt to regain my balance, and I lose my dignity. I must look like one of the Muppets.

Tavis is trying not to laugh.

"Don't laugh! I'm concentrating." Tavis, meanwhile, is doing it backward, forward, inside out, everything. All with an amazing grace and fluidity. I hate this man. He must be crap at something.

"You're doing fine."

I'm not. I can categorically state, I'm not. I look like one of those little five-year-olds you see hanging on to their father's hands and tiptoeing along on their Rollerblades to the sound of parental cooing.

"Try to get a bit more rhythm going."

It's all right for him to say that. I would love to get a rhythm going. My brain is doing all it can to bend my knees, but it doesn't seem to be passing the right messages to my legs.

"That's it!" Tavis shouts, shimmying backward and away from me. He draws his hand away until we are only touching by our fingertips. A little confidence is pushing down toward my toes. I'm starting to enjoy this. "Faster," Tavis says. "Feel the wheels. Good. That's good."

It's not bad. I'm picking up a bit of speed now. I can feel a cooling breeze on my face and in my hair. Ha, ha! Watch out, Granny! A few people notice the grim determination etched on my face and wisely move out of my way as we wind our way on the ribbon of path threaded through the sand and the palm trees, passing the fabulous, boxy beach houses of steel and glass that face off against the ocean.

"You're a natural," Tavis says.

And you know, I'm starting to feel the wheels. I'm doing more skating than slithering and it feels good—really good. This is what life should be for: sun, shorts and skates.

At that moment an octogenarian wearing a gold Lurex thong and very little else skates by, overtaking me on the inside. And I don't know what distracts me the most—the fact that I can see most of his wrinkly little hazelnut of a bottom or the fact that he's smoking a pipe—when absolutely *no one* in California smokes. Whatever it is, I'm suddenly aware that we're heading down a slope, a tiny incline to all those who aren't wearing Rollerblades, but something approaching Kilimanjaro to me. I'm gathering speed at an alarming rate, catching the old boy up quicker than I'd like to.

"Shitshitshit!" I can feel my arms flailing, but they are not helping to halt my progress.

Oh hell! I'm heading toward some sort of contemporary artwork—a graffiti-sprayed wall which several youths are working on. They're lounging around admiring their work, aerosol cans in hand.

"Stop!" Tavis shouts.

Which is really helpful. I would if I could, but he seems to have left out one vital part of my instruction. He didn't tell me *how* to stop! "I don't know how!"

The youths turn in my direction and a look of terror spreads across their faces.

"Don't these bloody things have brakes?"

"No."

"No?" Now I'm really worried.

"Make a *T*!" Tavis is belting after me.

"Make tea?" What?

"A *T*! With your feet!"

Oh! Why didn't he say so earlier?

"Get out of the way!" I shout at the hardened graffiti-sprayers.

They scatter on command, dropping their cans of spray paint and diving behind palm trees, and I'm heading—no steaming—toward their wall.

"Do a *T*! NOW!" Tavis sounds very panicked. "One foot behind the other."

I try to lift one foot to put it behind the other, but something suddenly is not quite right. My universe is inverted. The pavement is where the sky should be and vice versa. "Aarrgh!" comes involuntarily from my throat. And after a pleasant flight through the air, I land in an ungainly heap, a tangle of arms and legs, splayed out on the boardwalk.

Tavis comes up behind me, breathless. "Are you all right?"

I want to say, *Do I look all right?*—but all the breath has departed from my body.

To make matters worse, the man in his glittery G-string, still puffing serenely on his pipe, skates gracefully by.

Sixty-four

"Are you feeling better now?" Tavis is looking very chastened.

"Mmm-hmm." I nod but am not entirely convinced, and neither is Tavis. After he'd scraped me off the boardwalk, he examined all my limbs—rather thoroughly, I thought, for one who has only been a TV doctor—and then, having pronounced none of them to be broken, returned the offending and rather scratched Rollerblades to the rental hut and loaded me into his car.

It's not only me who's looking shaken either. "You had me worried for a minute there," he says as we head back toward Larchmont.

"Only for a minute," I say. "I must try harder next time."

He smiles at me. "I'm not too sure about your style, but I'd give you ten out of ten for artistic interpretation."

"Yeah, very funny." The graffiti boys, when they had eventually deemed it safe to come out from behind their palm trees, had given me deep respect and were spray-painting my name on their wall in honor. Upside down.

Tavis squeezes my hand. "You had a lucky escape."

I know. It was a stupid thing to do. Everyone else prepares for weeks for Oscars night—and not by going Rollerblading. Most take the more obvious route of the beauty parlor. My hands are trembling and my eyes feel all teary. And although I don't appear to have come to any physical harm, I feel sort of sore all over.

"Gil would have killed me," Tavis says with a rueful shake of his head. "I don't know what I was thinking of."

"No harm done," I say. I try one of my most winning smiles, but it feels a bit feeble. "I'm fine. Really."

"Sure?"

"All in the world is well."

He sighs, deeply, and I see a little tension seep out of his body. We stop at a red light and he turns to me. "It was fun, though."

"Yes."

He grins at me as he pulls away. "I think you've done it before."

"Yeah," I say. "Maybe I was a roller-disco queen in a former life."

We laugh and a little of my wobbliness vanishes and I relax back in my seat, eyes closed, enjoying Tavis's driving until he pulls up outside Daniella's house.

"There you go," he says. "Safe and sound."

"Yeah." Not for the want of trying.

Tavis twitches round in his seat and faces me. "Have a great time tonight," he says, sounding serious. There's a little shadow of sadness around his eyes. "Spare a wink for a friendly waiter."

"I will." I lean over and kiss him lightly on the cheek. His skin feels warm from the sun and tastes of the sea. "Next year you'll have a proper bona fide invitation—I'm sure of it."

"Get outta here," Tavis says. "Or you'll be late."

I risk another kiss. "And thanks for today. It was fun."

But as I go to get out of the car door, it jams. I give it a hefty push, but no good. "It's stuck." I have another push and shove.

"There's a knack to it," Tavis says. "Wiggle it around."

Wiggle. Push. Shove. "No. It doesn't want to know."

"Here," Tavis says and makes to get out of the car. "I'll get it."

"Don't worry." I dismiss him with a wave of my hand. "I can manage." And I spring up in my seat, deciding to vault over the top of the door as I've seen Tavis do a dozen times.

"Wait!"

I turn back to Tavis as I start my jump, and looking in the direction of his horror-struck gaze, I see that the seat belt is wrapped around my foot. But too late—*Houston, we have liftoff*—I'm launched. "Ooohhhh!"

In a scene reminiscent of the recent Rollerblading incident, there is far too much air between my feet and terra firma. "Aarrgh!"

When Tavis does this he always manages to look cool. It's not something I'm achieving. I can feel myself doing a cartoon scramble to try and turn myself the right way up, but whatever I was in a former life, it wasn't a cat, and I don't land gracefully on my feet, but straight on my face. My knees and elbows aren't far behind.

And neither is Tavis. He's out of the car and crouching beside me before you can say That was a stupid thing to do. He is ashen. "Are you hurt?"

"Yes." All over. And there's blood. Coming from my nose and possibly my lip. I'm not crying, but only because I'm too shocked.

"Can you stand up?"

Only if they rebuild me using metal pins and bionic technology. I will never again think that *The Six Million Dollar Man* was a load of old rubbish.

I ease my face from the pavement, leaving what look like vital bits of skin behind. "What do you think Gil will say?"

Tavis shakes his head. "I don't know," he admits. "But I bet it won't be nice."

Sixty-five

The white stretch limo pulls up outside Daniella's house.

I glance nervously at my friend. "He's here."

"You look fine," Daniella reassures me. "No one will be able to tell."

I touch my lip with a tentative finger. "Ow!"

Daniella winces.

"Sure?"

"Well," she says, "not many people."

I catch my reflection in the mirror. "Especially if they've got a squint or a glass eye?"

"Don't touch it," she says, looking worried. "Or it will bleed again."

The doorbell rings. I push Daniella toward the door. "You go."

She ducks behind me and pushes me forward instead. "You're going to have to face him sometime."

The doorbell rings again and I take a deep breath and open it. Gil's smile freezes. "What the hell happened to you?"

"I had an accident."

"You sure did," he says. Concern furrows his brow. "Are you okay?"

"Well . . ." I'm not sure what qualifies as okay. I have a black eye, a livid red graze on my cheek and a split lip. I've chipped a tooth and although it feels like I've had a razor inserted in my mouth, I don't think you can actually notice that. I may well have busted my ribs, I have no skin on either elbow or knee and one of my ankles is the same size as both of them put together. An awful lot of me is turning a deep navy-blue color. "Well," I say brightly, "I'm still ready to party!"

A look crosses Gil's face. It's no longer concern. It's a look that says, *You cannot go out like that!*

Daniella has put a pound of foundation on my face and force-fed me Extra Strength Tylenol. She's lent me a white gauzy stole which will disguise the worst of my elbows. The fabulous, fabulous dress that I wanted to look so wonderful in covers my knees and so long as I don't try to eat, walk or generally have too good a time, I should be okay.

Despite the fact that I'm laden down with his mother's diamonds and am wearing this killer movie-star dress, Gil can't tear his eyes away from my split lip.

"Are you in pain?" he says. He still hasn't moved toward me.

Loads of it. "Only when I laugh." I try to smile without making my lip bleed.

"Are you sure you want to go?" He does look concerned again—in a sort of hypnotized way. "We can miss it this once."

Miss the Oscars? Is he mad? If I was on a stretcher I'd still want to go. And believe me, it was a close-run thing.

"I'd like to go," I say, sounding feeble. "But only if you don't mind my looking like this."

I can see the decision cross his mind. "You look fine," he says, but there's no depth to the words. "You always look beautiful."

I risk a wider smile and feel my lip tear slightly.

"You'd better go," Daniella urges anxiously.

"Yes," Gil says. "Yes."

I set off and limp toward him. He takes my arm and I try not to complain as my raw elbow brushes against his jacket. Aaahhh! I want to cry. I've ruined everything. This was going to be perfect, and I've messed it up completely. And I'd like to be able to say this is all Tavis's fault, but it isn't, it's mine. All mine.

"How did you do this?" Gil says as he eases me toward the open door of the limo. The chauffeur looks at me and flinches as he sees my face.

Gil is still looking at me in mesmerized horror and waiting for detail.

"I fell," I explain.

"From the top of a ten-story building?"

"I tripped over. Onto the pavement," I mumble, thinking it's probably wise to miss out the vaulting-from-the-car episode.

"Poor you." Gil awkwardly tries to cuddle me and I wince. Shaking his head with bemusement, he helps to lower me into the car. "Did someone come to help you?"

"Yes," I say, without trying to incriminate myself further. I daren't tell him that it was my unreliable actor friend who helped me, otherwise I think his face would turn as black as his tuxedo.

Sixty-six

I get a thrill as we crawl up in the lavish, limo traffic of Highland Avenue and we see the gigantic, glamorous Hollywood sign hanging on the hill.

I think we were supposed to get here early before the crowds, but it hasn't worked out like that. When we arrive we're knee-deep in starlets working the heaving throng of the great, unwashed public—who have camped out for days on a square inch of sidewalk just to get a fleeting glimpse of their favorite stars. There's an equally great and unwashed crowd of paparazzi.

"Ready?" Gil says and he squeezes my hand. I realize it's the one bit of me that doesn't ache.

"Let's try to enjoy this," I say nervously, and I see his shoulders relax a little.

"You're right," he says. "I just hope no one thinks I did this to you."

And I can tell that he's only half joking.

We step out onto the red carpet, the crowd starts screaming and we're blinded by the lights of a thousand camera flashes. Maybe Gil is sufficiently well known to warrant a photograph, I don't know—but I'm certainly not. That doesn't stop the paparazzi though. They're calling at me to stand this way and that, just in case they discover later that I might be important.

The carpet, dotted with larger-than-life replicas of the Oscar statuette, stretches for miles and we form a slow procession toward the theater that's been purposely built for the Oscar ceremony. My heart is pounding as much as my head, and I can't believe that I'm really here.

I've been in the town for weeks now—movie-star headquarters of the world—and I haven't seen a single celebrity so far. Not one. Not even some measly TV soap celeb, or someone from *ER* or *West Wing* or *The Sopranos*—never mind a huge film star. Unless, of course, you count Noah Bender in his knickers in Gil's lounge. Now I'm in star heaven—they're running amok, twinkling brightly. They're all here: Nicole Kidman, Tom Cruise (though obviously not together), Sharon Stone, Dustin Hoffman, the dashing Denzel Washington, Russell Crowe (I'm trying not to faint), Robert Redford, the beautiful Ben Affleck and the permatanned Sylvester Stallone. The atmosphere is super-charged. There are more teeth and diamonds on show than I've ever seen in my life. How am I ever going to get them to believe this down at the Wing-Wah Chinese Takeaway?

I'm so glad that Gil has gone out of his way to make sure that I'm properly attired. I lean against him and gave him a little squeeze. A dozen flashbulbs record it.

"This is a feeding frenzy," I whisper.

"Welcome to LA," he says with a sardonic smile. We stop amidst the furor and he fixes me with his soft blue eyes. "Are you feeling okay?"

Just when I think we're going nowhere with this relationship, that we're never going to manage to get it right, I suddenly fall in love with him all over again. "Yes," I say. "I'm feeling fine."

We finally reach the entrance and join the crowd in the theater foyer, waiting for the ushers to show us to our seats in the orchestra level. I'm sure it's really nice in here, but I can't see anything for wall-to-wall people. It's hot and squashed and even though I'm fizzing with excitement, I can't wait to sit down again.

A young guy in a trendy tuxedo with a dragon embroidered down one sleeve comes toward us. He shakes Gil by the hand and I recognize him as the fourteen-year-old director with whom Tavis worked on the body-double shoot.

"Hey," he says to Gil. "I thought you avoided these like the plague."

"I have to come out every so often," Gil responds, "just to let them know I'm still around." Gil turns to me and so does the ridiculously youthful director. "This is Toby Portman. He's going to direct *The One That Got Away*."

"Can't wait, man." The Boy Wonder director claps his hands together. "We are going to put a boot to the butt!"

"We start casting in a couple of days," Gil informs me.

This is news to me. I know so little about Gil and his life. That's not good, is it?

"I have to go," Toby says. "I'll catch you later." He shakes my hand. "Nice to meet you."

"He's a hotshot," Gil says as soon as he's a discreet distance away. "I'm lucky to get him."

"He looks very young," I remark. Is it the same here as it is everywhere else with policemen? You know you're getting old in Hollywood because all the directors look like they're straight out of high school.

Gil shrugs. "It's Hollywood. You're over the hill by the time you're thirty. Maybe not even that old."

What a depressing thought. I feel like I haven't even begun the climb yet.

A slim, dark-haired woman heads toward us. She's wearing a full-length silk gown the color of emeralds. "Gil!" she says, and kisses my rather surprised-looking date.

"Katherine."

"I didn't expect to see you here," she says.

"No, no . . ." Gil stammers. "Me neither."

And I don't know whether he means he didn't expect to see her here or he didn't expect to be here himself.

"You look great," she says.

Gil's eyes take in her dress and everything else about her. "So do you."

"It's been so long."

Hello! I'm still here! "Hi," I say, feeling like I could give her a mock punch on the nose. And not for the first time in Hollywood, I wonder whether it's her own.

The woman smiles serenely at me.

"This is Sadie," Gil says. "She's English."

She's English? Is that all the description I warrant?

"Oh my," Katherine says just as a younger, handsome man comes to take her arm.

"We need to take our seats, honey," he says, nodding curtly at Gil.

"You remember David, don't you?"

"How could I forget?" Gil says.

I have the impression I'm missing a vital piece of information.

"We must meet up," Katherine says. "Have lunch sometime."

"Definitely."

The fragrant cloud of Katherine and her toy boy leave us.

I look at Gil for an explanation. "That was Katherine," he says.

"I gather." Nothing else is forthcoming. "Lunch?"

" 'Let's have lunch' in this town means 'I hope we never meet again as long as I live.' "

"She's an old girlfriend, right?"

Gil shakes his head. His lips are pinched and white. "No," he says. "She's an old wife."

"Another one?" I need to sit down. "You've been married twice?"

"Does it make a difference?"

"I think so." I'm not sure why just at the moment. "Why didn't you tell me?"

"Sadie," Gil says, and he sounds more exasperated with me than he should, given the situation. "Since you got here we've hardly had five minutes to ourselves. You don't even know what brand of cereal I prefer, let alone my past relationship history."

"Well," I say, "I happen to think one is a lot more relevant than the other!"

"We were married straight out of college. For two years. It was a sort of starter marriage."

"Thanks for telling me."

"And I like Cheerios. Although I do eat Golden Grahams on occasion."

Before I can retort, through the crowd I see another face—a more familiar one. Gina has spotted us and she and Noah are threading their way through the bodies toward us. I have a heart-sink moment. If Katherine was the starter marriage, this one is very definitely the main course. Everything might not have been going along swimmingly, but we certainly don't need Gil's current wife to come wading in on her five-inch stilettos.

"Oh no." Gil is obviously having his own heart-sink moment.

I see a gulp travel down his throat and his face turns even more white, if that's possible. I tug at his sleeve. "Gil? What is it?"

"You'll see," he says tightly.

The crowd parts and Gina is standing slap-bang in front of us. Noah is stage right, like some aging lackey. And now I know why Gil's face looks like one of those carved out of stone on Mount Rushmore. This is my worst nightmare come true. What a cruel coincidence. The female *faux pas* to beat all *faux pas*. Unlike me, Gina seems unperturbed. She's wearing my dress, my lovely sparkly dress, and for the record, she fills it out in places I could never hope to.

"Hi," she says brightly, all teeth and tonsils on show.

"What do you think you're playing at?" Gil mutters through his white lips.

"Oh!" she says, looking down at her dress for the first time. Her hand goes up to stifle a giggle. "Snap!"

I'd like to go snap too. Preferably to Gina's neck.

"You knew I'd chosen this dress for Sadie," Gil says tightly.

Did she? I wonder how. And then I realize this isn't a coincidence, it's Gina being spiteful and petty, and whatever her motive behind it, I don't want to get dragged into it.

"So I did," Gina admits with a roll of her eyes. "I must have forgotten."

"You look lovely," I say quietly.

"And so do you," Gina agrees. "You're even wearing Gil's mother's diamonds." She emphasizes her bare décolletage and heaving cleavage. "I used to love wearing those," she continues. "Even though they are a little outmoded."

My cleavage—what little there is of it—is heaving too. With rage. We all stand there exchanging meaningful silences.

"You *both* look fantastic!" Noah chips in. "Like twins."

Gina's jaw drops and she gives him a withering glare.

Noah shrinks but doesn't seem to know why. He holds his hands out. "I don't see what the problem is."

"She looks like she's been used as a punching bag!"

"I think it gives her face character," Noah says thoughtfully. "No one else has gone for that look."

"You're an idiot." Gina pushes away into the crowd with a loud and obscene expletive.

Noah shrugs. "I'd be pleased that someone else liked my dress enough to buy it too."

If it wasn't for my split lip, I'd risk a smile. "Thanks, Noah," I say. He's a truly nice man, despite his dependence on strong substances and his penchant for women's pants. "It's a bit of a girl thing."

The world-famous, aging rock star sidles up closer to me and whispers softly in my ear. "Do you think I could maybe borrow it sometime?"

I try very hard to see him in the same way that his legions of adoring fans do. "Can I get back to you on that, Noah?"

"Sure thing, doll," he says and wiggles away.

Sixty-seven

Tavis tugged uncomfortably at his bow tie. He was wearing a wing-collared shirt that was a size too small and it felt like it was strangling him.

The main party of Oscars Night is the Governor's Ball, which is hosted by the Academy. Everyone who is anyone goes, and very few who are no one. The ballroom is a shrine to glitz, hung with sparkling chandeliers the size of space stations.

"Are we ready, people?" the headwaiter asked. "Do we have our hors d'oeuvres?"

Tavis looked at the silver tray before him. He certainly did have his hors d'oeuvres—so did the army of servers lined up in ranks behind him. Each tray would be presented as if they were doing an audition for a major role, because tonight, people who could make or break futures were the revered guests, and you never knew just when you might be spotted and catapulted into stardom.

Tavis straightened his posture. If Brad Pitt could start out in Hollywood dressed as a chicken, parading up and down Sunset Boulevard to advertise El Pollo Loco restaurant, then there was no reason why he couldn't wait tables for the extraordinarily rich and the stellar famous.

"See you back at the ranch," Joe said and winked at him. "Happy hunting. Wait tables like you've never waited tables before."

Tavis set off through the crowd of shrieking and hugging ecstatic winners and the tight-lipped and resolutely stoic losers. Out of the corner of his eye, he spotted Gil McGann standing alone. He quickly scouted the room for Sadie, but couldn't see her. He hoped to God that she'd managed to get here. He felt terrible.

She'd protested that she was okay, but she'd looked in a pretty bad way when he'd left her at Daniella's and he felt that it was all his fault. He had to know whether she was still in one piece, so he worked his way toward her boyfriend.

With a few detours en route, Tavis eventually offered his hors d'oeuvres to Gil, who availed himself of a miniature hamburger. Tavis cleared his throat, but Gil's eyes were too busy working the room to notice him.

"Hi," Tavis said.

A shadow of recognition crossed Gil's face. "Hi there." A quick glance took in the waiter's starched white uniform.

"Is Sadie here?" Tavis asked.

Gil's eyebrows shot up in surprise and he fixed Tavis with a stare.

"I wanted to check that she was okay," Tavis said, aware that he was in danger of babbling. "She did get here?"

"She did," Gil said slowly.

Tavis felt his heart lift. "Wow," he said. "That's great. I was really worried about her. It was all my fault, man. My stupid car door . . ."

"Your car door?"

"I keep meaning to get it fixed." Tavis looked anguished. "If I had, she wouldn't have had to jump out."

"She jumped out of your car?" Gil said. "That's how she fell?"

"Yeah." Tavis was having a flashback. "I think she must have been more shaken than she thought."

"From what?"

Tavis paused briefly, but it was too late. He bit his lip. "From her Rollerblading accident."

"Rollerblading?"

"Yeah. It was a stupid, stupid idea. I'm sorry, man."

"You took her Rollerblading?"

"She was good at it . . . briefly," Tavis added.

"Briefly?"

"It was the guy with the thong and the pipe," Tavis explained. "I think it put her off."

Gil's face darkened. "The thong and the pipe?"

At that moment Sadie appeared. She was such a vision of loveliness, in the most fabulous creation, that Tavis nearly gasped. He checked himself in time. Even surrounded by some of Hollywood's finest, she still managed to create a little buzz as she approached. He could see heads turning, people commenting as she passed. When she came to Gil's side he could see why. She still looked stunning, but close up you could see that she was battered and bruised. Her split lip was crusted with blood and she had a great shiner that nearly closed her eye. When she tried to smile, her face creased in pain.

"Oh hell," Tavis said.

"Thanks," Sadie remarked.

Gil turned to her and there was no hint of a smile on his face. "You didn't tell me that Tavis had taken you Rollerblading."

"Didn't I?" Sadie squeaked.

"No," her boyfriend said.

Sadie pressed her lips together. "I'm trying to blank out the whole experience."

They both looked at Tavis.

"I'd better move on," he said. "So many people, so many hors d'oeuvres. The shrimp tempura are wonderful."

"Really," Gil said.

He offered his tray, but Gil remained impassive. Sadie gave a barely perceptible tilt of her head, but it was patently clear that she was saying, "Move on."

Tavis put on his most cheerful look. "Can't tempt you?"

"I'm very tempted," Gil said flatly. "But not by the hors d'oeuvres."

If Gil had his way, Tavis thought, he was certain to be catapulted somewhere tonight—but it certainly wouldn't be toward stardom.

Sixty-eight

This is just getting worse. What was supposed to be the best night of my life is turning into *Scary Movie*. Tavis looked so depressed, I thought he was going to fling himself into his tray of hors d'oeuvres and commit the culinary version of hara-kiri.

Gil, who wasn't very impressed with my cuts and bruises to start with, is even more unhappy now that he knows who the chief instigator of my injuries was, even though I can't lay the blame squarely at Tavis's feet. I look to Gil for support, but I get a tired, forced smile in return.

I feel that I don't belong here—not in this town, not in this room, not in this stupendous dress and not by Gil's side. For one wild moment, I'm wishing I was back home with my dull little job and my dull little life. I shouldn't be here amongst the Hollywood aristocracy. I'm an impostor, an interloper, a fake. I'm not part of this world.

To make matters worse, the other stupendous dress is heading toward me; Gina's threading her way through the crowd with a confidence that has always eluded me. The dress is filled out admirably by the smiling Gina, pneumatic assets fully pumped and on red alert. She's turning heads with her sheer beauty, not because she looks like she's been recently mugged. I can't handle this, not now and probably not ever. I'm feeling besieged by ex-wives who are more beautiful than me. My head hurts, but not as much as my feet and nowhere near as much as my heart.

I tug at Gil's sleeve. "I have to nip to the bathroom."

He turns to me. "You just came back," he says. "Are you okay?"

No, I'm not okay. I'm miserable. I want you to love me. I don't want to be in competition with your wives—ex or otherwise—

because I can never win. I want to spend some time alone, just you and I, getting to know each other. I don't want to be in this room full of people I don't know and never will, making small talk about things I don't understand. And it all makes me realize that I really don't belong here. I belong in rainy Britain with its cold weather and its hot tea, doing dodgy jobs for piffling amounts of money but with a great bunch of supportive mates, none of whom have pretend breasts.

"Yes," I say, returning Gil's tired smile. "I'm fine."

And before Gina can blast her way into my universe and my self-esteem again, I skulk off before sprinting for the loo like a greyhound.

Sixty-nine

"I saw Sadie rush off," Gina said. "What's the matter with her?"

"She's not feeling too well," Gil said. "The bruises she has are from falling out of a car after a Rollerblading accident this afternoon—I think. She's a bit shaken."

"Rollerblading?" Gina queried. "This afternoon? Before Oscars Night? What was she thinking? She should have been at the salon."

And suddenly Gil realized why Sadie had rushed off. He was so stupid. This was all getting too much for her. One ex-wife that she didn't know about popping up out of the blue, another soon-to-be-ex-wife turning up in her outfit. Of course she didn't want to see Gina wearing the same dress—the dress that had been ruined for her just as his wife had planned. And he cursed himself for being so uncaring. He looked at Gina and his heart went out to his funny, feisty English girlfriend and he knew that one of the main reasons he loved Sadie was that she was the sort of person who would spend the afternoon Rollerblading with a friend—albeit a threateningly handsome one—rather than sitting for hours on end getting whatever it was women got done in beauty parlors.

"You spoiled her night turning up in that," Gil said. "It was a spiteful thing to do."

Gina looked as if she was about to protest and then changed her mind.

"It's over between us, Gina. I've moved on. None of this hurts me. It just makes you look petty."

Gina opened and closed her mouth again.

"Why can't you be pleased for us? I don't love you any

more," Gil said, "and if you carry on behaving like this, I won't even like you."

Gina sighed. "Have you finished?"

"Yes," Gil said.

"I'm sorry. It was a stupid thing to do. Sadie's nice. I shouldn't have done it."

"Then go after her," Gil said, indicating the direction in which Sadie had so hastily departed. "Apologize. Make it up to her. You know, she could be a very good friend to you if only you'd let her."

"Let's take it one step at a time, Gil," Gina warned.

"You could do with a good friend," Gil said. "One with her feet on the ground."

"I'll find her and apologize about the dress," Gina conceded. "I still care for you, Gil."

"Then make it up to Sadie," he said.

Gina looked contrite. "I will."

And as she disappeared into the crowd again, he realized he was a fine one to talk. If anyone needed to make it up to Sadie, he did.

Seventy

I'm at the mirror in the ladies' room and I can't believe how terrible I look. I've had a good cry and emotionally I'm feeling a lot better. I'm trying to repair my ravaged makeup, and am hoping that, physically at least, I can patch myself up to reenter the fray. I try to think back to a time when I had no extraneous wives to contend with and now find that I have not only one but two. I'm trying to convince myself that being divorced twice isn't a bad thing—but I'm failing. Doesn't it indicate a certain flaw in the personality somewhere? A certain lack of staying power? And why did Gil have to be hitched to two such stunning women? Doesn't anyone in Hollywood have ugly exes?

I wave my lipstick as near to my split lip as I can cope with.

"Hey." One of Hollywood's triple-A-list actresses comes to stand next to me. "Could I steal your lipstick? I don't know where mine went."

I think I might hyperventilate. "Sure."

Taking my cheap lippy, she runs it round her trademark full lips. "Great color."

She's won an Oscar tonight and is clearly feeling mellow.

"Thanks."

She glances at my bruises. "What happened to you?"

"I fell out of a car," I say, deciding not to mention the Rollerblading accident.

"Poor you," the star of a dozen hit movies says. "I live in mortal fear of anything like that happening. I wrap myself in cotton for months before Oscars Night."

"I'm not an actress," I say. "It doesn't really matter what I look like." And as I say it, I realize that it doesn't matter at all. Not one jot. It doesn't matter if Gil has a dozen exes, because he's chosen to be here with me and he's chosen my fabulous dress and it's not his fault his wife is an old cow who decided to copy it. I'm here to have fun, and somehow in the stress of it all, I'd forgotten that.

"Lucky you," she says. "You can probably eat all that wonderful food too. They waft it all in front of us, but I'm not allowed any of it." She pats her washboard stomach ruefully. "If it isn't made out of egg white I can't touch it. I'm having to survive by trying to inhale the vapors."

I do my restricted version of a smile and notice that she is trapped in her dress by bones and fabulous corsetry that probably makes breathing, let alone eating, an art. "It's nice to see someone looking natural," she says, and I don't think she's being facetious.

"I think I look rather more natural than I would have liked."

She grins and hands my lipstick back. "Thanks."

"You're welcome."

"Nice meeting you." She heads toward the door. "Have some of those cute little burgers for me," she says over her shoulder.

And, do you know, I think I just might.

Oh no. Oh no. As I swing out of the ladies' room with renewed confidence, I see Gina heading toward me. And I really don't want her to burst my bubble so soon after I've managed to inflate it again. I'm feeling all floaty and buoyant and she looks suspiciously like she's brandishing a pin. I watch my arch enemy—it looks like she's searching for someone and I hope I'll go undetected, but she's definitely heading toward me. Damn. I look round for a means of escape, but I think there's only one corridor heading back to the main reception area and we're both on it. We're on a collision course whether we like it or not.

Huddling behind a group of dinner-suited men, I have a quick look round and see an anonymous-looking door. The sort of door you wouldn't notice unless you were on the hunt for somewhere to escape from the love of your life's wife. The sort of door behind which a superhero would strip off to his tights and undies undetected. Gina is bearing down on me but hasn't spotted me yet. Like a flash of lightning, I whip inside and close the door behind me.

It's some sort of store cupboard. I stand there, frozen to the spot and for some strange reason holding my breath. Mentally, I'm trying to work out where Gina would be now. She could be standing right outside. I press my ear against the door but can't hear anything. In films when people hide in cupboards like this to escape the baddie, there's always a hard floor so that you can hear their footsteps, or there's a conveniently large gap under the door so that you can see their shoes as the baddies conduct their futile search, or a strategically placed keyhole through which you can watch their progress. Here it's all plush shag-pile and tightly fitting doors with no keyholes, so that I can't see or hear a bloody thing. Just my luck.

I think I'll sit here for a while, take the weight off my poor old puffed-up ankle and bide my time until I can be sure she's gone. I fumble around and find the light and click it on. A low-watt bulb shows me that my cupboard is stacked with champagne. There could be infinitely worse places to hide! Although I daren't risk popping a cork in case it gives me away.

It's cool in here and I sit back on a convenient crate of fizz and rest my weary bones. I could, without too much prompting, lie down and have a lovely little sleep. It must be all the painkillers I've munched. I resolve to try harder with Gil. I can't let this clinging woman and a spurious ex-wife ruin a potentially wonderful relationship. I press my ear to the door again, but it's hopeless. All I can hear is the tinkling of a distant piano and a general hubbub of animated conversation. I can't hear any heavy breathing from my love rival so I guess I'm safe. It's time to face the music and dance again.

I stand up and stretch. If I had a big enough handbag, I could help myself to one of these bottles of fizz for posterity, but of course I don't. I've got one of those useless little evening purses that's only big enough for holding a lipstick fit for lending to a movie star. With a little smile to myself, I prepare to depart.

I go to turn the door handle, but in the place where a door handle might be useful is just smooth, polished wood exactly the same as the rest of the door. Oh. Just in case I'm going mad, I check again. No. Still no door handle. Bugger. There must be some way out of here. I lean against the door. It's absolutely and very firmly closed. This is ridiculous. It can't be closed. What good is a cupboard if you can't get out of it from the inside? I lean against the door again, this time with a bit of judicious shoulder pressure in the style of Eddie Murphy in *Beverly Hills Cop* movies. All it does is remind me that I have more than my fair share of pavement-eating disabilities.

Oh man! How can this be happening? I'm locked in a cupboard while all manner of wondrous things are going on around me. There's only one thing for it. A bit of pride swallowing and some well-aimed fists. I bang on the door and shout, "Help!" I might be a bit tentative, because no one comes. And now I wish Gina was lurking round outside, because she might at least let me out.

"Help!" This time I'm definitely louder and more desperate-sounding. "Helphelphelp!"

Nothing.

"Help! Let me out!"

But there's no one to let me out. Not Gina. Not Katherine. Not even the friendly A-list actress. No one.

"Help!" This is pathetic. There's a party with thousands of people going on just down the hall. If only they'd shut up for a minute, someone might hear me. What about Gil? Surely he must be missing me by now. "Helphelphelp!"

There's only one thing for it. I must try not to panic, conserve my energy and then try again in a little while. I hope that they all drink like fish and that someone has to come and get these reserve supplies. Ooo. That reminds me. If I'm going to be locked in a cupboard for the entire duration of the Governor's Ball, then I might as well be comfortable.

Choosing myself a bottle of champagne, I pop the cork—as close to the door as I can manage, but not close enough to put my own eye out. That really would put the top hat on the evening. I treat myself to a good long swig and position my crate so that if I swing my leg, I can repeatedly kick the door with my good foot. Someone is bound to hear this soon. And I settle down, bottle in hand, to wait.

Seventy-one

"I don't know where she is," Gina said wearily. "I've looked everywhere."

"She must be here somewhere," Gil said. The party was getting louder and louder and it was giving him a headache.

"Why? She could have gone home in a huff."

"Sadie doesn't do that sort of thing."

"How do you know?" Gina said. It was true, he didn't know. It just didn't seem like the sort of thing Sadie would do. Perhaps she was more upset than he realized. He'd have to explain the Katherine thing to her. He genuinely hadn't seen or heard from her in years. She wasn't another Gina—but Sadie wasn't to know that. He and Katherine had parted reasonably amicably when, tiring of living with a young, hungry producer who was a workaholic, she discovered she had a penchant for a young, hungry actor who was permanently unemployed. She moved out and, such is the way of the world, the young, hungry actor made it big on Broadway and they relocated to the East Coast so that he could work more. Gil wondered, with the benefit of hindsight, if that was when his phobia of actors had started.

Gil hadn't seen Katherine again until tonight. It was disconcerting, but his first wife was a balanced, independently minded woman—she could take care of herself. He wasn't sure that he'd ever been deeply in love with her, and she certainly didn't have the power to tug on his heart and his conscience like Gina did.

"Let's do one last circuit," Gil suggested. "Can you check the bathroom again?"

"Come on, Gil," Gina whined. "My feet hurt. I need more champagne. This is supposed to be a party. Face it, Sadie's gone."

"Do you really think so?"

"Of course. I wouldn't hang around if you treated *me* like you do her," she said.

"That's not what I needed to hear."

Tavis was doing another round of dishing out hors d'oeuvres. When he saw Gil and Gina, he went to give them a wide berth with the shrimp tempura. "Hey, Tavis!" Gil shouted, and very warily, Tavis approached them. Gil noted that he took in Gina and the dress. "Have you seen Sadie anywhere?"

"No," Tavis said, shaking his head. "Is she all right?"

"I don't know," Gil admitted. "She shot off." Gil flicked his eyes toward the dress in the hope that Tavis might catch his poorly concealed message. Tavis acknowledged it with a blink. "Any idea where she might have gone?"

Tavis shook his head. "No man, but I'll have a look around. Leave it to me. I owe you one."

Yes, you do, Gil thought. "Thanks," he said and a relieved Tavis hotfooted it out of the reception.

"So now what?" Gil said. "Do we stand and wait?"

"No way," Gina said. "I have an invitation to the *Vanity Fair* party at Morton's."

"You do?"

Gina shrugged dismissively. "Well, Noah does. But he went home ages ago. He hates other people's parties."

Gil couldn't say that he blamed him.

"Take me," Gina pleaded. "Take me in your limo. It's the most chic party in town."

"I don't want to go to another party."

"You do," Gina said. "It's Oscars Night. No one goes home before dawn."

"Except aging rock stars."

"And disgruntled girlfriends."

"Touché." Gil smiled.

"Come on. Let Sadie cool off. She'll be fine in the morning."

Gil bit his lip. "I don't know . . ."

Gina linked her arm through his. "I'll apologize to her—really I will. Take me to the party. I promise I won't drink too much."

"You won't?"

"Just a lickle-ickle champagne to relax."

Gil thought Gina was quite relaxed enough. "Okay," he sighed. "We can go. But just for a short while."

"I still love you," Gina said and kissed him softly on the cheek.

"Yeah? Well, let's hope Sadie does too," he said wryly.

He put his arm round Gina and escorted her toward the door, failing to notice that Tavis was watching them as he did.

Seventy-two

"I can't understand that man," Tavis said, loading a blini with a precarious heap of caviar. He wasn't even sure he liked caviar, but it was a taste he hoped to acquire in the future. He licked the fishy eggs, grimacing as he did so. "He's got someone like Sadie in love with him and yet he still seems to be sleazing around with a woman who's supposed to be his ex-wife."

Tavis and Joe were both relaxing amidst the debris of the grand ballroom and it was the first time they'd seen each other all night. They'd kicked back and loosened their bow ties and waiter's coats and were now sitting on the floor, backs against the wall, sharing the remains of a bottle of champagne, the leftover canapés and a joint.

"It's no good asking me," Joe said. "Heterosexual relationships are a complete mystery to me."

"And to me." Tavis shook his head. "I just don't want to see Sadie get hurt."

"It may be too late for that," Joe said. "Come on, buddy. Let's hit the dirt."

The cleaners had arrived and were starting to make a move toward returning the room to normalcy.

"I'll walk you to your car," Joe said.

"I need to go to the bathroom, man," Tavis said. "I'll see you back at the apartment."

"Okay. I'll fix us a nightcap." Joe waved goodbye.

"Hey, Joe!" Tavis called after him. "Thanks for making me do this. It was fun." Though Tavis had begun to realize that anything that involved seeing Sadie, however briefly, could be classed as fun. He wondered where on earth she'd disappeared to, as there had been no sign of her for the rest of the night.

"Yeah?" Joe shouted back. "So is getting a Brazilian wax." He disappeared through the kitchens toward the service elevator.

Tavis wandered down the corridor. Apart from the steady, quiet movements of the cleaners, there was no one around, which was markedly different from earlier on, when it had resembled feeding time at the zoo.

As he walked toward the men's room, he heard a thumping noise that stopped him in his tracks. It was coming from a nearby door. There it was again! Tavis tip-toed over and heard movement again. Perhaps it was one of the cleaners getting some stock or something. He decided to leave them to it. He'd done enough work for one night and his feet were killing him. Turning away, he headed off down the corridor. *Thump*. The noise came again. He couldn't ignore it. No way.

He marched back toward the door, listening to the thumping again and then turned the handle. As soon as he opened the door, he was met by a terrible scream.

The shock made Tavis think he was having a heart attack and there was nothing for it but to scream back.

Sadie was first to stop screaming. She looked at him through wildly blinking eyes. "What are you doing here?" she said.

"Shouldn't I be the one to ask that?" Tavis said, heart still pounding. "You're the one in the broom cupboard."

"You nearly scared me half to death," she said, and slumped back on a crate of champagne from where it seemed she had just risen.

"How long have you been in here?"

Sadie rubbed her face. "Too long." She hiccuped. "I dodged in here to avoid Gina, one of Gil's wives."

"He has more than one?"

"Loads," Sadie said. "It seemed like a good idea, but then I couldn't get out."

"He was looking everywhere for you."

"He was?" She sounded genuinely surprised. "Is he still here?"

"No," Tavis said. "Everyone's gone. I think he thought you'd run out on him."

"I must go to him," Sadie said, and when she stood up Tavis realized how much she was swaying. There was one empty bottle of champagne on the floor and another one clutched tightly in Sadie's hand.

"I can see what you've been doing to entertain yourself."

Sadie stared sightlessly at her bottle. "I was thirsty."

"I bet you were," Tavis said. "I searched the place," he admitted, "but I didn't even see this cupboard."

"*You* searched the place?"

"Yeah," Tavis said. "After Gil left." He smiled at her. "I didn't think you were a quitter." He took the bottle of champagne from her. "But then again, I didn't think you were dumb enough to get yourself locked in a cupboard."

"Well, now you know," Sadie slurred. "If I'm dumb enough to give up *everything* to come out here after a man who's still in love with his mad wife and has another one that he conveniently forgot to mention, then I'm certainly dumb enough to have a little trouble getting out of a closet."

"I'll take you home," Tavis said. "You need to sleep this off."

Sadie staggered out of the cupboard and he took her arm as they tottered down the hall. Sadie was limping badly and every few steps she managed to fall off her shoes.

"You're going to hurt yourself," Tavis said. Besides, it was going to take all night to get out of here if they went at this pace. He bent down. "Jump on."

"You are *not* giving me a piggy back," Sadie said, horrified.

"Jump on," Tavis instructed again. "No arguing. I'm your knight in shining armor. I just rescued you from eternity in a dungeon. My trusty steed is in the parking lot. Jump on."

"You're very stupid," Sadie said. "I'm very heavy."

"I lift weights," Tavis assured her.

Sadie hitched her skirt and took a run at him, but cannoned into him instead and fell down giggling onto her bruised knees. Champagne was a wonderful anesthetic, she'd discovered.

"Sadie, you'll have us both on the floor." Tavis tried to be stern. "Do it properly. Just a little jump."

"Hold my bag." She gave Tavis her little clutch purse, hitched up her skirt again and with an indelicate *ouff* jumped on his back.

"Jeez, Sadie," Tavis puffed. "You must have heavy bones."

"I have childbearing hips."

"Well, some guy will be glad of it one day," he said, panting heavily. "Let's go."

Sadie smacked his rump. "Giddy up, horsey."

"You can quit that right now, madam," Tavis wheezed.

And then he plodded off down the hall, Sadie slumped against his back.

"I don't want to go home," she said sleepily. "Take me somewhere, Tavis."

"I'm taking you home before you do me an injury," he grunted.

"Take me to the beach. Or to a party," she said. "I want to go to a party."

"You've been to a party."

"I spent it all stuck in a cupboard, so that doesn't count."

"I don't have any invitations. I'm the wrong guy." And that hurt more than he liked to admit. "You need your A-list boyfriend for that. I'm not even on the list. I'm a wannabe E-list."

"I don't care," Sadie mumbled. "I like being with you."

Tavis was aware that his heart had stopped beating and he didn't think it was because carrying Sadie was like having Dumbo on his back. He swallowed hard. "I like being with you too," he said softly.

She leaned her head against his shoulder. "I wish . . . I wish . . ."

"What do you wish?"

"Oh, I don't know." Sadie sighed. "I just wish things were different."

Tavis wished with all his heart that things were different too. He wished that he were rich. He wished that he were famous. He wished that Sadie was in love with him. And he wished wholeheartedly that he was the sort of man who could fall head over heels in love with her.

Seventy-three

Daniella is sitting on the terrace in her garden. She's wearing sunglasses and crunching her bowl of breakfast cereal and looking as if she's regretting that it's so loud.

I pad out to join her.

"Ooo," she says, lifting her head gingerly. "Are we the color of Spackle because we have a hangover?"

"We are," I say, sitting down next to her and trying to minimize the scrape of chair on paving stones. "Are we wincing at our breakfast cereal because we have a hangover too?"

"We are," Daniella says and abandons her spoon, which clunks on the table. We both shudder in unison.

"So what did you get up to last night?" I ask. "And with whom?"

"I stayed at home and got drunk," she says. "Alone. At least you had fun getting wasted."

"No," I say. "I sat in a cupboard alone—except for several crates of champagne."

"Which you felt moved to sample?"

I shrug. "I had nothing else to do."

We watch the sun shine for a bit, which sort of hurts, and we watch some birds being relentlessly chirpy. A few butterflies flit dizzily among the flowers. I cover my sunglasses with my hands. There are times when you can really grow to dislike wildlife.

"Why did you spend Oscars Night in a cupboard?"

"I was avoiding Gina."

"With a certain degree of success by the sound of it," my friend notes.

"With a little too much success," I agree. "Tavis had to rescue me."

"Tavis? What was he doing there?"

"He was a waiter at the party."

"That guy's becoming a regular feature."

"Isn't he."

"And where was Gil at this point?"

"I don't know," I say. I can't cope with revealing to Daniella that Gil seems to have a short memory when it comes to marriages. I need to get my own head round it first. "I tried to call him this morning but his phone goes straight to voice mail."

"They're never around when you need them." Daniella's moan sounds particularly heartfelt.

"If it wasn't for Tavis, I could have spent my entire life in that cupboard."

"Then it is your duty to show him that you're eternally grateful."

I shudder again when I think of Tavis lugging me through the maze of corridors on his back until we reached his car. "I tried to," I say.

Daniella lowers her sunglasses. "Really?"

"He wasn't interested."

After the "Katherine" revelation, I don't think a revenge shag would have been completely beyond the pale. I had a lucky escape because my chosen target deemed it out of the question. In the cold light of day, I'm rather relieved that Tavis is gay. "Tavis doesn't do girl, remember?"

"Do you think you're in love with him?"

"I don't know," I say, trying to avoid shaking my head. "I'm very confused. I love Gil—really I do, but Tavis makes me feel . . ."

"Horny?"

I tut. "Special."

"Horny's the same as special."

I sip my freshly squeezed orange juice and all my taste buds curl up in horror. "It doesn't even come close."

"Wow," she says thoughtfully. "One woman in love with two men. Isn't *that* the sweetest taboo?"

"Yes," I say. "It's a lovely idea and would certainly make a change from the usual arrangement, but the truth of the matter is that I'm currently struggling to hold on to one in the face of mounting competition, and the other one isn't interested in women at all."

"*Mounting* competition?" Daniella quizzes me. "Is that an English joke?"

"No," I admit. "Gil has two ex-wives."

"Just two?" Daniella says. "I'd say that was a miracle in this town."

"Well, it's more than enough for me to contend with."

Daniella sighs wearily. "I hate men," she says. "All of them. Short ones, fat ones, tall ones, slim ones, rich ones, poor ones. I even hate gay ones."

"This has something to do with the Mad Movie Mogul?"

"I met his wife yesterday," Daniella says. "She's a very nice woman. I liked her."

"But she didn't like you?"

"I don't know. She was fine—very civil. I don't know if I could have done that in her position." Daniella fiddles with her nails and stares off into the garden. "She told me a lot of home truths, Sadie. Things that I didn't want to hear."

I sigh. Why are relationships always so complicated? I think I'm going to get a cat and possibly a budgie and grow old and mad alone.

"She left him," Daniella continues. "Months ago—for someone else. And he never said a word. He just carried on letting me think they were still just playing Happy Families."

"What are you going to do?"

"I'm not sure yet," she says. "He called me several times last night and left messages, but I didn't answer."

"I guess if he's just got rid of one wife, he won't be in a tearing hurry to take another." Despite the perfect California climate, I feel a little chill trickle through my blood. I wonder what lessons I can learn from this for my own relationship.

"In my next life," Daniella announces, "I'm going to come back as a man—preferably a stinking rich, extremely handsome and well-hung one—and wreak havoc on the female population."

At the moment, I think that sounds like a damn fine idea.

Seventy-four

Tavis's agent never called him. He never returned Tavis's calls either. Which was pretty much par for the course for struggling actors in this town. It was what he had come to expect.

Now this was very mystifying. Not only had his agent called, but he'd gone as far as inviting Tavis into his office—for a discussion. Tavis hadn't been into his agent's office in two years, maybe more. They'd never exchanged more than three sentences. They'd certainly never had a "discussion." He was probably going to get dropped. Now that Doctor Robert was dead and buried and wasn't imminently looking like he was going to be— by some miracle of TV—resurrected and there was nothing else looming on the horizon, it could well be that he had become surplus to the agency's requirements. He was about to find out.

"Hey, Tavis!" His agent bowled out of his office. He was a short, fat Jewish man in his late fifties sporting more gold than Tiffany's window. Taking Tavis's hand, he pumped it until all his fingers had gone numb. "I haven't seen you in a long time," his agent growled. "You're always too busy to come and see me."

Tavis didn't like to point out that he hadn't ever been asked.

"I won't beat around the bush . . ." the agent said next.

That was it. The agent didn't want to represent him anymore. He knew it.

"Toby Portman called."

The Toby Portman?

"He said you did some good work for him."

I got my ass out for him, Tavis wanted to say. *And wiggled it around a bit. I was a butt double in a sex scene.* It wasn't good work. "Yeah?" he said aloud.

"Good work, bad fee. I got my cut." The agent shrugged at the infinitesimal amount. It had paid Tavis's rent for a month. "He liked you."

"He did?"

"He's casting for a new movie. Big budget. Great story. He wants you to read for the lead."

Tavis wanted to lie on the floor and kiss his agent's feet.

"Gimme the script," the agent said to his assistant. She handed it over and the agent slapped it into Tavis's hand. "Do good and the part's yours," he said brusquely.

Tavis was speechless. He knew he ought to say something, but he didn't know what.

The agent smiled. His teeth were like little razors. "You're on your way, kid." He slapped him on the back as if they were long-lost friends. "This is the big break I've been waiting for."

You've been waiting for? Tavis managed to find his breath long enough to speak. "Do you have any advice for me?"

"Yeah," the agent said. He was already walking away. "Don't fuck up."

Seventy-five

Even the ratty old spider plant seems to have perked up. Bay and Min certainly have. And all this, of course, is due to the appearance of Tavis.

He's lounging on the edge of my desk, looking all sort of tousled in a way that says he spent hours getting like that. "I called you last night," he says.

"I know." I'm tired. Bone tired. And I can't seem to perk up even though my favorite friend and rescuer has bowled up unexpectedly in my office. I say "my" office with a certain amount of largesse. Bay announced this morning that the IRS had phoned to ask about her employing illegal aliens and seeing as I am one and she is employing me, she's feeling very jittery. She says she doesn't want to let me go, but may have to before she has a visit from the men in black—the IRS ones, not the Will Smith ones.

To add to it, Delores steadfastly refused to budge out of Daniella's drive this morning for reasons best known to herself. If there's something seriously wrong with her, other than a severe case of lassitude, I might not be able to afford to fix her. I can tell already that this is not going to count as one of my better days. I don't think I can cope if both the men and the machinery in my life are going to give me grief. I want to lay my head down on my desk and pretend that none of it is really happening. If I'm soon to be without a man, without a job and without a car, what is there to keep me here?

"I got your message," I say to Tavis. "So what's the good news?"

He's clearly beside himself with glee. "Sadie." He lowers his voice. I don't know why, because both Bay and Min have ultrasensitive listening devices where their ears should be and don't miss a trick. "I have an audition," he says. "A great one. This could be my big break. My agent says if I don't fuck it up, the lead could be mine."

"Fantastic," I say, but Tavis can tell that it's not coming from my heart but from a much more shallow and forced place just under my skin.

"This is what I've waited for, Sadie," he continues, trying to elicit some enthusiasm from me. "One day all of my body could be famous—not just my butt."

"I'm pleased for you," I say. "Really I am."

"You don't look pleased."

"I am. I just haven't the energy to jump up and down for you."

"Have you fully recovered from your cupboard experience?"

I can feel myself flush a fetching shade of beetroot. "Yes," I say. "Thanks again for coming to my rescue. This role isn't for a superhero, is it? You'd be perfect."

"No, it isn't. It's for a sexy, romantic heartthrob."

He'd still be perfect, but I don't tell him that.

"So what's wrong?"

"Man trouble," I say. Bay and Min turn away—I've been bending their ears all morning about my relationship with Gil, and at a guess I'd say they'd heard enough.

"Oh, Sadie . . ." Tavis's smile fades.

"It's nothing." I can feel myself tearing up. "I'm just not sure that Gil and I are destined to be together." I wave his concern away.

"He doesn't treat you right," my friend says.

"Well . . ." I force a smile. "That's a man's prerogative, isn't it?"

"I'd like to give that guy a piece of my mind," Tavis says darkly.

I can't help but smile, and this time there's nothing forced about it. Tavis will make a lovely romantic hero. I do hope he gets the part.

Tavis glances at the clock on the wall. "I'd better go," he says, swinging his long legs off my desk and making Bay and Min go all unnecessary again. "Don't want to keep them waiting."

"Good luck, or break a leg," I offer. "Whatever it is you actor-types say."

" 'Good luck' is fine," Tavis says.

"Call me later," I instruct. "Tell me how it went."

"I will," he promises as he heads out of the door.

I watch his retreating back and my heart goes out to him. Funny. I feel very protective of him, and I wish that it was me suffering under pressure rather than him. Isn't that how people in love are supposed to feel?

"Hey!" I shout after him. "I'll be thinking of you."

Tavis smiles bashfully and my insides melt. If he does that in the audition they'll hand over the contract there and then. "Thanks."

He goes to leave again and suddenly I can't bear to watch him walk away. I'm feeling very emotional and I want this to be his big breakthrough. He deserves to do well and I truly wish him all the luck in the world.

"Hey!" I yell. "You didn't tell me what the film was called!"

My handsome friend turns and gives me a wave. *"The One That Got Away,"* he calls out.

And as my heart sinks to my boots, I realize that he is indeed going to need all the luck in the world.

Seventy-six

Tavis was sitting in a small reception area in the Cecil B. DeMille Building, and it was making all the hairs on the back of his neck stand up just being here. How could anyone not get a buzz out of being on a movie lot?

Paramount was the first studio in Hollywood and the only one left today after all the others had fled to the outer reaches of Burbank and Culver City. Its list of films read like the complete history of Hollywood—from the days of classic silent films through to *Sunset Boulevard* and *Star Trek Nemesis*. All had started life on this sprawling lot. Paramount was the place where you could still smell the glory days of cinema, feel the history in its walls, walk the sidewalks that had been trodden by Rudolph Valentino, Mae West, Marlene Dietrich, Gloria Swanson, Gary Cooper, Cary Grant—the list was endless. And it was still the place where wannabe movie stars flocked today. He worried at his lip and wondered, Was it possible to die of anticipation, longing and ambition? Tavis was sure if they kept him waiting for too long he'd have a heart attack.

He felt like a star waiting for his supernova. This was the stuff that dreams were made of and it had been his dream for as long as he could remember. Success was so close that he could taste it, smell it, feel it. It was an inch beyond his grasp.

It had been a long and bumpy road, but when everyone else had doubted him, he'd hung in there. Now he, out of all the struggling and equally talented actors in this town, had his big chance waiting just behind that very plain and innocuous-looking door ahead of him.

He'd never really discussed it with Sadie, but he felt that she understood. She, above anyone, seemed to know where he was coming from. And if the truth was known, he was starting to feel that he was only half existing when he was away from her. For someone like him, this was a terrifying thought. It was good to know that there was someone waiting for him, back in the real world, someone who was a good friend, someone who was rooting for him, someone who loved him unconditionally. *Loved?* Tavis halted on the word. *Loved!* Whoa!

Just then, the plain and innocuous-looking door opened and Tavis found himself staring at a familiar face.

"Hi."

"Hi," Tavis said. It was Toby Portman, the director who'd recommended him for the role. Tavis was tongue-tied and it wasn't a great time to be tongue-tied.

Toby clasped his hand, grinning broadly. "How are you doing?"

"Fine," Tavis breathed. "Just fine."

"This is going to be a great movie," Toby said effusively. "You've had time to look at the script?"

"Yeah," Tavis said. "I loved it." That wasn't strictly true. It was a bit sugar-schmaltzy for his taste, but it was destined to be a big box-office blockbuster, and that was all that mattered.

"Come on in," the director said. "Meet the producer. I don't think you know him, but he's followed your work closely and he's a big fan of yours."

"All right," Tavis said. That couldn't hurt. He just hoped it wasn't the usual Hollywood bullshit.

Tavis followed the director through the door. The door that could lead to stardom. The door that could change his life.

As he entered the office, he did a wide-eyed blink as a feeling of horror flooded through him.

"Hi," the producer said calmly.

Not only did Tavis know him, he also realized a big, steaming load had just been dumped on him.

"Gil," Tavis said with a nod and sat down opposite him. The atmosphere in the room grew decidedly chilly.

"You two guys know each other?" Toby said, mildly perplexed.

"Yes," Gil said. "We have a mutual acquaintance." The subtext was obvious. What Gil really meant was, *This guy wants to get jiggy with my girlfriend.*

Tavis could almost smile—so *that's* what this was about. Gil viewed him as competition. Gil, the hotshot producer, was jealous of him—the out-of-work actor. If he wasn't just about to be auditioned by him for the role of his life, this would have been laughable.

"Is something amusing you, Mr. Jones?" Gil said frostily.

"No." That sure wiped the smile off his face. Gil had clearly got him here just to exact some kind of sadistic revenge. Dangle the juicy carrot and then snatch it away. "I'm sorry."

"Perhaps you'd like to read for us."

Tavis nodded. His mouth was as dry as the Mojave Desert. His agent's words reverberated in his head. *Don't fuck up! Don't fuck up! Don't fuck up!*

"I'll feed you the lines," Toby Portman said, his glance shifting from man to man. "We'll take it from page one hundred. The restaurant scene."

"I got it," Tavis said, flicking through the script and sounding a lot more nervous than he would have liked.

Gil made a steeple with his hands and leaned on his desk, staring at Tavis.

"I'll take it from the top." Toby Portman started to read. " 'I know that you love her. Do you think I'm blind?' "

Oh no. This was a great way to start. Tavis glanced nervously at Gil. Maybe he should ask for another section; this just seemed too loaded. But then that would be unprofessional, and he was here to show that he was up to the job. Gil would know that. He was a professional too. Wasn't he? The producer's face was impassive as he watched and listened. " 'No. You should know better.' "

" 'You're always there for her. Just at the right time.' "

" 'Maybe you should try it yourself.' " Tavis licked his lips.

" 'Or maybe you should try butting out.' "

" 'S . . . Christie and I go back a long way.' " My God, he'd nearly said *Sadie*. " 'We're friends, man. Nothing more. Romantically, she doesn't know I exist.' " The words were starting to stick in his throat. " 'Maybe you should look after her better.' "

" 'Or what?' "

Gil's face was darkening by the minute, but his expression remained unmoved. Tavis hesitated.

Toby glanced up. "You okay?"

Tavis nodded.

"I'll take over," Gil said and he slowly turned the pages until he reached the appropriate scene. He looked levelly at Tavis. " 'I want you out of her life. I don't care how you do it. I never want *Christie* to see you again.' "

Tavis could hear his own heartbeat. "I can't do that," he said evenly.

Toby Portman flicked frantically through his pages. "Is that in the script?"

Gil tossed his script to one side. "I've heard enough," he said. "Thanks for coming." He stood up to indicate that the reading was over.

Toby Portman glanced at the producer, surprised. "We're finished?"

"I think so," Gil said firmly.

It was clear to Tavis that he was being dismissed. This was so unfair. It was so unfair as to be cruel. Gil had to know the situation between him and Sadie. He couldn't take that out on him in an audition. This was his life. His one big chance. He'd played it nothing but straight with Sadie, while Gil had been stringing her along since the moment she'd landed in LA.

Tavis stood up. Bile was rising in his throat. He should be able to take this—he'd stood in enough lines for hours on end at open castings that had ended in abrupt dismissal because his eyes were the wrong color or he was an inch too short. He should be able to take it. Rejection was a part of the job. If you can't take the heat, he told himself, you shouldn't be in the goddam kitchen. He could feel his hands bunching into fists. He tried to take his mind back to his acting classes, get his breath and his temper under control. The difference was, this time the rejection wasn't because he was the wrong shape, size or color—it was personal. It was because this man suspected that he was in love with Sadie.

"This is unprofessional, man," Tavis said to Gil, despite all his best instincts telling him not to.

"Thank you for your opinion, Mr. Jones," Gil said coolly. "Now get out."

Toby Portman was searching furiously through his script. Tavis walked toward the door and then thought better of it. He wheeled on Gil.

"You treat her like shit," he said. "You don't deserve her. What the hell are you playing at?"

"That is none of your business!"

"You've made it my business," Tavis said.

"Get out of here," Gil repeated. "Then get out of my life and out of Sadie's life."

Tavis squared up to the producer. "Make me!"

Toby Portman scratched his head. "What page are we on?"

Gil lunged toward Tavis and grabbed him by the shirt.

"She is one hell of a woman," Tavis said. "And if you can't see that, I certainly can." Gil was shaking him.

"Improvisation," the director shouted. "This is great. Keep going!"

Tavis swung Gil round by the lapels of his jacket while the producer flailed at him. Tavis drew back his arm. He hadn't punched anyone since kindergarten and it wasn't a great idea to resume his pugilist career on movie producers, but he was too far in now. "What are you afraid of, Gil? You're hanging onto that drunken wife of yours like a security blanket. Keep doing that and you'll lose her anyway."

Gil stopped in his tracks. "You're right."

Tavis dropped his arm.

Gil leaned back on his desk, breathing heavily. "You're right." He put his head in his hands. "You're absolutely right," he said, looking directly at Tavis. He wiped his hand across his mouth. "But I'll still make sure that you never work in this town again."

Tavis threw down his script and headed for the door.

As he reached it, Gil shouted to him. "Tavis," he said, "I'm not an idiot. I can tell that you love Sadie too. I might be hiding behind my wife, but what's your excuse?"

Without answering Tavis marched out of the door and slammed it behind him. The row of assistants stared up as he stomped out of the office.

Gil was still leaning against the desk, but his composure was slowly returning.

"That wasn't improvisation, was it?" Toby Portman asked tentatively.

"No," Gil said. "It wasn't."

"He's damn good though."

"Yes."

"He would have been perfect for the part," Toby said.

"Yes," Gil said with a humorless laugh. "He would have been."

Outside in the sunshine, Tavis leaned against the wall of the building, panting and snorting like some knackered old bull. The sun was still shining. The palm trees were still waving in the breeze, but something inside him somewhere had shifted. Jeez, what was he thinking of? He'd nearly punched a Hollywood producer. A man who had the power to make the rest of his life a misery. If that wasn't a fuck-up, he didn't know what was.

Tavis shook his head, trying to dislodge the images replaying in his brain. It was only sheer willpower that kept him from falling to his knees in despair. What on earth was he thinking of? He put his hands over his eyes. Sadie. Quite simply, Sadie.

Seventy-seven

Gil waited on the porch outside Daniella's house. He hoped Sadie had forgiven him, because he felt he'd done enough fighting for today. Maybe he should go and get a vitamin shot to give him a much-needed boost of energy.

Just as he was thinking of ringing the bell again, Daniella opened the door.

"Hey, Daniella," Gil said.

"Gil—hi. Come on in." Daniella stood aside while he went into her home.

There was a mess of papers strewn all over the kitchen table, almost obliterating a well-worn laptop. "I'm interrupting your work," Gil said.

"No, not at all." Daniella shook her head. "I'm glad of the break. I have writer's block," she explained. "I get it at least five times a day and it can only be cured by an excess of coffee and calories. Want some?"

"Sure." Gil nodded and wandered over to the table. He liked Daniella. She seemed sweet and uncomplicated—but then he was also the worst judge of women he knew.

The pages of a script with scribbles all over them were piled high. He slipped into her seat.

Daniella poured the coffee. "Cream and sugar?"

"Black's good," he said distractedly as, out of habit, he scanned the pages.

"You look like you need this," Sadie's friend remarked as she passed him the coffee.

"I'm not having a great day," Gil said. He didn't feel like going into the details of his fight with Sadie and his subsequent fight with Tavis.

"Sadie said you guys had a fight," Daniella said.

Gil's head snapped up to look at her.

"Hey," Daniella said. "We're buddies. She tells me everything."

"I came to see if I can make it up to her," he admitted sheepishly.

"Sadie's not home right now."

"Oh. I saw Delores parked outside."

"She was misbehaving this morning. Sadie said she couldn't persuade her to start, so she walked to the office." They exchanged a horrified look. "We'll never make a Californian of her."

"I hope we will," Gil said.

"You need to tell *her* that," Daniella suggested. "Not me."

Gil's eyes made another involuntary scan over the script. Mmm. It wasn't bad.

He flicked over a few more pages. "This is interesting," he said.

Daniella pulled up another chair. "You think so?"

"Mmm. How far have you gotten with it?"

Daniella inched closer to him. "I've finished the first draft and now I'm agonizing over the second."

Gil sipped his coffee without taking his eyes off the script.

"We need cookies," Daniella said. "Lots of them."

"Daniella," Gil said with a sigh, "you're a woman." That much he could work out. "You know about these things. Why can't I get it right with her?"

"You really wanna know?"

Gil nodded and helped himself to a cookie.

"There are too many women in your life, Gil. Ditch a couple. One in particular would be a good start."

"But I only love Sadie."

"Maybe it doesn't feel like that from her side."

"Gina needs me." Gil puffed out a breath. "I can't abandon her."

"Sometimes you have to be cruel to be kind," Daniella said. "Gina has to learn to stand on her own two feet."

"This is good," he said.

"The cookie, the script or the advice?"

"All of them," he answered with a smile. He spread the pages out before him. "Can I take it?"

"Only if you take the advice too."

"I'll read this as soon as I can," Gil said. "I think you have something here."

"Really? You're not bullshitting me?"

"Why would I?"

"Because you're a male of the species and a movie producer. I'm naturally suspicious of both."

Gil held up his hands. "No strings, I promise," he said. "I'll take a look and if I like the rest of it as much as I like the first few pages we'll go from there."

"Thanks, Gil," Daniella said, suddenly looking shy. "I appreciate it. This means a lot to me."

He walked toward the door. "Tell Sadie I came over. Maybe she could drop by tonight—if she doesn't have another engagement."

"How can she drop by? She doesn't have a car," Daniella reminded him.

"I could get Delores fixed up for her," Gil said, a spark of excitement in his eyes. "She'd like that."

"She'd love it," Daniella agreed.

"I'll do that," he said. "I'll get the garage to come and get it—*her*—later."

"Don't mess this up, Gil," Daniella warned.

"I won't," he assured her. "I'll make sure they do a great job."

"I wasn't talking about the car," Daniella said with a shake of her head. "I wasn't talking about the car."

Seventy-eight

I'm in a quandary—but then that's nothing new. I'm in my bed-room at Daniella's house lying flat out on the bed, and Alice, my lovely, long-lost friend from London, is on the other end of the phone. I love our girly chats, and I realize just how much I've missed her. I feel as if I've been away for ages.

I'm chewing my nails. "They want me back?" It bears repeating. And I have done so. Several times.

"I think you'd be mad to consider it," Alice says. She's not to know that my sanity has definitely been skewed since I got here.

"I don't know." I sound so pathetic.

"You don't know?" she echoes incredulously. "Why would you want to swap sun-kissed California for soggy old London?"

"Ooo, I don't know." I think it's just the fact that someone—*anyone*—wants me that's turning my head.

"Don't even think about it," my friend instructs.

"If you don't want me to think about it, why did you ring me up and tell me they want me back?"

"Because I thought you'd go, 'Ha!' and tell them to shove it where the sun doesn't shine."

"Ooo," I say again. "I don't know."

"Has all that California sun shrunk your brain?" my friend wants to know.

I think it probably has, but not for the same reasons that Alice may think. The job she's talking about is my "real" job. My real job back in the City with stocks and shares and all the other things I used to know about, with real money and real long hours. Not a job that involves giving out leaflets or serving drinks to drunken teenagers or trying to make actors' bottoms famous.

I'd get a real salary—a big one. Even more if I play hard to get. Hard to get? Who am I kidding? I've always been too biddable. But it would mean that I could stop living a hand-to-mouth existence and shop again. I have another nail nibble. "How much do they want me back?"

"They're begging you to go back," she says.

"That's nice."

"Nice?" I hear her tut. Loudly. "You seem to forget these are the same people who sacked you without a second thought."

"They're obviously regretting it," I suggest.

"Let them," Alice advises. "I hope they can't get anyone decent to work for them and that the whole company collapses."

I hoped so too, when I left—was forcibly ejected—but it never happens, does it? Life trundles on as it always does, with the bad guys winning and the good dying young.

"I'm missing London," I say. I can feel tears welling up inside me. "I'm missing everyone."

"No you're not," Alice says in her sternest voice. "And no one's missing you. They all forgot about you the minute you'd gone." She's about to start crying too. "I'll come out on holiday for a few weeks," she offers. "That'll make you feel better."

"You haven't got any money."

"I'll sacrifice my lounge carpet for you."

That is a true sign of friendship. I know how long Alice has been saving up for her lounge carpet and it makes me wail more.

"Don't do this, Sadie," she says. "I wish I'd never phoned. Stay and make it work."

"You're right," I say. "I know you're right."

"You could have a really good life out there." She's talking to me like I'm a clingy toddler. "Don't throw it away."

"No."

"How's Gil?" she says when I've stopped sniffling.

Not talking to me. "He's fine."

I'm not sure whether I'm pleased that he's taken Delores to get fixed as Daniella said or whether, as I suspect, he's actually repossessed her as he's technically the owner. Daniella thinks Gil is a warm and deeply desirable man, but I think that might have more to do with the fact that he thinks she could be the next hot-shot screenwriter than anything remotely objective about his suitability for me as a life partner. And, anyway, she's been hanging on to some crusty old Mad Movie Mogul for the past decade so I'm not sure that I trust her judgment either. She struggles with the fact that her man had one wife while glibly overlooking the fact that mine has had *two*.

"Look, there you are," Alice says encouragingly. "You've got a lovely man and a lovely life."

I've not. My life is like a broken vending machine—I keep pushing money in, but nothing comes out at the other end.

"Promise me you won't do anything silly?"

"Like flinging myself off the Hollywood sign?"

"No, like rushing back to take this crap job just because they've clicked their fingers."

I wipe my nose on my sleeve. "I wouldn't dream of it."

Seventy-nine

"I'm going home," I say to Bay.

"Home?" she echoes. "I take it you mean London home and not round-the-corner-to-Larchmont home."

I shake my head—or should I nod? "I've got a great job offer back in London," I say. "A *fabulous* job offer." I sound as if I'm saying this to convince myself rather than Bay. "I'd be a fool to turn it down."

"You'd be a fool to go back," Bay says, bosom heaving beneath her snakeskin Lycra.

"I don't want to get you into trouble with the IRS," I say. "I have to go."

"What about Gil?" Bay says.

"What about Tavis?" Min says.

"What about me?" I say.

Bay flounces about the office. "We can't allow this," she says. "You've only just got here. You're one of the family. I'll give you a pay rise."

"I don't want a pay rise."

"I do," Min says.

"This is a great opportunity," I say.

"What?" Bay snorts. "Working in some sweatshop office in the City? A crap Labor government, high taxes, dirty streets, getting mugged for a mobile phone, NHS hospitals where you're more likely to come out dead than cured?"

"I think that's a slightly biased view."

"You have a great opportunity here," Bay insists. "I'll retire," she offers. "You can run the office. Can't she, Min?"

"Okay by me," Min says graciously.

"You can't do that," I say. "You don't want to retire."

"Honey," she says in her best West Coast accent, "I have a toy boy fifteen years my junior. I can find *plenty* to fill my days."

I get a vision of Bay in her lurid Lycra ensemble in years to come as a Rollerblading geriatric.

"I can't stay here." I can hear myself weakening. "I keep forgetting to put sun cream on. My face will turn into a raisin."

"Get Botoxed," Bay says.

"A major earthquake is overdue by about forty years," I point out. "It could happen any day."

"And you could get hit by a London bus crossing the road in Kensington," Bay counters.

"Oh, that old chestnut." I admit that I always wear nice underwear in case I get hit by a bus, but how do you prepare for a disaster on the scale of an earthquake? I have no idea. Clearly I'm not meant to live here.

"You have two men in love with you," Min says. "That must be more than at home."

"Two men in love with me?" I'm struggling to think of one.

They both look at me open-mouthed.

"What?"

"Tavis is besotted with you," they say in unison.

"Tavis?" I can't help but laugh. "Tavis is gay."

"If Tavis is gay, then I'll eat my own leggings," Bay says decisively.

"My mind's made up," I say. "Nothing can persuade me otherwise." I bite my lips in case they foolishly think about quivering again. "London, here I come."

Eighty

"I'm going home," I tell Daniella.

"You are insanity itself," Daniella declares. She looks like she's about to stamp her foot.

"Don't go, Aunt Sadie." Alexis's chin is trembling.

"I have to, sweetheart." She starts to cry into Princess Sparkle Barbie's nylon hair and I feel like the biggest heel in the world.

"Now look what you're doing," Daniella says, cuddling her daughter. "You're breaking all of our hearts."

"I've booked my ticket," I say lamely.

"Fine," Daniella says. "Then there's no talking to you."

"I'm sorry." I can feel myself cringing. "I haven't told him yet."

"And are you planning to?"

"Eventually."

"And when is this ticket booked for?"

"Tomorrow."

"So 'eventually' will be when?"

"I think I might just leave him a note," I mumble.

"What has he done to deserve that?"

"Had more wives than he admitted to. Left me in a cupboard at the Oscars party."

"I think you're focusing on the negatives in this situation," Daniella says, in a very California way. "These are very small misdemeanors in the scheme of things."

They may seem like small misdemeanors to Daniella, but to me the whole thing just feels like bloody hard work. Should love be like that?

And I guess, to be truthful, it's starting to niggle at me that I have a much better time with Tavis than I do with Gil. We don't fight, we don't fall out, we don't have to creep round other people's feelings all the time. And he's a very good snogger—even if it *was* acting. I know that I would be hopelessly in love with that man if there was any point and Mr. Lovely-but-Hard-Work Gil could take a running jump. Surely there must be straight men out there like that? Just one would do.

"You know that this is running away, don't you?"

"Of course I do."

"Stay and sort this out with Gil," Daniella begs. "He adores you. Just because he's a jackass who can't get his act together doesn't mean that he doesn't love you."

"Thank you for those encouraging words." I smile when I want to cry. "I need to go for a walk."

"You'll get mugged."

Right now the thought of getting hit on the head with a hammer by someone doesn't seem like such an unpleasant prospect—it might even do me some good. "I'm going to tell Tavis."

Daniella's eyebrows rise. "Tavis—but not Gil. You don't think this might be significant?"

"I don't have a car," I point out, "and Tavis is working just around the corner. I can walk to Tavis."

"You're conveniently forgetting the miracle of telephone communication," Daniella says.

"Yes."

"I like Tavis a lot," Alexis pipes up. She is sucking Princess Sparkle Barbie's foot in contemplation.

"So do I," I say.

"But I like Gil a lot too."

"I think Alexis might have summed up the problem," Daniella suggests.

And although it pains me to admit it, I think she might have too.

Eighty-one

Zorba's is packed to the rafters. I can tell as I approach the restaurant that Tavis isn't going to have a lot of time for meaningful conversation. And sure enough, he's whizzing out of the door, arms stacked with plates of salad and grilled lamb and all things Greek. He distributes his dishes with a smile and a cheery comment for everyone and my heart goes out to him because I know that he is destined for so much more than this. I stand and watch him unobserved and I can't begin to articulate how I feel about him. *Oh bollocks,* is how I feel.

As he turns to head back toward the kitchen, I catch his eye. "Hey," he says. "What are you doing here?"

"I came to find out how the audition went."

His mouth twists into a bad shape. "I'm trying to remain positive about the experience," Tavis says.

"Which means?"

"That I didn't actually punch Gil."

"Oh dear."

"Oh dear indeed," Tavis says mimicking my accent.

"I was worried to death for you," I say. "When I realized that your audition was with Gil, I didn't know what to say. I guess he's not your number-one fan."

"I don't know why that is," Tavis says.

There's a moment when all the restaurant disappears, all the chatter stops, the stream of traffic looking for parking meters on Larchmont fades away and there is just Tavis and me. "Maybe it's because I am."

We look at each other. The moon is hanging high over the Hollywood sign. This is a Romeo-and-Juliet moment. I'm dying inside and I don't know why. Tavis takes a step toward me.

"Sadie . . ."

"Waiter!"

The noise comes back. "Right with you," Tavis says brightly. "We can't talk now," he says to me.

"I just have one more thing to say," I tell Tavis.

He looks like he really doesn't want to hear it.

"It's important," I add. I can feel that I'm shuffling my feet. "I've decided to go home."

"Hey, waiter!"

"Home?"

"To London," I clarify. "Real home. Tomorrow."

"You can't do this," Tavis says.

"There's nothing here for me," I say sadly.

"That's not true!" Tavis looks panic-stricken.

"I can't live on dreams and make-believe, Tavis. I need stability and commitment—all those things. I can't go where the wind blows me. I can't do one thing while dreaming about another. I'm too earthed."

"What does a fella have to do to get some more wine?" Tavis's customer yells.

"I have to go," Tavis says. "We need to talk about this. I'll come by the house when I finish my shift. It'll be late."

I shake my head. "I have too much to do, Tavis. I have to pack."

"We can't say goodbye like this," he pleads. "Let me take you to the airport."

"I don't know . . ." I've never been one for goodbyes.

"There are things I want to say." Tavis looks distraught.

"Like what?"

He rakes his hair. "I don't know," he says. "I need time to think about them."

"I have to leave the house around noon," I say. "Don't be late."

"I won't," he promises.

I turn to leave and give him a wave.

"Sadie . . ." Tavis's shoulders sag. "Think very carefully about this."

"I've been thinking about nothing else," I say—and I'm going to be thinking about it for the rest of the night too.

Eighty-two

Delores was barely recognizable. Gil stood in awe looking at her sleek, shining curves. "Wow," was all he could manage to say.

The garage had worked flat out on her through the night. She'd been stripped down, sorted out and spruced up to the nth degree. The rust was gone, the chrome sparkled and all of the mechanics were in working order. Even he had to admit that it was a far cry from the car he'd brought in. Gil winced as he handed over his credit card. The labor charges alone would have paid for a new Mercedes. But what the hell, this former heap of junk was Sadie's baby, and if it made her happy, then it was money well spent.

"I appreciate it," Gil said to the garage owner.

"No trouble, Mr. McGann. Anytime."

This was the same body shop that had repaired Gina's crumpled cars times too numerous to count. Gil's business had probably gone a long way to providing the man's pool home in the Hollywood Hills, so it was no wonder that they'd managed to pull out all the stops for Delores.

Gil checked his watch. It was nearly lunchtime and too late to take the car to Daniella's house, but he could go by Double Take and maybe let Sadie take her out for a spin on her lunch hour. He jumped in the car and headed off through the bustling traffic toward Wilshire Boulevard. He'd spent a long and sleepless night worrying about Sadie, Delores, Gina and Katherine. In the end he'd got up and read Daniella's script. Maybe Sadie's friend was right—there were too many women in his life. Even if one of them was a car. By the time dawn struggled through the curtains, he'd decided what he was going to do. One was to buy Daniella's script. The second was to ask Sadie to marry him.

*   *   *

Bay and Min exchanged nervous glances. "She's left," Bay said, licking her lips nervously.

"What do you mean, 'She's left'? " Gil said. "Did you fire her?"

"Of course not, you stupid man," Bay barked. "I wanted her to stay. It's a shame *you* didn't."

"Stay?"

"She's going back to London."

Gil felt as if he were in one of those horror films where suddenly all the world goes fractured and out of focus. "Sadie is?"

"You're supposed to be her boyfriend," Bay said. "Shouldn't you know these things?"

"She's said nothing." Gil could feel himself going hollow.

"She's leaving today."

"I've got to stop her," he said.

"Good luck," Bay said. "We both had a go and failed."

Gil headed toward the door. It were as if he were drunk and stumbling. Out on the pavement, the world was still the same. The car drivers were still impatient, the sun was still golden, the sky was still blue. But inside everything had changed. Gil could feel himself sweating. He fumbled for his cell phone, and pulling it from his pocket, he punched in Sadie's number. It went straight to voice mail. He'd go over to Daniella's right now. She must be still there. He didn't often pray to God, but he was prepared to give it a chance and pray that she hadn't left yet.

He jumped into Delores and eased her smooth, new, non-clonking transmission into gear. Before he could pull away from the parking lot, his cell phone rang. Maybe it was Sadie returning his call.

"Sadie!" Gil said as he snatched it up and answered the phone.

"No." The voice was slurred and he knew instantly who it was. "It's me."

"Gina," Gil said. "Not now. I've something very important to do."

"Noah has left me," Gina sobbed. "He threw my clothes in the pool. All my favorite clothes."

"No, Gina," Gil said. "I can't buy this now. Take a cab to the house. Get Maria to make you some coffee—strong coffee—and maybe a little something to eat . . ."

"I need you, Gil." Her voice veered between hysterical and sleepy. "I've only ever needed you."

"Go to the house. Do some yoga. I'll be back later."

"No one loves me," Gina wailed.

"They do," Gil said. "We all love you." One-handed he managed to pull out into the traffic. "I'll talk to Noah later. I'll talk to you both."

"I'm feeling all funny, Gil."

"Oh no!" Gil slammed the steering wheel. "Don't do this to me!"

"I'm so sleepy."

"Gina," Gil tried to stay calm. "What have you taken?"

"I don't know." She was sounding fuzzy around the edges.

"Have you taken something? Gina! Have you taken something?"

"Mmm-hmm," Gina sighed.

"Oh shit," Gil said. "Where are you? Gina! Where are you?" There was no reply from his wife bar weary sighs traveling down the phone line. "Are you at Noah's?"

"Mmm-hmm," Gina murmured. "Pool house . . ." and the line went dead.

Gil threw the phone on the passenger seat, floored Delores's throttle and headed up toward Beverly Hills and Noah's house. He patted Delores's steering wheel. "Come on, old girl. Show me what you can do," he said. "This is an emergency."

Eighty-three

Tavis paced up and down on the roof terrace of their apartment building. Joe, resplendent in an open Hawaiian shirt and reclining on a sun lounger, lifted one slice of cucumber from his eye.

"So what are you going to do?"

"I don't know," Tavis said, trying to control his breathing. "I'm thinking."

"Well, think quicker," Joe advized. "You're running out of time."

"Don't you think I know that?" Tavis snapped. "I don't know what to do. I don't know what to say." He looked at Joe, stricken. "What shall I do?"

"Man," Joe said with a sigh, "I am the last person to ask."

The phone rang. Tavis and Joe stared at it. "Maybe she's changed her mind," Tavis said hopefully.

"Yeah," Joe agreed. "And maybe Steven Spielberg wants you to replace Harrison Ford as the next Indiana Jones." Joe eased himself from the sun lounger, picking up the script which had fallen to the ground as he did so. "I'll answer in case it is Steven. You sound too hysterical." His friend answered the call. "Hi, Tavis Jones's residence."

Tavis made a face.

Joe covered the mouthpiece. "Next best thing," he whispered. "It's Toby Portman for you."

Tavis smoothed his hair and took the phone. "Hi."

Joe wrapped his arms round Tavis and pressed his ear to the phone too. Tavis tried without success to shoo him away.

"Hi, Tavis," Toby said. "Can you come down to my office?"

"Sure." Tavis could hear his heart beating. This couldn't be bad news. If Toby Portman even wanted to be in the same room with him again, this had to be good.

"Within the hour?"

"Oh man," Tavis said as a sinking feeling hit his stomach. He was due to go and take Sadie to the airport. He'd promised her he would. There was no way he could let her down now. He had a vision of Sadie standing waiting for him with packed luggage. He saw his final chance to say the things he thought he needed to say but which wouldn't formulate in his brain. "I can't be there. I have something really important to do."

There was a pause at the end of the line. Toby Portman clearly wasn't a man who was used to struggling actors saying no to him. "More important than kick-starting your movie career?"

"More important to me than anything," Tavis said.

"Then I'll get my office to call you with a more convenient appointment," Toby Portman said. But as Tavis hung up the phone he guessed that he probably wouldn't hear from Toby Portman again. It was one thing being marked down as difficult if you were Russell Crowe or Jack Nicholson, but who'd want to start out with a difficult Tavis Jones?

"More important than *anything*?" Joe said incredulously. "That's quite a statement."

"I guess it is." Tavis sighed.

"You realize you just turned down a meeting with Toby Portman for a woman?"

"I do," Tavis said.

"Are you insane?"

"Yes," Tavis said. "Or in love."

"It's the same thing," Joe said dismissively. He started fanning himself with the pages of his script. "You should be the one having an attack of the vapors."

"I'm fine. I'm cool," Tavis said. "There'll be other movies."

"There'll be other movies!" Joe fell back on his sun lounger, overcome with hysteria. "There'll be other movies!"

The sinking feeling wasn't about to leave Tavis's digestive system alone. "It's no big deal."

"No big deal!" Joe was squealing. "You've waited years for this! Years! Didn't you give women up because of this? What happened to single-minded Mr. Single?"

Tavis was beginning to wonder that himself.

"Jeez," Joe said, loosening his shirt even more so that the air could get to him. "You've lost your mind."

But Tavis knew that it wasn't his mind he'd lost, it was his heart—altogether a much more delicate organ.

Eighty-four

Daniella is standing at my bedroom door. Her arms are folded and her lip is wobbling. "You've got everything?"

"Yeah." I glance toward the suitcase I've had to borrow from my friend, because—what seems like a million years ago now—my own was stolen the night I arrived. "Daniella . . ."

"Don't get all sentimental," she says. "I'm going to cry."

"I just wanted to say—"

"Stop it," she instructs. "Stop it right now. We've had a fabulous time. We've become great friends. My child and my mother adore you. You've been a marvelous housemate—except for your annoying habit of being able to eat whatever you like and not put on weight. And now you're going to spoil it all by going home."

I cross the room and give her a big hug. "That's exactly what I was going to say."

"I hate the English," Daniella says with enthusiasm, "with your stiff upper lip and your 'jolly good, old sport.' You're so unemotional."

"I'm not unemotional," I say. "I'm trying to hold it all in."

"Why?" Daniella wants to know. "It's much better out all over the carpet. In ten years' time you'll get cancer or arthritis from holding all that pain inside."

"That's a very comforting thought."

"Let's change the subject," Daniella suggests. "I can't deal with this."

I hand an envelope to her. "I've written a letter to Gil," I say. "Will you give it to him for me?"

"This is exactly what I mean," she rails. "You should have

called him. What does the letter say? 'Terribly sorry, old sport. Have fucked off home to Blighty. Bad luck, what?' "

"That's unfair."

"Running out on Gil is unfair."

"I've tried his cell phone," I say. "Several times. There's no reply."

That leaves Daniella at a loss for words.

"I've put the spare set of keys for Delores in with it."

"Great," Daniella says. "That should double her value."

My eyes start to well up with tears and I press my lips together until I can feel them going numb. Daniella crumbles. "I don't want to fight."

"I'm not fighting," I point out. "You're saying mean things to provoke me into caving in and staying."

"Is that such a bad idea?" Daniella asks.

At this moment I don't know. I have no idea what the hell I'm doing or why, in fact, I'm doing it.

"Tavis should be here soon," I say.

"Good," Daniella says and she lifts my case and carries it into the sitting room while I trail obediently behind her. "I'll tell you something to cheer you up while you wait. If Gil likes this script as much as he says, then I'm on my way. I'm going to be a famous Hollywood scriptwriter and a woman of independent means. Then I can be free of the Mad Movie Mogul and find a nice man. Preferably much younger."

"You've worked hard for it, and I really, really hope that you succeed."

"I promise I'll bring him to visit you in London. I've never been to Europe."

"Well," I say, "it's about time that you did."

A car pulls up outside and we both crane our necks. "Tavis," Daniella says. And sure enough my Romeo is leaping out of his car and sprinting up the path to Daniella's door. My heart does a very passable impersonation of love again and gives a strange little twist at the thought that this might be the last time I see him.

"Let's hit the grit, sister," my friend says and heaves my case up. She opens the door to Tavis and dumps my case at his feet. He looks at it with a hint of disappointment in his eyes.

"Hi," he says. Tavis looks very scrubbed and polished and vaguely smart. I wonder if he's going somewhere important after he's dropped me at the airport. "I thought you might have changed your mind."

"No."

The disappointment spreads to the rest of his face, and I can't believe I'm doing this to my friends. Friends who looked after me so readily when I landed here as a penniless orphan.

Just then, another car pulls up outside Daniella's home—a huge black beast of a Mercedes that's probably a top-of-the-range one, stretched way beyond its normal measurements and fit for a Mafia don or First Division footballer. For one mad moment everything inside me surges as I think it might just be Gil. But it isn't. Out of the titanic car gets a short, fat, bald man. Despite the brain-scorching heat he's wearing a black rollneck sweater and a fluffy wool jacket and white loafers. In the middle of his chest hangs a gold medallion the likes of which I haven't seen since the 1980s.

"Good grief," I breathe as recognition hits in. He's much older than I imagined, and I can't begin to think what Daniella sees in him. But then money and power are potent aphrodisiacs, and beauty is only a light switch away. I turn to my friend, who has gone into a state of suspended animation. So this is the Mad Movie Mogul.

"What's *he* doing here?" Daniella hisses at me.

How should I know? "Maybe he's come to see if you've got a future together now that you know he's free," I suggest.

"I've longed for this moment, Sadie," she says under her breath. "And now that it's here, I don't know what to do." She looks at me with wide eyes that say *help me.*

"You said you wanted to be free of him, Daniella."

"I did, didn't I?" she says.

Tavis's jaw is trailing on the floor as he clearly recognizes who the Mad Movie Mogul is. He looks like he might prostrate himself at his feet.

"I'll have to get rid of him," Daniella mutters.

"Look," I say, "I hate goodbyes. Let Tavis take me to the airport. You stay here and sort out your future."

The Mad Movie Mogul arrives in front of us. "Hi," he says. "Daniella."

Daniella nods.

"You must be Sadie," he says and takes my hand. "I hope we'll be seeing a lot more of each other."

"Sadie's going home," Daniella says. "Tavis is just taking her to the airport."

The Mad Movie Mogul runs a critical eye over Tavis. "You're a fine-looking young man," he concludes. "You an actor?"

Tavis, still rendered speechless, nods.

Three Ms hands Tavis a gold-edged card. "Call my office," he says. Tavis nearly faints.

Now the Mad Movie Mogul is standing in front of Daniella. Despite his advancing years, charisma emanates from him. "I've been calling you," he says.

"And I've not been returning them," Daniella says.

As much as I'd like to be a fly on the wall for this conversation, time is marching on. "I have to go," I say to Daniella.

She gives me a hug. "I love you," she says. "You are completely and utterly wrong to leave. Isn't she, Tavis?"

"Yes," Tavis says with what sounds like a heartfelt sigh.

Daniella lets go of me and we exchange a kiss. "Keep in touch," she says, wiping away a tear.

"Come and see me soon."

"I will." She sniffs.

A taxi pulls up behind the Mad Movie Mogul's Mercedes with a screech of brakes, and for a brief moment I wonder whether it might be Gil, without wondering what he'd be doing in a taxi. The driver gets out and it's my Armenian robber who stole my suitcase on the first night. He walks toward us with it in his meaty hand, rendering me speechless. The case is dumped at my feet. "Mistake," he mutters in a thick accent. "I find you."

"You didn't rob me," I say. "You drove away with my case by mistake? And now you've tracked me down?"

The driver looks blank. "Armenian," he says.

I fumble in my purse for the biggest tip I can manage and hand it over. "Thanks. Thank you," I mumble.

With a curt nod, the Armenian cab driver pockets it and marches off.

"So this is closure," Daniella says with another sniff.

"I guess so." My manky clothes have come back so that I can restart my manky life. What comes around goes around. "Have these," I say to Daniella and push the case I borrowed from her filled with my designer clothes toward her. "I'm not going to need strappy tops in London."

"I'll keep them," she says, "but only in the hope that one day you'll come back for them."

I kiss Daniella again. "I'd better get going."

"Ready then?" Tavis says to me.

"As I'll ever be."

He picks up my battered old case. "Your chariot awaits."

"Thanks." Tavis and I exchange a rather sad, sickly grin and he throws my luggage into the back of his car. I'm really looking forward to going back to London and I'm sure that this is absolutely the right decision. Isn't it?

Eighty-five

Gina's eyes rolled back into her head. She was limp in Gil's arms and he shook her gently. He'd found her in Noah's pool house as she had said, slumped half on, half off one of the sun loungers. Her forehead was soaked with sweat and she was as white as a sheet. "Stay with me," he said, forcing her to look at him. "Open your eyes."

Gina struggled to comply.

"Come on, baby," he urged. "Don't go to sleep. Help is on its way."

He'd called the paramedics from the car and he was sure they'd be here any minute. All Gina had to do was hang on. She'd be fine. He was sure she'd be fine. His wife had gone this far before and she'd always pulled through. He just hoped that this time she hadn't pushed her luck once too often.

Gil glanced round the magnificent pool house and out toward the palatial mansion that had belonged to a string of beleaguered film stars. The sun sparkled on the still blue water of the pool that Noah had recently refurbished with a mosaic of BORN TO PARTY on the bottom. The palm trees swayed in the breeze, parakeets chattered in the trees, thousands of dollars' worth of red geraniums were grouped in ancient Turkish oil jars. It was an idyllic location, but it wouldn't be the first time someone had overdosed in this place. If anyone questioned the old adage that money couldn't buy you happiness they only had to come to Hollywood and look at the track record of the fabulously wealthy and famous.

Of Noah there was no sign.

The siren of the paramedics' ambulance announced their arrival and seconds later Gil heard their feet pounding across the handmade Italian terra-cotta tiles that bounded the pool area.

"They're here, baby," Gil murmured softly, stroking her hair. "Hang on. Just a little while longer."

"I'm sorry, Gil," she gasped.

The paramedics ran into the pool house and took Gina from his arms.

"Do you know what she's taken?"

Gil handed over the empty plastic pill container. It was white—the same flat color as Gina's skin. "And some booze too." He flicked his gaze toward a discarded bottle of vodka.

"We're gonna take you to the hospital, ma'am," the man said. They put an oxygen mask over Gina's face and loaded her onto a stretcher while Gil stood and looked on helplessly.

Gina reached for his hand and squeezed it with the strength of a child. "I won't do it again," she whispered. "Not ever."

As they wheeled her toward the waiting ambulance, he hoped that they'd be able to get her to the hospital in time and that those words wouldn't come back to haunt him.

Eighty-six

The journey to LAX is interminable. Tavis is driving so slowly that I'm not sure we'll ever get there at all. All the other traffic on La Cienega is whizzing gaily past us. We've hardly spoken a word and Tavis seems fixated by the tarmac. I just want to get there as I'm actually feeling physical pain at doing this.

As we get to the airport and the soaring concrete archway at the front of the terminal becomes visible, Tavis suddenly blurts out, "I wish you weren't going home."

I don't want to admit that I feel the same way too. "I have to," I say. "My relationship with Gil isn't going anywhere. I need to get out. This is the only way."

Tavis clears his throat. "There are other men in LA," he says. "Not many of them who aren't gay or insane," he continues, "but there are some."

"I only need one."

"Sadie . . ."

"Tavis . . ."

We both stop.

"You first," Tavis says.

"I think you're a wonderful bloke." I'm stammering and it isn't particularly attractive. I don't know where the eloquence of my Juliet performance has gone. "A really wonderful bloke."

Tavis looks bashful.

"And I did wonder . . . for a time . . . if I had feelings . . ." I glance over at him and his knuckles have tightened on the steering wheel. "I did wonder . . . if I had feelings for you."

"Sadie . . ."

I put my hand up to stop him. "I know what you're going to say."

"Do you?"

"Yes," I say firmly. "And I know that it's stupid to feel like that. I understand completely where you're coming from. I'm fine with that. Really. It's ridiculous to think that we could ever have had a . . . a . . ."

"Relationship?"

"A relationship," I confirm. "I know that you and I could never be anything more than just good friends."

"We couldn't?"

"No." I'm very clear about that now. I just wish it didn't hurt so much. "You're a very good friend," I say. "One of the best. And if you're ever in London I want you to ring me and we'll meet up and have dinner."

Tavis turns to me, despite the fact that we're swinging into the parking lot. "Have *dinner*?"

"Or something."

Tavis pulls into a parking space and he sits there for a moment staring out of the window. He takes a deep breath and turns to look at me. His eyes are so beautiful they'd make your heart stop.

"Sadie . . . Sadie . . ." then he reaches into the back seat for my case. "Let's go," he says, "before you miss your plane."

Eighty-seven

Gina had tubes everywhere and a monitor that sounded every beat of her heart with an irritating, tinny beep. Gil had never been so glad to hear anything so annoying in all his life.

The hospital room was white, stark and sterile. The shade was pulled down to block out the sun. It was like the hospital room in a movie. A nurse bustled round checking charts and drips and that Gina was comfortable.

His wife lay motionless on the bed, an oxygen mask covering her mouth. Her eyes were closed and her skin had gone from white to a pasty green.

"Is she going to be okay?" Gil said to the nurse.

"We're going to monitor her for a couple of days," she replied in a kindly voice that was perfect for a nurse. "She's a very lucky woman."

Lucky, Gil thought. Was Gina lucky? It was an odd choice of word to describe someone who had come back from the brink of death. And Gil wondered for the thousandth time why someone who could have so much and give so much would want to play Russian roulette with her life.

"She's out of danger?"

"We think so. Doctor will be in to see her later," the nurse said. "We're going to let her sleep for now. She'll be fine."

"She looks so pale."

"You don't look so hot yourself," the nurse said, offering him a gentle smile. "Why don't you go home and get some rest too?"

"I have things to do," Gil said.

"I'm sure they can wait," the nurse said.

"No," he said. "They can't."

"She doesn't know that you're here. Your wife will sleep for a while yet," she assured him. "You can slip away if you need to. I'll contact you as soon as she wakes."

"You promise?" Gil said. "The minute she opens her eyes?"

"I'll get right on the phone."

Gil scribbled down his cell phone number and handed it to the nurse. "Go on, now," she said. "Don't you worry."

He looked at Gina's face. She looked like Sleeping Beauty. Fragile and vulnerable. What was he going to do with her?

"I don't like to leave her," he said, and the sentence pulled him upright. Somehow it was always the same story.

Eighty-eight

"Ooo," I say. "That was quick."

Mercifully, there was no queue and I'm all checked in. We took so long getting here that now I'm very nearly late. My bag has gone off down the little chute, hopefully to reappear out of a similar one in London, Heathrow, a few cramped hours hence, and I'm clutching my boarding card.

Tavis still hasn't spoken.

"I'd better go through to the departure gate," I say.

He takes my arm and we walk toward the passport control desk. This is torture.

"I guess this is it," Tavis says.

I reach up and kiss him on the cheek. "I'm going to miss you," I say. And from nowhere, absolutely nowhere, tears spring to my eyes.

"Oh Sadie," Tavis says, and he folds me into his arms and pulls me against his chest. His lips are feathering my hair with kisses and as I look up to him, he kisses me full on the lips. A long, lingering kiss that brings the sensations of our steamy rendition of *Romeo and Juliet* flooding back.

"If things had been different," Tavis says as he holds me, "if *I'd* been different, I could have loved you, Sadie. I want you to know that."

I'm not sure if this makes me feel better or worse. I sniff my tears away. "I've got to go."

I ease myself away from Tavis's warm embrace. I think it's airports that engender this type of super-charged emotion. We hold hands, and I slip away from my dear, dear friend, our palms sliding away from each other until only our fingertips are touching.

Tavis is crying too. "I could have loved you very much."

I walk to the passport gate. "I could have loved you too."

I blow a kiss to Tavis and he stands looking so forlorn my heart is tearing in two. "Joe is a very lucky man," I say.

Tavis's eyes widen. The man glances at my passport and waves me through. Tavis rushes after me and we're separated by a panel of glass at head height.

Tavis jumps up. "Joe?" he says. "What's Joe got to do with this?"

I carry on walking toward the departure gate and Tavis keeps pace on the other side of the glass. We stop and stare at each other.

"What's Joe got to do with it?" he says again.

"Do I have to spell it out?"

"I think so," Tavis says.

"I hope that one day," I say, "I can find someone to love who's just like you."

Tavis still looks blank.

"Someone who's just like you—but who isn't . . ." How do you do "gay" with your hands?

"Who isn't . . . ?"

"Involved with someone else."

"Someone else?" Tavis says rather too loudly for my liking. Either side of our glass partition we seem to be gathering a crowd. "You think I'm involved with someone else?"

I lower my voice. "Someone else who isn't a man."

"A man?" Tavis says. "You think I'm involved with a man?" His eyes widen a bit more. There is the sound of a penny dropping from a great height. "You think I'm involved with *Joe*?"

The crowd are very interested by now.

"Yes," I say weakly.

"You think I'm gay!" Tavis is bellowing. "Oh my word! You think I'm gay!"

"Aren't you?" I wish there was a big hole that would swallow me up, but even though we're on a major earthquake fault and it had previously been my biggest terror, nothing seems to be so obliging.

"You think I'm Joe's *boyfriend*?" Tavis is pacing up and down tearing his hair. I think he's about to go into full rant mode.

"Yes." There doesn't seem much else to say.

"Don't you think if I was gay, I'd have better taste in men than Joe?"

"I'd never thought about it," I admit. "Joe's nice."

"Joe's nice!" Tavis shrieks. "I share his apartment, not his bed."

"How am I to know that?" I say in my defense. "You never said."

"You never asked!" Tavis pulls at his hair. "What makes you think I'm gay?"

I'm not altogether sure where this misapprehension came from. "Er . . ." I say. "You're an actor."

"I'm an actor!" he shouts. "And that's it? Not all actors are gay! Mel Gibson has seven children!"

He could be the exception that proves the rule. I don't voice this.

"You and Joe seemed very *happy* together."

"Of course we were happy. We've been through so much together. He's like my brother."

Ooo. "I told Alexis you had a boyfriend—right in front of you—and you didn't correct me."

"I thought that was your weird English sense of humor."

"I told Gil you were gay."

"Well, *he* clearly didn't believe you. Our fight was over you."

"You fought over me?"

"Oh, Sadie." Tavis looks as if he wants to pass out. "SadieSadieSadie."

"Oh." They had a fight over *me*!

"Jeez." Tavis paces up and down again. "Do I look gay?"

"If you mean do you dress like one of the Village People, no," I say snippily. "Look, Tavis, I'm not prejudiced. I don't mind. Really. It's your life."

"It's not my life," he says. "It *is not* my life! It could have been *our* life."

Now I don't know what to think. The audience around us is muttering.

"I'm not gay," Tavis shouts. The crowd behind him jumps. He turns on them. "*I* am *not* gay!"

"Shame," one very butch-looking man says and minces off.

"I can't believe this," Tavis says. "What do you think all that kissing was about?"

"You said it was acting."

Tavis sags.

"You said it was acting and that I shouldn't read anything into it."

"Goddamit," Tavis says. "So I did."

This can hardly be blamed entirely on me.

"I was frightened of commitment," Tavis says. "I didn't want anything to get in the way of my career. That's why I don't get involved with women. Or men!"

I've definitely got the wrong end of the stick on this one.

As an afterthought, Tavis adds, "And you were in love with Gil."

"I knew you were unavailable. I didn't let myself dare think . . ."

An announcement comes over the P.A. system. "This is the last call for passenger Sadie Nelson flying to London, Heathrow. Your flight is now boarding."

"My flight's now boarding," I say.

"I'll call you," Tavis says. "I'll come to London."

I'm rushing away and Tavis is following me, leaving the crowd behind. "I'm sorry," I say.

"I'm sorry too," he says.

We stop and touch our fingers together either side of the glass. I rest my cheek against the pane. "One day you'll be a big movie star and forget all about me," I say with a laugh. "You'll meet someone wonderful who isn't an idiot."

"I take it you mean a woman," Tavis says. He's trying to smile, but it's forced. "I can't believe we got this so wrong." He moves away from the glass. "Take care."

And as my heart does more backflips than a Russian gymnast, I stand rooted to the spot and watch him walk out of my life.

Eighty-nine

The lunchtime diners had drifted back to work and the afternoon was quiet. A few people sat out under the umbrellas on the sidewalk sipping coffee or beer. Tavis leaned on the bar and contemplated the mess that was his life.

Not only had he managed to lose the movie part, he'd also lost the girl, and he wondered if that counted as some sort of record. How could he have messed up so badly with Sadie? In trying to keep his heart intact and sending out "unavailable" signals, he'd somehow convinced her that he wasn't even interested in women. Joe would think it was a hoot. Tavis was less sure. He was going to have to get his own apartment and start doing "guy"-type things.

"Oh, Jeez," he said out loud to no one in particular.

As he looked up, Gil McGann walked into the bar. The producer sat down on the stool opposite Tavis. "Hey," Gil said.

"Hey." Tavis couldn't help but sound wary.

Gil sighed heavily before he spoke. "I take it Sadie's gone?"

"Yeah," Tavis said, wishing he didn't sound quite so miserable. "Did she get away okay?"

"Yeah," Tavis said with a half laugh. "She got away okay."

Gil leaned on the counter. He looked like a man who'd had all the stuffing ripped out of him. "Daniella told me that you'd taken her to the airport."

"Yeah," Tavis said, unsure whether Gil might want to punch him.

"That's nice," Gil said. "I should have done it."

"Well," Tavis said. "Yeah. Maybe you should have."

"Do you think she would have stayed?"

"Man," Tavis said, "I know nothing about how women's minds work."

"Me neither," Gil conceded. "I had Delores all spruced up for her." He flicked a thumb toward the door.

Tavis looked out. At the curbside, right by the restaurant, Delores sat in full glory.

"Wow," Tavis said in admiration.

"She drives nicely." Gil nodded toward the car. "Now."

"Sadie would have loved her," Tavis said.

"She loved her anyway," Gil said. "With all her flaws."

"Yeah," Tavis agreed. There was an uncomfortable pause. "Wanna beer?"

Gil nodded.

"Look," Tavis said. "I'm real sorry about the other day. I didn't mean—"

"No," Gil interrupted. "You were right. Absolutely right."

Tavis took a pull from his beer and put it down on the counter.

"You were only on the list because I wanted to see what you were made of. But Toby was right," Gil continued. "You're perfect for *The One That Got Away*."

"Yeah, well . . ."

"You've got the part," Gil said. "If you think you can work with me."

"I've got the part?" Tavis was incredulous.

"Toby Portman wants to see you to firm up the details."

"I've got the part?" Tavis was in danger of hyperventilating. All his dreams were coming true at once. Well, most of them.

"It was unprofessional of me to let personal feelings get in the way," Gil said. "Let's shake on a new start."

Tavis grasped Gil's hand. "Thanks," he said. "You won't regret it."

"I hope not," Gil said.

"This calls for a celebration." The two men toasted each other.

"To *The One That Got Away*," Gil said.

"*The One That Got Away*," Tavis echoed.

They both downed their beers. "I was right about Sadie, though," Gil said. "You were in love with her too."

"Yeah, well. She's gone now," Tavis said with a shrug. "Man, we were both dumb enough to lose her."

"I'm not so sure about that." I'm standing at the doorway, suitcase in hand. Both men turn to look at me. And I don't know who is more surprised.

"Sadie!" Tavis and Gil turn to each other.

When it came to it, my legs couldn't make me get on the plane. And despite the fact that I brought the entire wrath of the British Airways ground crew down on my head when I insisted on staying on this side of the Atlantic and they had to unload my manky luggage, I knew it was absolutely the right thing to do. I don't know what life holds for me, but I know that going back won't take me forward—if you know what I mean.

"What do we do now?" Tavis asks.

As I walk toward them, I'm thinking exactly the same thing. Daniella's right. This is the sweetest taboo. The sweetest, most exquisitely painful taboo. I look at Gil and Tavis and love them both. I love them both in different ways.

When I finally find my voice, I say, "I couldn't leave."

"I tried to find you," Gil says. He jumps down from his stool and comes to me, taking me in his arms. It feels as if he could hug the life out of me. "Gina had an emergency. I had to take her to the hospital. But she's OK. I think she's going to be OK. I did try to find you. I tried everything."

I give a tearful smile. This is the hardest thing I've ever had to do.

"And I've had Delores cleaned up for you," he says excitedly. "She runs like a dream."

"You are a wonderful man." I stroke his cheek. "A beautiful, kind and wonderful man."

Tavis is fading into the background. His eyes are dark and clouded and I can't tell what he's thinking.

Gil's phone rings and he lets his arms drop from mine to answer it. "It's the hospital," he says. "They said they'd phone as soon as Gina woke up."

I can feel my throat closing. Tavis and I exchange a glance.

Gil pockets his phone and looks at me. The expression on his face is bleak. "She needs me," he says plainly.

"She always has," I tell him softly. And she always will.

I take the keys for Delores from the bar and hand them to him. "Take my lovely car," I say and kiss him on the cheek. "Go to her."

Gil hugs me to him and I wonder if he will ever be able to let me go.

"I still love you," he whispers in my ear. "But I think you've always loved Tavis that little bit more." And before I can reply, he tears himself away and heads out of the restaurant.

I stand there and watch him leave, wondering what on earth I've done. But I know that Gil is right.

Tavis jumps over the bar and lands just in front of me. For the first time, he looks shy and unsure. "I got the movie part," he says, with an effort at a careless shrug that can't disguise his true feelings.

"And the girl," I add with a tearful smile. "If you want her."

He takes me in his arms and holds me tight. "Things don't get any better than this."

"Oh, I think they will," I say, resting my head against his chest. "This is Hollywood—and they just love a happy ending."